ADAPTATION

ALSO BY MALINDA LO

ASH
HUNTRESS

COMING SOON

NATURAL SELECTION (EBOOK ONLY)
INHERITANCE

ADAPTATION

MALINDA LO

Hodder
Children's
Books

A division of Hachette Children's Books

A Catalogue record for this book is available from the British Library.

ISBN: 978 1 444 91794 9

Printed and bound by CPI Group (UK) Ltd, Croydon, CR0 4YY

The paper and board used in this paperback by Hodder Children's Books
are natural recyclable products made from wood grown in sustainable
forests. The manufacturing processes conform to the environmental
regulations of the country of origin.

Hodder Children's Books
A division of Hachette Children's Books
338 Euston Road, London NW1 3BH
An Hachette UK company

www.hachette.co.uk

The slightest advantage in certain individuals, at any age or during any season, over those with which they come into competition, or better adaptation in however slight a degree to the surrounding physical conditions, will, in the long run, turn the balance.

– Charles Darwin, *The Origin of Species*

CHAPTER 1

The birds plummeted to the tarmac, wings loose and limp. They struck the ground with such force that their bodies smashed into dark slicks on the concrete.

'What the—' Reese Holloway pushed herself out of the hard plastic seat facing the floor-to-ceiling windows. Outside, heat waves rippled over the oil-stained runway. She glanced back at David, her forehead wrinkled. 'Did you see that?'

David Li looked up from his book. 'See what?' His dark brown eyes reflected the hard, bright daylight in tiny dots of white.

Reese tried to swallow the flutter of self-consciousness that rose within her as David met her gaze. She pointed at the windows. 'These birds just fell dead from the sky.'

David's eyebrows rose. 'No way.'

'Yeah.'

David closed the book over his right index finger and stood. 'Where?'

His shoulder brushed against her as he joined her at the

windows. She took a tiny step away and said, 'Over there – by those two workers.' A man in a blue jumpsuit pulled up in a baggage cart while another man, in an orange vest, ran toward him.

'You mean that dark stuff on the ground? Those are birds?'

'Were birds.'

'Damn.'

Blue Jumpsuit was gesticulating at the sky and the remains on the ground, apparently explaining the birds' fatal descent to Orange Vest.

'That was bizarre,' Reese said. The unforgiving glare of the sun on the neon-orange vest and the glistening lumps on the concrete gave the scene a surreal cast – like overexposed film. 'Have you ever seen birds just crash to the ground like that?'

'No,' David said.

Reese watched Blue Jumpsuit pull a plastic bag from a container on the baggage cart. He stuck his hand in the bag and squatted down to pick up the remains as if he were cleaning up after a dog. David went back to his seat, but Reese remained standing until the birds were removed, leaving only a smudge on the pavement: the stamp of their final moments. When she sat down again she felt unsettled, as if the ordinary world had been knocked off-balance and everything was now listing slightly to one side.

Beside her, David had returned to his book, and she saw the title angling across the cover in a retro-futuristic font:

The Left Hand of Darkness. She glanced at her watch. Their plane to San Francisco had been delayed, but it was due to take off, finally, in an hour. The waiting had made her twitchy, and her leg bounced with nervous energy. She bent down to pull out her iPod from her backpack, and as she fitted the headphones into her ears she surreptitiously watched David turn a page. He was wearing a short-sleeved shirt, and the skin of his arm had a golden tone like sunlight during Indian summer. She took a shallow breath and forced herself to look at her iPod, scrolling through her music. But as the song titles rolled past, she wasn't paying attention.

David was her debate partner. They had both joined the debate team at Kennedy High School their freshman year, but it wasn't until junior year last fall that their coach, Joe Chapman, suggested they might work well together. And they did. They worked so well together that they qualified for nationals. When Reese's mom found out, she was ecstatic. She even wanted to fly to Phoenix with them for the tournament, but her case ended up going to court during nationals – she was an assistant district attorney in San Francisco – so only Mr Chapman had come with them.

Reese was glad, because she would have been even more embarrassed if her mom had been there to watch her lose. Afterward, Reese had called her from the locker-lined hallway behind the auditorium to tell her the bad news. Her mom tried to comfort her. 'You can't win them all, honey.'

Reese pressed her fingers to the bridge of her nose as if that would pinch off the disappointment that was spreading through her. 'I know,' she said, schooling her voice to sound distant and detached.

But her mom wasn't fooled. 'I'm sorry,' she said gently, and Reese fought the urge to cry. She had wanted to win, of course, but it was the way they had lost that hurt the most. It had been all her fault. 'Do you want to tell me what happened?' her mom asked.

I screwed everything up because – because—

Reese couldn't even think the words to herself. 'It just didn't go well,' she said. Behind her the door to the auditorium opened, and David came out. Their eyes met briefly, but when he quickly looked away, chagrin rose in her, hot and uncomfortable. She blamed herself, but she knew David never would. Somehow, that made it even worse.

'I know you and David were well prepared,' her mom said, 'and sometimes it just doesn't go your way.'

'Yeah,' Reese said, but her mom's words didn't register. David had stopped about twenty feet away, turning toward a bulletin board covered with athletic announcements. They were the only two people in the hallway; everyone else was still in the auditorium watching the final round.

'Don't be too hard on yourself. I know how you are, honey.'

Reese clutched the phone with nervous fingers. Was David waiting to talk to her?

'Are you still there, Reese?' her mom asked.

'Yeah. Sorry.' Reese wrenched her gaze away from David

4

and stared down at the floor. A gum wrapper had been tossed onto the tiles, the foil glinting in the fluorescent lights.

'Oh, honey.' Her mom sighed. 'I'm sorry, but I have to go. We're heading back into court.' Her mom was in the middle of a big domestic-violence case. Her favorite kind – Reese knew her mom loved putting nasty husbands behind bars.

'All right,' Reese said. She saw David run a hand through his short black hair, making it stand straight up.

'I'll call you tonight to confirm your flight info. I love you, honey.'

'I love you too, Mom.' She hung up, and at that moment David pulled out his phone and dialed, turning away as he lifted it to his ear.

He wasn't waiting for her.

She was both relieved and let down, and the conflicting feelings sent a rush of heat through her body. Pocketing her own phone, she slipped past David and headed toward the lobby to look for their coach. David's voice echoed down the hall after her: 'Hey, Dad. No ... we lost.'

Now, in the airport as she sat beside him, the memory of that day – was it only yesterday? – and all its disappointments surged up again, slamming into the off-kilter tension that gripped her after witnessing the demise of those birds. *Get a grip on yourself*, she thought.

'I'm going to walk around,' Reese said abruptly to David. 'Will you watch my stuff?'

David nodded, and she stood, dropping her iPod into her backpack on the floor. She saw Mr Chapman threading his way through the seats toward them, carrying two bottles of water. He waved at her, and she waved back as she walked toward the center of the concourse. This trip could not be over soon enough. There were only a few weeks before school ended for the year, and thankfully no more debate practice. All of this weird crap with David would be done with, and she doubted they would be partners again next fall. *That'll be a relief*, she thought, ignoring the twinge in her chest that told her she was lying to herself.

Reese passed the podium, where a blue-and-white-uniformed flight attendant was dealing with a line of five or six travelers. A harassed-looking mother herded two toddlers forward while dragging a suitcase and pushing a stroller. Reese was trying to avoid the stroller, her sneakers squeaking across the glossy floor, when she heard someone scream, 'Oh my God!'

She turned to see a woman standing up, hands over her mouth and staring at the flat-screen TV hanging from the ceiling. The news was on as usual, and the Asian American anchorwoman had a hand pressed to her ear as if she were listening to a feed. Her face was grim. Reese took a few steps closer until she could read the headline at the bottom of the screen: *PLANE CRASH IN NEW JERSEY KILLS ALL PASSENGERS*.

Reese gasped.

The anchorwoman lowered her hand from her ear and

said: 'We have confirmed reports that an Airbus A320 has crashed outside Newark Airport. The cause of the crash has not yet been determined, but eyewitnesses have reported that the plane collided with a flock of Canada geese during takeoff. While airplanes are designed to withstand isolated bird strikes, apparently this was an entire flock – more than a dozen birds in all.'

A jolt went through Reese. *Birds?* In her mind's eye she saw the birds plunge to the tarmac again.

Other travelers began to gather beneath the TV screen while the anchorwoman repeated the bare facts. The plane had burst into flames when its fuel tanks exploded upon impact. One hundred forty-six passengers were presumed dead. Emergency crew on the scene were hoping to salvage some clues from the burning mess.

'This is crazy,' said a middle-aged woman standing near Reese. 'Those poor people!'

'What is this about birds?' said a man in a Red Sox cap. 'How could birds do this?'

The anchorwoman interrupted her own report, saying, 'We have news of a second crash, this time in the Pacific Northwest. A Boeing 747 has crashed onto the coast near Seattle.' The anchorwoman pressed her hand to her ear again. 'Information is still coming in. We do not know if there are any survivors of this second plane crash.' Her face stiffened, and she stopped speaking for a moment. Finally she lowered her hand and looked into the camera. 'Early reports indicate that this plane was struck by birds.'

Reese gaped at the television as a collective gasp arose from the travelers around her.

'We have Lamont Bell on the line from the Federal Aviation Administration,' the anchorwoman said. 'Mr Bell, what is the chance of two planes being downed by bird strikes within an hour?'

The man's voice sounded scratchy over the audio transmission, but it was clear that he was unnerved. 'It's not – it's very unusual. I've never in my entire career encountered two plane crashes of such magnitude due to bird strikes.'

'Are you saying that you believe the planes crashed due to a different, unnatural cause?'

'I – no, I'm not saying that. I don't know what caused the crashes. We shouldn't speculate.'

'Eyewitness accounts indicate the presence of large flocks of birds. Is it impossible that the plane crashes were due to bird strikes?'

'No, it's not impossible, but it's unlikely.'

'Then you do think something else is part of the equation?'

'I don't know,' Bell said, sounding exasperated. 'Look, I don't want to speculate.'

'Mr Bell, I'm afraid I have to interrupt you again,' the anchorwoman said. 'I've just received news that there has been a third crash, this time in Texas. Once again, reports do indicate that bird strikes may have been the cause of the crash. And—' She stopped speaking, turning to look off camera. Someone offscreen handed her a sheet of paper, and when she faced the camera again, she read directly from it.

'I've been informed that the FAA has grounded all aircraft in the United States while officials assess the threat level posed by these accidents.' She looked into the camera. 'I'm afraid we have some bad news for travelers today. I repeat: The Federal Aviation Administration has grounded all aircraft in the United States.'

Reese's stomach dropped, and the crowd around the TV monitor erupted with questions.

'What do you mean? Is my flight canceled?'

'This is bullshit!'

'What is going on? How could birds possibly do this?'

'It can't be birds – it must be terrorists.'

'That's insane. Terrorists can control birds now?'

As the questions piled one on top of another, louder and louder, Reese's heart began to race. The birds that had smashed onto the runway. Three plane crashes. *Three*. One is unusual; two is a coincidence; but three . . . how could it be an accident?

People were bumping into her, craning their necks at the TV, talking over the anchorwoman. Reese shoved her way out of the crowd, her skin crawling as disbelief warred with growing panic inside her. *What is going on?* She halted in front of a bank of monitors displaying the flight departure times. One by one, those times blinked out and were replaced by a single word, repeated over and over: *CANCELED*.

CHAPTER 2

Reese couldn't get through to her mom; the call went straight to voice mail. She checked her watch; it was 3:38 in San Francisco. She knew her mom was probably still in court, but Reese was stiff with anxiety. If terrorists were behind these plane crashes, how safe was her mom in a courthouse? David paced nearby, talking to his parents on his phone in Chinese.

Mr Chapman lowered himself into the seat beside Reese, frowning, and pushed up his black-framed glasses. 'This is a mess,' he said. Behind them, dozens of travelers were clustered around the podium, trying to rebook their plane tickets. CNN was still droning in the background, but Reese had stopped watching after the fourth plane crash in Colorado. She was filled with a kind of paranoid helplessness, and she kept glancing out the windows as if she were waiting for more birds to plunge from the sky.

'What are we going to do?' she asked, sounding more frightened than she intended.

Mr Chapman gave her a thin smile. She thought he was trying to be reassuring, but he didn't quite succeed. 'We just have to wait. You're too young to remember 9/11, but at first it was just a bunch of waiting. Waiting to hear from the president, waiting to find out who was behind it.' He shook his head and pushed up his glasses again, a nervous tic that betrayed his own tension. 'Hopefully, there will be some news soon.'

David ended his call and walked back to them. 'My parents are freaking out.'

'Do you want me to talk to them?' Mr Chapman offered.

'No, they'll be okay. They're just shocked like everyone else. My dad's company shut down for the day, and he's driving home now.' David pocketed his phone, then looked behind Reese at the gate area. 'Hey, something's happening.'

Reese twisted around. The cluster of people at the podium had turned back to the TV monitor. She couldn't see the whole screen from where she was sitting, but as the crowd quieted, the speakers in the ceiling could be heard clearly. A reporter said, 'In a moment, President Elizabeth Randall will make a statement from the Oval Office. We're about to — hang on, I believe we're going to that feed now.'

Reese jumped up to get a better angle on the TV. President Randall was seated at the desk in the Oval Office and looking directly into the camera through her trademark wire-rim glasses. Not a hair was out of place, though she wore a look of grave concern on her face.

'As you know by now, we've been struck by tragedy today

in our nation and in Canada and Mexico.' The president's Midwestern accent was stronger than usual. 'I want to reassure you that we are working around the clock to determine the cause of today's crashes, as well as coordinating with the Canadian and Mexican governments to analyze whether there is a pattern in these tragic accidents. At this time, we have suspended all flights in the United States, and Canada and Mexico have done the same in their territories. As of tonight, we know of seven crashes across North America, and we hope that by grounding all flights, we will avoid further tragedy. I know that many of you are frightened and confused by the conflicting reports coming out in the news about the causes of these crashes, and I urge you to remain calm and refrain from speculation. You can rest assured that I have ordered a thorough and complete investigation into these crashes, and I will make sure that you are informed of our progress as things develop.'

The president paused and a look of maternal solicitude swept over her face. She even tilted her head slightly. 'If you've been inconvenienced in your travel plans because of the flight ban, I'm sure you understand that this is in the best interests of our nation and your safety. As soon as it is safe to fly again, we will lift the flight ban. In the meantime, please join me in praying for those whose lives have been affected by these tragedies, here and throughout North America.'

The feed from the White House ended, and the news analysts reappeared. Reese sat down heavily, shaken by the president's words. Seven plane crashes due to bird strikes? It sounded insane.

Mr Chapman's face was pale as he said, 'I guess it's a good thing our plane was delayed.'

Reese almost dropped her phone when it suddenly vibrated in her hand. The caller ID read: *Catherine Sheridan*. Relieved, she scrambled to answer it. 'Mom! Did you hear the news?'

'Are you all right?' Her mom sounded both terrified and relieved. 'Where are you? You didn't get on the plane, did you?'

'No, it was still delayed when the flight ban started.' Reese rubbed a sweaty palm over her jeans. 'I'm fine. I'm still at the airport.'

'Good. Is your coach still with you?'

'Yes.' Mr Chapman had walked a few feet away to phone his wife. 'And David's here too.' He was trying to watch the news, though it was hard to hear over the din of travelers attempting to rebook their flights.

'I tried to call you earlier, but I couldn't get through till now,' her mom said. 'Everybody's going home early; they think it's a terrorist attack.'

Panic shot through Reese. 'Mom, are you still at work? You need to get out of there.'

'It's all right, honey. Don't worry about me. I'm leaving soon. Are you staying at the airport tonight?'

'Yeah. Mr C wants to wait till tomorrow morning to see what's going on. The airline said they'd issue 'alternative

13

transportation options,' whatever that means, if the flight ban isn't lifted by then.'

'All right. Just stay with Mr Chapman and call me the minute anything changes.'

'I will.'

'Promise?'

'I promise.'

The line at the Wendy's counter snaked back and forth across the polished concrete floor of the concourse. Reese guessed there were about twenty-five people ahead of her, which put her right at the edge of the seating area next to the overflowing trash bin. An abandoned Frosty was perched on its side and dripping onto the floor, forming a pool of beige liquid. Reese looked away from the mess, her gaze sweeping up toward the windows set high against the ceiling. The sky outside was dusky blue. She had been stuck in this airport since eleven o'clock that morning – almost nine hours.

Earlier, she had called her best friend, Julian Arens, to tell him she was stuck in Phoenix. He told her that all major airports in the United States were full of stranded passengers, and already some people were concerned the airports might run out of food. If the planes couldn't fly, they couldn't bring in supplies either.

'You're freaking me out,' Reese said, only half joking. 'Are you saying I should start hoarding those disgusting airport sandwiches?'

'They're probably gone by now,' he answered. By the

14

time she went to search out dinner, Julian was right. The deli cases that had once been full of sandwiches and salads were picked clean, and the only food left was the square-shaped burgers at Wendy's.

The line was moving at about the speed of molasses, so Reese pulled out her phone to pass the time, touching the icon for the Internet. The Hub loaded right away, with feeds popping up one after the other, all about the flight ban. It was mostly people complaining about being trapped in airports, but there was a lot of chatter about possible causes for the plane crashes too. Terrorism wasn't even the most outlandish one. She saw one feed declaring *Aliens did it, earthlings. Colonization is coming!* She let out a short laugh. Julian was always trying to convince her that E.T. had already visited Earth multiple times. One night in Dolores Park, while they were hanging out on the swings in the playground, Julian told her about meeting an alien abductee in Golden Gate Park the weekend before.

'He had an implant in his lower back – he totally showed me the scar and everything,' Julian said, gesturing with the stub of his cigarette.

Reese lit one for herself and said, 'Yeah, I'm sure *that's* what he was showing you.' She tossed the match down to the sand, watching as the flame sputtered out.

'You're just jealous you didn't get to see his ass.'

She remembered cracking up, almost choking on the smoke. Julian handed her the water bottle filled with vodka tonic, but she shook her head, wheezing as she laughed.

Her phone buzzed as she was scrolling through the feeds on the Hub; Julian had just texted her.

> Stuff is getting crazy out there.
> U have 2 check this out:
> www.short.349sy

She clicked on the link, which took her to a blog post on a website called Bin 42. The headline made her eyebrows rise: *Government cover-up of plane crashes continues with media blackout.*

If you've been on the Hub today, you probably noticed that everyone around the world is freaked out about one thing: these bizarre plane crashes. But you might also have noticed that your feeds about them keep mysteriously disappearing. We've uncovered evidence that every 15 minutes, feeds relating to plane crashes, bird strikes, and the causes of such are routinely wiped.

Who has the power to do this? Only one entity: the US government.

Here is what we've gathered over the course of the day (and be forewarned: this report may soon be wiped, too, so if you want to keep this info alive, we suggest you mirror it immediately to your own site or download a copy for yourself. Better yet, revert to ancient technology:

Print this out on paper!):

➤Official news and government reports state that only seven crashes have occurred in the US today, in New Jersey, Washington, and Texas. But continuous scanning of news feeds shows that at least 23 other planes have crashed today due to bird strikes within the continental United States alone.

➤Reports of these crashes are routinely posted online but removed shortly afterward. Caches of these news reports are eventually wiped as well. For a roundup of these reports (many now go to 404 pages), go here: www.bin42. com/34092

➤Video of plane crash sites has been circulating on file-sharing sites but is also routinely being removed. Don't be fooled! We have seen these videos and they are not doctored! A roundup of videos (some of which may no longer be online) are here: www.bin42.com/34093

➤Mainstream news sources are being forced to adhere to a media blackout, so don't go to the *New York Times* looking for confirmation – you won't find it. The only mainstream account we have of any of the other crashes is from the *Chicago Tribune*; here's a link to a screencap of that web page before it was taken down: www.bin42. com/34094

What does this mean for you? If you're safe at home, we advise you to check your emergency supplies and prepare for the worst. If you're a traveler stranded because of the flight ban, we suggest you find a way to drive yourself home. While there's no evidence that airports are unsafe (yet), there is also no evidence that the flight ban will be lifted anytime soon. Meanwhile, check back here regularly; we will attempt to keep this site online as long as possible.

Reese clicked on the link to the *Chicago Tribune* article. She saw a screencap of a story about three plane crashes in the Chicago area, all due to bird strikes. The article was accompanied by a photograph of one of the Chicago crash sites. A plane had plowed a deep furrow through a field of corn, culminating in a smoking black mess. The tail of the plane was still visible; the airline's logo could be seen through the smoke.

'Hey, the line's moving,' said a man behind her.

'Oh, sorry.' As she stepped forward she clicked back to the original Bin 42 blog, feeling uneasy. She went to the video roundup page. Most of the links were dead, but one video showed a young female reporter in a mountainous area. Wreckage was strewn behind her. Reese couldn't hear the audio, but the camera zoomed toward a person in a hazmat suit who was retrieving remains from the crash. Reese could barely see what he was holding in his gloved hands, but it stretched out toward the ground as if it was half liquefied.

Her stomach lurched. *What was that?* And why was the person dressed as if he were dealing with a biohazard? Her hands were clammy and the phone nearly slipped out of her grasp as she thumbed back to the blog post Julian had sent her.

But this time, she got an error message. It was gone.

'Can I take your order?'

Reese glanced up, startled. She had reached the front of the line, and a dead-eyed girl was waiting behind the counter. The overhead lights made her face look washed out and tired, and her ash-blond hair strayed in lanky strands from beneath her Wendy's cap.

'You wanna order something?' the girl prodded.

Reese swallowed. 'No.' She had lost her appetite.

David was sleeping on the floor in front of the plastic seats, his head resting on a rolled-up jacket, his back to the windows. Mr Chapman was napping nearby, slouched in one of the uncomfortable plastic chairs with his arms crossed and his feet stretched toward the glass. Night had fallen, turning the windows into a wall of dark mirrors. Reese saw herself reflected as a girl with flyaway dark hair and shadowed eyes in a pale face. Behind her the concourse was littered with travelers trying to sleep under the bright lights, legs propped up on carry-on bags, heads pillowed on lumpy backpacks.

She stopped beside David and looked down at him. One hand was curled beneath his chin, the other draped loosely

over his toned stomach where his Kennedy Swim T-shirt –
sharks of the bay – had inched up. He was captain of the
swim team and a soccer player in addition to being a
debater. An all-around golden boy. A familiar flare of self-
consciousness burned through her. Angry at herself, she
shoved away her feelings. What had happened between her
and David was in the past, and she should just get over it.
There was no use in thinking about it anymore; there were
more important things to worry about now.

She nudged David's shoulder with the toe of her beat-up
black Chucks. 'David.' He grumbled slightly but didn't wake
up. 'David,' she said more loudly, and nudged him again.

He rolled over onto his back, shading his eyes from the
fluorescent lights as he blinked up at her. 'What?' His voice
was clogged with sleep. 'What's going on?'

'I have to talk to you.'

'About what?' He pushed himself up, rubbing a hand
over his eyes.

'Hang on, let me wake up Mr Chapman.' She turned to
their coach and tapped him on the shoulder. 'Hey, Mr
Chapman.'

His eyes snapped open, and he jerked upright. 'What?
Reese?'

'Mr C, we have to talk.' She sat down next to Mr Chapman
while David leaned against the glass across from them. In
the window, Reese's Rhapsody of Emily concert T-shirt was
reflected in mirror image, and there was something
disquieting about reading the words backward.

'What's on your mind, Reese?' Mr Chapman asked.

'I've been checking the news on the Hub,' she began. She told them about the blog post that Julian had sent her, describing the *Chicago Tribune* article and the videos she had watched. 'I think we should get out of here,' she concluded. 'I think we should get a rental car and drive back to San Francisco.'

'The airline said they would start rebooking flights tomorrow,' Mr Chapman said. 'We should just wait.'

Before she could argue, David asked, 'What's on TV right now?' He looked past her at the concourse.

'What? I don't know.' She turned to glance at the nearest TV monitor, expecting to see the news, but instead she saw a line of men in orange prison uniforms moving across a yard. The scene changed to a close-up on one gray-haired man, his mouth shining wetly as he spoke. Across the bottom of the screen, she read the words: *Barred: Behind the Walls of America's Most Violent Prisons*. 'It's a prison documentary,' she said. 'They're on practically all the time.'

'It shouldn't be on now, not when there's more money to be made on a disaster.' David held his hand out to her. 'Let me see your phone.'

Startled, she said, 'That post is gone—'

'Just let me see it,' he insisted.

She unlocked her phone and handed it over. He pulled up the Hub, clicking through her history. 'Hey, what are you doing?' she asked.

'I'm looking for a mirrored site. From what you said

21

about Bin 42, I don't think they'd only post it in one location.'
She saw him entering something into her phone, swiping his
fingers across the screen. A moment later he held the phone
in front of her. It displayed a copy of the Bin 42 page. 'Is this
what you were reading?'

'Yeah, how'd you find that?'

'Magic,' he said with a grin that shot right through to her
belly. She tried to cover it up by rolling her eyes.

'Whatever. Just read that Tribune article.'

'Hang on,' he said. A second later she heard the tinny
sound of a video recording playing back on her phone.
When he finished, he handed it to Mr Chapman, who
watched it with a deepening frown on his face.

'We should leave, Mr C,' she said. 'Who knows how
long we could be stranded in Phoenix. I don't think the
news is telling us everything.' She lowered her voice. 'And
everybody's going to be trying to rent a car to get out of here
when they figure that out. We need to beat the rush.'

Mr Chapman's face was troubled as he handed the phone
back to her. 'I don't know whether I buy it, Reese. That site
– who runs it? Do you really think the government would go
to the trouble of covering all that up? Besides, it's doing an
awful job of it if that's the plan.'

Normally, Reese didn't believe half the stuff Julian tried
to convince her about, but tonight, Mr Chapman's skepticism
frustrated her. 'I don't know who runs it. But who would be
able to fabricate those videos so quickly? I think we should
get out of here. If we rent a car and start driving tonight, we

can be back in San Francisco by tomorrow.' The scene on the TV monitor changed again; now it showed a man in handcuffs being led out of a courtroom. She glanced at her watch. It wasn't even 10:00 PM yet. 'You know, David's right about the TV,' she said uneasily. 'The news should be on. Anytime there's a disaster, they cover it twenty-four/seven.'

They all turned to watch the prison documentary. The news network's logo was plainly visible in the corner. An inmate with bizarrely red eyes spoke to the camera, his face bearing a creepy, self-satisfied smile, and Reese shuddered.

Mr Chapman said, 'I suppose . . . it wouldn't hurt to check at the rental-car counter to see how much it would cost.'

'Great,' Reese said, surging to her feet. 'The rental-car center is open twenty-four hours; I checked. Let's go.'

CHAPTER 3

The rental-car center was packed with people who had exactly the same idea.

'So much for getting a jump on things,' Reese said as they made their way to the back of the very long line. They passed a snack counter along the way, and the refrigerator case was empty except for a few crooked signs that read TUNA SALAD or HAM AND TURKEY. Reese's stomach growled, and she wished she had bought that Wendy's burger.

By the time they made it out of the airport, driving one of the last available rentals – a Suzuki sedan with a long dent in the driver's side door – it was nearly morning, and Reese's hunger had settled into a gnawing hollowness that made her both tired and cranky.

Mr Chapman eased the sedan into the line of cars waiting to merge onto the I-10 as the horizon turned gray, then pink. David, sitting in the front passenger seat, scanned through the radio stations one by one, but none of them was reporting any news – not even traffic, which was moving at a crawl.

It took an hour to go seven miles. As they inched their way onto the interstate, Mr Chapman said, 'David, look at that map they gave us and find me another way to San Francisco. If it's this bad around Phoenix, I don't want to take this all the way to LA. It's just going to be worse there.'

Reese slouched in the backseat, checking her phone every few minutes for reception. She hadn't been able to get a call through to her mom, and the stress that had been tightening her neck all night was starting to make her head pound. Outside, the I-10 was practically a parking lot. A Toyota nearby contained a man and a woman and what appeared to be mounds of supplies: canned goods, toilet paper, blankets. A white VW that kept trying to cut them off was packed with five passengers, and the trunk was tied down over piles of suitcases. There were way too many people on the freeway for it to only be rush-hour traffic, and Reese couldn't shake the feeling that she was missing something. What was driving these people out of their houses at the crack of dawn?

'Hey, we can take the next exit to 17 North,' David said, breaking the silence. 'It'll take us to 93 North, and at Kingman we can switch to I-40, which goes west to 58, then meets up with 5 North to San Francisco. It even skips Las Vegas.'

'Great,' Mr Chapman said. 'I can't wait to get out of this and get some coffee.'

The sound of honking erupted, and a battered blue

pickup barreled down the shoulder of the road, causing more than one driver to scream out their windows at the truck. As it passed, Reese saw a man standing in the truck bed holding a giant sign. It read NEWS – AM 1438.

'Hey, try that,' Reese said, leaning between the two front seats. 'AM 1438.'

David switched to AM and cranked the dial until they found a scratchy signal that faded in and out. A man's voice was speaking: '. . . secure compounds inland. Reports of military convoys heading toward the heartland . . . President Randall . . . wait for confirmation. However, classified documents leaked onto the Hub show that the government is prepared to crack down on dissenters.'

Mr Chapman frowned. 'Who is this?' He moved his hand toward the radio.

'Wait a sec,' Reese cried, trying to make sense of the jumbled phrases.

The man's voice continued: 'Citizens are urged to prepare for disruptions in food supplies due to interstate lockdowns and the air traffic ban . . . terrorism but speculation is rampant about causes. So-called rogue states would not have the coord . . . too much for one little nation—'

The static roared, and Mr Chapman turned the volume down. 'Let's not get ahead of ourselves. Let's just get home.'

Arizona, Reese soon discovered, was one giant sprawl of desert, at least on either side of the highway. In the distance, mountains lent a jagged edge to the horizon, but they were so far away that they seemed like a mirage. The reality, here, was flat dirt: a light brown broken by occasional bushes that clung obstinately to their patches of ground and were permanently bent by the dry wind.

On the road, as far as the eye could see, was traffic. As the day wore on, Reese saw more and more cars packed full of gear: tents strapped to the roof, blankets and pillows piled high in backseats. She increasingly felt as if they had joined a tide of refugees – only she didn't know what they were fleeing from. At a Texaco just outside Phoenix, a man in a rumpled suit eyed her as she grabbed the last box of Hostess doughnuts, as if he wanted to take it from her. She hurried to meet up with Mr Chapman and David at the cash register, hunching her shoulders defensively. It was hard not to be affected by the sense of paranoia that seemed to infect their fellow travelers. Even the gas station attendants who took their money had developed a kind of squinty-eyed anxiety. If she could only get some real information, Reese thought, she wouldn't be so on edge.

But AM 1438 had long since faded to constant static, the only FM station that came in was playing old country music, and she still couldn't get online on her phone. At least she had managed to talk to her mom for a minute before the connection broke, but there hadn't been time to do more than say that they had left Phoenix. Now all Reese had was the view out the window, and it didn't tell her anything except she was glad she didn't live in a desert.

They reached Kingman at noon after a long morning of

stop-and-start driving. They intended to take the exit onto I-40, heading west toward California, but a few miles before they reached the interchange, traffic slowed even more. 'What the hell is going on?' Mr Chapman said in frustration. He had drunk three cups of awful black coffee that morning, and Reese was beginning to wonder if she or David should take over the driving. Mr Chapman was jittery and nervous from the caffeine and sugar, and hadn't slept any more than the two of them.

Half a mile before they reached the exit, Reese saw what was holding things up: a roadblock. A string of state police cars was parked right across the ramp to the I-40, their red and blue lights flashing beneath the hot midday sun. State troopers in khaki uniforms waved them past. Mr Chapman rolled down his window as they neared the roadblock, and heat blasted into the car. 'What's going on?' he called. 'We have to get onto 40 West to get back to California.'

One of the troopers took a step closer to them, looking down through his sunglasses. 'You'll have to drive up to Las Vegas and find an alternate route. Interstate 40 is closed here.'

'Closed? Why?'

'It's closed,' the trooper repeated. 'You'll have to drive north to Las Vegas.'

Mr Chapman stared at him, wrinkling his forehead.

'Move on, sir, you're blocking traffic,' the trooper said.

'Are you serious?' Mr Chapman asked. 'That's a – a four-hour detour.'

'Then you'd better get started.' The trooper's hand moved to the weapon at his hip.

For a moment Mr Chapman didn't move, and Reese's mouth went dry. What could you do when faced with a state trooper who had a gun? Mr Chapman rolled up the window and drove on, cursing beneath his breath. 'Sorry,' he muttered. 'This is crazy.'

They reached the outskirts of Las Vegas in late afternoon. Traffic picked up as they approached the city, and Reese hoped it meant that the worst was behind them. The map they had gotten at the rental-car counter didn't extend as far as Las Vegas, so at a Chevron off the freeway, Mr Chapman climbed out to refill the tank and buy a map. He left the nozzle in the tank as he walked toward the mini-mart, and Reese unbuckled her seat belt and stretched out her legs in the backseat.

David was studying his phone, and she asked, 'Any reception?'

He shook his head. 'I don't know what's up. Circuits are overloaded or something? And my battery's dying anyway.'

Reese took out her own phone and saw the battery indicator was at 50 percent. 'Crap, mine too. We should have charged them last night when we were in line.' Her phone charger was in her carry-on in the trunk, but without an adapter to plug into the car, it was useless. 'I'm going to turn mine off for now.' She looked up as Mr Chapman returned from the mini-mart, waving a map triumphantly. He headed back to the pump, tucking the map in his back pocket. 'Do you think we should stay in Vegas tonight?' she asked. She was tired. The nervous energy that had kept her alert all day was fading now that they had arrived in Las Vegas, and her lack of sleep was catching up with her.

'I guess it's up to Mr C,' David said. 'I can help drive. Do you have your license?'

'Yeah.' Reese heard a stranger's voice outside the window, and she twisted around to see a burly man in an army-green vest, his muscles bulging out of a black T-shirt, gesturing at Mr Chapman. He was backing away from the gas pump, hands raised, face white. The man in the khaki vest was pointing a gun at him.

The shock of recognizing the weapon was like having a bucket of ice water dumped over her head.

The man shouted: 'Give me your keys, now!'

Reese scrambled away from the window, her heart slamming into her throat.

Chapman was visibly shaking. 'They're – they're in the car,' he said, but the man didn't even glance inside the sedan.

He pulled the trigger.

The gunshot was so loud that everything Reese heard afterward seemed dull, as if it were coming at her from underwater. David was saying, 'Shit, shit, shit.'

Mr Chapman was on the ground. He had no face anymore.

She couldn't drag her gaze away. It was nothing like the movies. The lifeless weight of Mr Chapman's body, the utter stillness of it, could never be replicated on film. Her stomach heaved.

The gunman turned to look inside the car. Reese saw a snake tattoo writhing up the man's thick, sweat-soaked neck. Fear crashed through her in a frigid rush. She yelled, 'David!'

'Get out of the car!' the man screamed at them, pointing the gun at the window.

'David, lock the doors!'

David scrambled into the driver's seat, lunging for the door lock. The locks engaged with a *thunk* seconds before the man reached for the passenger's side door handle. He snarled when the door wouldn't open.

David fumbled with the keys that were still in the ignition. The engine roared to life. The man raised the gun again, pointing it at the handle. David floored the gas pedal, and Reese was thrown back hard against the seat as the car jerked forward. They heard a loud clank as the gas nozzle was yanked out of the tank, the hose snapping. There was a second gunshot, and Reese instinctually ducked down in the seat. The car bounced over a bump in the road so high she was sure David had just driven over a curb. She heard a horn blasting as the car turned sharply, throwing her onto the floor. The tires screeched. She heard another gunshot, popping like a firecracker – and then a giant boom.

'What the hell was that?' Reese was crouched on the floor of the car, the hair on her arms standing up as if she had stuck her finger in an electrical socket. She felt as if she was about to throw up.

'Jesus Christ,' David breathed, sounding stunned.

'What happened?'

'The freaking gas station blew up!'

Heart pounding, Reese pushed herself up to peer out the rear window. She saw the dangling end of a gasoline hose spitting fire. The pump where they had been parked was engulfed in flame, and fire licked across the oil-soaked concrete. People were running away from the inferno, abandoning their cars. She could no longer see Mr Chapman's body or the man who had shot him.

CHAPTER 4

The tires squealed as David wrenched the car onto the road, throwing Reese to one side again. Adrenaline surged through her as she clung to the top of the backseat, unable to tear her eyes away from the explosion.

The Chevron sign disappeared behind a plume of black smoke as a woman ran straight out into the road, her mouth open in a scream. A blue sedan slammed on its brakes to avoid hitting her, its tires burning black marks onto the pavement. Car alarms shrieked to life, a cacophony of sirens and honking horns.

Reese lost sight of the gas station as David turned the car abruptly, nearly tossing her onto the floor. 'Watch it!' she cried, but he didn't respond. She twisted around just in time to see him jerk the steering wheel to the left, barely avoiding another car. 'What are you doing? David!'

He raced through a light just as it clicked red, and car horns blared at them. Reese climbed through the gap between the front seats, bumping into David's arm as she awkwardly maneuvered herself into the passenger seat. Her hands shook as she fumbled the seat belt into place, just in time for him to slam on the brakes at the next red light. The seat belt cut into her chest and right shoulder as the car jerked to a stop. The sound of their frantic breathing filled the car.

They had entered a suburban neighborhood with cookie-cutter houses visible behind fences on either side of the road. But all Reese could see was their coach falling backward onto the gasoline-soaked pavement. The burst of blood as the bullet tore into his eye. 'Oh my God,' Reese said. 'We have to go back. Mr Chapman—'

'He's dead,' David said. Reese saw a vein snake down his temple as he clenched his jaw. The light turned green, and David accelerated through the intersection. 'Nobody survives that.'

'We can't just leave him there!'

'We should call 911. Is your phone working?'

She dug out the phone from her pocket and turned it on. So much for conserving the battery. There was only one bar of reception, and it was flickering. 'I don't think so.'

'Try anyway!' he snapped. An angry retort was on the tip of her tongue when she saw the slick trace of sweat on his cheek and realized he was just as freaked out as she was. She took a deep breath, trying to force down the panic churning inside herself. She dialed 911. David continued to drive as she waited for the call to connect. She heard the drumbeat of her own heart as she held the phone to her ear. Outside, there was no sign of the highway, only unremarkable houses, and empty streets.

Her phone beeped. 'Call cannot be completed as dialed,' said a computerized voice. 'Please try again.' She tried again, staring down at the device as the telephone icon fruitlessly spun in a circle.

'It's not working,' Reese said. 'Give me your phone.' He tugged it out and handed it to her with clammy fingers. But she had no luck with his either.

The next time David pulled to a stop, she looked up. They were at a red light, and they were the only car in sight.

'Where is everybody?' she asked. 'Why is this place so deserted?' All day they had been slowed down by traffic. The stillness here was unnatural.

'I don't know,' David said, sounding strained.

Reese looked down at the two phones. There wasn't even a single bar on either of them. 'There's no reception. We have to go back.'

David did not respond, and when the light turned green, he continued straight ahead.

'Did you hear me?' Reese asked.

'Yeah.'

'Then why aren't you turning around?'

His fingers tightened over the steering wheel. 'Because I don't know where we are,' he admitted.

'But you drove—'

'I don't remember which direction we came from,' he said through gritted teeth. 'I've been driving around trying to figure it out, but some of the streets are closed, and everything here looks exactly the same.' He paused. 'I'm sorry.'

She gazed out the windshield at the nondescript houses. They passed a strip mall with an empty parking lot. The windows of a convenience store were smashed, bits of glass spread all over the ground. Inside the building, she could see empty shelves; it had been entirely cleaned out. Nearby, a sign for I-215 came into view, pointing to the right.

'Turn there,' Reese said.

'Why?'

Because this whole neighborhood is creeping me out, she thought. But she said, 'Maybe if we get on a highway we'll be able to figure out the way back.'

David turned right onto a wide street. They passed quiet office buildings; another strip mall; another gas station. Its windows were also broken, and the gas pump hoses trailed onto the stained concrete. The area was disturbingly quiet – as if it had been evacuated. The entrance to I-215 came at a deserted intersection where red traffic signals blinked slowly.

David said, 'I think we came from . . .'

'That way,' Reese said, pointing to the on-ramp for 215 East.

'Yeah,' he agreed, and accelerated onto the interstate. The eastbound side was bordered on the south by a high wall, blocking off the neighborhood they had driven through. The three lanes were as empty as the streets they had just come from, but across the low concrete divider the westbound portion of the highway was packed with cars moving at a crawl. They were full of passengers, just like the ones outside Phoenix. Some cars were stuffed to the brim with suitcases and bedding as well. *It is an evacuation*, she thought.

Ahead of them, they saw a green sign for I-515 and two highways, 93 and 95.

'Weren't we on one of those? US 93?' David asked.

'I think so. We should take it south to go back to the gas station.'

But as they approached the exit, they saw that the southbound ramp was blocked off with movable concrete barriers and orange cones.

'New plan?' David said.

'Maybe we can turn around farther north.'

David headed for the 93 North exit, speeding up the elevated concrete ramp that swung around to the interstate. As their car swept up the curve, they could see the maze of the highway interchange beneath them to the left.

Reese gasped. 'Look!'

On the southbound side was a long convoy of military trucks. Behind the trucks were tanks, their gun turrets all pointed south.

'Where do you think they're going?' she asked, watching the trucks uneasily.

'It can't be anywhere good,' David muttered. 'Not with that many weapons.'

Reese twisted in her seat to look out the back window

and saw a plume of black smoke in the distance. She wondered if it was the fire from the gas station. The tanks were all heading that direction. 'Do you think we should turn around somewhere?' she asked.

'We'll get stuck in that – whatever it is,' David said tersely, gesturing at the convoy.

'But what about Mr Chapman? We have to go back and – and identify him.'

A bead of sweat worked its way down David's right temple. 'Keep trying the phones. We have to get through sometime.'

Reese gritted her teeth. It felt wrong to leave Mr Chapman there. But turning back meant spending more time in Las Vegas with its crazy carjackers and blockaded roads and army tanks. She definitely did not want to be in this city anymore. Every nerve in her body was telling her to *run* as far away and as fast as she could. 'All right,' she said finally. 'I'll keep trying, and if I can't get through, we'll find a landline the next time we stop.'

The freeway was lined on both sides by tall concrete walls that blocked the city from view. Beyond them Reese could only see flat rooftops and a few scraggly trees. There were a few other cars heading north, but otherwise the multiple lanes of the highway were wide open. On the southbound side, the military convoy continued for at least ten minutes – Reese kept glancing over at the tanks as she tried to call 911 – but after the convoy ended the road was deserted, as if it had been blocked off somewhere up north.

And then Reese noticed something else that was unusual. All the exits on the northbound side were closed off, though the on-ramps remained open. It was as if drivers were being purposely directed away from the southern parts of the city.

'We can't get off the freeway,' David said, echoing her thoughts. 'Are you having any luck with the phones?'

She took a shaking breath. 'No.'

When the concrete walls ended, Las Vegas emerged as a city of drab industrial buildings interspersed with towering hotels. Billboards popped up on the side of the highway, advertising another Hollywood remake of *Batman*. They passed multistory parking structures, all empty. In the distance, casino lights glittered red and gold.

It wasn't until they left the city behind, warehouses giving way to brown desert dotted with dark green brush, that the freeway exits opened up. It was after 5:00 PM now, and Reese had been checking their phones regularly, but reception never went higher than a single bar. As they departed Las Vegas, even that single bar disappeared. When the sun began to descend toward a range of mountains in the west, Reese said, 'Maybe we should find a place to stop for the night.' The thought of resting suddenly made her aware of how exhausted she was.

'How much money do you have?' David asked. He sounded as tired as she felt. 'I don't know if I have enough. I don't have a credit card.'

'I don't either.' She reached into the backseat to grab her

39

backpack. She pulled out her wallet and counted her bills. 'I have thirty-five dollars. That's not much.'

David slipped out his own wallet from his jeans pocket and handed it to her. 'Here. See how much I've got.'

She unfolded the soft, brown leather. 'You're rich. You've got forty-three bucks.'

He tapped his fingers on the steering wheel. 'Seventy-eight dollars. What can we do with that?'

She glanced at the gas tank. It was approaching a quarter full. 'We're going to need more gas.'

'You want to keep going?'

'What else are we going to do? I don't think we can afford a motel room.' She stared out at the barren landscape. It was like another world: abandoned and desolate. But with the sun sending long shadows across the ground, it was also eerily beautiful. 'Maybe we can find a town somewhere with a pay phone.'

'There was a sign for gas coming up. Ash Springs. We could ask for directions there.'

'I don't know.' Reese frowned out the window at the desert. 'What if the people there are freaks with shotguns? This looks like NRA country.'

David choked with laughter, and the unexpected sound of it cracked the tension that had held them tight since they fled the gas station. 'It's definitely not San Francisco,' he said. 'No liberal organic hipsters in sight.'

An involuntary smile tugged at Reese's mouth. 'And you're probably the only Asian person in a hundred-mile radius.'

'Never underestimate the Chinese. We're everywhere.'

Reese laughed out loud and looked over at David. He gave her a quick grin, and Reese noticed that his mouth was slightly crooked when he smiled, the right side angling up more than the left.

One of the phones in her lap beeped, and she scrambled to pick it up as David asked excitedly, 'Are you getting a call?'

Her brief moment of laughter was swallowed by sharp disappointment. 'No. My phone battery just died.'

At least she was too tired to be freaked out about it.

CHAPTER 5

As they approached Ash Springs, trees sprang up on the side of the road, pushing back the desert. When the town came into view, it was nothing more than a trailer park followed by a Shell station and a flimsy-looking two-story building. A couple of cars were parked in front.

David pulled up to one of the four gas pumps and turned off the engine. Reese opened her door, and the smell of the desert wafted inside: brush and dirt, soured slightly by the smell of gasoline. She and David got out, their doors slamming shut in two sharp cracks. The sun was setting.

'We have to pay first,' David said, reading the instructions on the pump.

'Maybe we should both go in,' Reese suggested. She didn't like the idea of splitting up.

'I agree.'

She walked around the car and noticed with a pang that the gas cap was still hanging down from the tank. Mr Chapman had never had a chance to screw it shut. She did so now, feeling a bit queasy. When she looked up, she saw David wince. 'Let's go,' she said, and headed inside.

Behind the counter, a bored-looking guy in a beat-up Pearl Jam T-shirt was turning the pages of a magazine. He glanced up when they entered but did not seem particularly interested in them. They wandered down the two short aisles, searching for maps. David found a road atlas that cost $16.95.

'It's too much,' Reese whispered. 'We have to buy gas.' Her stomach growled. 'And some food.'

He flipped the atlas open to the page on Nevada and scrutinized the tiny lines and letters. 'We're on 93 North, right?'

'Yeah.' Reese peered over his arm at the map. 'Look, there's Ash Springs,' she said.

With his finger, he traced a line that jutted west from 93 North. 'We can take this – 318 to 375, then to 6 and 95 North.'

'North? Don't we have to go west?'

'Ninety-five will get us to Reno, and then we can get onto 80 West. That goes straight to Oakland.'

She took the atlas from him and followed the white lines he pointed out. 'Okay,' she agreed, memorizing the road numbers. 'You want me to drive for a while? You could get some sleep.' David had the dazed expression of someone who had been trying to stay alert for too long.

'Aren't you tired?' he asked.

'Not as tired as you are. You've been driving all day.' He

looked skeptical, and she said, 'If I get too tired I'll pull over and go to sleep. But I think we should keep going as long as we can.'

'All right,' David relented. 'Let's go pay.'

At the counter, Reese set down two granola bars, a large bag of Doritos, a Diet Coke, and a bottle of water. 'Is there a pay phone around here?' she asked the attendant.

'Yeah, but it's broken.'

'Do you know where the nearest pay phone is?' David asked.

'You might find one in Rachel. Don't you have a cell phone?'

'No reception,' David said.

The boy shrugged. 'It's spotty out here. You know, military presence and all.'

'What military presence?' Reese asked.

'You're not from around here, are you?' the boy said flatly.

'We drove up from Vegas,' Reese said. 'Haven't you heard about what's going on?'

He shrugged. 'Some crazy shit with birds, right? Whatever. I still gotta work.'

David's eyebrows rose. 'Well, we're heading to 318 West,' he said. 'Do you know how to get there?'

'Sure. Everybody who comes through here wants to go there.'

'Why?' David asked.

'It's the Extraterrestrial Highway. You know, *aliens*. Area 51.' The boy whistled the *X-Files* theme song.

'Oh. Right,' David said. 'So is it far from here?'

'You can't miss the turnoff for 318. That'll take you to Rachel too. Just keep an eye out for the Alien Fresh Jerky sign.'

'Alien jerky,' Reese repeated in disbelief.

'Alien *fresh* jerky,' he corrected her. 'Can't miss it.'

'Thanks,' David said. He turned to head back out to the gas pump, and Reese hurried to keep up with him.

'This place is crazy,' she whispered.

'No doubt,' David agreed, and pulled the gas nozzle out of the pump. He hesitated for a moment before unscrewing the cap to the tank, and Reese knew he was thinking about Mr Chapman. She shivered, crossing her arms, and glanced nervously around the gas station. But there was nobody else there. Ash Springs was deserted except for them.

The sign advertising ALIEN FRESH JERKY appeared just as the sun dipped below the horizon. A green alien head – a pointed oval with black, almond-shaped eyes – peered out from the billboard. Near the sign was a brown shack that during the day might open into a farm stand but was now boarded shut.

Reese turned left onto 318, taking a sip of her Diet Coke. David had fallen asleep almost as soon as they had left the gas station, but the stop in Ash Springs – and the junk food – had refreshed Reese. Plus driving the well-lit streets of San

Francisco was completely different from this lonely two-lane road in the middle of nowhere. The empty highway at twilight had an eerie feel, and her hands were sweaty from clinging to the wheel.

After the sun set, darkness descended quickly, and she turned on the car's high beams. The center yellow dashes in the black road flashed by like Morse code. She heard David breathing in the passenger seat, and it felt as though the two of them were the only humans left alive in the world. She missed, fiercely, streetlights and skyscrapers and neon. There were dangers in the city, of course, but those were dangers she understood. She had no idea what was out in the middle of the desert. The blackness could be a beast that wanted only to swallow them whole.

When the road forked, she barely remembered to stay left in order to turn onto 375. She sped past a green sign that read EXTRATERRESTRIAL HIGHWAY and wondered what Julian would think about her driving down this road. He would probably be jealous. A couple of months ago he had tried to convince her to help him start a conspiracy news site called Black Mailbox, named after the object that was located off the side of the road near Area 51.

'That's super geeky, Jules,' she said. They were in the journalism room after a deadline, drinking Diet Cokes and playing basketball with crumpled-up sheets of page proofs.

'Geeky is awesome,' he said, and emphasized his point by expertly tossing a paper ball into the trash can, which they had hooked onto the back of the door.

46

'The mailbox isn't even black – you said it's white now. If it's going to be the name of a *news* site, shouldn't it at least be accurate?' Reese balled up the proofs of her most recent story, 'GSA Launches Anti-Bullying Awareness Week.' It banged off the edge of the trash can and fell to the floor. She groaned.

'It doesn't matter what color it really is. It's known as the black mailbox. And it's not an *alien* mailbox – it's just a regular mailbox where you go if you want to see UFOs over Area 51.'

'But the UFOs are *alien* spacecraft, aren't they?'

'Maybe, maybe not. They could just be top-secret military fighter planes or something. Like the B-2 bomber. It was tested at Area 51. Black Mailbox is an awesome name.'

She had agreed to help him – they even discussed how she would play skeptic to Julian's believer on their site – but shortly afterward she and David had qualified for nationals, and all her time was taken up with debate practice.

And then she had gone and messed up during the semifinal round. All that work for nothing.

Reese glanced over at David. The dashboard lights didn't illuminate much; he was mostly a shadow in the seat beside her, his head lolling against the passenger side window. In the dark bubble of the car, her thoughts drifted back to the night before semifinals. She had tried to stop herself from thinking about it too much – it wouldn't do her any good to obsess over it – but she was all alone with David in the middle of nowhere. She couldn't help herself.

They had won the quarterfinal round decisively. Mr Chapman took them to dinner at a Southwestern restaurant to celebrate, and Reese remembered the blue corn enchiladas and garlicky guacamole with an audible hunger pang. After dinner they returned to the Holiday Inn, where most of the debaters were staying, and Mr Chapman went to bed, telling them to get some sleep before the big day. But she and David were too excited to sleep. They bought sodas from the vending machine by the pool and staked out two deck chairs, spreading out their notes to quiz each other.

The pool area was crowded with other high school students. Some were swimming, but most were debaters like them, cramming in last-minute research before the big event. It was only the Holiday Inn – thoroughly and efficiently pedestrian in its decor – but Reese remembered the pool as if it had been decorated for a glittering party. She remembered lights hung in delicate strands around the perimeter, reflected in the water as hundreds of wavering stars. She remembered David leaning toward her, watching her with smiling eyes while she shuffled through notes and charts.

When the pool closed and all the students were forced to head upstairs, David walked her back to her room on the sixth floor even though he was on the fifth. The hallway carpet had a pattern of tiny, brownish-gold diamonds on a background of dark red, probably designed to withstand heavy foot traffic and spills, and Reese found herself staring at it intently as they neared her room. At the door, she shifted her backpack to one shoulder so that she could dig

48

out her keycard, and David reached out to grab the bag before it slipped to the floor.

'Thanks,' she said. She had to open the front pocket of the backpack, and for some reason David didn't let go of it. She looked up at him, and it was as if some kind of invisible switch inside her flipped. Her skin went hot, and her brain went blank. Her heartbeat accelerated. David's straight black eyelashes were like the bristles of a fine paintbrush. His cheeks were tinged light pink.

The elevator at the end of the hall dinged open, and a crowd of debaters surged into the corridor. One of them called out, 'Just kiss her already!'

The other students snickered, and Reese's face burned with mortification. David jerked away from her, letting go of her backpack so suddenly, it banged sharply against her knee.

Reese spun around and slammed the keycard into the lock. She burst into the room and shoved the door closed just as she heard David call her name. Laughter ricocheted down the hallway. One of the kids called out, 'She's playing hard to get!'

Reese backed away from the door and sat down on the edge of the bed, dropping her backpack onto the floor. Her whole body shook. For months – ever since he broke up with his girlfriend back in November – her feelings for David had been building up. She had tried to ignore them, because they scared the living daylights out of her – she did *not want* to like someone. She did not want to be thinking about

David when she was supposed to be doing something else. Maybe other girls liked that nervous, fluttery feeling in their stomachs, but she hated it. It made her feel out of control.

She had promised herself a long time ago, after overhearing one too many fights between her parents, that she wasn't going to get involved in anything romantic. Her parents had divorced when she was nine, but for years afterward they would reconcile and then split up again. Every time things went south – which they inevitably did – Reese saw the way it wrecked her mother. Reese didn't want to be like that. And that meant she wasn't going to date anyone, and she definitely wasn't going to *like* anyone.

She had never factored in the possibility that someone might like her. That the pull of that person might overrule her intellectual decision to deny her feelings.

David was knocking on the door, calling out, 'Reese? Reese, let me talk to you.'

'Leave me alone,' she said, her voice hitching into a sob.

'Reese?'

'Leave me alone!' she yelled, and finally David went away. She should have been relieved – now he would definitely never be interested in her since she had overreacted like a freak – but instead she felt as if a dragging weight had been chained to her feet. She stared at her hands as hot tears fell onto her palms, and told herself to get over it. It was better this way. Safer.

The next day, she screwed up royally during semifinals.

She could barely look at David, much less concentrate on the debate topic. No wonder they had lost.

She was still stuck in that memory, sinking lower and lower, when a shape flew directly into the headlights.

It was a bird, its wings flapping seemingly in slow motion, two pinpricks of yellow glowing where its eyes should be. 'Shit!' Reese screamed.

She slammed on the brakes. The car, moving at sixty-five miles per hour, skidded forcefully down the asphalt. She flew forward, and then the seat belt jerked her back, contracting painfully across her chest. She heard David shouting. The brakes emitted a long, unending shriek.

The smoothness of the highway abruptly ended. The tires struck desert, and she felt the jarring impact right down into her bones. Loose rocks rumbled beneath the car; dust flew up into the high beams. The car had gone off the road, and now it was rolling downhill. Reese pumped frantically at the brakes, but it didn't seem to make a difference.

There was a jolt so big, her head struck the roof, and the car banged down, hard, into an unseen ditch. It flipped, and her stomach flipped with it. The high beams bounced crazily over the desert. She saw the ground lit by the unnaturally bright lights; rocks smashed against the windshield. Something smashed into her head.

Everything went black.

CHAPTER 6

Reese heard a strange gurgling sound, like liquid being forced through a pipe. She tried to move, and it sent a shock of pain through her – pain so intense that she screamed and screamed – and then realized that the gurgling sound was the sound of her breath. Was she drowning? Panic erupted in her. She tried to swim, but her body was pinned beneath something hard and sharp, something that cut into her abdomen. The scream in her throat broke into a sob.

The darkness returned.

Next came the light, bright as the full moon, startling as a lightning flash. As it advanced, the ground rumbled, and she wondered if she had been in an earthquake. She thought: *All those stories are true. I'm going toward the light.*

The shriek of metal being torn apart exploded in her ears. The entire world rattled. She blinked; all she could see was blinding white light.

A machine groaned, and she heard voices she could not understand. She was suffocating in a haze of pain. She whimpered. Something was wrong with her – with all of her. Her whole body felt distorted, as if she were in a real-life fun-house mirror, and parts of her were swollen monstrously out of proportion. Was she dead? A screeching, metallic roar invaded all of her senses, blotting out thought.

All the pressure that had been holding her body immobile suddenly released. She fell out into the night air. It was cool and dry.

The smell of the desert. Hands beneath her body. Fingers pressed into her stomach, and she cried out. The gurgling sound returned.

She couldn't breathe.

She felt motion beneath her, around her, but her body was so still. She could not move. She tried to wriggle her toes, but she did not know if she succeeded. Terror engulfed her. She tried to speak, but her mouth would not open. She heard a low beeping sound, like a heart monitor. Someone touched her hand, and she felt a pressure on her wrist. Something cool slid into her, and the world went blank.

A door slammed. Wheels rattled along a tile floor. A fan hummed on. Wind swept over her skin. When she opened her eyes, she could see – but she could not understand what she was seeing.

She was in a yellow sphere. It reminded her of a planetarium, except it was much, much smaller – only big enough for one person. The walls of the sphere undulated in and out as if they were breathing. Was she hallucinating? She could not feel her body. There was no more pain. She felt entirely disconnected, as if her consciousness were the sole part of her that existed. The only sound was the whisper of the wind: a gentle inhalation in the background.

Red cracks began to appear in the soft, rippling walls, arising from nothing and branching out like veins across the surface of an egg yolk. She stared at them in amazement. She spun around and realized that she *could* spin around. She was suspended in the center of this yellow bubble with its red rivers snaking across curved, luminescent walls.

Gradually she became aware of another sound. It was strangely distant, as if it were coming at her through a wall of water. It reminded her of documentaries about deep-sea divers: this sound of half-swallowed, echoing ringing.

The red veins were moving faster. They spread and spread like a time-lapse video of red coral growing, and as the red covered the yellow, she felt heavier and heavier, and the golden glow of the sphere's walls dimmed and dimmed until all there was, was nothing.

Twenty-seven
days later

CHAPTER 7

Reese opened her eyes and saw a grid of grayish-white ceiling tiles above. She blinked a few times, inhaling shallowly. The room smelled antiseptic, like a hospital. She turned her head to the right; there was a window not far away, but the blinds were closed. Daylight glowed from behind them. To her left was a computer and monitor on a cart, along with some kind of medical machine. Several tubes emerged from it, connected to an IV drip hanging above her head. Another tube ran from that drip to her left arm.

I was in an accident. She remembered the eyes in the headlights, the car leaping off the road, slamming into the ground. The weight of something terrifyingly heavy pushing against her body. The machine and the lights and the pain – and David.

What happened to David?

Dizziness swamped her, and she closed her eyes. The room seemed to be spinning, and she curled into a fetal position as nausea swept through her.

If she had survived, that meant he had too. Didn't it?

Her gut clenched. She didn't want to think about the alternative, and it was several minutes before she had calmed herself enough to open her eyes again. She was now staring directly at the computer next to her bed, and the monitor was dark. Her mouth felt fuzzy, as if there was something nasty on her tongue.

Where am I?

Slowly she pushed herself up to a seated position and then swung her legs over the edge of the bed. The movement made her stomach heave, and she doubled over for a minute, gasping, as she waited for the nausea to subside. She saw speckled gray linoleum below her bare feet, and pale remnants of bruises ran up her left shin and over her knee.

The sight of the bruises sent a cold shock through her. She stared at her legs. The right leg was bruised too, but even more stunning was a long pink scar running diagonally across her knee and thigh. When she touched it, she felt a slightly raised ridge there, and goose bumps rose all over her skin.

She took a few slow breaths. The IV tube swayed. She straightened up and held out her arms, examining each of them. The IV needle was inserted into her left arm just below the elbow crease, held in place with white tape, but otherwise the arm seemed normal. On her right arm, the area around her elbow felt tender, but she couldn't see whether there were any bruises there. On her right wrist she wore a plastic bracelet imprinted with a code: PLATO PA83 HOLLOWAY. She was wearing an open-backed hospital gown printed with a pattern of tiny blue diamonds.

She looked around the room, hoping that something here would give her a clue to where she was. There were two doors: one closed, the other slightly ajar with a hint of tile floor beyond. She guessed it must be a bathroom. The walls were painted an industrial shade of beige, and the only furniture was the bed and the bedside table that held the computer. She scooted off the bed, stepping onto the floor.

Her feet and legs tingled the way they did after they had fallen asleep, and she hissed with pain as she limped the few steps to the computer. She turned the monitor around, looking for any identifying markers, but there was only a serial code that meant nothing to her. The computer itself was clipped below the tabletop, and she felt around the edge of the rectangular box until she found what must be the power button. She pressed it, and the machine hummed on. For a moment she was elated, but her excitement was short-lived. The first thing that appeared on the screen was a login box prompting her for a password.

She abandoned the computer and wheeled the IV-drip pole away from the wall, using it like a walker as she headed to the window. The pins-and-needles sensation in her legs subsided a bit as she walked gingerly across the floor, but they still felt jellylike. At the window, she tugged on the string attached to the blinds, and they rattled up.

Outside, the sun beamed white-hot over a small parking lot where a lone, dirty Jeep was parked. Past the small, paved surface, the desert rippled with heat. In the distance she saw a long, low building with tan, windowless walls. Far beyond that a lumpy mountain range defined the horizon, and above it all the pale blue sky seemed almost bleached of color by the sun.

She was still in Nevada – she had to be. This desert looked exactly like the other hundreds of miles of desert she and David had driven through after leaving Phoenix. As she pressed her face to the glass, she caught a glimpse of her eyes barely reflected in the window, ghostlike. She drew back, unnerved, and her reflection disappeared.

Behind her she heard the door opening, and she spun to see a woman in a lab coat entering. She had dark brown hair worn in a precisely cut bob. 'I see you're awake,' she said, an eager look on her face. 'I'm Dr Evelyn Brand. You should be careful with that IV; let me help you get back into bed.'

'Where am I? Where's David?' Reese asked. Her voice sounded rough, unused.

The doctor briskly crossed the room. The door clicked shut. 'You shouldn't be walking around with that drip attached to you,' Dr Brand said. She put a cool, dry hand on Reese's right elbow and firmly propelled her back to bed, pulling the IV pole behind them. Startled, Reese let the doctor swing her legs up and tuck the thin blanket over her.

'Let me take a look at you,' Dr Brand said, pulling out a stethoscope. Her eyes were such a light brown that they were almost gray.

'Where's David?' Reese asked again as Dr Brand pressed

the stethoscope against her chest. 'He was in the car with me. Is he all right?'

'Don't worry. David Li is fine,' Dr Brand said. The knot of dread in Reese's belly loosened. David was alive. 'But you both had a very nasty accident. Your car flipped over, and we had to cut you out. It's a good thing you crashed where you did.'

The stethoscope slid cold and hard over Reese's skin. 'What do you mean? Where did we crash?'

Dr Brand gave her an apologetic smile. 'That information is classified. I'm sure you remember approximately where your car crashed, but I can't tell you much more. Because of that, you'll need to remain in your hospital room for now. I can't authorize you to wander through this facility.'

Reese stared at Dr Brand, stunned. 'But . . . what happened? Did I have surgery? I saw a scar on my leg.'

'You broke your leg and fractured your arm, and you had some serious internal injuries as well. Your spleen was ruptured, probably from the impact of the steering wheel, and you had a concussion.'

Reese was confused. She felt as if her brain were thinking in slow motion. 'I broke my leg? Shouldn't it be in a cast, then?'

'If you were at any other hospital, yes, but we've used some very advanced medicine on you – medicine that isn't available to the general public. Normally, you'd have been in a cast for three to six months, but because of the treatment you received, you can walk already.' Dr Brand wound the stethoscope back around her neck and put her hands in the pockets of her lab coat. 'How are your legs feeling?'

'They...they feel sort of like they were asleep.'

Dr Brand nodded. 'That's normal. You might have some of that tingling sensation for the next few days off and on, as well as some nausea as you come down from the medication. In order to speed your healing processes, we put you in a medically induced coma, so there will be a period of adjustment from that.'

Dr Brand sounded so calm, as if all this information was entirely ordinary, but Reese felt a pricking of unease all over her scalp. 'A coma? How long was I asleep?'

'Twenty-seven days.'

Reese's heartbeat quickened. 'Twenty-seven days?' She finally seemed to wake up fully. 'I need to call my mom. Does she know I'm here? Why isn't she here?'

'We already told her about you, but visitors aren't permitted here. There are no telephones in the hospital rooms, but we'll make arrangements for you to call her yourself soon.'

'When can I go home?'

'You'll need to stay here for another couple of days so we can monitor your recovery, but you'll be able to go home soon. Since you had a concussion, you'll likely have some headaches for a few weeks, particularly after stressful situations, so you'll want to take it easy. Does your head hurt right now?'

'No.' Something that Dr Brand had said floated to the

surface of her consciousness. 'You already called my mom? How do you know who she is?'

Dr Brand smiled. 'We did recover your driver's license. Clarice Holloway – that's you, isn't it?'

The smile on the doctor's face was disconcerting. An odd feeling flashed through Reese, as if she had seen Dr Brand somewhere before, but she couldn't figure out where. 'I – I don't go by Clarice. My name is Reese.'

'I'm sorry. I didn't know.' Dr Brand gave her a sympathetic look. 'Are there any other questions I can answer for you?'

'Can I talk to David?'

'He's still asleep. But as soon as he's awake you'll both be debriefed and we'll get started on the paperwork to get you out of here. I'm going to leave you now, but – actually, I'll bring you some magazines, how about that? I'm sure you'll want to catch up on what you've missed while you were asleep. I'll be right back.'

Dr Brand left the room as briskly as she had entered it, her shoes tapping smartly across the floor. Reese leaned back against the pillows, a dull pain beginning to blossom at the base of her skull. She closed her eyes, the doctor's words echoing in her memory. She was in a classified facility. She had received advanced medical treatment. David was alive.

Mr Chapman was dead.

Her eyes flew open just as Dr Brand returned. 'Here you go,' Dr Brand said, laying the magazines on the edge of the bed. 'A lot has happened, but—'

'I have to tell you something,' Reese said.

Dr Brand looked startled. 'What is it?'

'When we were in Las Vegas – David and I – we were with our debate coach, and he was shot outside a gas station. We were just there to buy some gas, and this carjacker came and shot him. David and I left – we had to leave because the guy was about to shoot us. But then we could never find our way back to the gas station. We meant to call the police, but the phones never worked. You have to tell someone. You have to call his family or the police or something. His name is Joe Chapman; he's a teacher at Kennedy High School in San Francisco.' As she spoke, the dull throbbing in her head began to expand into sharp jabs of pain. She grimaced.

'Calm down, Reese.' Dr Brand glanced at the IV drip, then pulled a hypodermic needle out of her pocket. 'If you become overexcited, that can also trigger the headaches.'

Reese sat up too quickly and winced. 'But you have to call the school! You have to tell them.'

'I heard you. I'll contact them. Let me give you a little painkiller, all right?' Dr Brand did something with the needle and the drip, and a cool sensation washed through Reese's arm and into her body. The headache began to dissipate, but she also began to feel numb, as if her emotions had been turned off. 'Just rest,' Dr Brand said. 'I'll call the school.'

Reese succumbed to the drugs, relaxing down into the pillows. 'Thank you.' Her speech sounded slurred. The doctor smiled at her again, patting her hand, and then left.

After the door closed she rolled onto her side, accidentally knocking the magazines Dr Brand had brought onto the

66

floor. Groggily, she leaned over the edge of the bed and gazed down at them. There was a *Time* magazine on top, and on the cover was a photo of an airport on fire. Bright orange flames licked into the sky, where a giant cloud of black smoke plumed up from the inferno. The headline, in bold red font, screamed: *The Truth Is Out There*. The subtitle read: *Riots, conspiracies, and clues – what really happened during the June Disaster?*

Twenty-seven days, Reese thought. She had been unconscious for almost a month. Fighting against the wave of numbness brought on by the painkiller, she leaned over the edge of the bed and reached for the magazine.

The Truth Behind the Terror

By Patricia Martinez; Alan Thompson, Ellen Wu, Mark Ritter/Washington; Steve Elliott/Denver

Conspiracies can be doggedly enduring. The Kennedy assassination, the moon landing, even 9/11 have all been subject to detailed and often frighteningly convincing conspiracy theories. But rarely have those theories translated into real-world consequences as quickly and as fatally as those that followed the plane crashes of June 19.

That afternoon, shortly after President Elizabeth Randall addressed the nation and urged us all to remain calm, conspiracy theorists lit up the Internet with calls for disclosure. Jason Briggs, the pseudonym of the man behind the conspiracy-fueled website Bin42.com, was one of the first to issue warnings to Americans. Stock up on supplies, he suggested. Get to your bunkers and lock your doors.

Had it not been for a perfect storm of events, Briggs's exhortations might have been dismissed as the ravings of a crackpot. But as the first twenty-four hours of the ultimately seven-day-long flight ban ticked by, the evidence seemed to pile up, and it was all on Briggs's side.

In Chicago a plane crashed but was not acknowledged by the FAA. Bits and pieces of video footage from the crash site leaked onto the Hub, but were repeatedly removed. Members of the hacker collective Black Hat claimed that they detected US government interference blocking traffic on the Internet backbone. Cell phone and broadband service was disrupted in up to 85 percent of the United States. In Las Vegas a plane crashed onto the Strip, leading to a forced evacuation of a large portion of the city. Stranded tourists with slot-machine tokens in their pockets were herded by the National Guard into a caravan and shipped off to a tent encampment in the middle of the desert, where they were unable to call their loved ones.

And then came the straw that broke the camel's back. At Denver International Airport, less than eighteen hours after the flight ban was instated, a disagreement between several travelers turned violent. When Transportation Security Administration officers intervened, the situation escalated, ultimately resulting in a riot that ended only after the deployment of tear gas.

After that, the gloves came off. Mobs began to descend on supermarkets and warehouses, looting freely and invoking Bin 42's theories as justification for their actions. For the first time since the Civil War, the United States Army rolled into major urban areas believed to be on the verge of instability, including Los Angeles, Denver, and Boston. Curfews were instated across the country, even in sleepy small towns.

Briggs – and his website – had become the vocal leader of a new conspiracy, one that has become disturbingly mainstream. The theory? The United States government is hiding the cause of the June 19 crashes because the government itself had a hand in it.

But is Briggs right? Or were the disastrous events of June simply the tragic result of bureaucratic mismanagement compounded by misinformation spread by crippled communications systems?

White House press secretary Carolina Lopez categorically rejects the assertion of Bin 42 and its cohorts. 'These websites have no real evidence,' Lopez says. 'President Randall understands that people are on edge right now, but stirring up fear with these conspiracy theories doesn't help. We are working day and night – in cooperation with the Canadian and Mexican governments – to pinpoint the cause of these bird strikes.' Lopez notes that the United States was not the only nation affected by the deadly bird strikes that caused a dozen planes to crash, killing more than two thousand people in North America over the course of twenty-four hours.

'There is just no way that the United States government could be behind this event,' says Peter Vikram, professor of history at Harvard University and author of *Conspiracists United: A History of American Skeptics and Their Beliefs*. 'These kinds of theories cropped up after 9/11 also, because believing in a government-organized conspiracy can be comforting. It gives order to a series of frightening events that otherwise seem entirely random. If we know whodunit, then we can catch the killer. Unfortunately, in this case, there is no single villain; there are many. That's the real trauma that the United States is facing now – coming to understand how we could have done the things we did, motivated only by fear of not knowing why the planes crashed.'

Jason Briggs denies that he and his cohorts are fear-mongering. 'That is bulls—' he states in an e-mail interview. 'We are releasing the truth as the evidence comes to us. Everyone can judge for themselves. Of course the Randall Administration isn't going to admit that they're culpable – that would be political suicide for the president, and she's only halfway through her first term.'

The so-called evidence that Briggs has been amassing on Bin 42 draws from citizen reporting of alleged cover-ups of crash sites as well as theories incubated by conspiracists over decades about classified military projects. Several threads lead directly to beliefs about UFOs.

Briggs is unapologetic about the connections to those fringe theories. 'Anyone who dispassionately examines the evidence will come away with a conviction that the government is involved in a cover-up about UFOs,' he writes. 'I'm not saying there are aliens walking the Earth right now, but there is something there that the government doesn't wish the public to know.'

Millions of Americans clearly agree with him. Traffic to Bin 42 quadrupled once the Internet went back online, and chatter on the Hub has centered almost exclusively on those theories. The Randall Administration's efforts to turn the public's attention to rebuilding and moving on after the June Disaster have been largely met with skepticism.

Outside the White House every morning, protesters pace back and forth. Written in large, hand-lettered block capitals, their signs declare, 'Birds don't destroy planes, people do,' and 'Tell us the truth, President Randall!'

But perhaps the truth is greater than the conspiracies detailed online. Perhaps the real issue is not whether the government orchestrated the plane crashes, but instead, do we trust our elected officials? And if we don't, why have we elected them in the first place? Democracy, at its root, is based on the faith that our representatives have our best interests at heart. If we as a nation no longer believe that they do, that may be even more disturbing than the idea that aliens are among us.

CHAPTER 8

I thought you'd like to put on some real clothes before you and David are debriefed,' Dr Brand said, wheeling in a damaged suitcase on a dolly.

The top was bashed in and the zipper broken, but Reese recognized it as her carry-on. The sight of it, all squashed and misshapen, was disturbing. She and her bag had been in the same accident; had she been as damaged when she was pulled from the wreckage?

'How are your legs feeling?' Dr Brand asked.

Reese sat up, averting her eyes from the battered luggage. 'Better than yesterday.' Her limbs felt more solid than when she first woke up from the coma, but every so often they still felt a little rubbery.

'Good. No problems with breakfast?' Dr Brand had unhooked Reese from the IV that morning, when she had brought her a bowl of nearly tasteless oatmeal.

'No. It was kind of disgusting, though.'

Dr Brand gave her a sympathetic smile. 'I'm sorry about

that. We have to be careful at first, getting you back on solid foods. When you go home you'll want to stick to a bland diet for a few days. You should get dressed now. I'll come back in about half an hour.'

Reese knelt on the floor next to her suitcase. Bungee cords were wrapped around it to keep it closed, and when she unhooked them, the suitcase seemed to sigh as it expanded. She opened it up. Her toiletries kit was smashed flat in the center, and dark stains seeped out through the fabric of the bag. She lifted it out and saw that toothpaste and lotion had exploded all over the top layer of clothing.

She didn't feel like she had been in a coma for twenty-seven days. Even after reading the *Time* magazine from cover to cover and trying to absorb all that had gone on while she had been unconscious, she still felt like she had been asleep for one night only. But now as she lifted out the soiled blouse and skirt she had last worn at the debate tournament, the weeks that had passed since the accident became gut-wrenchingly real. Her clothing smelled of toothpaste and time, as if the suitcase had been in storage. She pulled out a blue T-shirt printed with a silver alien head – Julian had given her that – and held it to her nose. A combination of mint and the scent of some place closed-off and cool, air-conditioned and dark. There was something familiar about that smell.

She was swept by a wave of dizziness. She sat down, the linoleum floor pressing cold and hard against her bare thigh. A dull ache began to pulse behind her temples. She took a few deep breaths, trying to calm the sudden, uncomfortable racing of her heart. Her legs tingled, and unconsciously she rubbed the scar on her knee, her fingers tracing the ridge as if she were following a map over her own skin.

The scar didn't seem to be as raised as it had been yesterday.

She looked down, shifting so that her right leg stretched out in front of her. The scar was still there, but she could swear it had lightened, and somehow it seemed shorter. She remembered that it had slashed almost halfway up her thigh, but now it faded away only a few inches above her knee. *That's weird.* Had her medication distorted what she had seen?

She massaged her temples with her fingers, waiting for the dizziness to pass. She wished her mom were here. Homesickness pulled at her with a physical ache in her belly. What had Dr Brand said? The headaches would increase under stress? That almost made her laugh. How could being in a near-fatal car accident and waking up alone in a hospital be anything other than stressful?

Breathe, she told herself. *You're going home soon. Everything's going to be fine. You can freak out when you get home. Today you're going to see David.*

David. For the first time since that night before semifinals, she didn't feel self-conscious about the way she might act around him. She just wanted to see him, alive, with her own eyes.

She began to rummage through her broken suitcase and

pulled out underwear and a bra, socks and a pair of jeans. It was good to put on her own clothes, even though they felt strange sliding over her skin. The jeans were loose on her, hanging lower on her hips than they used to, and when she slipped her arms through the alien T-shirt, even that seemed a bit baggy. *Liquid diet.* She got up to go to the bathroom and check her appearance, but when she went inside and turned on the light, there was no mirror over the sink. She hadn't noticed that yesterday. She looked at the back of the door, but there was none there either.

The door to her room opened, startling her.

Dr Brand was back. 'Reese? Are you ready?'

'Just a minute.' Reese hurriedly ran her brush through her dark brown hair before leaving the bathroom. 'I'm ready.'

The hallway outside Reese's hospital room was as blank and nondescript as the room itself: beige walls, linoleum floor, speckled drop-panel ceilings. She could have been in any office park, except that each door was fitted with a camera and keypad instead of a normal lock.

Dr Brand paused at the end of the hall in front of a door marked CONFERENCE B. She entered a code while standing in front of the camera, and then a small green light came on at the base of the keypad. She pushed open the door. 'Go on in. I'll be right back with your paperwork.'

Reese stepped into the conference room. It was a plain, rectangular space with an oval table in the center, surrounded by rolling chairs. A blank white board hung on the wall to her right, and across the room was a window with the same mini-blinds that hung in her hospital room.

David was standing at the window.

He met her halfway across the room, his arms sliding around her tightly. 'Are you all right?' she whispered, her face pressed against his shoulder. He smelled like her suitcase: air-conditioning and a slight layer of dust. His clothes had been in storage too.

'I'm fine,' he said. She felt his voice reverberating through her, his breath on her hair, and in that instant an odd sensation pushed at her: a feeling of discordance. As if two instruments sounded but were not in sync.

She pulled back, disoriented, as her body tingled into awareness of how close she had been to him. David's face blurred in front of her, and she grabbed the back of a chair for balance.

'Reese? What's wrong?'

'I think I just need to sit,' she said carefully. He put his hand on her elbow and guided her to the table. She could feel the imprint of his fingers on her arm long after he let go and sat beside her, his knee brushing gently against her leg. 'It must be a side effect of the drugs.' Her voice sounded shaky. 'Dr Brand told me there would be some. Side effects. Have you felt any?'

'Some weirdness in my legs, yeah. I don't think anybody wakes up from a coma feeling totally on top of the world.' He smiled slightly, and she noticed that his face was thinner. There were hollows in his cheeks she had never seen before, and they gave his cheekbones a new prominence that made him seem older. His black hair had grown out so that it swept softly over his forehead.

She realized she was staring at him. She flushed and glanced away. Outside the window she saw a vista that appeared to be nearly identical to the one outside her room. The same tan desert, baking under the sun. 'I can't wait to go home,' she said. Her words came out sounding more fervent than she intended, and homesickness flooded her again, thick and hot.

'Me too,' David agreed heartily.

The door opened, and Dr Brand entered with a man in a black suit. He was tall, with short dark hair and sharp blue eyes that darted from Reese to David. 'This is Special Agent Bradley Forrestal,' Dr Brand said as she took a seat. 'He'll be telling you about what's next.'

'Good morning,' Agent Forrestal said, flashing them a brief smile. He set a metallic briefcase on the table and opened it, pulling out a laptop and sitting down. 'Dr Brand says you're both recovered enough to go home tomorrow. I'll be escorting you back to San Francisco, and I'll be your contact once you're home if you have any questions about the treatment you've received here.' He withdrew two stapled documents from his briefcase and slid one to Reese and the other to David, then passed them each a pen. 'Before you leave we just need you to fill out some paperwork. It's all basic information, and at the end there's a nondisclosure agreement for you to sign. Basically, it says that you agree to not talk to anyone about the treatment you've received here.'

Reese began to flip through the document. 'Why can't we talk about it?'

'I'm sure Dr Brand explained to you that you're in a classified military facility. Neither of you is authorized to discuss anything you've seen here, that's all.' He gave them a fake smile – the kind, Reese recognized, that adults give teens when they're only pretending to level with them. 'I'm sure you understand – you wouldn't want to compromise our national security, would you?'

The condescension in his voice made Reese bristle. 'I sure wouldn't, sir,' she said with exaggerated sincerity.

David swallowed a snicker.

Agent Forrestal looked slightly puzzled, but Dr Brand leaned forward, her eyes narrowing on the two of them. 'There are real repercussions to sharing your knowledge about this facility with anyone, even your parents. We've spoken with your parents, and they understand that they can't ask questions about where you received your treatment. I hope you do too.'

Dr Brand's tone was cool, but her words left no room for argument, and Reese was somewhat ashamed of her snarky comment. 'Yeah, of course I understand,' she said.

'David?' Dr Brand said.

His eyes shifted from Reese to Dr Brand. 'Yes, I understand.'

'Good,' Agent Forrestal said. 'Then let's fill out that paperwork and get you two home.'

Reese filled out the form – name, birth date, parents, address, school, various questions about her health – and then flipped to the last page, where there was a line for her signature above her name. *Clarice Irene Holloway.* She scrawled her name across the line and pushed the documents back to Agent Forrestal as David did the same with his.

'Can I call my mom?' Reese asked.

Agent Forrestal glanced at Dr Brand. 'Do you have a phone set up for that?'

'I do. It's just down the hall in the empty office.' She looked at Reese. 'When you're ready, I'll take you.'

'Is there anything else we have to do here?' Reese asked Agent Forrestal.

He shook his head. 'You're all set. I'll see you both tomorrow morning, bright and early.'

CHAPTER 9

Reese hadn't been outside in twenty-nine days. When she stepped through the door out of the hospital and into the bright morning, she was assaulted by heat. She sucked in a breath of dry desert air and raised a hand to shade her eyes from the blinding sunlight.

She had awoken before dawn, eager to go home, but now she turned back to look at the place where she had spent almost a month unconscious. The hospital was a one-story, prefab building painted tan, with a plaque affixed to the door that read BUILDING 5 – PLATO.

That word, *PLATO*, had been on her wristband too.

When she got dressed that morning, the bracelet had snagged on her long-sleeved T-shirt. She had forced it over her knuckles and dropped it in her suitcase along with a copy of the nondisclosure form she had signed the day before. What did PLATO mean?

'Hey, you coming?' David called. He was waiting for her about ten feet away.

'Yeah, sorry.' She followed him and Dr Brand down the concrete path, dragging her bungee-corded suitcase behind her.

Agent Forrestal was in the parking lot with the Jeep. He loaded their battered luggage into the vehicle, and then David and Reese climbed into the backseat.

'Have a safe flight,' Dr Brand said. As the doctor's gaze flickered over them, Reese felt a strange reluctance to leave. *Of course I want to leave*, Reese thought, watching Dr Brand head back to the hospital. Talking to her mom the day before – finally – had made this place feel like a cage. She had tossed and turned all night, overcome with impatience to get out of there. Yet the sight of Dr Brand walking away from the Jeep made Reese uneasy, as if something was unfinished.

Agent Forrestal turned on the Jeep's engine, and Reese started at the sound of it.

'You okay?' David said.

She tried to shrug off the weird feelings. 'Yeah. I just can't wait to be home again.'

As they drove down the dusty road away from the hospital, Reese saw a couple of other buildings nearby, marked with signs identifying them as BUILDING 3 – PLATO and BUILDING 2 – PLATO. In the distance were more structures, some with curved roofs that reminded her of airplane hangars; others with windows flashing in the sun. They were all beige or tan, their walls blending in almost perfectly with the surrounding desert, as if they were meant to disappear into the background.

It was a quick drive to an airstrip, where a single small plane was parked, its door already opened into a short stairway. Another man in a black suit, whom Agent Forrestal introduced as Special Agent Daniel Menzel, helped load their suitcases inside. Then David and Reese climbed in. At first she could barely see because the interior of the plane was so dark compared to outside. She fumbled her way into the seat behind David – there only appeared to be about six of them – and squinted as her eyes adjusted. She reached to pull up the window shade, but her fingers touched only glass. There was no shade. All the windows were painted black.

'The location of this facility is classified,' Agent Forrestal said. She glanced up, and his face was a dark shadow framed by the bright sunlight coming through the door. 'That's why the windows are black.'

She pulled her hand away from the glass, and despite the desert heat, a chill snaked down her spine.

California smelled of dry grass and oak trees, a scent that immediately made Reese remember summers at her grandparents' house in Marin, hiking around Phoenix Lake as her mom argued good-naturedly with her grandfather about criminal law. Her eyes watered as she inhaled deeply, homesickness now throbbing like a drumbeat inside her as she climbed down from the plane.

They had landed at an airport, but it didn't look like a regular airport. It wasn't until they were herded into a black

83

town car and began driving away that she saw the signs for Travis Air Force Base. Reese had never heard of it before, but after they left the base and turned onto the freeway, she realized they were north of Oakland. She gazed out the tinted windows as they drove south toward San Francisco. Nothing seemed to have changed. There were the rounded brown hills in the distance, dotted with gnarled live oaks; the bay, gray and windswept; the sprawl of Oakland; and then the Bay Bridge, with traffic just as backed up as always.

But as they left the Bay Bridge behind and the freeway curved up in a concrete ramp over the edges of the city, she saw an electronic billboard mounted on the side of the ramp with a message scrolling across it: 9 PM CURFEW ENFORCED WITHIN SAN FRANCISCO CITY LIMITS. VIOLATORS WILL BE ARRESTED.

'Hey, look at that,' she said, pointing it out to David. 'That's crazy.'

David leaned across the seat toward her to look out the window. 'I didn't think anything happened here. Did Dr Brand give you those magazines to read too?'

'Yeah, but they didn't focus on San Francisco.'

Agent Forrestal glanced over his shoulder from the front passenger seat. 'It's a precautionary curfew. There was rioting in Fremont and parts of Oakland, and the city of San Francisco wanted to prevent any further outbreaks of violence.'

'How long is the curfew going to last?' Reese asked.

'No idea. It was eight PM at first; they raised it to nine pm last week.'

They exited the freeway at Cesar Chavez, and at the bottom of the ramp traffic barriers were piled up on the side of the road, as if they had only recently been pulled aside. It reminded Reese of Las Vegas: the blocked interstate, the exploding gas station, Mr Chapman. She turned to David. 'I forgot to tell you – I told Dr Brand about Mr Chapman. I told her to call the police.'

'I told her too,' David said. 'Hopefully, she did.'

'Are you referring to your debate coach, Joe Chapman?' Agent Forrestal asked. 'Dr Brand informed me about what you said. We've passed on your information.'

'Did you find out what happened to him afterward?' Reese asked.

'I believe his body had already been identified and returned to California.'

Hearing Mr Chapman referred to as a 'body' made Reese sick to her stomach. She turned her head to look out the window, rolling it down to let in some air. They were paused at a stoplight, and on the corner yellow police tape was wrapped around a collection of Dumpsters. A biohazard sign was taped to the side of each one. The Dumpster lids were closed, but something was poking out of one of them. She could swear it was a wing from a bird.

They arrived at Reese's house in Noe Valley first. She was already reaching for the door handle as Agent Menzel pulled the car over in front of a yellow Victorian. She glanced back at David before she opened the door. 'Um, bye,' she said, feeling awkward.

'Bye,' David said. 'I guess I'll see you around?'

'Yeah. I'll see you around.' She got out of the car and then impulsively leaned inside again. 'I'm really glad you're okay.'

He smiled. 'I'm glad you're okay too.'

She backed out self-consciously and closed the door, nearly banging into Agent Forrestal as he climbed out of the passenger seat.

'I'll bring your suitcase,' he said. 'You go on up.'

Reese's mom opened the door before Reese finished walking up the steps from the street. The sight of her in the doorway sent a torrent of relief through Reese, and she took the last few steps two at a time until her mom crushed her into a tight embrace. She smelled of jasmine shampoo and laundry detergent, and Reese's eyes stung with tears as the tangled knot of anxiety and homesickness inside her began to unravel, making her limbs feel watery. For a long time her mom held her, and Reese heard her directing Agent Forrestal to leave the busted suitcase in the front hall.

'Here's my card if you need to be in touch,' Agent Forrestal said.

'Thanks,' her mom said, and reached one hand out to take it. Finally Reese heard Agent Forrestal's footsteps recede, and the town car drove away.

Reese pulled back, wiping a hand over her damp eyes. 'Hi, Mom.'

'Welcome home, honey. Come on inside. Nanna made a pot of soup for you.' Her mom put an arm around her shoulders and they stepped through the doorway into the cool, dim front hall.

Everything looked the same. There was the Victorian hall tree with its speckled mirror and burnished oak surface; there was her favorite blue scarf hanging on one of the hooks next to her mom's purse. It was as if nothing had changed at all. Her mom dropped Agent Forrestal's card on the hall tree table and ushered her down the hall past the living and dining rooms into the kitchen. 'Sit,' her mom said, nudging her into one of the chairs around the wooden table. Dazed, Reese sat, the chair creaking beneath her. 'How are you feeling? Are you hungry?'

Reese hadn't eaten since breakfast, and that had only been a bowl of tasteless oatmeal and some orange juice. She looked at the clock on the wall; it was 2:40 in the afternoon. 'I feel all right, but I could eat,' Reese said. The house smelled of chicken soup, that rich scent of onions and celery cooked into a meaty broth, and Reese knew, suddenly, that her grandmother hadn't just dropped off the soup. She had come over and made it here, probably keeping her mom company while they waited for Reese. 'Where's Nanna? Is she here?'

Her mom ladled soup into a bowl. 'She was, but she didn't want to overwhelm you on your first day back. She and your grandpa will be over tomorrow night when you're more settled.' Her mom set the bowl on the table and handed

Reese a spoon. 'Dr Brand said you need to eat bland food for a few days.' The fragrance of the soup pulled a growl out of Reese's stomach so loud that her mom laughed. 'I guess you are hungry.'

The spoon in Reese's hand trembled as she took her first sip. The flavors exploded over her tongue: salt and fat and the delicate sweetness of carrots over the rich, round taste of chicken. She had never eaten anything so good; it was as if she had acquired an entire new set of taste buds, and she couldn't drink the soup fast enough.

'Nanna must have really hit it out of the park with her chicken soup this time,' her mom said wryly, sitting beside Reese. 'Or else they weren't feeding you properly at that fancy military hospital.'

'I was being fed through an IV,' Reese said between spoonfuls. 'So, not really.'

Her mom frowned. 'Well, I'm glad to have you home. They didn't call me until three days after you disappeared; your father and I were frantic.'

Reese's father lived in Seattle, and Reese didn't see him too often. She liked it that way. She noticed her mom eyeing the expression on her face.

'He really was worried, honey.'

'I'm sure.'

'You have to give him some credit. He's been trying.'

'I know.' Her dad had sent her a bunch of gifts for her seventeenth birthday in April. A shiny new laptop loaded with every conceivable app she might need, gift cards for music and books and movie tickets, a video picture frame that played a message in which he declared how much he missed her. It was so over the top that it felt like he was trying to buy her affections.

'When you're settled in, I think you should give him a call. He was very supportive while you were gone, and I would have gone crazy if I had to deal with it by myself. I know he would love to hear from you.' Her mom sat back in her chair. 'Do you have any pain anywhere? Dr Brand said you were pretty seriously injured.'

'I'm okay,' Reese said as her mom scrutinized her, although she felt the beginnings of a headache behind her eyes.

Her mom's eyes narrowed. 'I think that we should get you checked out by your doctor.'

'You mean Dr Wong?' Reese said, referring to the family doctor she usually went to.

'Yes.'

'Why? Didn't Dr Brand tell you what happened?'

'Yes, but she said she can't release your medical records because the treatment is classified. I just want to get you checked out so that we have some record of this. I'll call to make an appointment.' Her mom was quiet as Reese finished her soup, but as she scraped up the last bits of broth, her mom said, 'I also heard from the school. They told me about Mr Chapman.'

Reese paused with the spoon midway to her mouth. 'They did? What did they say?'

'They said he was shot outside Las Vegas.'

The headache began to push more firmly at the insides of Reese's skull. 'Yeah.'

'There's going to be a memorial tomorrow. Do you want to go?'

'Tomorrow?'

'They wanted to wait until you and David were back, in case you wanted to go. It will be at two o'clock in the afternoon at Cypress Lawn cemetery in Colma.'

Reese dropped the spoon into the empty soup bowl. Her head was really beginning to pound now.

'Are you sure you're all right? This is a lot to deal with. Is there anything you want to talk about?' Her mom reached out and rubbed Reese's neck, her fingers pressing against the tense muscles. But instead of making her feel better, it made her dizzy, and the pounding in her head began to sound like cymbals banging over and over again. 'Reese?'

She pushed herself away from the table. 'I'm sorry, I think – I have to go to the bathroom.' She sprinted out of the kitchen and up the stairs to her bathroom, stomach heaving. She flicked on the light and slammed the door shut, bending over the toilet, but nothing came up. Her stomach made bizarre gurgling noises, and she heard her mother outside, asking if she was sick. 'I'm fine,' she said, but she stayed on the floor for another few minutes until her stomach had calmed down. Maybe the rich soup had been too much for her after the tasteless liquid diet.

When she stood, she saw herself in the mirror, her face

pale and drawn. It was the first time she had seen herself since Phoenix, and the sight shocked her.

She had known that she had lost weight, but seeing it written on her face in hollowed-out cheeks and dry lips was disturbing. Now her hazel eyes looked too big for her face, and deep purple shadows stained the skin beneath them. Her hair was longer too. It fell almost to the middle of her back now, in tangled, dark brown strands. She looked like she had been caught in a windstorm, and she wondered why her mom hadn't commented on her disheveled appearance.

She hadn't showered in the bathroom at the hospital, but now the urge to take a shower was overpowering. She felt the accumulated dirt of the last month crawling over her like a second skin that needed to be scrubbed off. She pulled off her shirt, fumbling with her bra and jeans, dropping everything on the floor. She reached out to turn on the water and caught a glimpse of her body in the mirror.

She turned back. There was a long, pink scar running down the left side of her torso from her armpit all the way to her bellybutton, and another one mirroring it on her right side. It was like she had been cut open and sewn back together. Her heart pounded. She looked down at her legs, searching for the scar over her thigh, but it had thinned to an almost invisible white line. She spun around and peered over her shoulder at her back. Purple-gray bruises bloomed over her shoulder blades. She tried to touch them, but she couldn't quite reach. Suddenly she saw something near her hairline, and she stepped closer to the mirror, pulling her hair away from her face. She could barely make it out because her scalp was white too, and the scar faded almost completely into it, but it was there: a pale line that skirted the edge of her forehead, around her temples, and disappeared behind her ears.

Reese couldn't breathe. She gripped the edge of the counter as steam from the shower filled the bathroom. Dr Brand had told her she had broken her leg and ruptured her spleen, but why did she have so many scars? Goose bumps prickled over her skin. She couldn't remember anything from the time between the accident and the day she woke up. It was all one giant blank spot, and when she tried to think about it, pain pierced her head.

Slowly, the mirror fogged up with steam. Her sharp reflection began to blur behind a cloud of mist, until she was only an indistinct human shape, her features erased.

She took a deep breath. She pulled back the shower curtain and stepped into the tub, flinching as the hot water stung her skin. She forced herself to stand under the spray until she adjusted to the temperature. She closed her eyes and ducked her head beneath it too, feeling the hot water streaming down the length of her hair, her back, her legs. She tried to forget about the blank spot in her memory that suddenly seemed so overwhelmingly huge, but she couldn't. She was certain, somehow, that there was something there that she needed to recall.

She remembered the bird in the headlights, and she

remembered waking up twenty-seven days later. But the more she tried to focus in on that *thing* that had happened between those events, the more it slid away from her, slippery as an eel.

CHAPTER 10

Cypress Lawn was one of Colma's bigger cemeteries, but Reese's mom almost missed the entrance to the parking lot. The tires squealed as she abruptly turned into the second entrance off El Camino Real. 'Sorry,' her mom muttered. She followed the road uphill, passing a planting of annuals that spelled out CYPRESS LAWN on the way to a sprawling, concrete building on the hilltop.

All around them, the hills of Colma were blanketed with headstones. The dead of San Francisco – five million of them and counting – were buried here, just a few miles south of the city. Hardly anyone had been buried in San Francisco itself since the 1940s.

'There's the sign,' Reese said, pointing toward a placard that read CHAPMAN MEMORIAL.

Her mom parked the Prius on the side of the road behind a line of other cars. Reese was about to get out when her mom put a hand on her arm. 'How are you doing, honey?'

Reese knew she was supposed to be somber and saddened by the fact that she was going to a funeral – and she was – but she also felt uncomfortably exposed. As if she were about to walk into a packed auditorium wearing nothing but her underwear. How was she supposed to act at the funeral of her debate coach, who had been shot only a few feet away from her? She didn't want to inadvertently do something wrong. 'I'm fine, I guess,' she said, but she knew it was unconvincing.

'If you start feeling sick or anything, we can go at any time.'

'Okay.'

Her mom turned off the car. 'All right. Let's go.'

Reese got out. It was clear but windy, and she was glad she had worn long sleeves and pants. As they headed toward the mausoleum, she saw a tall figure leaning against the hood of a blue car parked up the road. David. She was relieved to see him; she wouldn't have to face this alone.

'Can I meet you inside?' she said to her mom, pausing before they reached the iron gates to the courtyard. 'David's over there.'

'All right. I'll save you a seat,' her mom said.

Reese walked toward David, her arms crossed against the wind. He was dressed almost identically to her – black trousers and a black button-down shirt – and as she approached he lifted his head to look at her, his face solemn. 'Hi,' she said. 'What are you doing out here?' The wind gusted over the hill, making the American flag hanging near the mausoleum flap like birds' wings.

'Hey,' David said. 'I just needed a minute.' He pulled something out of his pocket and held it out to her. 'I brought this.'

She reached out and took it. It was a photo of the two of them with Mr Chapman, taken in Phoenix right before the semifinal round. Mr Chapman was standing between them, his arms around their shoulders. Both she and David had strained smiles on their faces. She had forgotten about the photo. The morning it had been taken, she had wanted to crawl into a hole rather than be anywhere near David. But now she was grateful that Mr C had corralled them into posing together. Seeing the photo nudged something inside herself, and sadness welled up thick and dark. The photo shook in her fingers.

'I thought we could give it to Mr Chapman's wife or something,' David said.

'That's a great idea.' Tears pricked at her eyes.

'Hey,' David said softly. He reached out and squeezed her shoulder. His hand seemed to linger on her, and her breath caught in her throat. She looked up at him. His eyebrows drew together in concern. 'Are you feeling all right?' he asked. When he let go of her, she was leaning toward him, slightly off-balance.

She choked on a laugh. 'My mom asks me that every five minutes.'

He smiled slightly. 'Mine too.'

The tension of the last few minutes dissipated somewhat,

and she handed the photo back to him. He was going through the same thing she was. Maybe she should tell him about the scars. 'David . . .'

'Yeah?'

She hesitated, pulling her hair over one shoulder as the wind buffeted her. 'I saw something in the mirror when I got home. There were scars all over me. Did you – do you have scars from the accident?'

He studied her face. 'Yeah, of course.'

'Do you have scars all around your head?'

'Where?'

She ran a finger along the edge of her face. 'Here.'

He came closer, raising a hand to her head. Her scalp tingled from his touch.

'Do you see it?' she whispered, her pulse speeding up as his fingers traced her hairline.

'Just barely.'

She felt his breath on her ear, and the rush of the wind over the hills of tombstones seemed to echo the buzzing sensation that lit through her body.

David went very still. 'Reese . . .'

All of her senses seemed to zero in on that moment: the brisk wind on her face, the throb of blood in her veins, the thrill that traveled directly from David's fingertips into her body. 'What?' she said, the word hanging in the air between them like a bubble of hope.

His hand fell away from her and he stepped back. His expression was slightly apologetic. 'We should go in. I think the service is going to start soon.'

The bubble burst. She had forgotten already: After her behavior at nationals, he was obviously not going to be interested in her. The fact that they'd had this crazy accident together didn't change a thing. They were just friends. Besides, she told herself, she didn't want anything more anyway.

Nonetheless, disappointment settled over her thickly. She swallowed it like a bitter pill. 'Of course. Let's go.'

Just through the iron gates was a courtyard with memorial plaques mounted on the walls, each one bearing a person's name and dates of birth and death. Several rows of chairs had been set up in the courtyard, all facing a podium that was hung with a wreath of lilies. There were already about a dozen people there, and Reese saw the high school principal along with a few teachers she recognized. David went to sit with his parents in the third row, and Reese saw her mom waiting a couple of rows back. Reese sat down beside her, feeling worn out even though the service hadn't begun yet. Her mom squeezed her knee and whispered, 'That's Mr Chapman's wife up there.' She indicated a woman in a black dress who was standing near the podium. She didn't look sad; she looked empty. Reese clutched the edges of her seat as a wave of something desperate and lonely swept against her. She hadn't expected the funeral to affect her so strongly. Her mom put an arm around her shoulders, and Reese leaned against her gratefully.

Other students from the debate team were scattered throughout the audience, and some of them twisted around to look at her, unable to hide their curiosity. The feeling of being exposed came back, and Reese shrank into her seat. She slumped in relief when the service began because that meant her classmates could no longer stare at her. But when Mrs Chapman went to the podium to speak, Reese had to lower her gaze to the ground so that she didn't become overwhelmed by the grief on Mrs Chapman's face. Reese couldn't remember her emotions ever being so volatile before. It was as if a storm were brewing inside her: the wind swirling dark clouds in an accelerating spiral. She managed to hold it together through the entire service, and she even went with David to deliver the photo to Mrs Chapman, who embraced her in thanks. The woman's body felt brittle as a bird's. Reese had to excuse herself afterward, muttering that she was looking for the ladies' room. Someone directed her toward the mausoleum entrance and she went inside on shaking legs, worried that she was going to throw up.

She hurried down a broad corridor lined with memorial plaques up to the twenty-foot-high ceiling. She caught sight of the RESTROOM sign at the end of the hall, and she quickened her pace until she was practically running, her sneakers slapping dully on the marble floor. She turned the corner and saw the ladies' room to her right. She ducked inside. There were two stalls and she slipped into the empty one, slamming the door shut. She bent over, her breath wheezing in her lungs. A droplet of sweat trickled off her temple and plunged into the toilet. Someone flushed in the next stall, and as water stormed through the pipes, she began to calm down.

Out there, she had been afraid she would fly apart, as if she were a rag doll being fought over by children, the seams stretching to their breaking point. It was better in here, alone. There was no one to see her, and no one for her to see. She felt herself knitting back together again.

She waited until the bathroom had emptied and then came out, turning on the tap to splash water over her face. Over the sink a sign had been affixed that read DANGER: DO NOT DRINK THIS WATER. *Ugh*. Not a good thing to see in a mausoleum bathroom. She straightened, pulling some paper towels from the dispenser to dry off her dripping face and hands. Some strands of her hair had gotten wet, and she ran her fingers through it in an attempt to straighten out the windblown mess. She heard footsteps approaching, and a woman she recognized from the memorial service entered the bathroom. Reese gave up on finger combing her hair and left as the woman went into one of the stalls. She wasn't eager to go back to the memorial, though, and as she stepped out into the hallway she glanced to the right.

A man in a black suit was framed briefly in the archway to the next corridor.

She stared at the now empty archway. Who was that? He reminded her of Special Agent Forrestal.

She walked toward the archway, but when she reached

100

the threshold of the room beyond it, there was no one there. It was a roughly square space, the walls lined with glass cases filled with urns and framed photos. Though she was surrounded by the dead, there was nothing frightening about it. It was peaceful there. Glass doors on the right led out to a grassy courtyard, and wide corridors full of more memorial plaques branched off to the left and continued straight ahead. She looked out the doors, but the courtyard was walled in and empty. Maybe the man had gone down one of the corridors.

She took the one to the left. It was roofed in stained glass depicting blue flowers growing among waving green grasses, and the sunlight that shone through it made the corridor glow. She began to walk as quickly and silently as possible, hoping to catch a glimpse of the man again. She passed a room tiled in blue and green like a Moroccan courtyard. She passed a stone tomb carved out of the wall, as if it had been lifted whole from a medieval European crypt and transplanted here, to be surrounded by the ashes of Californians. The mausoleum seemed to go on forever: a palace of the dead, silent but for the whisper of her footsteps. She was a world away from the funeral now, focused solely on catching another glimpse of—

There.

She ducked into an alcove, pressing her back against the marble wall, pulse racing. She leaned forward to peer around a vase filled with silk flowers.

A man in a black suit with a coiled wire curving over his

ear was standing about fifteen feet away, half-hidden by a statue of a woman draped in classical Greek robes. She held her breath. He was standing so still, and she couldn't see his face – and then he lifted a hand to the wire in his ear, and the very faint sound of his voice drifted to her. He turned his head slightly.

Reese flattened herself against the wall before he saw her. She hadn't been able to get a good look at his face, but there was something about him that freaked her out. She heard his footsteps clicking across the marble, and she froze, worried that he was going to walk right past her and ask what she was doing following him.

But as the minutes ticked by, the footsteps faded. He hadn't found her.

She peeked out again and couldn't see him. She took a deep breath and ran back the way she had come, her hair flying out behind her.

She wanted to talk to David, to ask him if he'd seen a man in a black suit anywhere, but by the time she returned to the courtyard, there was no sign of him. 'He had to leave,' her mom told her when she asked. 'He said to tell you goodbye.'

'Oh.'

Her mom gave her a concerned look. 'Are you all right? You just turned white.'

Reese tried to erase the disappointment from her face. 'I'm fine.' But as she and her mom made awkward small talk with the other students and teachers at the funeral, she couldn't help but think that David must be avoiding her now. She told herself it was easier this way – no more complications – but it didn't work. It still stung.

CHAPTER 11

Reese had known Julian her entire life. Their moms had been friends in college, and for as long as Reese could remember, they had shared summer vacations up at the Russian River, weekend trips to Disneyland, and holiday meals that mingled family related by blood or by friendship. Julian's mom was African American and his dad was Jewish, while Reese's mom was a lapsed Catholic, so there were a lot of traditions among them. Reese thought of Julian's parents almost as extensions of her own mom, and Julian was more than merely a friend; he was like a brother to her. But when he opened the door to his house later that afternoon, even she was startled by the strength of the joy that crashed through her at the sight of him: brown eyes alight, full lips widening to reveal a flash of white teeth in a smile that could knock you over.

And then he reached out and punched her in the shoulder.

'Ow!' She rubbed her shoulder indignantly. 'What

was that for?'

'You freaked the *hell* out of us,' Julian said, and hugged her.

She squeaked in surprise. He was taller than she remembered; her head came only to his chin now, and he held her so tight that all her breath seemed to squeeze out of her. When he let her go, she said, 'I missed you too.' They both broke into laughter.

'Come on in,' Julian said. 'What's with the all-black? Are you turning into a goth?' He assessed her appearance again. 'A preppy goth?'

'I just came from a funeral,' she said.

Julian's face sobered. 'Oh, sorry.' He shut the door quietly. 'I forgot. You mean for Mr Chapman?'

'Yeah.' The front hall was dim, and the house was unusually silent. 'Where are your parents?' she asked, changing the subject.

'They're out back working on the "farm",' he said, giving the word air quotes. Julian's parents had bought the three-story Edwardian in the Mission District two years ago partly because it had a giant backyard, and Julian's mom – who was a city planner in her day job – had a dream to start an urban farm collective. 'I think they planted about a zillion strawberry plants while you were gone, and they're desperately trying to keep them alive.'

Julian began to head upstairs, and Reese followed him. 'When did you find out about Mr Chapman?'

'A couple of weeks ago.' Julian's room was on the third

floor and overlooked the street through big bay windows. It was messy as usual, with his bed half-covered by a dark blue quilt and clothes piled up in random clumps on the floor. Photos of UFOs covered the wall over his desk. Julian lifted his backpack off the beanbag chair and gestured for her to sit. 'The school sent an official letter to everybody's parents.'

She lowered herself into the chair, the beans whooshing beneath her. Julian sat in his desk chair, tipping it back on its rear legs. Behind him the star-field screen saver on his computer was running, almost hypnotic as the tiny white dots sped forward on an endless loop.

'So,' Julian said, 'you wanna tell me about it?'

Her knees knocked together as she considered what she could say. 'After the accident I was mostly out of it, so there's not much to tell.'

'But what happened exactly? The letter only told us that Mr Chapman was shot in a carjacking.'

She told him about renting the car at the Phoenix airport; the traffic and roadblocks that led them to Las Vegas; the horror of the carjacking and the surreality of the gas station explosion. 'We tried to call 911, but the phones weren't working. So David and I decided to try to get back to San Francisco. That's when we had the car accident. I was driving. It was late at night and in the middle of nowhere, and this bird flew at the headlights and I flipped the car over.'

'A bird?'

'Yeah.' She heard the note of curiosity in his voice and

said, 'It was probably just a coincidence. I mean, if you're thinking about those plane crashes.'

He raised his eyebrows. 'Have you heard about the other bird stuff going on?'

'What bird stuff? I was in a coma for twenty-seven days.'

'But you know what's been going on, right?'

'I read this issue of *Time* magazine that sort of summarized it, but—' She narrowed her eyes at him. 'What?'

'Birds. They've been all over the news. Birds crashing into skyscrapers; dozens of birds dying randomly in some suburb in Virginia. Birds. So when you said a bird crashed your car—'

'It didn't crash the car. I crashed the car; the bird just flew straight at me.'

He spread his hands, shrugging. 'Same thing. It caused you to crash the car.'

'Maybe. I guess technically that's true.'

'So what happened after?'

'I can't really talk about that.' His questions were making the back of her neck tense.

'Are you serious?'

'Yeah, I can't talk about it. But I'm fine now, and I'm back. So what's been up with you?'

He gave her an incredulous look that turned slowly into excitement. 'You crashed your car in the middle of nowhere in Nevada because a bird hit you, and now you can't talk about what happened? Do you realize what that sounds like?'

She was uncomfortable. 'Uh, what?'

The front legs of his chair banged down onto the wooden floor. He jumped up and searched among the photos tacked to the wall. He pulled one down and held it out to her. She took it and scanned the image; it was a satellite photo of what looked like a desert. There were some mountain ranges along the perimeter, a line that indicated a road running down the center, and a few pale boxes that looked like they might be buildings. 'What's this?' she asked.

'Area 51,' Julian said. 'Is that where you were?'

A chill washed over her, but she said, 'That's kind of jumping to conclusions, isn't it?' She handed the photo back to him. He dropped it on the desk and sat down in his chair again, elbows on his knees as he leaned forward and watched her. She noticed a shadow running along the brown skin of his jawline. Was he growing a *beard*?

'You suck at lying, Reese.'

She flushed. 'I'm not lying,' she insisted, but his eyebrows just rose in disbelief. The star-scape screen saver on Julian's monitor behind him abruptly stopped speeding ahead. A message window popped up – and then another and another. 'Hey, you're getting some e-mail or something,' she said, grateful for the distraction.

He spun around. 'Shit.' He scooted his chair closer to the desk and began to click on the messages.

'What is it?'

'They're videos. I'm doing some video editing for Bin 42. I wasn't expecting to get any today – this must be – whoa.'

She scrambled to her feet and went to look over his shoulder at the monitor. 'What is it?'

'Freaking birds. I told you, this shit is everywhere now.' The video was panning over a mound of dead birds, everything from sparrows to pigeons and crows, their eyes glittering as the camera moved.

'Oh my God,' Reese exclaimed.

The camera zoomed out to show what seemed to be a vast warehouse with exposed pipes overhead. A machine that looked like a giant oven was located at one end of the cavernous space; the birds were mounded up on the floor in front of the machine as if they were about to be shoveled inside. The video ended with a jerk, and Julian clicked on the second one. It showed the exterior of a nondescript building with a single door on which a biohazard sign was affixed. The warehouse was surrounded by a deserted parking lot and empty fields. In the distance were low, brown hills.

'This must be the outside of the location with the bird pile,' Julian said. 'Keith wants me to edit them into one video.'

'Who's Keith? Why are you editing footage of dead birds?'

Julian glanced at her sideways. 'You know that Bin 42 website?'

'Yeah, they interviewed the guy who runs it in the Time article I read.'

'Well, I know the guy – that's Keith.'

'You *know* him?' Reese perched on the edge of his desk.

'How? And I thought his name was something else, not Keith.'

'He didn't tell them his real name. You never know whether the government is listening. Remember when I did that story for the *Kennedy Leader* about conspiracies?'

'Yeah, the one you wrote to get an A in journalism without having to work too hard.'

He grinned. 'Yeah, that one. Well, that's when I contacted Keith. He was kind of flattered that an award-winning high school newspaper wanted to interview him.'

'Award-winning? Did you actually say that?' She laughed.

'I put it in the e-mail. You know you have to present yourself in the best possible light. Anyway, after that we kept in touch, and since the June Disaster he's had a lot of video footage to deal with, so I offered to help him out.'

Julian hit Play again, and the camera panned over the dead birds. She watched it out of the corner of her eye and grimaced. 'I saw a couple of birds crash onto the ground when I was at the Phoenix Airport. It was bizarre. You never see dead birds fall out of the sky like that. Where do they go to die, anyway?'

'Sometimes they die in big groups and end up freaking out the locals.' Julian dragged the video files into his video-editing program. 'Every year there's some hysterical news story about a mass bird die-off, but these things happen all the time.'

'Really?'

'Yeah. But these birds are not dying normally.'

'Did they really hit the planes? Like, fly directly into them?'

'The ones on June nineteenth? Yep.'

'What do you think caused that?'

He shook his head. 'Nothing good. Birds crash into planes all the time, and planes can withstand sucking a couple of birds into their engines, but entire flocks? It's weird.'

'Was it terrorists?'

'That's one theory, but how the hell would terrorists be able to train massive numbers of birds to attack airplanes? That's a pretty far-out theory. But I think that's why the government has been exterminating wild flocks of birds. Mostly Canada geese, but pigeons and crows and other common birds too. The animal-rights people are going insane.'

They heard the doorbell ring, and Reese glanced at her watch. 'That must be my mom. She was just running a few errands and said she'd be back to pick me up. My grandparents are coming over for dinner tonight. We have to eat early so they can get home before the curfew.' Reese scooted off the edge of the desk. 'Hey, what was it like here when I was gone?'

'It got a little crazy. My sister came back from Berkeley for a week because everybody thought the East Bay was going to riot, but the National Guard was called in and it wasn't too bad there. San Francisco was mostly normal, although they did cancel Pride.'

'Wow, really?'

'Yeah. Sucked because it was actually hot that weekend too. But other than that, it was just a bunch of paranoid people cleaning out the grocery stores. The Mission was really quiet for a while – it was weird to go out and see all the taquerias closed. And trash didn't get picked up for days, which meant everything stank in the heat wave, but after the flight ban was lifted, the garbage trucks came back too.'

They heard Julian's mom calling upstairs. 'Julian! Reese!'

'Come on,' Julian said, slinging an arm around her shoulders. 'I'll let you off the hook tonight, but don't think you're gonna get away with it for long.'

'Get away with what?' she asked as they headed downstairs.

'Hiding whatever happened to you after your accident. The truth *will* come out.' He attempted to raise one eyebrow at her, but he still hadn't mastered the trick, which meant he looked more ridiculous than devious.

She laughed to cover the burst of unease that shot through her. 'I'm sure it will.'

CHAPTER 12

That night she dreamed of a yellow room. Red streaked down the walls like dripping paint, and she felt enclosed in a warm, pulsing cocoon. Her heartbeat sounded in a deep, reverberating bass, and it was as though she wasn't merely inside the yellow room but was the room itself. The walls were her skin; the red was her blood.

She awoke, heart pounding, as dawn light slipped through the window blinds. She threw off her blankets, kicking them onto the floor as she sat up, gasping for breath. Her T-shirt was stuck to her sweat-dampened skin. She went to the bay windows and pushed one open, letting in the cool morning air. Outside, the street was quiet and empty. It was barely six am and not even the dog walkers were out yet. As she leaned against the windowsill, she mulled over the dream. There was something so deeply familiar about it that it felt etched in her bones. Had she had the dream before? She couldn't remember.

She heard an alarm go off elsewhere in the house. It was

Monday morning, and her mom had to go to work. Today, Reese was supposed to call SF Radar, the website where she had begun a summer internship in early June, to tell them she was back and ask if she could finish out the month of July. The thought of it made Reese feel exhausted already. She left the window open but climbed back into bed, pulling her pillow over her head, and eventually managed to fall asleep again.

When she awoke the second time, her bedside clock said it was 10:06, and her mom had left a note propped up next to a new cell phone. *I got this phone for you. Don't forget to call SF Radar. I love you, Mom.* Reese groaned and forced herself to get up.

Downstairs the coffeepot was still on, and as she poured herself a cup she saw the newspaper lying on the kitchen table. She sat down with her mug and pulled the *Chronicle* toward her. There was a photo of President Randall just below the masthead. She was walking across a concrete floor in a warehouse, wearing goggles and plastic gloves, and the headline read: *President Randall Visits Bird Disposal Facility.*

WASHINGTON – President Elizabeth Randall was accompanied by members of the Defense Department on Sunday during an impromptu visit to a bird disposal facility outside Washington, DC. Since the plane crashes of June 19, the Defense Department, in cooperation with the National Guard and the Centers for Disease Control and Prevention, has spearheaded a nationwide effort to exterminate potentially dangerous birds, primarily focusing on Canada geese. However, as public reports of bird violence by other avian species – including crows and pigeons – have increased, the bird disposal teams have begun to cull other birds as well.

After the visit, President Randall spoke briefly to the press, stating: 'I'm here to assure the American people that we are working very hard to make certain that no other bird strikes will occur. As you can see, we're following stringent practices to contain any possible diseases that the birds might bear, and we will continue to test the birds for signs of what might have caused the bird strikes on June 19.'

Outside the facility, members of People for the Ethical Treatment of Animals and other animal-rights groups staged a protest, dressing in bird costumes and demanding that the Randall Administration stop the exterminations. 'There is no evidence that the birds they're killing have anything to do with the June Disaster,' said Andrea Reynolds, a spokesperson for PETA. 'This is just senseless murder of innocent creatures stoked by baseless fears, and the Randall Administration should be ashamed of itself.'

Joseph Morales, a zoologist at the National Zoo, does not believe that the birds involved in the plane crashes were diseased and thinks that the exterminations may not be necessary. 'I think that the likeliest cause of the bird strikes was an electromagnetic storm that disrupted the birds' magnetoreception capabilities,' Morales said. 'Testing them for some kind of disease or genetic abnormality wouldn't prove much.'

Nonetheless the Randall Administration will continue with the targeted exterminations for the time being. 'Our number one goal is to make sure that Americans are safe in the skies,' said Homeland Security Chief Sandra Rinaldi. 'Right now, culling flocks of Canada geese is one step to that safety.'

Reese couldn't bring herself to call the internship. She had lost so much time while she was in the coma that it was already the second half of July, and school started in less than a month. She didn't want to be cooped up in an office for the next three weeks, making copies and writing boring arts listings. She decided to put off the phone call and instead went for a walk.

It was overcast outside, and fog still clung to Twin Peaks in the west. She turned away from the cool mist and headed northeast toward Dolores Park. She had taken this route countless times on the way to Kennedy High School, which hugged the northern edge of the park. But it had been over a month, she realized, since she had last been here, and as she trudged up the hill on Church Street she began to notice tiny differences. Ragged strands of yellow police tape were caught in the branches of the Chinese banyan trees. Someone had affixed duct tape in giant Xs across all the windows of a nursery school, as if to prevent breakage. And as she passed a mural of wildflowers, she noticed that something had been added. A black bird with outstretched wings had been graffitied onto the mural, the eyes spray-painted in dots of neon orange. She zipped up her hoodie and dug her hands into the pockets, hurrying past the image on her way up the hill.

The sun was attempting to break through the cloudy sky, but it shone only weakly over the bowl of Dolores Park. San Francisco spread out to the northeast like a toy city cupped in the palm of a giant's hand. She skidded down the grassy slope past a few hardy sunbathers, cutting across the pockmarked lawn toward the café on the corner of Eighteenth and Dolores, across from Kennedy High School. It was a Monday morning and not very warm outside, but the café still had its share of patrons with their laptops. She bought herself a coffee and lightened it with cream, then began to walk back up Dolores Street to find a seat in the park. She was approaching Nineteenth Street when someone came careening around the corner and smashed right into her.

Reese went sprawling, the concrete slamming into her knees and the palms of her hands. Her coffee splashed, steaming hot, all over the sidewalk. The shock of impact left her speechless.

A girl with bright pink hair came running at her. 'I'm so sorry! I'm so sorry, I didn't see you!' She knelt down beside Reese, propping a skateboard against the side of the building nearby. The bottom of it was inked with a picture of a spiderweb, but in the center of the web a long-lashed eye had been drawn. 'Are you okay?' the girl was saying. She touched Reese's arm, and Reese flinched. Pain shot up from her hands as she lifted them. Her palms were torn open, dirt from the sidewalk embedded in her flesh. 'Oh shit, I'm so sorry,' the girl said again. 'Let me – I'll go get some water. Hang on.' She got up and sprinted away.

Reese's heart was racing. A woman with a pierced lip walked by talking on her cell phone, but she barely noticed Reese. A man wearing ripped jeans and pushing a stroller paused and asked, 'Are you all right?'

But the girl with the pink hair was back. 'I've got it, I've got it,' she told the young father. She picked up Reese's hand and pressed a damp napkin to the skin. 'Does it hurt?'

The girl gazed at her with anxious gray eyes. She had a trim nose – just slightly upturned at the tip – and lips the color of coral, full and perfectly shaped. Her hair was short and dyed hot pink, cut in a trendy, mussed style. She wore a white tank top and khaki cargo pants, and the strap of her hot pink bra peeked out, bright as her hair. A light sheen of sweat shone on her throat, her pale skin gently flushed as if she had been running. Which, Reese realized, she had.

'Are you okay?' the girl asked again.

'I – I think so.'

'I am so sorry,' she repeated. 'I totally didn't see you coming. I should have looked.'

'I wasn't looking either.'

The girl dabbed at Reese's bloody palms with the napkin. 'But I was going too fast. I know I shouldn't go that fast.'

Reese stared down at her hands, at the girl's hands cradling hers. Her short nails were painted deep purple. Reese could feel the places where they touched so clearly that it disoriented her, tipping all of her awareness into the girl's fingertips. If Reese hadn't been sitting already, she would have stumbled, and now she leaned toward the girl as if the ground had tilted. Her own heartbeat seemed to echo the pulse she swore she could feel through the girl's skin.

The jarring peal of a telephone cut through the weighted air between them, and Reese started, pulling away from the pink-haired girl. Her right pocket was vibrating, and she realized it was her new phone – she didn't recognize the ring yet. She pulled it out, glad that she hadn't landed on it. It was her mom.

'Hi,' Reese said, breathless.

'Hi, honey. I called Dr Wong's office, and she can fit you in on Wednesday at noon. Does that work for you? Did you call SF Radar?'

'Not yet. So Wednesday's fine.' The girl sat back, wrapping her arms around her knees. She watched Reese with a half smile on her face, and Reese felt a flush creeping up her own neck. She broke the gaze, looking instead at the girl's sneakers. Purple Converse high-tops.

'All right, I'll make the appointment. Tonight I won't be home till around seven. I'll pick up some takeout on the way.'

'Okay.'

When Reese hung up, the girl said, 'I'm a klutz. Do you forgive me?'

'What? Of course. I'm totally fine.' Reese tried to get up, but she didn't want to put her cut-up hands on the ground, so she had no leverage.

The girl moved swiftly, cupping her hand beneath Reese's elbow to help her up. 'You should wash that out,' she said. 'Are you sure you're okay? That was kind of a bad crash. Can I replace your coffee at least?'

'No, it's all right.' Reese bent over to pick up the now empty coffee cup, avoiding the pool of hot liquid on the ground.

'You're sure?' The girl flashed her a brilliant smile. She had the face of a movie star, polished and sharp and knowing. The gray irises of her eyes were almost crystalline in the sunlight.

Reese felt dazed, as if the sense had been knocked out of her along with her breath. It was disorienting, and she shook her head. 'No, I'd better go home and wash off.'

'All right,' the girl said. 'Bye.'

'Bye.' Reese turned away, heading south on Dolores. It wasn't until she was five blocks south that she realized she was still carrying the empty paper cup. Rattled, she tossed it into the next trash can.

When she got home, she went into the bathroom to wash her hands. As she lathered soap over her palms, she wondered who the girl was. Reese guessed that they were about the same age, though the girl might be a little older. She rinsed the soap off, lingering over the memory of the girl's smile. She was . . . *pretty* wasn't exactly the right word. It was too bland for this girl.

Reese stared down at her hands. After washing away the dirt and tiny pebbles that had been stuck to her palms, she could barely see the cuts at all. There were only a few shallow scrapes, nothing that could have bled as much as she remembered. She reached into her pocket with damp fingers and pulled out the napkin that the girl had gotten for her. It was pink now, soaked through with her blood. She looked back at her hands, and then again at the napkin. She felt a crawling sensation over her skin. She put the napkin down and pulled her hair back from her face as she had done the day she returned home, examining her reflection in the mirror.

There was no longer a scar there.

With a growing sense of urgency, she pulled off her shirt. There had been scars on both sides of her body, but now . . .

She couldn't breathe. The long white lines that had marked her from armpit to belly were gone. She turned, remembering the bruises on her back, but there was no trace of them either. She unlaced her sneakers, kicking off her shoes so that she could take off her jeans. But even as she peeled them off, her stomach sinking, she knew what she would find in place of the ridge that had cut over her knee and thigh the day before yesterday.

Nothing.

CHAPTER 13

Reese spent hours researching cuts and scars online, but other than being forced to view some pretty gruesome images, she didn't learn anything that cleared up what had happened. In fact, the stuff she read led her to believe that it was impossible for injuries to heal that quickly or for scars to vanish overnight the way hers had. That would be the holy grail for plastic surgery.

She gazed down at her palms. Since she had washed them earlier that afternoon, even the small scrapes had disappeared.

Her fingers curled into fists and she dropped them into her lap. Her computer was still open to an image of a scarred knee. She had learned that nearly every wound leaves some type of scar, except in the case of animals capable of regenerating their tissue, such as salamanders. There were cases of humans, usually young children, regenerating fingertips that had been sliced off, but otherwise human regeneration was a thing of science fiction . . . or extremely advanced medical research, the kind that might be done by the Defense Department.

Reese had also found a news article that reported the Defense Advanced Research Projects Agency, or DARPA, was working with a biomedical corporation in Massachusetts on regeneration technology to treat soldiers who had been seriously injured in combat. Had she been given that kind of treatment? Was that what Dr Brand had meant when she said they had been treated with advanced medical procedures? Had David had the same treatment?

She dug her fingers into the tense muscles in her neck, trying to ease the pain that was throbbing in her head. She wanted to tell David about her hands and ask him if he had experienced anything similar, but she had lost her old phone in the accident and, consequently, his phone number. She was reluctant to e-mail or leave him a message at his page on the Hub; she had never communicated with him that way before. They had always texted each other, and to do something else now seemed weird.

Her stomach twisted into knots. Weird. Only because she was still completely embarrassed by the way she had acted at nationals that night in the hotel. When they were driving away from Phoenix, after Mr Chapman was shot and even while they were in that military hospital, the awkwardness between them had seemed to disappear. They had been in a bizarre situation, and there wasn't any time for her to be embarrassed. But now that they were at home and everything was supposed to be back to normal, the awkwardness was back too.

Don't be a dork, she chastised herself. *You're overthinking this.* She opened the Hub and clicked through her friends to David's page. He hadn't updated in over a month. His last post said: We rocked quarterfinals! Heat spread over her skin. She opened a message window, her fingers hovering over the keys. She wrote the note at least a dozen times before she settled on the final text.

> David,
> Remember when I asked you about the scar
> on my head at the funeral? Something
> strange happened. The scars disappeared. I
> looked up info about scarring and wounds
> online, and I don't think this is normally
> supposed to happen. I think this is related
> to whatever happened to us in the hospital.
> Have you experienced anything similar since
> we got back?
> Reese

That's good. There was no trace that she was still thinking about that night in Phoenix. She had clearly moved on.

But she stared at the message for several tense minutes before she pressed Send. Now she just had to wait for him to respond.

By the next morning, there was still no response. Filled with a jittery impatience, Reese cleaned her room, even lining up the pens in her top desk drawer according to brand. By midmorning she had vacuumed and dusted as well and knew that she had to get out of the house or else risk going crazy. She decided to head back to the corner of Nineteenth and Dolores, hoping that seeing the place where she had crashed into the pink-haired girl would give her some insight into how her hands had healed so quickly.

When she arrived at the corner, the ground where she had fallen didn't look any different from any other stretch of concrete. There was an amoebalike shadow on the sidewalk that was probably the remains of her coffee, but if some of the darker flecks nearby were bloodstains, she couldn't tell for sure.

Frustrated, she crossed the street to sit on the low concrete wall at the Nineteenth Street entrance to the park, staring at the building across the street where the girl had propped up her skateboard. That girl. Reese's thoughts circled around her repeatedly, as if there was something there she didn't quite understand. She could remember the girl's face so clearly that when she saw her walking down the sidewalk twenty feet away, at first she thought she was just imagining it.

But then the girl saw her too, and she stopped, recognition lighting her face. 'Hey,' she called. 'It's you.'

Reese blinked. The girl was wearing a red hoodie with a racer stripe down each sleeve, unzipped over a gray T-shirt printed with the image of a melting ice-cream cone.

She walked toward Reese and asked, 'Revisiting the scene of the crime?'

Reese was startled to see her. But it was a good kind of startled. 'The crime scene's across the street.'

The girl grinned. 'How're your hands doing?'

'They're fine,' Reese said without thinking. And then she remembered the reason she had come back to the park, and she asked, 'Do you remember – they were cut up pretty bad, weren't they?'

A puzzled expression flitted over the girl's face. 'What do you mean?'

'I mean – I—' Reese stopped. What was she going to say? That she thought she had miraculously quick-healing hands? That sounded ridiculous. 'Nothing. Never mind.'

The girl cocked her head. 'Hey, what's your name anyway?'

'Reese.'

'Hi, Reese. I'm Amber.'

'Hi,' Reese said. The single syllable seemed to hang awkwardly in the air between them, and then Amber smiled.

'So, what are you up to? Can I buy you that replacement coffee now?'

Reese was surprised when a tingle of excitement went through her. 'Um, sure.'

'Cool. Let's go to the café on the corner. It's the least I can do after knocking you over.'

Reese slid off the low concrete wall and joined Amber as she walked down the street toward the café, chattering about how she had only recently bought that skateboard and was still getting used to it. Reese found herself losing track of the conversation. Every time she looked at Amber, she became transfixed by the way the shocking pink of her hair clashed with the red hoodie, or the way the sunlight shone on her pink lip gloss.

When they entered the café, Reese saw the other patrons' glances skitter off her, drawn to Amber. She turned to Reese and asked, 'What do you want?'

Reese was taken aback. 'What?'

Amber smiled coyly. 'Coffee?' She pointed at the menu hanging on the wall.

'I – I'll have a regular coffee.'

They took their drinks back outside to the sidewalk patio, choosing a table in a patch of pale morning sunlight. 'So where do you go to school?' Amber asked, peeling the lid off her large cappuccino.

'Across the street. Kennedy.' Reese took a careful sip of her coffee. It was so hot, she almost burned her tongue. And it needed cream. She had forgotten to add that when they were inside. She settled for pouring in three packets of sugar.

'High school?'

'Yeah.'

'Sorry, I'm new to San Francisco. What year are you?'

'I'm a – I'm going to be a senior.' Reese looked down at the black metal table. Through the mesh, she could see Amber's purple Converse swinging in the air. 'What about you? You just moved here?'

'Sort of. I went to high school on the East Coast; I graduated in June. I'm taking a year off before college, and 'my uncle has an apartment here. He's traveling for the summer and is letting me house-sit for him.'

'Wow, that's cool. What are you going to do in your year off?'

'I haven't really decided yet.' Amber dipped a finger into the foam of her drink and licked it contemplatively. Reese noticed all the people seated nearby swiveling their heads to look at Amber. 'My mom wants me to major in chemistry or microbiology in college, so she's encouraging me to find an internship or something. But I don't know if I want to be a scientist.'

'Is your mom a scientist?' Reese took another sip of her coffee, but now it was too sweet. She put it down.

'Yeah. How about yours?'

'She's a lawyer.'

'Do you want to be a lawyer?'

'I'm not sure.'

'What do you like to do now? Like, are you in a band or anything?'

'A band?' Reese laughed.

Amber grinned. 'Why not? You could be in a band. You have that look – you know, with your belt and that T-shirt.'

The sun suddenly seemed excessively hot. 'Uh, no,' Reese said, glancing down at herself. She was wearing her metal belt and a blue tee with the word amplify stamped on it over a faded image of a fist. She had bought it out of a bin at Community Thrift last winter. Actually Julian had picked it out for her, saying, 'You should wear this to debate.' Reese

128

watched Amber take a sip from her cappuccino, her purple nails almost black against the white paper cup. 'I think *you* have that look. I'm, um, on the debate team.'

'Aw, that's so sweet.'

'Sweet?' Reese was skeptical. 'That I'm on the debate team?'

'That you think I look like I'm in a band.'

'Oh.' Reese felt a twinge of embarrassment. 'Um, yeah. Well, pink hair?'

'Do you like it? I've had it for a while. I'm getting kind of tired of it.'

'It's – it makes a statement.'

Amber laughed, and everyone in the vicinity turned to look at her again. 'I can't carry a tune, and I don't know how to play a single instrument. But I'm good at dyeing my hair. How about you? Ever think of going pink?'

Reese smiled. 'I can honestly say that I have never thought of going pink.' Amber's smile turned into something of a smirk, sending an unexpected quiver through Reese.

'You should think about it,' Amber advised. Before Reese could come up with a response – she felt like she was missing something in the conversation – Amber leaned over and picked up Reese's coffee, taking a sip. She made a face. 'Ugh. How can you drink that?'

Reese let out a half-strangled laugh. 'I put in too much sugar.'

'Do you want another one?' Amber started to get up.

'No, no, it's fine.'

'Okay,' Amber said dubiously. 'You want some of mine?' She pushed the frothy drink toward her.

Reese shook her head self-consciously. 'No, thanks.'

Amber sat back in her chair, crossing her legs. 'So, where do you live? I don't know the city very well yet. Is there anything I should do while I'm here?'

As the morning progressed, they talked about San Francisco, its neighborhoods and tourist traps; the way the fog rolled in at night and turned summer into crisp, chilly autumn within minutes; the fact that cafés were crowded all day, even during the middle of the week when people were supposedly at work or school. But every time the conversation drifted toward the June Disaster or how it had affected the city, Reese found a way to change the subject. She didn't know how she could possibly explain that she had been in a medically induced coma for almost a month. It was a little soon, she thought, to bring that up.

As people began to come out of the café carrying plates of sandwiches and salads, Amber pulled out her phone and said, 'Oh my God, we've been talking forever! It's past noon.'

Reese picked up her coffee cup and was surprised to find that it was empty. 'I guess I should go,' she said, reluctant.

Amber stood, slinging her bag across her chest. 'Yeah, I have to go too. But this was really fun. We should hang out again. Maybe you can show me around or something.'

'Sure. That would be cool.'

'What's your number?'

Reese dug out her new phone and stared at it. 'I don't know. I just got this number.'

Amber laughed. 'Here. Call me.' She grabbed Reese's phone, their fingers brushing against the gleaming plastic, and quickly dialed. Amber's phone began to ring, and she handed Reese's back to her. 'Great, I got it,' Amber said. 'What are you doing tomorrow?'

She remembered the appointment with Dr Wong, but she didn't want to tell Amber about it. 'I'm not sure yet.'

'Well, just text me when you're free. I'll be around.'

'Okay.'

'Cool! It was great to talk to you.' Amber dropped her phone into her bag and then stepped closer to hug her.

Caught off guard, Reese returned the hug awkwardly, their bodies pressing briefly together. Amber smelled like cupcakes, and long after she had waved and headed off in the opposite direction, the scent lingered in Reese's memory: buttercream and the sweetness of sugar.

CHAPTER 14

After dinner, the phone rang. Reese's mom looked up from her laptop and said, 'Can you get that, honey?'

Reese had been loading the dishwasher while wondering what she should say to Amber tomorrow. So, you wanted me to call you? *Hey there, tour guide reporting for duty?* She dried off her hands and was about to pick up the phone when she saw the caller ID: Rick Holloway. Her father. She let it ring another couple of times – and caught her mom giving her a pointed look – before she answered. 'Hi, Dad.'

'Hi, sweetie. I've been hoping to catch you. How are you feeling?'

'I'm fine,' Reese said automatically. She took the phone out of the kitchen, heading into the living room, where she sat down on the leather armchair.

'Your mother told me that she made an appointment for you to see Dr Wong tomorrow.'

'Yeah.' Maybe she should offer to take Amber on a tour of

Alcatraz or something. Didn't newcomers to San Francisco want to do that?

'Well,' her dad said, 'I think that's a good idea.'

'Sure,' she said, half-listening. Then again, visiting a creepy old prison didn't really sound like a great introduction to the City by the Bay.

'Have you been having any headaches or any other pain?'

'It's not that bad.' What else was there to do? Fisherman's Wharf? The only times Reese had been there were when out-of-towners came to visit, and they insisted on dragging her and her mom to see the disturbing pile of barking sea lions.

'I want you to watch out for them, though. Head injuries can have long-lasting consequences.'

'I'm fine,' she said curtly. A strained silence ensued, and she felt a stab of guilt for not being friendlier.

Her father sighed. 'You know, Reese, I want to be here for you. You can call me anytime. I know I haven't been so great in the past, but I really want you to give me a chance. When your mom called to tell me about your accident, I thought—' He cut himself off and laughed bitterly. 'I thought, What a dick I've been to you and your mom.'

Reese almost dropped the phone. All thoughts of tourist possibilities vanished from her mind. She had never heard her father talk like that before.

One of her most vivid childhood memories was of coming home from school during the third grade to find her mom sobbing on Julian's mom's shoulder because Rick – her husband at the time – had been discovered having an affair.

133

Reese hadn't entirely understood it then, but over the years she put together the story from overheard conversations and a few uncomfortable discussions with her mother. Her father, it seemed, was a bit of a philanderer. Reese had looked that word up in the dictionary when she heard Julian's mom use it, and she remembered her mother's retort: 'However you dress it up, he's still a cheater.'

Two years ago, Reese's father had been profiled in the *Seattle Times*. It painted a picture of Rick Holloway as a successful entrepreneur who spent a good portion of his money on romancing young women. In an interview with the Times, he didn't apologize for it, saying simply that he appreciated feminine beauty, and he was lucky enough that some women appreciated him too. The article had been published along with a series of photographs of her dad attending various galas, accompanied each time by a different woman. All of them were in their early twenties, beautiful as models, wearing skimpy dresses and heels so high, Reese couldn't figure out how they could possibly walk. There was no mention at all of his ex-wife and teenage daughter.

Reese remembered reading the article online in her room, door closed, hoping that her mom never, ever saw it.

'I want you to know that I love you,' her father continued over the phone. 'And I hope you can find a way to forgive me.'

In the silence, she could hear him breathing. Waiting. Her fingers tingled as she held the phone so gingerly, it could have been a bomb. 'Dad, I—' She didn't know what to say.

'I know I just laid that on you. But remember what I said, and believe me. I mean it.'

She took a breath. 'Okay.'

'I'll let you go now. Call me whenever, all right?'

After they hung up, she sat there, stunned, cradling the phone in her hands and studying the edges of the coffee table. The wood was a little beat-up from where she had crashed into it several times as a kid on her Big Wheel, which she shouldn't have ridden in the house but did anyway.

Her mom came into the living room and sat down on the couch. 'Are you all right?' she asked, reaching out to take the phone away from her.

'Yeah. He – he apologized to me.'

'Well, that's something.'

Reese looked up at her mom. She was wearing horn-rimmed glasses and a tentative smile. 'Has he ever apologized to you?' Reese asked.

The smile disappeared. 'Yes. He has.'

'Do you forgive him?'

Her mom's face paled. 'Now that's a different story. Some days I do. Some days I don't. How do you feel about it?'

'I don't know.' Years ago she had carefully constructed a mental box into which she stuffed all her thoughts and feelings about her dad. She had nailed that box up tight and tried to forget about it. Now it was as if her father himself had arrived with a crowbar to pry it open. Even though he had apologized, it didn't make her feel better. It made her remember all the times he had screwed up and not apologized. All those times she had heard him tell her mother she was overreacting instead of admitting that he had done something wrong. Her head began to tighten, and Reese rubbed a hand over her forehead, closing her eyes.

'Well, you don't have to figure it out tonight.' Her mom glanced at her watch. 'In fact, it's getting late. Why don't you sleep on it and see how you feel in the morning?'

Reese had been keyed up before the phone call – all nerves, running through a hundred different options for tomorrow – but now sleep seemed like a brilliant idea. When she was asleep, she wouldn't have to think about anything her father had said.

CHAPTER 15

She woke up with the haze of the dream hanging over her: red streaking down golden walls that were gently heaving like lungs. Her mouth was fuzzy and her head throbbed, making her feel clumsy and heavy as she got out of bed.

Her father. The memory of his phone call rose up unbidden, and she groaned. She didn't want to think about him. One apology didn't make up for the past. She threw off the sheets and headed downstairs, hoping coffee would clear her head.

Her mom had left a note on the coffeemaker: *I'll be home at 11:30 to take you to Dr Wong.*

She poured herself a cup of coffee and saw her phone sitting on the counter nearby. She was going to call Amber today, but she still hadn't figured out what to say. She felt as if she were taking a step down a new path, one she hadn't planned on and therefore had no map for. She normally didn't make friends easily, but this was...different. She wanted to call Amber. Anticipation sparked in her. But she

137

would wait until after the doctor's appointment. She didn't want to seem too eager, although she wasn't entirely sure why.

Her stomach growled. She had been so hungry since she got back. She took out eggs and bread to make herself breakfast, and her mouth watered as she melted butter in the pan, dropping in the eggs with a sharp sizzle. When they were cooked over easy, she layered them on top of toast and sliced in, watching the yolk ooze out in an orange slide of viscous liquid.

Exactly like her dream.

Her head started to pound so hard, she dropped the fork onto the plate, splattering the yolk all over the table. She doubled over, her stomach threatening to flip inside out as sweat rose on her skin. *What is going on with me?* One minute she was fine, and the next she felt like she might vomit. She took several quick breaths, trying to calm herself down. When she felt stable enough to stand, she made her way to the first-floor bathroom and pulled out a bottle of ibuprofen, washing down three pills with water from the faucet that she cupped in her hand.

In the mirror she was wild-eyed, water dripping from her chin. She wiped her face off with the towel and ran a hand over her tangled hair. She was still hungry, but she didn't think she could eat those eggs anymore.

'Overall, you seem very healthy to me,' Dr Wong said.

Reese was sitting on the paper-covered exam table dressed

in a flimsy hospital gown that fastened with Velcro. As she shifted in place, the paper beneath her rustled. She stared at Dr Wong. 'I'm . . . fine?'

'Yes.'

'That's a relief,' Reese's mom said. She was seated in the chair by the door.

'What about my headaches?' Reese asked.

'You could have post-concussion syndrome. Have you been feeling irritable or emotional lately?'

Reese was startled. 'Yes.'

Dr Wong nodded. 'Those are symptoms of PCS, which isn't unexpected, since you've suffered a brain injury. We'll have to keep an eye on that. I'm going to send you down to the lab to draw some blood, and I'll run some tests.' She handed Reese a form. 'Meanwhile, why don't you start keeping track of your headaches, and I'll check in with you again when we get the test results next week.'

After Dr Wong left, Reese got dressed. 'Well, I'm glad we did this,' her mom said. Reese didn't answer; she'd have to look up that PCS thing later on. Could that really explain what she had been feeling? 'Let's go down to the lab,' her mom said. 'I have to get back to work soon, but I'll drop you off on the way.'

All the way home, Reese felt the press of her phone in her pocket, silent and still. She didn't know what she would say to Amber, and the uncertainty was making her increasingly jittery. Upstairs in her room she turned on her computer instead, checking the Hub for messages from David, but there was nothing. Her stomach sank. She sat on the edge of her bed and swept her finger over the touch screen on her phone, pulling up Amber's number. She settled on something simple, and texted: Hi. What are you up to?

When she hit Send, the fact that she would have to wait for an answer from Amber too almost made her physically sick. Impatience gripped her like a fever, and she began to pace back and forth. But it was only a few minutes before her new phone rang, playing an extremely loud and obnoxious melody. She hadn't yet set the ringtones. She silenced it and saw the message on the screen: Nothing much. Wanna come over and hang out? I'm at 659A Sanchez.

Reese couldn't breathe for a moment. She tapped back: OK. And then she stood there in the center of her room and realized she had now committed herself to going over to Amber's house. Heat flushed her skin. She had to change; she couldn't wear the ratty old T-shirt she had worn to Dr Wong's office. She went to her closet, flipping through shirts and skirts and pants. She put on a new pair of jeans, then decided they looked too new. She pulled on a pair with a hole in the knee. She laced on her blue Converse sneakers and then stood in front of her closet to assess her sorely inadequate collection of tops. Why did she only seem to have worn-out Cal shirts, or tees screen-printed with the names of obscure bands that made her look like a pretentious idiot? She finally settled on a plain blue ringer tee and a hoodie for when the fog rolled in.

She stopped in the bathroom and examined her reflection.

She needed to brush her hair. When she finished, her hair looked smoother, but it was too long. Irritated, she pulled it into a ponytail. That was better. Her eyes had dark smudges beneath them – she hadn't been sleeping well recently – but there was nothing she could do about that. She thought it would look ridiculous if she put on makeup. But she did put some lip balm on. She shoved her phone and her wallet into her pockets and ran downstairs, grabbing her keys from the hall tree as she left.

Amber was staying in her uncle's top-floor flat on the crest of Sanchez Street west of Dolores Park. She answered the door in a white tank top with a towel around her neck, her hair damp with some kind of pale blue cream. 'Hi!' she said brightly, giving Reese a stiff-armed hug. 'I don't want to get this stuff on you. I'm bleaching my hair. Come on in.'

She headed upstairs, and Reese followed, shutting the front door behind them. Amber was barefoot, and her jeans hung low on her hips. Reese saw the tops of Amber's blue polka-dotted underwear peeking out. She caught herself wondering if Amber's bra matched and then blushed furiously. She tried to focus on climbing the stairs without tripping on her suddenly shaky legs.

The flat was furnished in the kind of pristine minimalism that reminded Reese of photographs in decorating magazines. The stairs led into a wide front living room with windows overlooking the street. The floor was made of some kind of expensive-looking dark wood, and there were only a few items of furniture. A modern, rectangular sofa in a nut-brown suede; a glass-and-steel coffee table; a white shag rug beneath. The back of the living room opened into a kitchen with stainless-steel appliances and slate-gray countertops.

'I'm in the bathroom!' Amber called.

Reese followed her voice down the long hallway that stretched from the living room to the back of the flat. The first door was half open and seemed to lead to Amber's bedroom; Reese caught a glimpse of an unmade bed and blue curtains before she moved on. The second door opened into the bathroom, where Amber was bending her head over the tub with a detachable showerhead in her hand.

'Sorry,' Amber said. 'This took longer than expected. I was trying to finish up before you got here.'

'It's fine.'

'I'll be done in a sec. What'd you do this morning?'

'Um, not much.' Reese watched Amber rinse off her hair, mesmerized by the sight of the blue coloring coming off in the stream of water. The droplets slid down Amber's neck and dripped onto her tank top. Her bra did match.

When Amber finished, she toweled off her head and straightened up. 'What do you think?' Her hair was no longer bright pink. It was now white-blond and sticking up all over the place.

'It's . . . different,' Reese said.

Amber frowned. 'Do you like it?'

'I – yeah. I like it.' It made Amber look older, more sophisticated. Then again, it was hard to look sophisticated with pink hair.

Amber turned to the mirror, examining her reflection soberly. She ran a hand through her hair, tousling some of it, smoothing down other bits. 'It'll do.' Then she looked down at her wet shirt and laughed. 'I made a mess, though.' She lifted the bottom of her tank top and pulled it off, brushing past Reese as she exited the bathroom.

Reese watched as Amber went into her room and emerged a moment later, tugging on a new, dry tank top. This one was blue, with spaghetti straps. Amber stopped in the hallway, hands on her hips. 'What? Do I look weird or something?'

'No. Sorry. I'm—' She shook her head. 'Never mind. You look fine.'

'Do you want something to drink?' Without waiting for an answer, Amber headed back to the front of the flat.

'Sure,' Reese said, following.

'Have a seat,' Amber said as she opened the fridge. 'We have…let's see. Diet Coke? Water? Beer?'

'Whatever you want.' Reese sat on the edge of the sofa. It faced the big picture window, and she had a million-dollar view of multicolored homes stacked on the hillside, all the way down to a glimpse of the downtown skyline.

Amber joined her with two Diet Cokes cradled in one arm and two glasses of ice. 'Too early for beer?' she said with a grin, and sat down beside Reese, folding her legs up beneath her.

'Thanks.' Reese picked up one of the cans. The soda fizzed as she poured it over the ice, and when she took her first sip, the bubbles on her tongue felt like tiny little sparklers. Everything here – the couch, the view, Amber and her new blond hair – everything was so sharp, so crisp. She felt as though she suddenly had superpowered vision.

Amber was studying her with a little smile on her lips. She was wearing pink lip gloss; it shone in the light pouring through the windows. It would be tacky, slightly sweet, Reese thought. Like candy. The thought made her feel warm all over, and she took another sip of her Diet Coke.

'So,' Amber said conversationally, 'what do you think of the view?'

'It's – it's great.'

'Yeah. I love it. I could just sit here staring out the window for hours.'

Silence descended on them, and Reese became aware of the sound of a clock ticking in the distance. She heard Amber's breath beside her; the rustle as she shifted on the couch, leaning forward to pour her own soda; the ice rattling in the glass. She even heard the sound of Amber swallowing.

Amber said, 'I'm glad you could come over.'

'Me too,' Reese said. Was this her cue to offer to play tour guide? The idea of taking Amber to Alcatraz or Fisherman's Wharf now seemed completely ridiculous. She wouldn't want to go there. She looked at Amber. She thought she could see the view reflected in her gray eyes.

Amber leaned forward. 'I wasn't sure if you were into girls.'

The words snapped back at Reese. 'What?'

Amber smiled slightly. 'Girls. I thought so, but maybe not.'

144

Reese felt as though her head were suddenly inhabited by a thousand buzzing bees; all she could hear was static in her ears, trying to drown out the emotions erupting within her. Confusion, denial, the delirious sensation of seeing Amber bend toward her with her mouth slightly open, her hand stretched out – and then Amber had simply placed her frosty glass on the coffee table, barely brushing her hand against Reese's knee as she sat back again.

'I'm straight,' Reese managed to say, her heart beating so loudly, she thought Amber surely must hear it.

Amber quirked one eyebrow up. She hadn't bleached her brows; they were perfectly shaped dark brown arches. She leaned forward again and Reese almost backed away, but Amber was only reaching for her soda. She took it out of Reese's cold, damp fingers and put it on the table next to her own, the glass clinking gently.

'I don't think you're straight,' Amber said, and part of Reese was simply shocked by her directness. Who even said that?

'What?' Reese said again. She had to work on being more articulate.

Amber took her hand, and Reese let her lace her fingers with hers. 'You heard what I said.' She pulled at her, like a girl tugging on the string of a balloon that has floated nearly all the way up to the sky, and just like that balloon, Reese felt herself drawn downward, half-floating, half-sinking, toward Amber.

The lip gloss did taste like candy. It was slick and hard at the same time, and as soon as their lips touched, Reese thought she was going to fall apart from shaking so much. Amber laughed a little, releasing Reese's hand and cupping her face to keep her steady. Reese felt like an awkward schoolgirl; she didn't know where her hands were supposed to go. Her body was bent at a strange angle, and she wanted to move it. She scrambled, not wanting to stop kissing Amber; she twisted around and her leg smashed against the coffee table.

'Hey, be careful,' Amber said laughingly, against her mouth, and she pulled Reese's arms around her waist, and her body was soft and curved and warm and full of breath and heat. Her mouth opened, and her tongue was cold from the icy soda, which was so odd, because everywhere else she was undeniably, unmistakably hot.

And then Amber, pushing her back ever so gently, said softly, 'See, I told you, you're not straight.'

CHAPTER 16

Reese walked home in a daze. The entire city, covered in late afternoon light, seemed to glow. Every street, every building, even the steel streetcars, became wondrous things: artifacts of a day when her entire world turned upside down.

As she passed the hardware store on Twenty-Fourth Street, she halted, transfixed by the display in the window. Long rolls of paper had been covered with paint in different shades of red, from pink to darkest maroon. That color – the second-brightest pink – was the same color as Amber's lip gloss. And that one – the third red from the right – was the exact shade of the red that dripped down the walls in her dream.

The thought struck her so forcefully that she gasped. She put her hand out to touch the window, as if she could feel the sensation of the paint through the glass. The cool, hard surface gave away nothing. She backed away, her handprint clinging to the window momentarily, and then, as if she were being led by someone she could not see, she went into the hardware store and found the paint aisle.

There were so many colors here. She ran her eyes over the hundreds of paint chips displayed on the wall, seeking out the single shade of red that she had recognized. She began to pull out the paint chips in the red spectrum, moving faster and faster as she discarded the wrong colors in a growing pile on the floor. Sour cherry, brick red, holly berry, Ivy League crimson, love knot, strawberry fields... she had never known there could be so many shades of red or so many bizarre names for paint. Finally she found the color she was looking for: bittersweet root.

'Can I help you?' said a clerk from behind her.

She jumped, looking up. 'No, I found it.'

The clerk glanced at the pile of paint chips nearby.

'Sorry,' she said. 'I'll clean it up.'

He shook his head. 'Don't worry about it – I'll put them in the right place. Do you want a sample of that color?'

She glanced at the little paper chip. 'Isn't this a sample?'

He smiled. 'Never painted a room before, have you?'

'Um, no.'

'That's just a paint chip. A sample is some of the actual paint.'

'Oh. Sure, I'll take a sample.'

She left the hardware store a few minutes later with a tiny can of bittersweet root in a brown paper bag and headed home.

Upstairs in her room, she cracked open the paint can on her desk. It looked lighter in liquid form than on the paint chip. Tentatively she dipped a finger in the paint and held it up to the light. The red crawled down her finger in a bloody line, dripping onto the desktop. 'Crap,' she muttered, and grabbed a tissue to wipe it up. She put the lid back on the can of paint and went to rinse off her hands. As the water washed the color down the drain in a pink stream, she was suddenly confused by why she had taken the sample. What was she going to do with it? She wasn't planning to paint anything that color.

She returned to her room and lay down on her bed, tracing a damp finger over the shape of her lips, remembering the way it had felt to kiss Amber. Warmth flushed her body. Did this make her gay?

She had never really kissed anyone before. There was that fourth-grade kiss on the playground, but that had been on a dare and she didn't think it counted. It hadn't particularly bothered her, though; her friends seemed to think her lack of kissing experience was more important than she did. Sophomore year, during a party at Tyler Pon's house when his parents were gone, they had tried to get her to kiss someone. It hadn't gone well. Tyler was a junior on the soccer team and the party was full of athletes, but because Tyler's younger sister Madison was on the newspaper, everyone on the *Kennedy Leader* got invited too. Kennedy wasn't like the high schools on TV, with their strict divisions between jocks and nerds and theater geeks, but friendship circles still tended to form along shared interests. So Reese spent most of the party hanging out with the other journalism

149

kids in the relatively quiet family room in the back of the house, while the music got louder and louder in the living room at the front.

Madison was obsessed with finding a boyfriend that year, and she couldn't stop talking about which boys were cutest and whether or not she should go into the living room and talk to them. Julian thought she was amusing and egged her on, but Reese was barely paying attention. She had drunk a cup of the disgustingly sweet vodka punch and it had made her sleepy, and the L-shaped couch was so comfortable. She stirred when Madison grabbed her foot and shook it. 'What?' she mumbled, opening her eyes.

'Everyone's going around saying who's the cutest guy at the party,' Madison said. 'You're up, Reese.'

Reese propped her head up on her hand, blinking at Madison. She was dressed in a fuchsia tank top and a white jean miniskirt, and her hair was pulled back in a ponytail on top of her head. 'I don't know,' Reese said. 'Does it matter?'

Madison shook her head dramatically. 'Oh, Reese. You *know*.'

'Maybe she doesn't,' said Briana Martinez, who was sitting on the rug and leaning against the edge of the sofa. 'Don't push her.' Bri had short black hair and was wearing a T-shirt that said dyke on it as part of her attempt to shock the soccer players.

'Who would you pick?' Reese asked.

Bri grinned. 'If I had to pick a dude, I'd go with Julian here.'

Julian was lying on his stomach and playing a game on his phone. 'Sorry, Bri, you're not my type,' he said.

'Come on,' Madison said, pouting at Reese. 'I think you're just embarrassed to say who you like.'

'I'm not embarrassed,' Reese said. 'Why would I be embarrassed?'

'Crushing on someone would ruin your reputation as the distant but intense loner with a heart of gold,' said Julian.

'That is *not* my reputation,' Reese objected, and threw a pillow at him.

'It totally is,' Bri insisted.

'Yep,' said Robbie Revilla. He wrote music reviews for the *Leader* and dressed like a goth rock star. 'They're right. Own it, Reese.' He raised his plastic cup of punch to her and took a sip.

Reese's head was too fuzzy to come up with an appropriate comeback. So she changed the subject. 'If I had to pick a dude,' she said, quoting Bri, 'I'd go for David Li.'

Madison squealed, bouncing up onto her knees. 'David Li?'

'Sure, why not? He's cute.'

'He's like Captain America.' Madison laughed. 'I can't believe you would go for him!'

'She has a hero streak in her,' Julian said. 'Writing all those op-eds about asshole cops harassing students. I could see it.'

'Do you like him?' Madison asked.

'Who?' Reese said deliberately.

Madison rolled her eyes. 'David Li, you dork.'

'I don't *like* anybody,' Reese said.

'Would you go out with him?' Madison pushed.

'No, I don't date anyone.'

'Right on, Reese,' Robbie said. 'We're too young to be tied down.'

Bri gave Reese a curious look. 'You wouldn't date *anyone*?'

Reese shrugged. 'I'm not interested. I like being on my own.'

Madison asked, 'But if you were interested, you'd date someone?'

Reese sat up. 'Jeez, I don't know. Why?'

Madison smiled. 'No reason, just asking. Have you ever kissed anyone?'

Reese thought for a minute. 'Yes. In fourth grade I kissed Eli Campbell on a dare at recess. Does that count?'

Bri cracked up. 'No. It does not count.'

'Have *you* kissed anyone?' Reese countered.

Bri turned red. 'None of your business!'

'Dude, it's okay, you can out me as your secret lover,' Robbie said, waggling his pierced eyebrow at her.

Madison giggled. 'So Bri's totally kissed someone. Robbie, despite his supposed preference for being single, dated Stephanie Chen last fall. Julian's dating that guy he met over the summer. And I at least had a real kiss at the Fall Formal. You know what that means?'

'What?' Reese asked dubiously.

Madison smiled. 'You should kiss someone tonight!'

Bri and Robbie both seemed to think it was a great idea, but Reese shook her head. 'No. That's ridiculous.'

Her objection made Julian take notice. 'Why?' he asked. 'You should do it. It's not like you have to date the guy.'

'Or the girl,' Bri put in.

'You guys are crazy. What am I supposed to do, just walk up to someone and be like, "Hey, you wanna kiss me"?'

Robbie started laughing, but Madison was seriously considering the question. 'No, we'll set it up for you,' she said.

Reese's eyes widened. 'What? No.'

Madison seemed excited. 'Yes! It'll be great. Who do you want to kiss? I'll go ask them!'

Reese shook her head. 'I don't think that's a good idea.'

'She likes David, what about him?' Bri suggested.

Madison shook her head. 'He's dating Riley now. Haven't you seen them going at it?'

'Hmm,' Robbie said. 'You should get a David lookalike. Your brother!'

Madison made a face. 'Ew. I'm not asking my brother.'

'You guys, I don't want to do this,' Reese said, but her objections were falling on deaf ears. When Madison fixated on a crazy scheme, she had a way of making it happen. Reese figured Madison would be editor in chief of the *Leader* by the time they were juniors.

'Eric Chung,' Julian said. 'I bet he'd do it.'

'Oh my God, that's perfect,' Madison said. 'Julian, you know Eric, will you go ask him?'

Reese swung her legs over the edge of the couch, her face darkening. 'You guys, I'm *not* doing this.'

Madison finally looked at her. 'I'm just saying maybe you should try it.'

'Why? What does it matter if I've kissed anyone before?'

Madison scrunched up her face, puzzled. 'Don't you want to?'

'No!' Reese turned red. 'Look, it's not my ultimate goal in life to kiss anyone or find a boyfriend. That's your deal, Madison, not mine.'

Madison's face went white. 'What are you saying? That I'm some boy-crazy idiot? I'm just trying to have some fun. You're overreacting.'

Reese's entire body stiffened as heat suffused her skin. 'I am *not* overreacting,' she snapped, and before Madison or anyone else could respond, she got up and left.

She couldn't go to the living room – it was packed full of drunk kids dancing to hip-hop – so she headed to the back of the house. The kitchen was a mess, the counters strewn with paper plates and crushed plastic cups. The punch bowl, still half full of the unnaturally pink drink that tasted like a gallon of syrup mixed with paint thinner, was surrounded by empty beer bottles. A couple was making out in the corner, and they didn't even look up as she banged into the trash can, causing a tower of pizza boxes to crash onto the floor. She saw the back door behind the couple, and she brushed past them and pulled the door open, letting it slam shut behind her. She thought she heard the couple squeak in surprise.

Outside, the yard was deserted. It was March, and it was freezing. Fog cloaked the neighborhood in the kind of damp chill that soaked through to your bones, but the cold air felt good on her flushed cheeks. She pulled her hood over her head and zipped up her sweatshirt, crossing her arms as she gazed across the long, dark yard. Her breath steamed out, mingling with the fog that crept through the light from the kitchen door. The neighbors were still awake, their windows visible through the mist in fuzzy yellow squares.

She barely had time to take a few breaths before the door opened behind her and Julian said, 'Reese, you okay?'

'I'm fine,' she lied. Madison's words still burned, making her tense and defensive.

Julian dragged a couple of metal deck chairs toward her and sat down in one. She didn't say anything more, waiting for him to give up and leave. But instead he took something out of his pocket and struck a match. His face was lit by a flame as he cupped his hand around a cigarette. 'When did you start smoking?' she asked.

When the match sputtered out he laid it carefully on the armrest. 'Couple weeks ago.'

She watched him smoke. He seemed fairly proficient at it. 'Sean smokes, doesn't he?' Sean was the guy Julian had started dating recently; he was only a year older but had run away from home and was trying to make it as a musician. Julian had met him at a queer youth event at the Center.

Julian flicked the ashes at the ground. 'Yeah. So?'

'So it's a bad habit to start.' Reese sat down in the other chair, watching as Julian exhaled plumes of smoke into the fog. She had gone with Julian to one of Sean's gigs at a dive bar where they had snuck in the back. The band sucked, but Reese could see why Julian liked Sean. He was all swagger, spiky dark hair and eyeliner and lips like a girl's.

'Give me a break. I live in a house full of organic everything – even the freaking soap is organic. Maybe I need some carcinogens to balance things out.'

She laughed, and just like that, her anger dissipated. She sighed. 'I should apologize to Madison.'

'She didn't mean to push your buttons.'

'I know.' They sat in silence for a while as the fog shifted in the dim light. The night sky had an orange cast, reflecting the lights of the city in the cloud cover.

'I'm sorry,' Julian said finally. 'About the kissing thing.'

She shrugged. 'Whatever. It doesn't matter.'

'Why are you so against it?'

Frustration flared in her. 'I'm not against it!' She groaned. 'I'm just not interested. I don't want to date anyone.'

'Why not?'

'I don't need the drama.'

'You mean like with your mom.'

She was startled at first, then remembered that Julian had been there for a lot of the fights, or at least for the aftermath.

156

His mom usually helped pick up the pieces. 'Yeah. I'm not going to be like my mom.'

'What if you meet someone you like?'

She shook her head. 'Doesn't matter. I'm not getting involved.'

'That sounds kinda grim, dude.'

'Maybe for you. For me it sounds rational.'

'Love isn't rational.'

She could barely see his expression in the dark, but she could hear the grin in his voice. 'Don't be so melodramatic.'

'I'm just saying: Someday you're gonna meet some guy and he's gonna change your mind.'

'Yeah? You're psychic now?'

He shook his head. 'No. I just know you.'

Her eyes grew hot. She blinked and inhaled a lungful of fog. 'Hey, give me a cigarette,' she muttered.

'You don't smoke.'

'You can teach me.'

Thinking back on that night, Reese remembered that Julian had never suggested she might meet a girl who would change her mind. Had the possibility never occurred to him? It had never occurred to her. Amber was as unexpected as an August heat wave in San Francisco, and about as irresistible. Reese hadn't consciously known a thing about what she was getting into when she texted Amber earlier that day. But if she was honest with herself, she realized now that some part of her – the part that operated solely on instinct – had been aware. How else could she explain her compulsion to change her whole outfit before going over? It was completely unlike herself.

But her fashion crisis was far from the most unusual thing she had experienced today. What did it mean that she had spent the afternoon making out with a girl? Did that mean she liked all girls or only Amber? Did she actually like Amber or just kissing her?

Reese rolled onto her side and pulled the pillow over her head, unable to answer any of those questions.

CHAPTER 17

Reese was online surfing for San Francisco tourist information when there was a knock on her door. 'Yeah?' she called.

Her mom opened the door. 'David's downstairs.'

At first Reese thought she had heard her mom incorrectly. 'What?'

'David. Your friend. He's waiting for you in the living room.'

She scrambled to her feet and ran down the stairs. He was standing in the bay window, looking out at the dark street. 'David?'

He turned. 'Hey. I got your message.'

She had nearly forgotten she had sent it. 'Oh.'

'Sorry I didn't respond sooner; I haven't been checking the Hub lately. And I thought it would be better if we talked about it in person. I don't have your phone number anymore.'

She swallowed. All that stressing out over his lack of response for nothing. 'You want to sit down?'

He sat on the couch while she took the armchair. 'So, your scars disappeared?' he said.

She glanced over her shoulder, but there was no sign of her mom. She would freak out if she heard about this. 'Yeah,' Reese whispered. 'That scar I showed you on my head at the funeral? It's gone. So are the rest of my scars. What about you?'

'The same thing happened to me. I thought it was just because of the treatment we got. You know, it was supposed to be really advanced, so maybe—'

'I thought so too,' she interrupted, and then lowered her voice again. 'But there's more. I fell on the sidewalk the other day – someone ran into me. I scraped up my hands pretty badly, but by the time I got home there was nothing wrong with them. It was like they healed within half an hour. I thought maybe I had just imagined the scrapes, but . . . I don't think I did.'

He leaned toward her. 'You think that's related to the scars?'

'Maybe.' She told him about her research online and the report about the DARPA initiative on regeneration. 'What if that's what they did to us? What if they made it so that we can regenerate our tissue?'

His mouth opened slightly. A lock of hair fell over his forehead as he scooted closer to her. He reached out and took her hand, and she stopped breathing. 'This hand?' he asked.

'Both hands.'

He cupped both her hands in his, turning her palms up as if he could read the lines on her skin. Her memory flashed back to the moment on the sidewalk with Amber after she had fallen, when Amber had cradled her hands as well. It wasn't exactly like déjà vu; it was more like she was living in two parallel dimensions at once, and though the experiences mirrored each other, they were slightly different. David's hands were larger than Amber's; his thumbs curved over Reese's palms and traced the hollows of her hands. Her pulse raced within her wrists, and she wondered if he could feel it. A thrill ran directly from where his thumbs touched her all the way to the center of her body, as if he had turned on a live wire connecting the two of them.

He raised his gaze to hers. His pupils were dilated so that his brown eyes were almost black. She was overcome by a feeling of doubling. Her own body was taut with tension, but she could also feel something – someone – else. Another body, with a different interior landscape than hers. A different sense of balance. It was so disorienting that her head spun, and the whole world seemed to bend.

'Reese?'

She squeezed her eyes shut, but that only made it worse, so she opened them again, and David's face was hovering over hers. She had slid down the chair, her head limp against her shoulder.

'Reese, what happened?' He let go of her hands and brushed the hair away from her sweat-dampened forehead.

'I just need a minute,' she said.

He drew back, and she pressed her fingers to the bridge of her nose. The sensation of the other body was gone, but it had left her with a throbbing headache.

'Are you sure you're feeling all right?' David looked worried. 'Do you want me to get your mom?'

'No!' Then again, more quietly: 'No. I'll be fine. I just get headaches sometimes. It's a side effect of the accident.' Was she having hallucinations with her headaches now? She had heard that migraines sometimes were accompanied by hallucinations.

'Do you get them often?' David asked.

'I get them when I'm – when I'm stressed out.'

'Maybe I should call your mom. Do you want me to bring you some water?'

'No.' She didn't want her mom to notice. 'But maybe I should go lie down.'

'You sure?'

'Yeah. I'll be fine. I'm just . . . tired.' She could barely remember waking up that morning. Maybe everything that had happened had just caught up to her, and having David here in her living room after the afternoon with Amber— The pain sharpened.

'Okay.' He stood up, preparing to go, and pulled out his cell phone. 'What's your number? I just got a new cell phone.'

After she gave him her number, she walked him to the front door, pulling it open. Fog was stealing down from Twin Peaks, swirling through the street in ghostly fingers.

'It's cold. How did you get here?'

He stepped outside, hands in his pockets. 'I drove. I'm just parked down the street.' He began to go down the steps but turned halfway. 'Call me if something else happens. I mean it.'

'I will.'

She watched him until she lost sight of him on the sidewalk, and then she went back upstairs, her head pounding in time with her heart. Her laptop was still open, the screen saver sending multicolored spirals across the monitor. She ran her fingers over the touch pad and the browser lit up, showing a site listing the top ten tourist destinations in San Francisco.

What was she doing with Amber? Besides the obvious, she heard Julian quipping. She picked up her phone, clicking through her contacts to find Amber's number. Amber had already texted her earlier that night, saying that she wanted to see her again. Reese hadn't replied yet, but now she did.

> Tomorrow morning I'll take you to
> the beach. Pack a sweater. Your
> tour guide, R.

CHAPTER 18

'Oh my God, it *is* cold,' Amber said, wrapping her arms around herself as they crested the sand dune and looked out at Ocean Beach.

'I warned you,' Reese said. They had ridden the N Judah all the way to the end, sitting side by side, thigh pressed against thigh. She tried to play tour guide, pointing out the sights along the way, but the N Judah didn't exactly run through the most interesting parts of the city, and Amber herself was so distracting: warm and sweet-smelling, the curve of her lips shining in the sunlight that poured through the streetcar windows.

Amber had kissed her when she arrived at her house earlier that morning – just flat-out kissed her – and Reese had nearly fallen over on the front step. Now all she could think about was kissing her.

Except it was kind of hard to do that when they were slipping and sliding down the cold, sandy hillside toward the ocean, the wind tugging at Reese's ponytail and whipping it around her face. But even though it was cold, it was clear, and Reese was thankful that the beach wasn't swathed in damp fog. Amber ran ahead to the firmer-packed sand and stood there with her back to Reese, looking out at the ocean as it roared onto the land in bubbling white foam, leaving trailing strands of seaweed behind.

'Wow,' Amber breathed. 'This is very cool.' When Reese came to stand beside her, Amber slid her arm through Reese's, pulling her closer so that their hips touched. 'It feels a lot bigger than the Atlantic.'

'Oh yeah, you're from the East Coast, right?'

'Yeah. I went to school there – at this private school in Massachusetts for a while.'

'Do you miss it?'

'School? Or the East Coast?'

'Both.'

'I don't miss school. I don't miss the East Coast. I like where I am.' Amber gave Reese a smile that made Reese's heart race. 'Wanna find a place to sit down?'

'I brought a blanket.'

'I know.' Amber grinned and stepped away. Her hand slid down Reese's arm until she caught Reese's fingers in hers, tugging her along the beach.

They found a relatively sheltered spot where the sand dune created a kind of windbreak, and they spread out the blanket, anchoring it with Reese's backpack and themselves. The beach was mostly deserted, except for a few people walking their dogs, and once they lay down on the blanket it wasn't nearly as windy as it had been when they were standing at the edge of the waves. When Amber leaned over her, Reese felt as if they were entirely alone. A smile pulled at Amber's mouth, and when they kissed, Reese could feel the smile imprinted on her own skin.

Kissing Amber was like falling into the sea: Her body surrendered to the pull of the tide, buoyed by the saltwater, every breath tasting like the ocean. Reese lost all sense of where the surface was. All there was, was this. Amber's lips, her tongue, her hands stroking back Reese's hair, curling around her head and holding her steady. If their first kiss had been a bit awkward, that was gone now. Now it felt as if they had been dancing this dance together always, and somewhere within herself Reese noticed this. When they parted so that they could breathe in the salt air, Reese rose up on her elbows and pushed Amber onto her back so that her pale eyes reflected the blue sky.

Amber giggled, whispering, 'What are you waiting for?'

Reese looked down at her, drunk with kissing, and said, 'I don't know your last name.'

Amber put her hand on Reese's neck, her fingers sliding against the pulse in her throat. 'My last name is Gray. What's yours?'

'Holloway.'

There wasn't much gloss left on Amber's lips, but they still seemed to shine as they curved up. 'Reese Holloway,' she murmured.

Reese felt so full at that moment, as if her heart had

expanded to at least twice its normal size, and it was pushing at the walls of her body in a deep, insistent rhythm. 'Amber Gray,' she said, the name almost swallowed by the crash of the surf.

Amber pulled Reese's head down to hers, her mouth brushing against Reese's ear. 'It's nice to meet you.'

The next afternoon, Amber came to Reese's house. She had invited herself over, saying coyly that she wanted to see where Reese slept at night, and Reese couldn't say no.

After Amber arrived, she wandered through the ground floor, peeking into the living room, the kitchen, the office in the back where Reese's mom sometimes worked from home. 'Where's your room?' Amber asked.

'Upstairs,' Reese answered.

Amber smiled at her and held out her hand, and Reese took it and led her toward the stairs.

Nerves fluttered in her stomach as Reese opened the door to her bedroom. She had straightened up that morning, even dusted the furniture, but now the door banged into the edge of her suitcase, which had become wedged into the corner between the door and the closet. She kicked at it, trying to shove it out of the way, and Amber asked, 'What happened to your suitcase?'

'I – it was in an accident.'

'You were in an accident? Or the suitcase?'

'Both, I guess.'

Amber came into the room and went directly to the bay

window, peeking through the blinds at the street before sitting on the edge of the desk. Her eyes traveled over the space: a giant Rhapsody of Emily poster on the wall beside the door; a big bulletin board covered with notes for the national debate championships; a bookcase filled with books and debate trophies; her desk and desk chair; her bed, covered in the floral-patterned quilt her grandmother had made. And in the corner, the suitcase. 'Nice room. Very organized,' Amber said. 'What happened in the accident? Were you injured?'

Reese shut the door. 'Yeah, but I'm fine now. It's not worth talking about.' She dragged the suitcase toward the closet, pulling open the sliding door to push the suitcase inside. But there wasn't enough space on the floor. Her laundry basket took up most of the room, and shoes and bags were piled up around it. Embarrassed that Amber was seeing all of this, she hastily dragged the closet door shut, but it was too late – Amber was standing beside her, fingering the edge of a red dress that peeked out from among Reese's darker clothes.

'What's this?' Amber asked.

'It's a dress, obviously.'

Amber shook her head playfully. 'Oh, Reese. Can I see it? The color's nice.'

'I don't wear it anymore.' Reese pulled it out, remembering the last time – the only time – she had worn it, at a fundraising gala she had gone to with her mom more than a year ago. They had sat at a round table in a hotel ballroom, listening to speakers talk about violence against women. The dress was dark red, with spaghetti straps and a simple bodice that flowed into a knee-length, fluttery skirt. Her mother had picked it out for her, and Reese had shivered in it all night. The ballroom had been overly air-conditioned, and the dress wasn't exactly cozy.

'Can I try it on?' Amber asked. 'It's pretty.'

Reese was surprised. 'Go ahead. You can have it.'

'Let me try it on first. It might not fit.' Amber pulled off her T-shirt and unbuttoned her jeans, pushing them off her legs, and Reese froze as she watched Amber shimmy into the red dress. It got stuck halfway on, and Amber said, her voice muffled by the fabric, 'Can you help me out? I think I might be too big for it.'

Reese remembered the times she had gone shopping with Madison, who liked to try on every single prom dress in Macy's even if she didn't have the money to buy a single one. They crowded into tiny dressing rooms together, and Reese helped Madison button and zip and smooth out those gowns. But never – not once – had she felt as self-conscious as she did now, when she put her hands on the hem of the dress – *her* dress – and tugged it over the curves of Amber's hips and breasts. Her hands trembled as she tried to zip up the back, but it wouldn't budge, and the stubbornness of the zipper broke the spell that had fallen over her. She laughed in relief. 'I don't think it's going to work.'

'Ugh. That's a bummer. I really like the color. Well, will you unzip it?'

Reese realized she had relaxed too soon, because once the

zipper was down, Amber took off the dress, and then she was standing there in Reese's bedroom wearing only her underwear. Though they had done plenty of kissing, this was the first time she had seen Amber undressed. Reese forgot to breathe. Amber's bra was pale pink with white stripes, like a pastel candy cane, with a froth of white lace on the edges of the cups. It was nothing like the bras that Reese's mom bought for her. This was a confection, meant to be seen. Reese wore plain, taupe-colored bras selected by the gray-haired bra-fitting lady at Nordstrom, who had a measuring tape slung around her neck and came into the fitting room with her to prod her breasts into proper formation. 'Enjoy it while you're young!' she would say in her dry, slightly accented voice. Reese always thought she must be Russian, and the bra lady's words echoed inanely in her head now as she looked at Amber, who still hadn't put her clothes back on. She was watching Reese with an expression that was half a question, half an answer. She took the few steps across the room to Reese and kissed her.

A few moments later, Reese let Amber pull off her own shirt, and there she was, kissing a girl, skin to skin, and she wondered, *Is this what it feels like to be a lesbian?* Amber's body, like her own, but so unlike her own. Soft. Her skin warm, flushed.

Reese's phone rang, and at first she barely heard it, enveloped in the haze that descended on her when Amber was so close, but then Amber picked up the phone and silenced it.

'Hey—' Reese said, reaching for the phone.

'Later,' Amber said, and put the phone in the top desk drawer. Then she took off her bra.

The world spun, and Reese had to sit down on the edge of her bed. Amber's hands slid around Reese's back and unfastened her bra too, and they lay down, breast to breast, as goose bumps rose all over Reese's skin.

Reese pulled Amber closer. She couldn't get close enough. It was extraordinary: the feel of Amber's skin on hers, the places their bodies fitted together, the way she felt like she would melt if Amber didn't touch her, and maybe even if she did—

But when Amber's fingers slid beneath the waistband of Reese's jeans, she froze. An unexpected panic raced through her, and before she knew what she was doing, she grabbed Amber's hand and pulled it away, whispering, 'Not yet.'

Amber stopped. She laid her head on the pillow, facing Reese, and smoothed back Reese's hair from her flushed cheeks. 'Okay,' Amber said, and kissed her gently on the corner of her mouth. 'Okay.'

CHAPTER 19

Amber left at five o'clock so that she could avoid running into Reese's mom. 'I could stay and meet her,' Amber suggested as she put her shoes on.

Reese, leaning on the edge of her desk, crossed her arms. 'I don't think I'm ready for that.'

Amber finished tying the laces on her sneakers. 'All right. No need to rush.' She got up from the bed and went over to Reese, cupping her face in her hands to kiss her lightly. 'So, when will I see you again? Tomorrow?'

Reese rested her forehead against Amber's. 'I can't tomorrow.'

'Aw, why not?'

'I have to do some stuff with my mom, and tomorrow night we're having dinner at a friend's house.'

'How about Sunday then?'

'Yes,' Reese agreed, sliding her hands around Amber's waist.

'I'll miss you.' Amber's mouth was so close to Reese's that

she could feel the movement of her lips when she spoke.

Sunday seemed an eternity away, but part of Reese was relieved to have the break. Things were moving so fast – too fast. Now she felt as if Amber was waiting for her to say *I'll miss you too*, and the words stuck in her throat. It was easier to pull her closer, fingertips pressing on her back, and kiss her instead. When they parted a few minutes later, Reese said, 'I'll see you on Sunday.'

After Amber left, Reese went slowly back upstairs to her bedroom. It seemed like a new landscape. The quilt on her bed was rumpled; the red dress lay in a lurid puddle on the floor by the closet. The suitcase still glowered in its broken, bungeed heap in the corner. She had to unpack it sometime. It might as well be now.

She knelt on the floor beside it and unhooked the ends of the bungee cords. The suitcase sagged open. She took out the shattered toiletry kit and didn't even bother to look through it, simply tossing it in the trash. She went through her clothes, piling the salvageable items into her laundry basket and throwing away the rest. She found debate materials too, down at the bottom of the suitcase. A pile of papers, including information about the national tournament, which she recycled. A notebook that she had used during debates to take notes on the opposing team. The cover was warped, and she threw it away. And wedged into one bent corner of the suitcase she found a thin plastic bracelet with a label stuck on it. Her stomach clenched.

It was the bracelet she had worn in that drab hospital

room in the middle of Nevada. The letters printed on it were clear and sharp.

PLATO PA83 HOLLOWAY

What did those letters and numbers mean? She was trying to work out some kind of acronym or code when she remembered the nondisclosure agreement she had signed. Maybe that contained an explanation. What had happened to that? She flipped through the pockets of her suitcase but couldn't find it. She thought back: She had stuffed it inside, she recalled that clearly, but where? Her gaze alighted on the recycling bin where she had thrown her debate notes. She dragged it over and shuffled through the papers again. There it was. She put the bracelet on the floor and began to skim through the nondisclosure agreement, searching for any sign of what PLATO PA83 might mean. But the more she read, the less she understood – and the more freaked out she became. Phrases leaped out at her as if they were highlighted.

Classified Nondisclosure Agreement
An Agreement Between Clarice Irene Holloway
and the United States

I have been advised that the unauthorized disclosure of classified information by me could cause damage or irreparable injury to the United States . . .

I have been advised that any unauthorized disclosure of classified information by me may constitute a violation

174

of the United States criminal laws, including the provisions
of Sections 641, 793 . . . the provisions of the Intelligence
Identities Protection Act . . . I recognize that nothing in this
Agreement constitutes a waiver by the United States of
the right to prosecute me . . .

Whosoever, through gross negligence . . . shall be fined
under this title or imprisoned . . . In time of war, with intent
that the same shall be communicated to the enemy . . . shall
be punished by death or by imprisonment . . .

She had signed this document without reading it – Agent
Forrestal and Dr Brand had made it sound so completely
routine – and now she wondered what exactly she had
agreed to. A lifetime of keeping her accident a secret? And
why was the punishment so severe? She had never signed a
nondisclosure agreement before, but she didn't think that
death or imprisonment was a normal repercussion.

She scrambled to her feet and went to her desk,
dropping the bracelet and the agreement next to her laptop
and pulling open the drawer to grab a pen. She saw her
phone sitting there where Amber had put it, the voice-mail
indicator blinking. She picked it up and pressed the voice-
mail button.

'Hi, Reese, it's David. Just wanted to see if you're feeling
better. Also, I think I had one of those headaches today. Call
me when you get a chance.'

He sounded tense in his message, and Reese was about to

call him back when she heard the front door open downstairs and her mom's footsteps in the hall.

'Reese?' her mom called. 'Are you home?'

Reese put down the phone next to the agreement. Maybe she could get some more information about it before she called David. She went downstairs.

For as long as Reese could remember, she and her mother had a standing date on Friday nights to watch a movie and eat whatever they wanted, as long as they didn't have to cook it. Tonight her mom had brought home Thai takeout and the latest Jane Austen movie. Reese could barely pay attention. It was yet another rendition of *Pride and Prejudice*, starring one of Hollywood's newest it girls, and as this Lizzy Bennet wandered across the English countryside, Reese tried to figure out how she could ask her mother legal questions without raising her suspicions. She waited until the credits began to roll before saying, 'Can I ask you something?'

Her mom was sitting in the armchair, legs propped up on the coffee table with a mostly empty martini glass in her hand. 'Of course, honey. What is it?'

'I was researching something today, and I found this nondisclosure agreement that seemed weird to me. It said that if the person talked, they could be punished with death or imprisonment. Is that enforceable? Doesn't that seem insane?'

Her mom's eyebrows rose. 'Death or imprisonment? I've never heard of an NDA referencing that. Lawsuits, yes, but not . . . what kind of NDA was this? For a corporation?'

'For the government. The United States government.'

'I don't think anyone could be imprisoned or killed, honey. That does seem a bit extreme. Can you tell me more about it?'

'Well, it listed these laws – one of them was the Intelligence Identities Protection Act. Do you know anything about that?'

Her mom swung her legs off the table and put down her martini glass. 'Not really. That must relate to treason and those kinds of issues. I suppose in the case of treason, people can be executed. They have been, in the past, but not without a massive trial. It's very, very unlikely to happen.'

'What about imprisonment?' Reese pushed. 'Could that happen?'

Her mom gave her a curious look. 'It's more likely than state-sanctioned execution, but . . . why are you asking this? What are you researching?'

'It's just something that Julian and I are working on for this blog he wants to start about conspiracies,' Reese lied. She hoped her face didn't give her away. Her mom was pretty good at scoping out liars.

'What does an NDA have to do with it?'

'I just found one online, and it seemed – it seemed related.' *Crap*. She was screwing this up.

Her mom's eyes narrowed on her. 'Sometimes in the case of someone who is privy to information they were not authorized to receive, they are asked to sign an NDA after the fact. Does that sound like the agreement you found online?'

'Um, yeah. Exactly like that.'

'I see.' Her mom paused. 'Well, I'll tell you this, honey. A minor – someone who is under the age of eighteen – can't be forced to sign an NDA like that.'

'Really?'

'Only in very specific circumstances would an NDA hold up for a minor. In situations involving health care in a life-threatening situation *maybe*, and only in some states. Or, I don't know, in the case of something so top secret it truly would cause harm to the government. But even then, death or imprisonment is highly unlikely. I don't think any court of law would uphold that kind of an NDA forced on a minor without parental approval.'

Reese shifted in her seat uncomfortably. Her mom totally knew what she was talking about. 'Thanks, that's very helpful.'

But Reese wasn't entirely reassured. Now she found herself wondering, if the NDA wouldn't hold water in court, why had the government asked her to sign it? Were they just trying to scare her? Or had she really seen something at that hospital that was so important, it needed to remain classified at all costs?

After her mom went to bed, Reese entered the term *Area 51* into the search engine. She remembered Julian's first assumptions upon learning where she had crashed the car, and the more she thought about it, the more curious she became. A billion results seemed to pop up in response to her query: websites, images, wiki entries heavy with footnotes and external links. She was drawn to the photos first, clicking through one after another of brown desert, pale buildings seen from above, distant mountains, and clusters of signs:

WARNING: Military Installation.
It is unlawful to enter this installation
without the written permission of the
installation commander.
Maximum punishment:
$1000 fine
six months imprisonment or both.

The landscape in the background behind the signs did look familiar, but was that because everything in that part of Nevada was similar?

She decided to try a different tactic. She could retrace online the route she and David had driven from Las Vegas and see if it ended up in the vicinity of Area 51. She started her search at Ash Springs, where they had bought gas. The interactive map allowed her to zoom in on the image of the gas station, and then she followed the highway north until she saw the turnoff for the Extraterrestrial Highway. When she passed her mouse over a square dot on the landscape, it expanded into a sharp image of the Alien Fresh Jerky sign.

Zooming out, she followed the light gray stripe of road to the west. She didn't know exactly how far they had driven before the accident, but the only thing between the Alien Fresh Jerky sign and the next highway – which she knew she hadn't reached that night – was a cluster of flat-roofed buildings and a few empty airstrips. There were multiple pinpoints on the map, left by tourists eager to share their findings. The markers opened into images of a dusty road leading through the desert to nowhere. One photo showed a white truck parked on a hill. All the photos were labeled with the same words: area 51.

Was that really where she and David had spent those twenty-nine days?

On impulse, she searched for *Area 51* and *PLATO*. The string of websites that resulted was dizzying, containing layer upon layer of confusing and sometimes contradictory conspiracy theories about extraterrestrial visitors. The more she read, the more she felt as if she had tumbled through a rabbit hole into a dimension in which the ordinary world was less realistic than this universe of shadowy conspiracies.

On Bin 42, she found a post detailing something called Project Aquarius, supposedly established by President Eisenhower in the early 1950s to investigate all UFOs and contact with extraterrestrial biological entities. The post provided a list of black projects associated with Aquarius. Sigma's goal was to establish communications with aliens; Pounce would evaluate UFOs for space technology; Redlight would recover an extraterrestrial craft; Snowbird would rebuild it. But another project jumped out at her. Project Plato was reportedly established in 1960 with the goal of establishing diplomatic relations with aliens. It also involved cooperation between the United States government and the extraterrestrials to abduct humans for the purpose of biological research.

She picked up the hospital bracelet and studied the words stamped on it: plato pa83 holloway. If it was the same Plato, that would mean, first of all, that she believed these conspiracy theories. She didn't know if she was ready to buy in yet. Second, it would mean that extraterrestrials existed and had in fact visited the Earth, an idea that seemed too far-fetched to be plausible. How could the arrival of extraterrestrials have been kept secret for so long? Third, it raised a ton of questions about what exactly had happened to her – and David – at the hospital.

That was the part that terrified her the most, because even if she didn't believe these websites, the fact remained that something had been done to her and David at this place that seemed to correspond to Area 51. And she had no real idea what had been done – only that it was so classified, she couldn't even admit to having been at that hospital. A chill swept over her as she eyed the bracelet.

She suddenly remembered that she was supposed to call David back, but when she picked up her phone, she saw that it was after midnight already. It was too late; she'd have to call him in the morning. While she was holding the phone, it buzzed. She nearly dropped it in surprise. A text message from Amber came through.

> Just found out citywide curfew's
> being lifted Sunday. Can I take you
> out on a date? Dinner and dancing,
> like the olden days. I will look up
> some places. XO, A.

It was surreal to be holding the bracelet in one hand and the phone in the other. The collision of the two worlds was jarring. Reese opened the top drawer of her desk, dropping the bracelet in and slamming it shut. Then she texted back: Yes.

CHAPTER 20

Dinner at the Arens house was an island of normalcy in the middle of an increasingly bizarre world, and Reese tried to relax into it. Daniel and Celeste Arens were great cooks, and Saturday night they made honey-barbecued beef ribs and a lemony green salad – 'From our farm,' Celeste noted proudly – and roasted sweet potatoes. The ribs were delicious, sticky and spicy-sweet, but Reese still couldn't forget about the unsettling conversation she'd had with David earlier in the day. She had told him about her mom's assessment of the nondisclosure agreement as well as what she'd found out online. 'Do you think I'm crazy?' she asked, forcing a laugh.

'No, but you might think I am.'

'Why?'

'I thought I saw Agent Menzel yesterday.'

Reese's fingers tightened over her phone. 'You mean one of those agents who brought us back from Nevada?'

'Yeah.'

'Where?'

'Down the street from my house. But when I went to look, he was gone.' He sounded frustrated. 'I swear, I'm not making this up. I've been feeling like someone was following me for a couple of days now, but I've never been able to see who it was.'

Reese remembered her sighting of the man in black at Cypress Lawn cemetery; she had never told David about it because he had left before she returned to the memorial service. 'I thought I saw someone at Mr Chapman's funeral,' she said now. 'I wasn't sure, because I never saw his face.'

'Have you seen anyone since then?'

'No.'

On the way to dinner Reese kept her eyes peeled, but she hadn't seen anything out of the ordinary. She jumped when Celeste picked up her empty plate and asked if she wanted dessert. The dining room was a world away from where she had been in her mind.

'You look like you've been daydreaming,' Celeste said. 'Anything in particular?'

She shook her head and saw Julian give her a curious glance. 'No, sorry. I'm just tired. Of course I'd love dessert.'

It was a strawberry-rhubarb crisp served with vanilla ice cream, and Reese concentrated on each bite, willing herself to focus on what she was eating instead of who might be lurking outside. The fruit had softened into tangy, tender spoonfuls topped with the crunch of brown sugar and oatmeal. As the ice cream melted cool and sweet over the crust, Reese felt the tension in her muscles easing. By the time she scraped the bottom of the bowl, she felt almost normal again.

Julian's older sister, Serafina, was home that night too, and after dinner the three of them retreated to the family room to play video games. Sera refused to play anything except Cannon Ball, in which they competed to shoot the most number of bubbles out of the sky before being crushed by falling cannons. With three players, it got pretty competitive, and after a few heated rounds Reese excused herself to refill her water glass, leaving Julian and his sister battling it out to the next level.

She was outside the archway to the kitchen when she heard her mom talking to Celeste. 'He apologized to Reese,' her mom was saying.

Reese halted at the sound of her name.

'How did she take it?' Celeste asked.

'She seemed a little stunned.'

'Well, how do you feel about it?'

'I don't know.' Her mom sounded upset. 'I'm always going to love that man, you know. I can't help it.'

There was silence for a while, and then Reese heard her mother sigh. Celeste said, 'I know.'

Reese was about to move away from the door, feeling distinctly uncomfortable, when her mom said, 'You'd think he would quit while he's ahead. I was all set to forgive him after he told me he was going to apologize to Reese, and then he had to tell me that he still loves that other woman. Lydia.'

Celeste made a soothing noise. 'Oh, Cat—'

'What is he thinking?' her mom demanded, her voice rising. 'He told me that we're the only two women he's ever loved, and that he wants me to understand he can love more than one woman at a time. How am I supposed to take that?' Her words were slightly slurred, and a glass banged down on the counter. 'Do you think that's possible?'

'I don't know. Maybe for men? I don't see how it's possible for women. I think you love one person, and you commit to it. Honestly, you know how I feel about Rick's various reasons. Do you think he's making any real progress?'

Her mom groaned. 'I don't know. He's seeing a therapist – I can tell by the way he's changing his sentences. He's using 'I' statements now. He's trying. I just don't know how much longer I'm willing to stick it out. It's been so long. Twenty years?' A chair scraped across the floor. 'Shit, it's getting late. I have to get home before the curfew.'

Reese hastily backed away from the door, but she had only made it across the front hall before her mom and Celeste appeared.

'Oh, Reese, I was just coming to get you,' her mom said. She rubbed a hand over her reddened eyes. 'I think we'd better get home. It's almost nine.'

'Okay.' Reese wished she hadn't overheard that conversation. It was like accidentally seeing your parents make out; you could never un-see it.

Celeste gave her a shrewd look. 'Are you all right, sweetie?'

'Yeah, I'm fine,' Reese said, pasting a thin smile on her face. 'Julian and Sera were kicking my ass in Cannon Ball.'

'Do you think you could drive us home?' her mom asked. 'I had two glasses of wine and the cops are gonna be out tonight.' She slid an arm around Reese's shoulders, and Reese wobbled. It was as if she could feel her mom's tipsiness in her own body: a kind of blurring sensation, along with a pleasant warmth in her stomach. 'It would be bad news for the assistant DA to get pulled over on a drunk-driving charge,' her mom whispered conspiratorially. 'Even though I'm not drunk. I just had two glasses of wine.'

'Maybe three,' Celeste said.

'*Maybe*,' her mom admitted.

'Sure, Mom. I'll drive.'

'Oh, good. That's one benefit of you growing up.' Suddenly her mom seemed on the verge of tears, and she squeezed Reese closer. The blurred feeling intensified, and the room briefly swam before Reese's eyes. 'You're growing up so fast,' her mom said, her voice thickening. 'I just want you to be happy, honey.'

'I am,' Reese said, embarrassed and confused. Why did she feel so weird?

'Don't scare the child,' Celeste said. 'She's not an adult yet.'

Julian and his sister came into the hall, and when Reese's mom saw them she exclaimed, 'Julian! You're so tall now – and so handsome. Are you growing a beard?'

187

Her mom left her side, and the blurriness abruptly ended. Reese took a step back, breathing shallowly as her vision returned to normal. Had she just had another hallucination, like that night David had come over?

Her mom was cupping Julian's face in her hands, making him squirm as she praised him. 'And Serafina,' she continued, moving to caress Sera's smooth brown cheek. 'So lovely. You look just like your mother.'

'Thanks,' Serafina said with a grin.

'All right, all right, let's get going,' Celeste said, herding Reese and her mom toward the door. 'I don't want to bail you out of jail in twenty minutes when you miss the curfew. Bye now.'

'Bye, Celeste. Tell Daniel to stop working and keep you company. It's Saturday night,' Reese's mom said, kissing her friend on the cheek.

Julian made a face in the background, and Sera covered her mouth with her hand.

'Bye, you guys,' Reese said, taking the car keys from her mother.

But when she climbed into the driver's seat, she realized this was the first time she had driven a car since the accident in Nevada. She was paralyzed as she flashed back to the bird's eyes in the headlights, the screeching tires on the dark highway. Her skin grew hot as she tried to force back the memories. There was no time for this; she had to drive them home.

Her mom fastened her seat belt and made a funny noise

that Reese recognized as a sniffle. 'Mom? Are you all right?'

She laughed shortly. 'I'm sorry, honey. I'm such an embarrassment. I'm supposed to drive you home, not vice versa.'

'It's fine, Mom. Don't worry about it.'

'You're a good girl,' she said, patting Reese on the knee.

'Uh, thanks.' Reese glanced over at her mom. She had folded her arms and was looking straight out the windshield, and there was a wet gleam in her eyes.

'We'd better get going. Curfew.'

'Right.' Swallowing her anxiety, Reese punched the power button to start the Prius. At least it didn't sound like that rental car.

Her mom was as silent as the car during the drive home. Reese clutched the steering wheel with clammy hands, her eyes darting repeatedly from the rearview mirror to the road ahead. No birds. No traffic, even, other than a single set of headlights several blocks behind.

They stayed the same distance behind for some time, until Reese's heart was pounding in her throat. Finally, when Reese turned onto her block, the headlights veered away. She sighed in relief. The street was deserted. But as she followed her mother up the front steps, she couldn't escape the feeling that she was being watched.

CHAPTER 21

On Sunday night, Reese met Amber at an Indian restaurant on Valencia Street. It had about a dozen tables, half of them taken when Reese arrived, and the surfaces were covered with stainless-steel dishes and fragrant foods that she didn't recognize. The crowd was mostly young and local, and Amber was already seated at a table in the window. She waved at Reese as she entered.

'Hi,' Reese said, sitting across from her. Amber's pale hair stood out against the wall behind her, which was painted in two wide stripes the colors of turmeric and cinnamon.

Amber stood up to lean across the table and kiss her on the lips. 'Hi, yourself.'

Reese blushed, glancing out the corner of her eye at the couple seated at the next table, but they didn't seem to have noticed. She picked up the menu. 'Have you eaten here before?'

They ordered the vegetarian *thali*, an assortment of eight little dishes served on a round tray, accompanied by rice;

paratha; and a puffy, hollow bread. Reese had eaten Indian food plenty of times before, but her mom stuck to buttery chicken korma and tandoori, so the arrival of their dinners made her eyes widen. There were three kinds of curry, one including dark brown pods that Amber identified as fresh chickpeas. There was a pickled lime that Reese ate in tiny bites, savoring the unfamiliar, mouth-puckering tang. She tore into the puffy bread, deflating it, and dipped it into the spicy soup.

Amber seemed to find her appetite amusing. 'I'm glad you like it so much.'

Reese spooned up a mouthful of saffron rice. 'It's amazing.'

Amber's eyes crinkled at the edges as she smiled. 'I knew you had good taste.'

'You're fishing for a compliment, aren't you?'

Amber's smile turned mischievous. 'I would never do that.'

'Right. Of course not.' Her dry tone made Amber's eyes light up.

'How about this: I found this place, so you can pick next time. I'm sure you'll impress me.'

The idea of *next time* caused Reese's stomach to do a nervous flip. 'Um, okay.'

Amber observed her for a moment. 'I just freaked you out, didn't I?'

Reese's cheeks reddened. Was she that transparent? 'I'm not . . . I've never done this before. Dated anyone.' The heat on her face spread to her neck. Now she sounded like a dork.

'Hey, it's all right.' Amber reached out and stroked a finger down the back of Reese's right hand, which was gripping her fork tightly. Reese dropped it onto the plate. 'We can do whatever you want. There's no rush.' Amber leaned forward and laced her fingers through Reese's. 'I'm sorry if I moved too fast,' she said in a low voice. 'I . . .' She trailed off, gazing at Reese with a faint blush on her face. For the first time Reese had noticed, Amber looked self-conscious. She took a deep breath. 'I've never felt this way about someone before. The way I feel about you. It's like – this is going to sound weird, but it's like we're in a movie, and every time I'm with you, the camera zooms in for a close-up and we're the only two people in the frame. Do you know what I mean? You're my close-up.'

Reese had stopped breathing. Heat rolled through her belly, sweet and slow, and holding Amber's hands across the table wasn't enough. She got up, leaning over the empty dishes, and cupped her hands around Amber's face and kissed her. She tasted of salt and spice, and she let out a soft gasp that made Reese tremble. This time the couple at the next table did notice, but Reese didn't care.

After that, it was as though a dam had been breached. 'Did you always know you were queer?' Reese asked, taking a tiny bite of the syrupy rice pudding dessert.

'Queer, huh?' Amber said. 'You can't use that word everywhere.'

'What do you mean?'

'In some parts of the world it still means, you know, *queer*. Wrong. San Francisco's kind of the exception to the rule when it comes to queer things. How about you? When did you realize?'

Reese shook her head. 'You're not going to believe me, but seriously, I have never thought about it.'

'Really? You've never had a crush on a girl before?'

'No.'

'Wow.' Amber grinned. 'Do you have a crush on me?'

Reese laughed. 'You're shameless.'

'I think shame is pretty pointless. And you didn't answer my question.'

'I thought I did, earlier.' Reese smiled at her.

Amber sat back, looking unusually shy. 'I guess you did.'

'But you didn't answer my question either. When did you know?'

Amber shrugged. 'I've always known. I don't think it's useful to limit yourself to one gender.'

'So you like guys too?'

'Not so far. But never say never.'

'Are you out to your parents?'

'Yeah. They don't care.'

There was something odd in the way Amber said it, but Reese didn't want to push.

'Do you think your mom would be okay with it?' Amber asked.

'I think so. My best friend is gay. He's my mom's best friend's son, so she's had a gay kid around for a long time.

And besides, we live in San Francisco.' Reese took one last bite of her dessert and glanced at her watch. It was already nine o'clock.

'Ready for part two of our evening?' Amber asked, counting out money for dinner.

'Let me give you some,' Reese said, pulling out her wallet.

Amber shook her head. 'Next time, remember? You can take me out for sushi.'

'Oh I can, can I?' Reese laughed. 'I thought I was supposed to pick. Where are we going now?'

'Dancing,' Amber said coyly, and slid out of her chair.

'Do we need fake IDs? I don't have one.'

'They'll let us in,' Amber said confidently.

They went to a bar on an otherwise quiet corner off Valencia, where a neon sign jutted into the street. Dozens of women clustered on the curb, laughing and smoking and talking. The sound of pulsing music burst into the night every time the door opened. As they approached, Reese saw a bouncer checking IDs. 'Are you sure about this?' Reese said.

'Don't worry about it.'

The bouncer was probably only a few years older than they were. She had a buzz cut and a nose ring, and she carried a flashlight in one hand. A tattoo spiraled up her forearm, and Reese wondered if she was really as tough as she looked. 'ID,' she said shortly.

Amber smiled at her, and Reese watched as the bouncer blinked once, twice, meeting Amber's gaze. 'You can't just let us in?' Amber said. The bouncer hesitated. Then Amber reached out and ran a finger over the tattoo on the bouncer's arm. 'What's that? A snake?'

The woman visibly shivered. 'No, it's personal.'

Amber leaned in just a little bit, so that she was bending over her wrist. 'It's nice.'

The door to the club opened, and three girls burst out onto the street, laughing loudly, and the beat of an old nineties rap song pounded into the air. They brushed past Amber, knocking her against the bouncer, who caught her around the waist and didn't let her go. Reese felt a flare of jealousy sting her. *This is stupid*, she thought. She was about to reach out for Amber's hand when the bouncer said, 'Fine. Just this once.'

'Thanks,' Amber said, and then she stepped out of the woman's hands and reached back to pull Reese up the step and into the club.

It was so dark inside, she could barely see. The bar, which ran the length of a long, rectangular room that resembled a hallway more than a dance floor, was strung with Christmas lights, but the ceiling lamps were turned down so low, they were practically useless. There was a throng of women pressing toward the bar, and along the opposite wall was a long bench that looked oddly like a church pew, with more women seated there.

Reese realized they must mostly be lesbians, because there were plenty of them being awfully touchy-feely with one another. There were girls with short, spiky haircuts;

there were girls with long curls and darkly made-up eyes. Most wore jeans and tees or tank tops, though a few wore little dresses that exposed bare arms and backs covered in tattoos. Still, Amber stood out, and as women turned to look at her – and then at Reese – Reese felt a strange tremor over her skin, as if she were being touched by dozens of people all at once.

There was a jukebox in the corner, and Amber shouted over the din of the music, 'Wait here!' Reese leaned against a pile of kegs near the jukebox as Amber pushed through to the bar, past the neon sign pointing toward the restroom, slithering between an older woman in a tie and a younger one in a miniskirt.

The weird sensation on her skin changed as she watched the crowd. The creepy feeling of being touched faded, but now it was as if she could hear something just beyond the vibrating bass of the music that shook the room: whispers breathing in her inner ear, raising the hairs on her body. She shook her head and moved away from the jukebox, wondering if there was some kind of distortion effect from it. She bumped into a woman standing nearby, and she had a flash of tense muscles, a clenched gut. A burst of pain lit through her head.

'Hey, watch out, it's a little cramped here,' the woman said.

'Sorry,' Reese mumbled, and backed away, bumping into the kegs. She hadn't had a headache for days, but now she could feel it coming: the nerves in her neck tightening until her vision swam. She bent over, hands on her knees as if she had just run a marathon. She saw her feet down below, the dull metal sheen of a keg of beer, the edge of the jukebox, and a pair of black ankle boots that stopped in front of her. Amber crouched down to Reese's eye level, concern on her face.

'Are you all right?' She was holding a drink in each hand.

Reese straightened up, blood rushing away from her head. 'Yeah,' she said breathlessly.

Amber looked at her closely. 'What's wrong?'

'Nothing,' she said, but her body was hot and shaking. Her stomach heaved, and she muttered, 'I have to go—' She bolted for the bathroom.

Miraculously there was no one in line, and Reese rushed inside, slamming the door between her and the crowded club, sliding the bolt home with trembling fingers. She leaned over the toilet, her hair falling forward in a dark sheet. She tried to hold it all to one side, but strands kept sticking to her sweat-dampened neck. She heard knocking on the door behind her, and Amber's muffled voice called, 'Reese? What's going on?'

'I just need a minute!' Reese gasped.

'Are you sure? Can I come in?'

'Just . . . give me a minute.'

The bathroom was tiny: barely enough room for the toilet and a sink that jutted out of the turquoise-blue wall. A yellow light glowed in the ceiling, making the little rectangular room seem like it was underwater. As Reese's breathing began to slow, she noticed that the wall was covered with graffiti. Over the toilet, there were dozens of scrawled phrases. *For a good time, call Joanie. Sheila is a cheater. Don't be a bitch, T.*

The letters blurred before her eyes. The room spun around her. She sank down onto the floor, pulling her knees up and resting her cheek on them. She tried to breathe steadily. She hated throwing up. She really didn't want to throw up here. Next to her on the wall, half hidden by the edge of the toilet and visible only to those who had to kneel down on the floor, someone had carefully written out a poem.

Haiku for J

You broke my heart and
Changed my life. Now I'm a dyke
Lovesick on the floor.

Reese stared at the words, wondering if 'J' had ever seen this poem. She reached out and touched the outline of the *L* in the word Lovesick. There was something about the feel of the wall beneath her fingers, cool and dry and solid, that made her calm down. She kept her hand on the wall and looked around as the pressure in her head lessened. Dozens of women had poured their hearts out onto the ocean-colored walls, and their words leaped out at her, almost vibrating with raw emotion. It was like she was sitting at the bottom of a teardrop.

198

She could still hear the music from the club, but the closed door blocked out most of it, and now it was more like being surrounded by a heartbeat. She could feel it reverberating from the wall into her hand and through the blood in her veins, as if the sound of the bass connected her to the words etched into the wall. She didn't know where the feelings on these walls ended and where her own began.

Her fingers splayed wide, framing the haiku between her thumb and index finger. Impulsively, she pulled out her phone and took a picture of it: the blue wall, the black letters, the white curve of the toilet on the right. The image was grainy and probably too poorly lit to be readable, but she didn't want to leave this place without a record of it. She felt as if something inside her had unexpectedly awakened; as if a third eye had opened in her forehead and she was only beginning to learn how to see.

Amber knocked on the door again, and now she sounded worried. 'Reese? Are you sick in there?'

Reese pushed herself up, tucking the phone back in her pocket. She took a deep breath and looked at herself in the mirror. Her face was pale and washed out, but she didn't look too awful. She tucked her hair behind her ears and opened the door.

Amber was standing outside, her hand raised as if she were about to knock again. Relief filled her face. 'Are you all right? What happened?'

'I'm sorry. I was worried I was going to be sick. But I'm fine.'

'Was it the dinner?' Amber asked, horrified.

'No, I just got a bad headache. It happens sometimes.' Behind Amber there was a line of women, some of them looking pissed off at being forced to wait for so long. Reese stepped out of the bathroom. 'I have to get some fresh air. I'm sorry.'

Reese kept her head down as Amber led the way through the jostling crowd. If she didn't make eye contact with anyone, somehow it felt safer. But still she felt their gazes on her, and her stomach threatened to give itself up again. When they finally squeezed out the door, popping into the cool July night, Reese felt as if her synapses were expanding in reaction to the air, and she sucked in several deep breaths in relief.

'Do you need some water or anything?' Amber asked.

'Maybe that would be good.'

They went across the street to the corner store, and Amber bought her a bottle of water, handing it to her with an anxious expression. 'Was the headache really bad? Did you feel nauseated too?'

'Yeah.'

'Does this happen a lot?'

'It hasn't happened lately.' Not since the night David came over to her house. Thinking about him when she was with Amber was unsettling, and she pushed the memory away.

Amber bit her lip, watching as Reese drank the water

gratefully. 'Well, this wasn't exactly how I wanted the night to end up. Maybe I should walk you home.'

'Let's go to the park. I feel like I need to be in an open space or something.'

'Okay.' Amber reached out and took Reese's hand. Her touch sent a noticeable shiver all through Reese's body, and Amber's eyes widened.

'Reese?'

The voice came from behind her, and Reese turned around. 'Julian?' she said, startled.

He was standing in the light of the streetlamp on the corner about ten feet away. 'It is you.' He took a few steps toward them, and his eyes flickered from her to Amber, who was still holding her hand.

Reese's cheeks burned, and she let go. 'Hey,' she said.

'Hello,' Julian said, curiosity plain on his face.

They could still hear the thump of the music from the club and the chatter of the girls across the street. Someone broke into raucous laughter. Amber said, 'Hi. I'm Amber.'

'I'm Julian.' He glanced at Reese with his eyebrows raised high. 'So, what are you doing tomorrow morning?'

Reese sighed. 'Having breakfast with you?'

He grinned. 'Sounds good. I'll be over.' He turned to continue where he was going, and added, 'Have a good night, *ladies.*'

The swing set in Dolores Park was deserted, the light from the nearest streetlamp barely reaching into the sandy playground. The chains creaked as Amber lowered herself into one of the swings. 'Push me,' she said.

Reese put her hands on Amber's waist and pulled her back, then pushed. Amber's legs kicked, and she let out a rippling laugh. Reese backed up, her sneakers shuffling through the sand, and reached out to push Amber again. For a while, there was no sound except for the whoosh of wind in Amber's wake, the creak of the swing set, and the sound of cars driving past on Dolores Street. Overhead, Amber's body made a shadow against the dark sky. It was a clear night – at least in this part of the city – and in the distance the lights of the downtown skyline twinkled. Reese took the swing next to Amber's and pumped her legs until she was flying up into the sky. The wind felt good on her face, blowing away the last bits of her headache.

'Reese,' Amber called.

Reese looked over to see Amber extending her hand. She reached out and grabbed it when they swung close enough together. It tipped Reese off balance, and she careened wildly as Amber's fingers locked on to hers. Amber shrieked with laughter.

'Kick!' Reese cried. They tried to coordinate their motion, but it was too late, and the swings rapidly decelerated until their feet scraped against the ground.

Amber was still breathless with laughter when Reese tugged Amber's swing closer, their legs tangling together. Reese reached for Amber and pulled her head to hers, kissing her, and Amber's laughter stopped abruptly. Reese slid out of her swing, her knees in the sand as she knelt between Amber's legs and wrapped her arms around her back. She felt the bones of Amber's shoulder blades shifting beneath her hands as Amber slid her arms around her; she felt the pulse of Amber's heartbeat against her own. This was better than soaring in the night sky. This was knowing the texture of Amber's breath as well as she knew her own, as if they breathed from the same set of lungs. *I am you*, Reese thought, *and you are me.*

There were so many things Reese didn't know about Amber. She didn't know her parents' names or where she had been born or even whether she would stay in San Francisco after the end of the summer. But she knew this: She was falling for this girl, this beautiful, beautiful girl, and she wanted to fall. She wanted to leap right now, arms spread wide, gravity pulling her down, the wind tearing at her hair. She didn't care if she crashed, as long as Amber crashed with her.

CHAPTER 22

Reese dreamed of the yellow room again.

It was like floating in a silky yolk, her entire body buoyed by the viscous weight of the liquid around her. She watched the red veins climbing and spreading across the walls with a detached, intellectual curiosity. Would it split into two branches there? Or three? And what would happen when the red covered the yellow, turning this golden sunset into a bloody sphere?

She spun around, entranced by her weightlessness. She was like the jellyfish she had seen once at the Monterey Bay Aquarium, their bodies glowing like alien ships drifting in space.

She heard the dull echo of that sound she couldn't quite place. A repeated, underwater kind of beep, but more sonorous and stately. If a bell could be rung from the bottom of the ocean, that was what this sounded like.

This time in her dream, the red veins began to accelerate. Tendril upon tendril of creeping red vine spread over the walls, and heat suffused her body. She began to sweat, and her heart began to race, and she raised her hands and pounded against the now-red walls. To her shock, they gave beneath her hands. They were slick and warm, and when she spread her fingers into them, her fingertips sank into the surface, stretching it out. She was like a creature in a horror movie attempting to break free from a cocoon. She shoved her face into the rubbery exterior, her hands and body stretching the pliable surface over her skin. She was about to break through – she felt the wall beginning to rip – and then the dream ended, and she was sitting up in bed, her skin hot and damp.

Her breath tore out of her lungs as if she had been sprinting. It was Monday morning. Her clock read 9:06. Sunlight streamed through the cracks in the blinds, casting a ladder of light across the hardwood floor. Her room looked so extraordinarily normal in comparison to that other room, with its creeping veins and disturbingly textured walls.

Her gaze fell on the small can of red paint on her desk. She got out of bed and picked it up, turning it around in her hands. BITTERSWEET ROOT was stamped on the lid. She pried it open with the assistance of a pair of scissors and dipped her fingers into the liquid, watching it drip back down in lazy droplets. She looked around her room. The walls were painted blue-gray. She walked to the wall where the Rhapsody of Emily poster hung beside the closet and smeared her paint-tipped finger over the blue-gray. The red was a dark cut against the lighter wall. The sight of it vibrated through her like the bass in the club. As if some kind of physical memory was awakening.

This was what she had to do. She had to paint the room she saw in her dream. Just like that bathroom with its ocean-colored walls. The compulsion was so strong, she wanted to start right away, but she only had this one tiny can of paint.

She set it on the floor so she could get dressed to go to the hardware store.

Julian was sitting on the front steps when Reese returned, carrying two bags full of paint cans and brushes. 'I was about to think you were standing me up,' he said: 'I tried calling you, but you didn't answer.'

She had forgotten he was coming over. 'I didn't bring my phone with me.' She put the bags down to unlock the door.

Julian peeked into the bags. 'What are you doing with all this paint?'

'I'm going to paint my room.'

'What color?'

'It's . . . kind of complicated.' She carried the bags inside and left them at the bottom of the stairs.

'Complicated?'

'Yeah. Can we talk about it later?'

He came inside and shut the front door. 'Oh-*kay* You're acting a little weird, you know.'

A flash of impatience swept through Reese. She wanted to get started on the painting, but now Julian was standing in the hall holding two cups of coffee, and she knew he wouldn't leave without an explanation. She took a deep breath. 'I didn't sleep that well.'

He handed her a cup of coffee. 'Here. Drink this.'

'Thanks.' She took the paper cup and headed into the living room, dropping onto the couch.

Julian followed, sitting in the armchair and propping up one foot on the coffee table. 'So, are you gay now?'

She choked on her coffee. The hot liquid burned down her throat, and she had to gasp for cool air.

'Sorry,' Julian said, smiling. 'Maybe I should've given you a warning.'

'I'm not gay,' she said, throat raw. 'I'm just...not straight.'

'I knew it!' he crowed. 'I totally knew it. And there's a word for that, you know. Bisexual.'

'I don't know,' she said reluctantly. 'That seems pretty definite. Like: Yeah, I like both.'

'Don't you?'

The question made her squirm, and she peeled the lid off her coffee and blew on it. 'I guess, but I don't want to put a label on it.'

He took a sip from his drink. 'I felt the same way when I first realized I was gay. I didn't want to name it.'

'Really? Why?'

'I think because I wasn't comfortable with it yet.'

She hunched over, gazing down at the milky coffee. Julian always remembered how she drank it. 'Yeah,' she said finally. 'Maybe that's it. Not that I think it's wrong – I don't. But it's really new.' She took a careful sip. 'Besides,

207

bisexual . . . it makes me think of girls on reality TV making out in front of guys.' She made a face. 'I don't want people to think that about me.'

'People are always going to think something about you that isn't real. It doesn't matter what they think. Nobody ever knows what to think of me. I'm not black enough for some folks, and I'm not Jewish enough for others. I mean, my favorite food is bacon. And then you throw in the gay thing, and it messes it up even more.' Julian sounded strained. He sighed. 'This is getting too heavy. What's up with this chick Amber? When did you meet her?'

She smiled faintly. 'Last week. And . . . thanks. For telling me that.' She and Julian had been friends forever, but she couldn't remember talking about this stuff with him before.

Julian waved it off. 'It's the way it is. So: Amber. How am I supposed to be your best gay if you don't tell me all the dirty details?'

'Don't only straight girls have best gays? How is that going to work if I'm not straight anymore?'

'I wouldn't know.' He gave her an arch look. 'I apparently am not friends with a straight girl.'

She laughed. 'I ran into her near Dolores Park. I mean, I literally ran into her – or she ran into me. She wasn't looking where she was going. When I went back the next day, I saw her again, and she wanted to buy me a cup of coffee. We started talking, and then it . . . sort of went from there.'

'Where does she go to school?'

'She doesn't. She graduated in June and is taking the year off.'

'So she's an older woman.'

'Whatever, she's a year older.'

'And what do her parents do?'

'Her mom is a scientist.'

'Where?'

'I don't know.' Reese had never thought to ask.

'What about her dad?'

'She never said anything about her dad. I think her parents are divorced or something.'

'Where does she live?'

'She's staying in her uncle's apartment on Dolores Heights.'

'What's she doing in San Francisco?'

'Hanging out for the summer.' Reese frowned. 'What's with the third degree?'

Julian's face softened. 'Sorry. I just want to make sure she's not a serial killer or something.'

'She's not a serial killer. But thank you.'

'And you like her?'

Reese blushed. 'I like her.'

He smirked. 'So are you done with your plan to not date anybody?'

'I totally meant it when I decided that,' she protested. 'You know I did.'

'But you're done?' he pushed. 'Like, you're dating this Amber chick?'

'I went on *one* date with her,' Reese objected, putting down her coffee.

'You've only seen her once?' Julian was incredulous. 'You looked pretty tight.'

'We've only gone on one official date,' Reese explained, and as she said the words she saw Julian's face light up.

'How many *un*official dates did you have? And how long did they last?'

'I'm not telling you everything, jeez. What about your 'I never kiss and tell' policy? But yeah, I guess I'm dating her.' Saying the words suddenly made it real, and her stomach flipped. 'Shit. I'm dating a girl.'

Julian broke into laughter and had to put down his coffee cup so he didn't spill the liquid. 'Aw, I always knew you were family, Clarice.'

She laughed and threw one of the couch pillows at him. 'Don't get all sappy on me.'

He ducked, and the pillow bounced off his shoulder. 'Hey! Watch it.'

Reese took another sip of her coffee. 'So are we done with the processing? I want to get started painting.'

'Wow, you're like Martha Stewart on a mission.'

'I just want to get it done.'

He raised his hands in surrender. 'All right, chill. Do you have any plans tonight?'

'No. Why?'

'You know how I told you I was doing some work for Bin 42?'

'Yeah.'

'Someone sent me a lead on something in the Bay Area. There's a warehouse north of the city where the government might have stored some wreckage from one of the plane crashes.'

'From June nineteenth?'

'That's the theory. I want to go there tonight and check it out, and I need you to come with me. I want to get video footage of the warehouse and hopefully whatever's inside, and I need you to back me up.'

'You need me to drive,' she said dryly. 'Isn't that it?' Julian still hadn't gotten his license.

He grinned sheepishly. 'Well, we have to get there somehow, and it would be great if we could use your mom's car.'

She turned the coffee cup around in her hands. 'When would you want to go? And where exactly is this warehouse?'

'It's west of Petaluma in the middle of nowhere – maybe a two-hour drive from here. I looked it up online. I think we should wait till after our parents are asleep to leave.'

Reese didn't think there was much chance that her mother would give her permission to drive two hours north in the middle of the night to sneak into a government warehouse. That meant she'd have to lie about where she was going or steal the car keys after her mom went to sleep. 'I have a better idea,' Reese said. 'David has his own car. I could ask him to drive us.'

211

'David Li? You think it's a good idea to bring in someone else?'

'Well, he's kind of already involved,' Reese admitted reluctantly.

'What do you mean?' Julian gave her a pointed look. 'What haven't you told me?'

She hesitated, thinking of the nondisclosure agreement. Even if it didn't hold water, she wasn't sure if she was ready to ignore it. 'Ever since I got back, some weird things have been happening to me and David. Remember when you showed me that photo of Area 51?'

Excitement rose on Julian's face. 'Are you saying that I was right about where you had your accident?'

'Well, the car crashed near where Area 51 is supposed to be.'

'I knew it!' Julian cried.

'I don't know for sure that's where I was,' Reese cautioned him. 'But the fact that it happened during the June Disaster, and I almost hit that bird – I know it's a lot of circumstantial evidence, but I feel like there's some connection there, you know?'

Julian was shaking his head, his mouth twitching.

'What?' she demanded.

'Do you know how funny this is? You're trying to convince *me* that there's something shady going on. I'm already there. What exactly is this weird stuff that's been happening to you and David?'

She stalled for time, taking another sip of coffee while she tried to figure out how much she should – or could – tell him. He gave her an expectant look. 'I really want to tell you, but I don't think I should,' she said, settling on the truth. Julian would see through her anyway if she lied.

The anticipation on his face changed into sober thoughtfulness as he studied her. 'Okay,' he finally said. 'You think David will really go for this?'

Relieved, she said, 'Yeah, I do. He wants to know what's going on with us as much as I do.'

'Then how about you get him to pick us up at midnight?' Julian stood to leave.

'Do you want to wait while I call him?'

'Nah. I have to get home and make sure my recording equipment is ready. Just text me after you've talked to him.'

'All right.'

Reese followed Julian to the front door. As he opened it he added, 'Wear black. And bring a flashlight.'

CHAPTER 23

Reese was right. David didn't hesitate to say yes, and they quickly agreed that he would pick her up first at midnight, and then they would head over to Julian's. After she texted Julian the details, she took the paint upstairs and looked around her room. She decided to start with the wall next to the door, where the bulletin board hung beside the closet.

As she unhooked the bulletin board to lay it on her bed, a couple of photos that had been stuck beneath others tumbled to the floor. She bent to pick them up. One was of herself with her mom and grandparents at the Marin County Fair when she was thirteen. It startled her to see how young she looked, all braces and awkwardness. The other picture was of her and David after the first debate tournament they had won last winter. They both had giant smiles on their faces, and David was holding up their trophy. She remembered how excited they had been. Afterward they went out with the whole team to IHOP and vowed to win all the way to nationals. Too bad that hadn't worked out. The memory of how she screwed everything up still hurt, and she forced herself to drop the photos on the bed and ignore the twinge of embarrassment that pinched her.

She spread newspapers on the wooden floor in front of the now blank wall. At the hardware store, she had bought a large can of bittersweet root and two cans of yellow paint. One was called morning sunrise; the other, slightly lighter in color, was downy gold. She pried open the can of morning sunrise with a flathead screwdriver and unwrapped one of the new brushes, running her fingers over the stiff bristles before dipping it into the paint. She swept the color, glistening and bright, over the blue-gray wall in a curving streak of yellow. She felt as if her hand were being guided by instinct, and the more she painted, the closer she came to remembering what was so familiar about that dream.

After most of the wall was covered in morning sunrise, she switched to downy gold, using a clean brush. The bottom layer wasn't dry yet, so the two colors smeared together. When she saw the new color that created, her stomach lurched. *That* was it. That was the color of the room in her dream. Excitement hummed through her. She painted the lighter yellow all over the wall, mixing it in with the darker shade in quick strokes. When the whole wall was yellow, she knew she was ready to add the red, but she had to wait until the yellow paint dried or else the mixed colors would turn into orange.

Impatient, she went downstairs to make herself a sandwich for lunch. As she ate it in the kitchen, staring out at the backyard, all she could see was the yellow room in her dream. She could picture exactly how the red veins spread down the walls, but now she also remembered a thin layer of iridescent gel over the red, like a caul protecting a newborn. How could she paint that? She glanced around the kitchen and her eyes alighted on a box of plastic wrap. She opened it and peeled off a piece. The edges stuck together, and as she stretched the plastic flat, her fingers sliding against the sleek surface, something inside her clicked.

She was the newborn within the caul.

She had been inside the yellow room with its bleeding, pliable walls.

She couldn't breathe for a minute as the truth uncoiled through her: After the accident she had been in this place that she dreamed of. She knew it in her bones. It was an incubator, and after she emerged, she was different.

She ran back upstairs, clutching the box of plastic wrap. The yellow wall gleamed at her, still shining wet in some places, but she couldn't wait any longer. She opened the can of bittersweet root and began to drag the red across the yellow, like the branching limbs of a tree. She loaded the brush so heavily that paint began to drip down the walls, sliding over the electrical outlet. She put down the brush and went to get the screwdriver to remove the faceplate so that she could wipe off the paint.

There was a red light blinking inside the wall, attached to the outlet.

She froze. *What is that?* The red light was part of a tiny device that looked like a round battery. She reached into the wall and pried it loose; it seemed to be stuck with some kind of adhesive. In the palm of her hand, the device continued to blink like a little red eye, opening and closing. A trail of cold crept down her spine. She flipped it over. Engraved into the bottom of the battery were minuscule letters that she had to squint to read: EC&R.

Her phone rang, startling her. She dropped the device, and it clattered onto the wooden floor. Cursing, she picked it up and put it in her pocket, then answered the phone. It was Amber.

'Hey, what are you doing?' Amber asked.

'What? I'm – nothing,' Reese said. *Was that a bug? Is someone listening to me?*

'Are you at home?'

'Yeah. Why?'

'I'm outside.'

Reese went to the window and pulled up the blinds. Out on the sidewalk, Amber was standing with a bouquet of flowers in one hand.

'I brought you something,' Amber said through the phone, sounding coy. 'Can I come in?'

Reese could feel the pressure of the tiny object in her pocket. She had to get this thing out of the house. 'I'll be there in a sec. Hang on.' She hung up and ran downstairs to the kitchen, unlocking the back door. She headed for the potted geraniums and shoved the blinking device deep into the soil before she went to let Amber in. She would have to examine it later.

* * *

217

They were gerbera daisies – orange and fuchsia and purple – and even though Reese had already glimpsed them from her bedroom window, seeing Amber hold them out to her sent a warm glow through her. 'Nobody's ever brought me flowers before,' Reese said. She was pretty sure there was a goofy smile on her face.

Amber leaned in to kiss her on the cheek. 'I'm happy to be the first.'

She followed Reese into the kitchen, where Reese took down a vase for the flowers and filled it with water. 'How come you're covered with paint?' Amber asked.

Reese glanced down at herself, faintly surprised to see yellow and red smeared all over her shirt. 'Crap. I've been painting.'

'Obviously,' Amber said, laughing. '*What* have you been painting?'

'My room.'

'Really? Can I see?'

Reese hesitated, arranging the flowers in the water. 'It's not finished yet. And it's kind of weird.'

Amber came behind her, sliding her arms around Reese's waist. 'I promise I'll like it.'

Reese turned to face her. 'I bet you say that to all the girls,' she teased her.

'No,' Amber said, shaking her head seriously. 'Only to you.'

Heat flared in Reese's belly. The light from the kitchen window drew out darker flecks in Amber's gray eyes so that they looked like granite, solid and steady. 'Okay,' Reese said. 'I'll show you.'

When they entered Reese's bedroom, Amber gasped. The paint was still wet, and the red drips that streaked down the wall ended in gleaming little droplets. Amber's mouth parted slightly, and a shadow seemed to pass over her face, as if she were seeing something that struck a nerve in her. She turned to look at Reese, who was standing in the doorway with the vase full of daisies.

'You painted this?' Amber said, her voice hushed.

'Yes. I told you it's weird.'

But Amber said, 'It makes me think of rebirth.'

Reese's heartbeat quickened. 'Rebirth?'

'Yeah.'

'How did you come up with that?' Reese entered the room and put the vase on her desk.

'I don't know; it's just a feeling I get. It's intense.' She took out her phone. 'Do you mind if I take a picture?'

'No, why?'

'I think it's really cool.'

'Oh.' Reese was flattered, and the phone's camera clicked.

'Have you ever painted before? Like, art stuff?'

'No. Not outside of school.'

'You said you weren't finished. What else are you going to do?'

'I'm going to put plastic wrap over part of it.' Hearing the words out loud made Reese realize how odd they sounded.

Amber gave her a quizzical look. 'That's an interesting decorating idea.'

Reese shook her head. 'It's not decorating.'

'What do you mean?'

Before she could stop herself, she was explaining the whole thing. 'I had this dream – I keep having this dream over and over again. I see this yellow room with these bleeding walls, and . . . this morning I woke up and knew that I had to paint it. I actually got the idea after seeing the bathroom in the club last night.'

'The bathroom?'

'Yeah. It was all blue. It reminded me of the dream. Except, of course, the colors are different. I know this sounds totally bizarre.' She wondered if she had made Amber think she was crazy.

'No, it's really interesting,' Amber assured her. 'Do you have a lot of dreams like this?'

'No. Just this one.'

'When did you start having this dream?'

'After the accident,' Reese said, and then stopped. There was something in Amber's face – an excitement – that Reese didn't understand. But as soon as she noticed the odd expression, it was gone.

'The one that damaged your suitcase?'

'Yeah.'

Amber gave her a concerned look. 'What happened in the accident? Was it really bad?'

'Yeah.' Reese sat down on the edge of the bed, unsure of

what else to say. She couldn't tell Amber the whole truth, not only because of the nondisclosure agreement, but because it would sound insane. And she didn't want Amber to think she was crazy. 'It was bad,' she finally said. 'I had internal injuries, and I was in the hospital for a while.'

'But you're better now?'

'Yeah,' Reese said, even though she wasn't entirely sure that was true.

'Good.' Amber sat down beside her, and the bulletin board slid over to knock against her.

'Sorry.' Reese reached over to move it out of the way.

The loose photos that had fallen off earlier fluttered onto the bedspread. Amber picked them up. 'Oh my God, is this you?' she asked, examining the Marin County Fair photo. 'You're so cute – and so surly.'

'Hey, I was thirteen,' Reese said, taking it from her. 'Give me a break.'

Amber still held the photo of Reese and David, and she looked from the picture to Reese. 'Who's this? You two look cozy.'

Reese reached for the photo, but Amber wouldn't let go. 'Give it back to me,' Reese said.

Amber quirked an eyebrow at her. 'Who is this guy?'

'My debate partner.'

'He looks like more than that.'

'He does not.'

'Look at the way his arm is around you,' Amber insisted. 'And you're practically draped all over him.'

221

'We were just happy because we won that day.'

'Sure you were,' Amber teased her.

'You're being ridiculous,' Reese objected, ruffled.

'It's fine with me if you still like boys. It's a free country.' Amber held out the photo. 'As long as you still like me.'

There was more than flirtation in Amber's expression; there was challenge. Warmth rippled through Reese. She took the picture and threw it on her desk before she pushed Amber back onto the bed. 'I still like you,' Reese said, and kissed her.

Like every time, time melted away. A minute could have passed, or an hour. There was only Amber: her mouth and the movement of her body against her own. Reese felt as if she could kiss her forever, and she would never grow tired of it.

Someone coughed.

Reese knew that cough.

She scrambled away from Amber, who was lying stretched out on the bed, her shirt hiked up to reveal her bare stomach. Reese looked up, and her mouth went dry. Her mother was standing in the open doorway. 'Hi, Reese,' her mom said.

She pulled down her own shirt. 'Hi, Mom.'

Amber sat up, her face turning white. 'Shit,' she said, and then her hands flew to cover her mouth.

Reese's mom broke into laughter. 'I just wanted to let you know I'm home, since you didn't seem to notice.' Reese turned red. 'I'll be downstairs. Come down and say hi when you've collected yourselves.'

222

CHAPTER 24

Reese's hands were clammy as she entered the living room, Amber in tow. Her mom was sitting on the couch, pretending to read a newspaper, but when she saw them she dropped the paper onto the coffee table. 'Hi there,' her mom said, as if they hadn't already greeted one another upstairs.

'Hi, Mom. This is Amber.'

Her mom stood up, extending her hand. 'Hello, Amber. It's so nice to meet you.'

Amber stepped forward and shook her hand. 'Hi, Mrs— Mrs—'

'Cat. Please, call me Cat. I'm nobody's Mrs anymore.'

Amber smiled. 'Sounds good to me.'

'Would you like to sit down?'

'I'm really sorry, but I have to get home,' Amber said. 'My mom's in town for a few days, and I'm supposed to meet her for dinner. I, um, lost track of time.'

'Well, you're welcome anytime, Amber.'

Amber seemed surprised. 'Uh, thanks, Mrs— um, Cat.'

She began to head for the front door and added, 'It was great to meet you.'

'The pleasure's all mine.'

Reese rolled her eyes at her mom. 'I'll be right back,' she said, and followed Amber down the hall.

Out on the front steps, Amber whispered, 'I hope she doesn't hate me!'

'She doesn't.'

Amber looked skeptical. 'If you say so. Will you call me later and tell me what she says?'

'Yes.'

Amber went down the steps toward the sidewalk, waving. Reese closed the door, took a deep breath, and returned to the living room.

Her mom had a mischievous look on her face. 'She's cute.'

Reese stared at her. This was definitely not the reaction she had expected.

She grinned at Reese's expression. 'What? I grew up in San Francisco. You don't think I've ever kissed a girl?'

Reese's mouth dropped open.

'So,' her mom continued, 'is she your girlfriend?'

'Oh my God,' Reese muttered. She sat in the armchair and dropped her head into her hands so that she wouldn't have to look at her mom.

'Well, is she?'

'I don't know. Maybe.'

'How long have you two been together?'

'I've only known her for a week.'

'That's all? You looked like you knew each other pretty well.'

Reese felt like her face was on fire. She heard the couch creak as her mom shifted over and laid a hand on her knee.

'You know I love you no matter who you fall in love with,' she said gently.

The word *love* made Reese cringe. 'You make it sound so serious.'

'Well, isn't it?'

Reese stared at the edge of the coffee table, unable to look at her mother.

'Are you sleeping together?'

'Jesus Christ—'

'The lord isn't going to help you with this, honey. Are you using protection?'

Reese's head snapped up. 'Mom, even if we were sleeping together, which we're not, she's a *girl*. What are you talking about? I'm not going to get pregnant.'

Her mom frowned. 'There are still STDs you can get from having sex with a woman. If you're having sex, we need to talk about—'

'We're not having sex,' Reese interrupted, completely mortified to be having this discussion with her mother.

'Not yet.'

'Oh my God, can we *not* have this conversation?'

Her mom raised her hands. 'All right, all right. I just want to make sure you're being safe, honey.'

'I'm fine,' Reese insisted.

Tears sprang to her mom's eyes and she reached out to cup Reese's face in her hand. 'You know you can tell me anything, honey. You don't have to keep secrets from me.'

Reese was astonished. 'I'm not—' And then she realized what her mother meant. 'Mom, I didn't know myself. I didn't know until I met Amber. I haven't been keeping it a secret from you. It's still new to me.'

Her mom's lips trembled. 'Come here,' she said, and Reese moved onto the couch and into her arms. She heard her mom's heartbeat beneath her ear, pulsing in the same rhythm as her own.

And then a door seemed to open between them, and she could do more than merely hear it. She sensed her mom's heart beating from the inside. She breathed the air drawn into her mom's lungs. She experienced the movement of the muscles in her mom's hands as she stroked Reese's hair. Beneath it all was a deep sense of protectiveness that was anchored so firmly in her mother's physical being that Reese couldn't miss it if she tried.

Her mom said, 'I love you, honey,' and Reese recognized, then, that it was love she was feeling. She wanted to sink into it, soft and warm and cocoonlike. It was astonishing and comforting and completely, strangely, familiar. Of course, she had been in her mother's body before. She didn't remember it consciously, but it was there, a muscle memory long buried, now recalled the same way she would never forget how to ride a bike. There was nothing frightening about it because she knew that her mother loved her. There was no reason to be afraid of this connection that was open between them.

She said, 'I love you too, Mom,' and she meant the words with every fiber of her being. Tears slid out of her eyes.

'Oh, sweetie,' her mom said. She drew back a little, and the connection between them stretched thin. 'It'll be all right.' Her mom reached for the tissues. Now they were almost completely separated.

Reese wiped her tears away, unexpectedly chilled. Her mom rubbed a hand over her back, but it wasn't enough to bring back that sense of being completely surrounded and supported by her. Reese took a shallow breath, wanting to go back to that feeling but also exhausted by the aftermath. It was a little like being hungover. As she glanced at her mom, she realized that her mom hadn't experienced any of it. She looked the same as ever, although her eyebrows were drawn together in concern.

'Is there anything you want to talk about?' her mom asked.

The question forced Reese to gather her thoughts together. She scooted over on the couch to toss the tissue in the wastebasket in the corner of the living room, and her mom's hand fell away from her back. It was like a spiderweb breaking, the strands floating in the air for one long moment before blowing away.

She felt her body settling into itself again. Her blood, her bones, her breath. Her skin containing it all.

What the hell had happened at the hospital in Nevada? She didn't think those experiences with David and at the club were hallucinations anymore. They were like previews of what had just happened with her mom.

'Reese?'

She shook her head, focusing on her mom sitting nearby. They had been discussing Amber. 'I'm just – it's a lot, you know, to deal with. I didn't exactly plan to, um, come out to you like that.'

Her mom smiled gently. 'I'm glad I know.'

'Me too.'

'Now why don't you tell me why you've painted a gigantic red-and-yellow mural on your bedroom wall without asking my permission first?'

'I'm sorry,' she said, rubbing a hand over her forehead. 'I just had this dream and I really wanted to see it in three dimensions. I've been thinking about it for days and I had to paint it.'

Her mother leaned back, crossing her arms. 'You had to paint it on your bedroom wall? I would have bought you a canvas, you know.'

'I had to do it. I don't know how to explain it.' Reese tried to figure out how to put the compulsion she had felt into words. 'I've been having this dream ever since I got back. I kept seeing these colors in my head, and I had to see them in reality. I think it has something to do with what happened to me after the accident.' All of a sudden she remembered the tiny device she had found stuck inside the electrical

228

outlet. She stood up. 'Mom, I have to show you something.'

Her mom looked surprised. 'What is it?'

'It's outside in the backyard, but you have to promise not to say anything while we're out there.'

She stood slowly. 'You're starting to alarm me, honey. What's in the backyard?'

'Just promise you won't speak outside. We'll come back in afterward and you can ask all the questions you want, but not out there.'

Her mom seemed doubtful, but she agreed. 'All right, I promise.'

Reese led the way through the house and out the back door. It was overcast outside, and the wind was already beginning to blow the fog inland, dampening the air with mist. Her mom followed her to the potted geranium, where Reese dug into the soil and pulled out the device. The light was still blinking red. She handed it over. Her mom's mouth hardened into a thin line as she examined it, turning it over in her fingers. Then she went back to the geranium and shoved it into the dirt again. With a finger over her lips, she gestured for Reese to follow her back into the house. To Reese's surprise, she kept going toward the front hall, where she grabbed her keys and phone.

'Let's go for a walk,' she said.

Confused, Reese followed her outside and down the front steps. Her mom turned west, heading up the street into the wind, and Reese hurried after her. 'Mom? Where are you going?'

'Where did you find that device?' she asked.

'It was in the wall of my bedroom. I found it when I was painting. I took off the faceplate on the electrical outlet so I wouldn't get paint on it, and that's where it was.' Her mom was silent, and Reese asked, 'Mom, why are we walking—' She cut herself off, fear sending ice down her back. 'You think the rest of the house is bugged?'

'I don't know. But that is definitely a recording device. I've never seen one exactly like it before; it's pretty advanced. But why would someone be bugging your room? And how do we know that only your room was bugged?' Her mom stopped at the end of the block. She turned to study Reese's face with sharp eyes. 'I trust you to tell me the truth, honey. Is there anything else I should know?'

Reese looked away. The fog was massing at the western end of the street in a bank of pale gray mist. She thought of all the things she had said in her room, the things she had done while that thing was listening. Horror washed through her.

'Reese?'

She wanted to tell her mom everything – even the crazy parts about Area 51 – but simultaneously she was afraid to say a thing. She didn't want to get her mom involved in this until she knew what she was dealing with. She silently cursed herself for showing her the bug and tried to think her way out of this situation. She faced her mom. 'I don't know what's going on,' she said truthfully. 'Maybe it's related to that nondisclosure agreement I was asking you about. I got it at the hospital. Maybe they're just trying to make sure that I comply with it.'

Her mom shook her head. 'I knew that was related to you. You need to show me that NDA, all right?'

'I will.' The wind blew mist in Reese's face, and she shivered.

'Is there anything else?'

'No. I swear.'

Her mom's eyebrows rose, but Reese kept her gaze steady. She was not going to tell her about her plans with David and Julian for tonight; besides, they hadn't done anything yet. And now, more than ever, she wanted to drive out to that warehouse. Maybe it was a tenuous connection, but she would rather do something than wait around for someone else to figure things out. She had always hated waiting.

'All right.' Her mom pulled out her phone to make a call. 'Jose?' she said a moment later. 'Hi, it's Cat. I need a favor. I need you to come sweep my house.'

CHAPTER 25

Jose Gutierrez was an investigator who worked for the district attorney's office. He and Reese's mom spent several hours going through the entire house, opening up every switch plate and electrical outlet, sweeping their hands under tabletops and behind any conceivable hiding place. Reese accompanied them silently, handing over tools and keeping track of loose screws as they searched. They found two more devices: one in the kitchen and one in the living room. Because there was no device in her mom's bedroom or office, Reese had to face the fact that whoever was listening was listening only to her. Somewhere in the back of her mind there had been the tiniest possibility that this was related to her mom's work; that somebody out there might be trying to spy on the assistant district attorney. But no. They were spying on her.

The knowledge was frightening, but the more she thought about it, the angrier she became. She had done nothing wrong. If this was related to the treatment she had received after the accident in Nevada, she hadn't said a thing to anyone except David, and he had been there. *They have no right to do this.*

Her mom asked Jose to check the Prius too. By then it was almost eleven o'clock, and Reese began to worry that she was cutting it too close to midnight, when David was due to arrive. Thankfully, Jose finished by eleven and took the three recording devices away with him, and her mom headed upstairs to bed. 'I'm going to change the locks tomorrow,' she said to Reese, who was quietly fuming in the living room. 'I don't know when those things were planted, but whoever did it is not getting inside again.'

Her mom's light went out at eleven thirty, but Reese waited until five minutes before midnight to sneak down the stairs. It wasn't until she was slipping out the front door that a horrible thought entered her mind. If her house had been bugged, what about David's? What if someone had bugged his car? She halted in the doorway, frozen with indecision. There hadn't been a bug in the Prius; maybe they wouldn't bug David's car. But could she risk it? It was *his* car, after all, and if they were listening to him, wouldn't they plant something in his vehicle? She glanced upstairs, but all was still quiet.

Her mom's purse was hanging on the hall tree. Quickly, she reached inside and rooted around until she found the keys, and then went outside to wait for David.

He pulled up a few minutes after midnight. She heard him unlock the doors for her, but instead of getting in she

233

walked around to the driver's side window and gestured for him to roll down the glass. She could see his puzzled expression in the light of the nearby streetlamp. 'What's going on?' he asked. 'Why aren't you getting in?'

'I'm going to drive. You should park and leave your car here. I'm sorry I didn't tell you earlier; there wasn't any time.'

'What? Why?'

'I'll explain in a minute. Just go park and come back here. I'll get my mom's car out of the garage.'

He cocked his head at her, as if about to ask more questions, but there must have been something in the look on her face that convinced him, because he gave in. She went to the garage and entered the code to open the door, praying that the noise wouldn't wake her mom upstairs. At least the Prius was quiet.

It didn't take David long to park, and once he got into the car she began to drive toward Julian's house. 'Are you going to tell me what's going on?' he asked.

She explained about finding the bug in her room and her mom sweeping the house and her car for others. 'I thought it would be safer if we drove this car because I don't know if yours is bugged.'

'Who do you think put those devices in your house?' he asked.

'I don't know, but I plan to find out. My mom is going to have them tested, but she said they were pretty advanced.' David didn't speak as she continued to drive through the empty streets of the Mission District. There wasn't much traffic, and she didn't see anyone behind them. 'Have you seen Agent Menzel since the last time we talked?'

'No. I haven't seen anyone.'

'Do you think you were – um—'

'Seeing things? I don't know. Maybe if they're recording us, they don't have to follow us, and I was just being paranoid.'

'Well, if someone's following us, they're going to be pretty obvious tonight. We're driving out in the middle of nowhere; they're going to be the only other people on the road.'

She pulled up outside Julian's house, and David turned to her. 'Reese, I have to tell you something.'

There was a note in his voice that made a shiver of anticipation run across her skin. 'What?'

There was a knock on the passenger window. Julian stood outside, waving at them. Reese unlocked the doors and Julian climbed into the backseat, oblivious to the strained silence in the car.

'Hey, I thought David was going to drive,' Julian said.

Reese rubbed a hand over her eyes; her head felt a little funny. She hoped she wasn't getting a headache. 'Change of plans,' she said, and explained again about the bug.

'They're totally violating your rights,' Julian said. 'That's messed up.'

'Yeah.' She put the car into drive, trying to ignore the pressure in her head. 'Where do I go?'

'Golden Gate Bridge first, to 101 North,' Julian said.

'So what do you think is in this warehouse?' David asked.

'My lead told me the remains of an airplane might be stored there. I'm looking for that, mostly, because the government is still insisting that only seven planes or something crashed in the US on June nineteenth.'

'How many planes do you think crashed?' Reese asked.

'At least a hundred. Anything from small private planes to airliners.'

'A hundred?' David sounded shocked. 'Wouldn't that be kind of hard to hide?'

'Well, not all of them crashed in the US. I don't know what sort of security measures Canada and Mexico are taking, but even here there are plenty of ways to hide things.'

'Why do you think they'd be hiding it?' David asked.

'To cover something up, obviously.'

'But what?' David pushed.

'The cause of the plane crashes, mostly. If you don't have remains to examine, you can't determine the cause of the crash.'

'The cause is those birds, though,' David said. 'The government just issued a statement saying that the bird strikes were due to a virus that mutated through bird populations and caused them to go berserk. I saw it this morning on the news.'

'There's no evidence that this virus exists,' Julian said. 'In independent testing of the bird remains that have been found, there's nothing there that could cause those birds to do that.'

236

'Then what do you think it was?' Reese asked.

'There are a bunch of theories, some relating to magnetoreception capabilities being disrupted by radio waves.'

'What?' David said skeptically. 'Explain that in English?'

'Birds navigate using magnetoreception – they can sense the Earth's magnetic field, and that's how they know where they are. When birds migrate long distances, they're not flying around randomly; they know where they're going because of this ability. But you can disrupt the birds' magnetoreception with radio waves at a specific frequency. When the birds are disoriented, they go crazy.'

'But why would someone do that?' Reese asked. 'And who could do that over all of North America?'

'Exactly,' Julian said. 'It's a bullshit idea. Especially because if it were true, it would require some massive coordinated effort to shoot radio waves at birds.'

'Then what do you think happened?' she asked.

'I don't know. That's why it's important to establish that more planes did crash on June nineteenth. Maybe if we can amass enough evidence of that, we can convince Congress to push back against the Randall Administration and demand more investigation.'

'Right now she's saying that it's solved,' David said. 'I saw that this morning too. President Randall said the investigation is over, and once the Canada geese population is exterminated, everything will be fine.'

'People are buying this?' Reese said.

'Would you rather believe your president or think that she's lying to you?' David asked. 'I think most people want to believe that their leaders are telling them the truth.'

'That's bullshit too,' Julian said.

'What do you mean?' David asked.

'I'm not saying that every elected official is a liar, but the United States government does plenty of stuff without telling us about it.'

'Like what?' David asked.

'Oh God, don't get him started,' Reese warned.

'Like the NSA,' Julian said. 'Dreamland. Project Blue Book. Depending on how deep into conspiracy you are, the Kennedy assassination and the moon landing. Not to mention all the crap that gets uncovered that the government has to apologize for later. The Tuskegee experiment. Abu Ghraib. We don't know shit about what our government is doing.'

'You believe all that?' David asked.

'No,' Julian said. 'I think the moon-landing conspiracy is total bullshit, for one thing. But I don't believe everything the government tells us is the truth either.'

'Reese, what do you believe?' David asked.

'Honestly?' She glanced over at him. 'Right now I have no idea.'

The Golden Gate Bridge was cloaked in fog. The steel struts and wires, painted orange and lit from below, disappeared into the mist scarcely ten feet above the car. Reese had to slow down because visibility was so poor, but after they went over the Waldo Grade and descended into Marin County, the mist lifted, revealing the lights of strip malls on either side of the freeway.

It was another hour's drive north before they reached the exit to Petaluma that led to the warehouse Julian had mapped out on his phone. There had been hardly any traffic on the freeway, but now as they drove through Petaluma's deserted downtown and headed west on Bodega Avenue, they became the only car in sight. The dark countryside on either side was broken only by the occasional streetlamp illuminating a dirt road or the corner of an isolated farmhouse. It was so much like the stretch of the Extraterrestrial Highway Reese had driven in Nevada that her muscles began to stiffen with tension, bracing for something to come flying at her out of the dark.

'I think we're almost to the turnoff,' Julian said from the backseat. In the rearview mirror she saw his face lit by the light from his cell phone. 'Right after we pass Middle Two Rock Road, you're going to turn left on the next street.'

A pair of headlights came into view in the mirror, the reflection flashing in her eyes. 'What is it?' David asked.

'Probably nothing.'

'You sure?'

'There's a car behind us. It just turned onto the road.'

'The turn's coming up,' Julian said. 'Two hundred feet.'

It was a dirt road that was barely visible even in the light of the high beams. The car's tires crunched over the edge of the pavement and onto the gravel-strewn dirt. She drove slowly and asked, 'How much farther?'

'We're almost there,' Julian said. 'There should be some buildings coming up straight ahead. There they are.'

In the distance, at the edge of the high beams, they saw a shed followed by a larger structure with a corrugated metal roof. A wide dirt parking area opened up off the road, and she circled the car around so that it pointed back the way they had come. 'For a quicker getaway,' she said with a forced laugh, and turned off the car and its lights. A sliver of a crescent moon barely lit the countryside, but a field of bright stars was scattered over the clear sky.

'Hey, Reese, I brought this for you to use,' Julian said, handing her an electronic device about the size of a pack of gum.

She took it from him, turning on the dome light so she could see. It was a video recorder. 'Is this going to pick up anything in the dark?'

'I downloaded a plug-in that tricks it out so that it'll work. You just point and shoot, but try to hold it steady so I don't get sick when I'm editing the footage.'

'Why do you want me to be the camera guy? I thought you'd want to be in control of it.'

'It's backup. I have another camera I'm going to use.' He showed her a bigger video camera.

Reese opened the car door. The air was cool but not uncomfortable, and it smelled of dry grass and cattle manure.

'Wait,' Julian said. 'Put this on.'

He handed her something woolen, and her fingers discerned the shape of a ski mask. 'Are you serious?' she said.

'Yes. We can't be on camera,' he said, and handed one to David as well.

She pulled the ski mask over her head. It was too big, and she had to tug it up so that she could see through the eyeholes, leaving an empty poof on top of her head. She got out of the car, nudging the door shut. The sound of it closing was loud as a firecracker in the stillness.

'Shh!' Julian whispered.

'There's no one here,' David said, pulling on his ski mask.

'You never know,' Julian said.

'You're creeping me out,' Reese said. She fumbled with the tiny video camera and managed to turn it on by touch. The screen lit up, showing the ground beneath her feet outlined dimly in green. 'Wow, it works.'

Julian hovered over her shoulder, checking out the image. 'Good.' He bent down to rummage in his backpack and pulled out a flashlight, handing it to David. 'You can be in charge of this.' Then Julian turned on his own camera, lifting it up to eye level to pan around the moonlit parking area.

Straight ahead of them was the big building with the metal roof. There was a large sliding metal door in the center of it and no other discernible entrance.

'Let's go,' Julian said.

Their footsteps crunched over the ground, the only sound other than the steady chirping of insects. David reached the sliding door first, but the handle was locked and it wouldn't budge when he tried to pull it open. Julian had already moved on, walking around the perimeter of the building.

'Come on,' he called to them. 'We're not getting in the front door.'

David shrugged. 'Doesn't hurt to check.'

The building was much bigger than it appeared from the parking lot. The side they had seen first turned out to be the shorter end of a long, rectangular building. They passed several smaller doors at intervals along the wall, all of them locked, and above their heads windows reflected the crescent moon.

Julian paused about two-thirds of the way down the building and turned back to look at Reese. 'Maybe we could lift you up there to look inside.'

'What?'

'We'll pick you up – David and me. You can get up high enough to look inside.'

Nervous energy shot through Reese. 'Are you crazy?'

'Maybe you'll see something,' Julian said. 'Please?'

She sighed. 'Fine. Don't drop me.'

'Awesome,' Julian said. 'Here. You just have to stand on our shoulders.'

'Um, easier said than done?'

'We'll kneel, and you can climb on,' Julian said. 'It's just like a cheerleading pyramid.'

'That's gonna help me how? Since I've never been a cheerleader?'

'Here, take this flashlight,' David said, handing it to her.

She shoved it into one pocket of her jeans and then put the mini camera into the other so that she would have her hands free. 'Now what?'

David knelt on the ground beside the wall and cupped his hands. 'I'll help you up.' She put a foot in his hands and almost tumbled onto her butt as he began to lift her. 'Can you take your shoes off?' he asked.

She unlaced her sneakers and stepped onto the ground in her socks. 'You guys ready?'

Julian knelt beside David. 'Yeah.'

She put her foot back in David's hands and tried to balance herself against the wall of the building as he pushed her up. 'Oh my God,' she said as she rose into the air. Her right foot sought out Julian's left shoulder.

'Ow,' Julian said as she leaned her weight on him.

'Wimp,' she said.

Somehow she managed to shift her left foot out of David's hands and onto his right shoulder, and then she was balanced precariously a few feet off the ground, her hands splayed flat against the wall. She was acutely aware of how easy it would be to lose her balance and fall onto her ass – or worse, her neck.

'Are you ready?' David asked.

'Yeah,' she said, though she didn't feel ready at all.

'On the count of three,' David said.

She heard him counting, but when the moment came and David and Julian straightened up, she almost fell backward. 'Shit!' She leaned forward, her sweaty hands sliding over the wall in search of the bottom of the window. She grabbed onto the windowsill and clung to it tightly. When David and Julian stopped moving, the bottom of the glass came to her chin.

'Can you see in?' Julian called up.

'Just barely.' The interior of the warehouse was lit only by the moonlight coming in through the windows. 'I'm going to take out the flashlight.' She reached slowly for her left pocket, hoping that she wouldn't lose her balance.

'Take out the camera,' Julian said.

'Hang on.' She clicked on the flashlight and shone it through the window. She saw large canvas-sheeted items laid across the floor of the warehouse in long rows, but they could have been tractor parts, for all she could tell. 'There's stuff in here, but I can't see what it is. It's all covered up.' The flashlight beam didn't travel too far, either, which meant most of the warehouse remained in shadows: just lump after lump in the dark. She turned off the flashlight and carefully put it back into her pocket before pulling out the video camera. She balanced it on the edge of the window with one hand and pressed the Record button.

A light seemed to shine out of nowhere through the windows on the other side of the building. She froze as it slowly arced across the warehouse, revealing more of the covered lumps, and then she heard the sound of a car engine. 'Somebody's here,' she said. 'I just saw headlights.'

'Shit,' Julian said. 'You have to get down.'

Adrenaline raced through her as she repocketed the camera. 'All right, I'm ready.'

Her hands slid against the metal wall as Julian and David knelt again. There was a clumsy maneuvering of feet and hands, but finally her feet were on the ground again. Julian was already preparing to go back the way they had come, but she had to put her shoes back on. 'Wait a minute,' she hissed, and Julian stopped while she quickly laced on her sneakers.

'Let's go this way,' David suggested, pointing away from the parking area.

Julian hesitated momentarily but then swung his camera up and followed. They walked as quietly as possible down the length of the building while listening for the approaching car. At the end of the building, Reese peered around the corner and saw more warehouses – there were at least three of them – and, in the distance, the headlights of a car that suddenly blinked out. The engine shut off, and she heard two *thunks*: two car doors closing. Julian crowded up behind her and whispered, 'They're in the parking lot. We have to get back over there.'

'But they'll see us,' David said.

'Come this way,' Reese whispered, sprinting across the gap between the first two warehouses. She paused on the far side, ducking into the shadows as Julian and David caught up to her. 'Maybe we can circle around the parking lot from the other side. Then they won't see us.'

'What other side?' Julian asked. 'There's only one side!'

'Shh,' David said suddenly, and they pressed themselves against the wall of the second warehouse and waited. They heard footsteps on the dirt: a very light *crunch crunch crunch*. The sound stopped. Reese held her breath.

A beam of light shone out from a powerful flashlight. It swept across the field behind the warehouses, and Reese saw rolling grass and a dilapidated wooden shed in the distance. A cow mooed. The light shut off, and the footsteps began again.

And they were coming directly toward them.

Reese gestured wildly to David and Julian, pointing away from the sound of the footsteps, and then she took off, feet pounding on the dirt. She heard David and Julian running after her. She heard someone shouting – a man – and the flashlight came on again, the beam bouncing on the ground at her feet. She saw the end of the warehouse on her left. As she rounded the corner, a semitruck loomed up in front of her, parked on the edge of the field. The flashlight beam danced over the side of the truck, revealing the image of an atom along with three letters that stopped her cold: EC&R.

David banged into her, whispering fiercely, 'We can't stop here.' He grabbed her hand and pulled her onward. She ran as if her life depended on it, legs pumping as she glanced over her shoulder. She saw Julian sprinting right behind her, his backpack flopping on his shoulders. Behind him, two men were running with the flashlight. They wore suits, and she saw the gleam of their polished shoes hitting the ground.

Suddenly the hard-packed dirt gave way to a grassy field,

and she nearly tripped on a furrow in the earth. David jerked her up, and she bit back a cry as her shoulder burned. 'Where are you going?' she gasped.

'Back to the car. It's across the field.'

The field was strewn with rocks and other things that Reese identified as cow pies by the odor that rose when her sneakers slipped onto something soft. She heard Julian utter a sound of disgust. But the field also seemed to have slowed down the two men, because the flashlight beam was falling back bit by bit.

Abruptly, her sneakers hit bare dirt again. A town car was parked almost directly in front of her, and she jerked David's hand to drag him out of the way. Julian paused and flipped up his camera. 'What are you doing?' she cried.

'Just a sec,' Julian said, sweeping his camera over the license plate.

'Come on!' Reese said, unlocking the doors. Julian spun around and sprinted for the car just as the two men reached the edge of the field. They all piled inside, and Reese punched the ignition button. The wheels scratched in the dirt as she accelerated out of the parking lot, driving as fast as she could.

CHAPTER 26

'Are they following us?' Reese asked, pulling off the ski mask with a crackle of static electricity. She could see headlights in the rearview mirror, but they were so far back, she didn't know if they were from the town car.

'I don't know,' David said, twisting in the passenger seat to look behind them.

Julian was in the backseat, his mask pushed up onto his forehead as he scrutinized the video camera. 'I got footage of that car. It has a government plate.'

Reese groaned. 'We're screwed.'

'Don't freak out yet,' Julian said. 'Give me the mini camera. I want to see if you got anything from the warehouse.'

Reese pulled it out of her pocket and held it over her shoulder. 'You can't see anything. Just a bunch of lumps. But did you see what that semitruck said? EC and R? What does that stand for?'

'EC and R?' he repeated. 'Is that what it was?'

'Yes. I remembered because I just saw those letters. They

were on the bugs we found in my house.'

'EC and R is a major defense contractor,' Julian said. 'Eberhard, Carlyle and Reed. They've handled a ton of the projects rumored to be under way at Area 51.'

Reese glanced at him in the mirror. By the light of the video camera, his face looked haunted. 'Why would they have planted those devices in my house?'

Julian drew in a deep breath. 'I don't know. Maybe they just manufactured them and had nothing to do with putting them there.'

'You really think so?' Reese said skeptically.

'Maybe it's time for you guys to tell me what really happened to you during your accident,' Julian said.

'We can't talk about it,' David said. 'We signed nondisclosure agreements.'

'My mom said they might not hold water in court because we're minors.'

'So tell me,' Julian insisted. 'Tell me what happened to you.'

She eyed the rearview mirror; the headlights were still behind them but had not come any closer. 'What do you think, David?'

'It's a risk,' he said.

'Dude, we got tailed to some secret military warehouse in the middle of nowhere, and we're probably still being followed by men in black,' Julian said. 'Not to mention the fact that Reese's whole house – and maybe yours too – was bugged. I think we've moved beyond *risk*.'

David let out his breath in a short laugh. 'You've got a point.'

'I think we should tell him,' Reese said.

'Do you think it'll help?'

'We're not getting anywhere on our own.' As she drove down the dark road, keeping an eye on the car behind them, she told Julian the whole story.

It was past four am by the time they arrived back in San Francisco. After they dropped Julian off at his house in the Mission, Reese drove back to Noe Valley. The streets were deserted, and Reese saw no sign of the car that had trailed them in Marin. She had lost sight of it on the freeway, and she wondered whether it had really been following them at all.

'Why would they chase us away from that warehouse and then let us go?' she asked. 'It doesn't make any sense.'

'Maybe they just didn't want us to see what was there,' David said.

She made a frustrated sound. 'We couldn't see anything anyway. It was all covered up.'

'We saw that semitruck,' he pointed out. 'Maybe we could have seen something more if they hadn't shown up.'

'I guess we'll see what Julian's cameras picked up.' They took the last few blocks in silence. It wasn't until she had pulled into the garage and turned off the car that she noticed David watching her with a strange expression on his face, as if he were trying to make a decision. 'What is it?' she asked.

She remembered what he had said right before they picked up Julian. 'What were you going to tell me earlier?' The dome light cast David's eyes into shadow, but she saw the way his jaw tightened before he spoke.

'I have to tell you something,' he said again, 'and you might think it's a little crazy.'

'After what happened tonight, you really believe I'm going to think it's crazy?'

He smiled slightly. 'Maybe I'm the one who thinks it's crazy.'

'What is it?' A note of fear crept into her voice.

He gazed out the windshield at the dark garage. 'Sometimes I hear conversations in my head, and I don't know where they're coming from.'

She was taken aback. 'You're hearing things?'

'I don't know. I don't *think* I'm making this stuff up, but...the only people who hear voices are crazy, aren't they?'

'What are the voices saying?'

He shook his head. 'That's just it. It doesn't make any sense – they're not saying anything important. It's like I'm surfing through TV channels or something, and I randomly hear snatches of dialogue.' He looked at her. 'You think I'm going insane, don't you?'

'I don't think that.' She looked down at her hands, where those scrapes had healed so quickly. She thought about her headaches and the bathroom at the club and that moment with her mom. 'I've been feeling a little crazy myself.'

251

'What do you mean?'

Her stomach tightened nervously. 'Sometimes this thing happens to me where I – I feel like I can sense someone else's body from the inside.' Her fingers curled into fists. 'It's like I'm inside their body or something. It happened with my mom last night.'

'Like . . . possession?'

'Like a horror-movie kind of possession? I don't think so. It was like I was feeling everything she was feeling, but I couldn't control her or anything.'

'When does it happen?'

'Sometimes when I'm touching someone else, but sometimes . . . not.' She thought it had happened that night when David came over and examined her hands in the living room. But she didn't think it had ever happened with Amber. It made no logical sense, and it frustrated her. 'Maybe it's just as random as you hearing voices.'

He shifted in the seat next to her. 'Has anything else weird been happening to you?'

'Well, I keep having this dream.' She told him about the yellow room.

'What do you think it means?'

'I think it's a memory of what happened after the accident.'

'You were in a yellow room?'

'Yes. But it's not a room with four walls and a door. It's like a bubble. It's like—' She hesitated. 'This sounds ridiculous, but if you could imagine being in an incubator, except one made of some kind of living material, that's what

I think it felt like.'

David stared at her. She could sense the sudden increase in tension between them as clearly as if he had reached out and touched her. 'The walls,' he said in a low voice. 'Are they bleeding?'

Her mouth went dry. 'Yes. You remember it too.'

The dome light went off, plunging them into blackness. The streetlamp outside the garage barely penetrated the dark. Reese almost leaped out of her skin when David's hand brushed hers. 'Reese,' he said.

'Wh-what?' The air in the car seemed to move as if it were a pile of metal filings, all pointing at her.

His jacket rustled as he shifted in the passenger seat. 'We're different. Since the accident. You and me.' His words hung in the charged air. His fingers laced through hers.

Her breath caught in her throat.

'Is it happening to you now?' he asked.

His pulse was strong in her hand, echoing the pace of her own. And then, as if that third eye had blinked open in her again, she could see him from the inside out.

It terrified her. With her mom, there had been nothing to be afraid of. She trusted her mom; she loved her. But she wasn't sure if she wanted to *know* David like that. It was much too intimate. All her defensive walls snapped up, pushing back against him. She jerked her hand away.

In a dizzying rush, she was just herself again: backed up against the car door, her body trembling. 'No. I don't know,' she said. 'It's getting really late. I should go upstairs.' She pushed the door open awkwardly. The dome light came on again, and David was a shadow turned toward her.

'All right,' he said.

She couldn't tell if he was disappointed or confused. She wasn't sure she wanted to know.

She climbed out of the car on rubbery legs, and as she was about to shut the door she saw a lump on the backseat. She ducked back into the car; it was Julian's jacket. She pulled it out and inspected the rest of the car, making sure nothing else had been left behind for her mother to discover, buying some time before she had to face David again.

He was waiting outside in the chilly night. When she emerged from the garage, she entered the code on the number pad to close the door.

'We have to talk about this,' David said.

She clutched Julian's jacket to her chest. 'I know.'

His face was unreadable as he said, 'I'll call you tomorrow.'

'Okay.' She turned stiffly and climbed the steps to the front door, not allowing herself to think about what she had sensed when he touched her.

CHAPTER 27

Reese couldn't sleep. David's words rang in her memory. We're *different*. She knew it was true. She ran a hand along the side of her body, tracing the phantom scar that had once slashed across her ribs to her belly button. They had cut her open, and when they sewed her back together, something fundamental had changed.

She didn't know how to deal with it or even how to understand it. The more she thought about it, trying to puzzle out why or how her strange new ability worked, the more frustrated she became.

Restless, she flipped onto her side and pillowed her head on her arm. Julian's jacket was flung over the back of her desk chair. The early morning light was seeping through the blinds. She could just make out the red and yellow paint on the wall, now completely dry. She sat up, remembering the last part of the project. She threw off the blanket and picked up the roll of plastic wrap, turning on the overhead light. She found scissors and clear tape and began to stretch the

255

plastic over the center of the wall in the shape of a rough star.

When she was finished, she stepped back to look at the entire wall, with the glistening plastic center layered over bittersweet root, morning sunrise, and downy gold. She remembered watching the birth of a calf, once, in biology class. The furry head, damp and frighteningly large, emerging from the cow's birth canal. The ears and neck and shoulders slipping out of the wet, glistening caul.

Reese could almost remember how it felt: like an amphibian heaving itself out of the primordial goo of the sea, crawling onto the shore. Damp, new, exhilarating.

Rebirth, Amber had said.

It was just before seven o'clock in the morning. Her body hummed with alertness. She couldn't go back to sleep now. She decided to go to Amber's house and surprise her and then take Julian's jacket back to him. She wrote a note for her mom so she wouldn't worry when she woke up to find an empty house, then grabbed her keys and left.

Outside, the fog hadn't burned off yet. The mist still curled over Twin Peaks, and the radio tower was obscured by damp white clouds. She wrapped her scarf around her neck and pulled Julian's jean jacket over her hoodie for added warmth.

Along the way she remembered that Amber had said her mother was in town for a few days, and Reese realized she hadn't asked about the logistics of that. Was Amber's mom staying in the flat with her? She should probably call her when she got there, instead of just ringing the doorbell. She wished she had a key, so she could sneak upstairs into Amber's room and kiss her awake. The thought of it pulled deliciously at her belly, and she turned onto Amber's street with her phone in her hand, ready to dial.

As she glanced in the direction of Amber's house, she saw someone emerging from the building's front door. It was an older woman dressed in a gray skirt suit, her dark hair cut in a bob.

It was Dr Brand.

Reese halted. *What is she doing here?*

But the jolt of recognizing Dr Brand was nothing compared to what Reese felt when she saw Amber come out of the house and hand the woman a manila envelope.

Reese instinctively ducked behind the hedge that bordered the steep front steps of the house next door, her heart slamming against her chest. All her anticipation for seeing Amber vanished, smothered by the shock of discovering that Amber somehow knew Dr Brand. Reese twisted around so that she could look in the direction of Amber's house, but the foliage was too dense. She stiffened as she heard footsteps heading toward her, and then Dr Brand spoke.

'That's all? You only saw the painted wall, right? There was no other evidence of the adaptation chamber anywhere?'

'No, that was all,' Amber said. 'I think she's starting to remember, but I don't think she really knows what it means yet.'

Their voices grew closer, and Reese was afraid that they

257

would walk right past her and see her crouched on the steps, but at the last minute they stopped. A car alarm beeped, and someone opened a car door.

'When are you coming back?' Amber asked.

'I'm not sure,' Dr Brand answered. 'I'll take this photo with me and consult with the others. I didn't think she would remember so quickly.'

'What do you want me to do in the meantime?' Amber asked.

There was a pause, and Reese held her breath. Amber was only a few feet away, and if she walked any farther to the right she might see Reese.

'You've done an excellent job so far,' Dr Brand said. 'I think you should just continue with your assignment. Let me know if anything else comes up.'

'All right,' Amber said. 'Have a safe flight.'

The door closed, and a moment later the engine turned on and the car drove away. Reese waited until she heard Amber's footsteps return to the house. After the front door opened and closed, Reese pushed herself up and walked blindly down the hill toward the park. She didn't look back.

Reese felt like she was going to throw up. If Amber knew Dr Brand, and Dr Brand knew Amber, that meant—

Reese didn't want to think about it, but she had to. Was Amber a spy? Had she been lying to her the entire time? Her stomach heaved. Dr Brand's words echoed in her mind:

You've done an excellent job . . . you should just continue with your assignment.

She inhaled raggedly as tears came to her eyes. She smelled exhaust on the wind, oil that turned her stomach. When she hit Church Street she crossed over to the park and headed to a bench on the Twentieth Street rim. She sat down and stared at the city. Everything looked blurry, as if she were gazing through rain. She realized it was because the tears she had held back were running free now.

Her phone buzzed. Automatically she tugged it out of her jeans pocket. It was a message from Julian, but she didn't feel up to reading it. She shoved it into the jacket pocket. Her fingers brushed against crinkly plastic. She pulled out a pack of cigarettes and remembered that the jacket was Julian's. She rubbed away the tears on her face, feeling disoriented. Nothing made sense.

With trembling fingers, she pulled a cigarette out and stuck it between her lips. She found the matchbook Julian had tucked inside the box. She struck a match and it died in a breath of wind. She tried again. Five matches later, she was disgusted with herself for failing to light the cigarette and vaguely nauseated at the idea of smoking, period. But she was nothing if not stubborn, and halfway through the matchbook she lit a flame that caught. The end of the cigarette glowed as she inhaled.

She coughed. The taste of it was acrid. A fleck of tobacco clung to her lip, and she brushed it off. She exhaled a plume of gray smoke. A guy in a blue jacket passed her and stopped, turning back. 'Hey, can I bum a smoke?' he asked.

She held out the pack.

'Thanks,' he said.

She was barely half-finished with the cigarette, and already her head was feeling hazy from the nicotine. All she could smell was tar and ash. She was about to grind out the end of it on the ground when her phone rang again. This time when she pulled it out to check, the call was from Amber.

Her stomach fell. She put the phone down on the bench beside her, staring at the photo of Amber that had come onto the screen. Reese had taken it the day they went to the beach, and Amber was lying on the blanket and looking up at her, a half smile on her face. The lip gloss on her mouth was smudged.

Feeling woozy, Reese pulled out another cigarette, lighting it from the glowing end of the first. The phone stopped ringing, and nausea twisted through her. She wasn't used to smoking, and it was beginning to make her sick. But she couldn't seem to stop. There was something soothing and yet simultaneously self-destructive about it. It gave her something to do. People came to the park and smoked all the time. She was totally normal. She hadn't just discovered that her girlfriend – and she realized, in a horrified, heartbroken way, that she *had* begun to think of Amber like that – had been *assigned* to her by some kind of covert government agency. The very thought of it was ridiculous. Her hand visibly shook as she tapped ash from the cigarette onto the ground.

Her phone dinged: the sound of a voice-mail message arriving.

She couldn't resist. She picked up the phone and touched the message icon on the screen. 'Hey, it's Amber. I hope your mom wasn't too upset yesterday! I wanted to call and see if we could get together today. I miss you. Call me back.'

Heat bit at Reese's fingers, and she yelped. The cigarette had burned down to the filter. She dropped it on the ground, rubbing it into the dirt with her shoe. It lay there like a gray slug, broken and blackened at the tip, and for a moment she thought she really was about to throw up. She bent over, her head between her knees, the phone clutched in her left hand, and took several shallow breaths. Sweat rose on her skin as her stomach churned.

She saw the shoes of pedestrians pause slightly as they walked past her. She could practically feel them sizing her up, hesitant about asking if she needed help. A girl bent over on a park bench, apparently sick. They must think she was homeless. Or drunk. She laughed bitterly to herself, knowing that the hysterical sounds coming from her must only further confirm the strangers' opinions.

When her stomach no longer felt like it might flip over, she slowly straightened and put her phone and the cigarettes back into the jacket pocket. Below her, the bowl of Dolores Park was mostly empty; it was still pretty early in the day. But joggers were circling the perimeter, and commuters were walking briskly toward the Muni stop nearby.

A small beige van had pulled up on the paved road that ran into the park behind the playground below her. Two men in matching yellow biohazard suits climbed out. They each held a plastic sack and a long pole with an apparatus at the end like a pair of tongs. She watched in growing apprehension as they approached a couple of dark lumps on the ground, piled behind the big green trash Dumpsters. When the men plucked the lumps from the ground with their devices, Reese gasped.

They were birds.

Their wings unfurled limply toward the ground as the men deposited them into the bags one after another.

Reese glanced around the park, shocked that nobody else had noticed. The men walked back to their yellow truck with the dead birds swinging in the plastic bags. They put the bags inside the van and climbed in. The sound of the engine turning on was distant and small, and nobody noticed that either, and for the first time Reese understood how the government might be able to pull off any number of conspiracies.

It was easy when most people simply didn't pay attention.

Reese walked home slowly. Her stomach was gradually settling down, but her legs were shaky. When she arrived, the house was silent. There was a note on the hall table.

Reese,
Call me if you know what you want for dinner. And don't

262

forget to call SF Radar. I know you've been avoiding it.

Love, Mom

She trudged upstairs to the bathroom and turned on the tap, cupping her hand in the stream and rinsing her mouth several times. The taste of the cigarettes lingered, stale and gritty. Feeling as if she were in a trance, she crossed the hall to her bedroom, pausing in the doorway as she saw the painted wall. The wall that Amber had photographed and then shown to Dr Brand.

A snippet of Dr Brand's words floated back to her: *no other evidence of the adaptation chamber*. What did that mean? Reese entered her room, her gaze sweeping over the plastic affixed to the wall, the open electrical outlet, the bulletin board propped against her desk – where she saw the vase of daisies that Amber had given her.

The sight of the flowers stabbed at her.

All those hours with Amber. Discovering how to kiss her. Their date at the restaurant, where Amber had said, You're my close-up. That didn't even make any sense. Had she been lying the whole time?

Reese went to the desk, picked up the vase in trembling hands, and carried it down to the kitchen. She pulled the flowers out and savagely stuffed them into the trash can as tears splattered onto her hands.

CHAPTER 28

Reese spent the day in bed. When her phone rang, she pulled the blankets over her head to muffle the sound. When her mom came home from work, Reese heard her calling her name, but she didn't answer. Eventually her mom came upstairs and opened the door to her room. 'There you are. Are you all right, honey?' She sat on the edge of Reese's bed and put a hand on her forehead. 'You're burning up.' She forced Reese to take two ibuprofen and drink some water. Reese lay back down after swallowing the pills and blinked at her mother. Nothing felt real. Her mother looked anxious. 'I'll get you some soup for dinner. I think you're coming down with something.'

Reese turned over, facing the wall. Her whole body ached as if she had been pummeled in a fight. She curled her legs up, tucking her hands close to her chest. Her mother stood and left the room.

She must have dozed off, because the sound of her door opening woke her up, and she blinked her eyes against the lamplight. Her mom entered with a tray on which a bowl of soup steamed. It smelled of ginger and lime, and her mom said, 'I got you tom yum soup.' Reese sat up and drank the soup, spoonful by spoonful, until the salty, tangy warmth seeped into her body, erasing the unsettling feeling that she wasn't all *there* anymore.

After that, her mom turned off the lamp, and Reese sank into sleep. Dreams rose up and faded away, as if her brain were sorting through a series of movies and trying to select one for her to focus on. She felt as if she were on a merry-go-round, dream slipping into memory and memory slipping into dream.

She saw Amber in her bedroom, sliding out of her own red dress, her skin glowing as if she were made of light. And then David opened the door, and behind him was an endless marble corridor of memorial plaques. He was speaking to her, but she couldn't make out the words. The walls around David slipped and slid, and then she was no longer in the mausoleum but in the yellow room, where she floated, hands folded over her chest. Safe. The sonorous tone of the bell rang underwater, echoing the beating of her heart.

Reese opened her eyes in the dark. It was the middle of the night. Amber was a liar.

She felt like a fool.

Reese woke up to the sound of the coffee grinder downstairs. Her stomach growled, and as she rolled over she felt as if the entire center of her body had been hollowed out by hunger.

She threw the covers back and stood too quickly. Dizziness made her sit down again on the edge of the mattress, one hand to her head. She took a deep breath and tried again, moving more slowly this time.

In the bathroom she brushed her teeth vigorously, trying to rid herself of the lingering taste of yesterday. She spit into the sink and glanced at herself in the mirror, water dripping from her lower lip. Her face was so pale that the light sprinkle of freckles on her cheeks seemed abnormally dark in comparison. Her eyes were slightly puffy from crying in the middle of the night. She dried off her face and went downstairs.

In the kitchen her mom was reading the newspaper and waiting for the coffee to finish brewing. When she saw Reese, she dropped the paper and came over to feel Reese's forehead. 'How are you doing? You don't seem to be burning up anymore.'

'I'm hungry.' She brushed past her mom to open the pantry cabinet.

'Well, that's a good sign. Sit down, and I'll make you some eggs before I go to work.'

Reese moved to the table and slid heavily into a chair. Her mom had been reading the arts section of the *Chronicle*, and the front page lay beside it, discarded. There was a photo of President Randall just below the masthead, shaking hands with Canada's prime minister. *President Randall Attends Canadian Memorial for June 19 Crash Victims in Toronto.*

'Have some juice first,' her mom said, placing a glass in front of Reese. She started, and her mom gave her an inquisitive look. 'I'm a little worried about you, honey.'

Reese picked up the juice and took a sip. 'I'll be fine, Mom.'

Her mom watched her for a moment longer and then pursed her lips. 'All right. How about some scrambled eggs?'

'Sure.' She stared at the top news story as she heard her mom open the fridge.

TORONTO – On Tuesday, President Randall attended a memorial for Canadian victims of the June 19 crashes at Toronto's St. Michael's Cathedral. Approximately two hundred Canadians died in plane crashes in New Jersey and outside Toronto last month. 'I'm here to express the American people's sympathy and shared grief over these senseless deaths, and to assure Canadians that we in the United States are doing everything we possibly can to get to the bottom of what happened,' President Randall said in a brief press conference after the service.

It's all a bunch of lies, Reese thought. She pushed the paper away and dropped her head into her hands. She was grateful when her mom set a plate of food in front of her because it gave her something to do. She wolfed down two scrambled eggs and was buttering her second piece of toast when the doorbell rang. Her mom, who had been packing up her briefcase while surreptitiously watching Reese eat, glanced toward the hallway. 'That's weird. Who would be here at eight in the morning?'

She went to answer the door. Reese dropped the toast onto her plate, her palms growing clammy. She had a bad feeling about this, and as she heard her mom open the front door, her apprehensiveness solidified into dreadful certainty.

Amber's voice floated into the house.

Reese heard her mom inviting her in. Their footsteps came down the hall. She stiffened in her seat as her mom returned to the kitchen and said, 'Look who stopped by.'

It made Reese's stomach twist just to look at her. The smile on Amber's face faded into one of confusion. 'Reese? Are you sick?'

Her mom glanced from Amber to Reese as she picked up her briefcase and travel mug of coffee. 'I have to get to the office, so I'll leave you two alone. I'll let you know when the locksmith is coming; I'm hoping to meet him here this afternoon. Call me if you need anything.' She squeezed Reese's shoulder briefly before she left.

Reese almost wanted to call her back, but she couldn't speak. The front door opened and closed. Her heart was pounding, and she was cold everywhere, and her stomach was threatening to reject the entire breakfast she had just inhaled.

Amber came over to her, concern forming lines on her forehead. She leaned over as if to kiss her, but at the last moment her lips only skimmed Reese's cheek. 'Hey,' Amber said, pulling out a chair from the table and sitting beside

268

her. 'Why didn't you call me back? I was worried your mom freaked out about us and took away your phone or something.'

Reese thought: *She doesn't know that I know.* Reese wanted to fake it herself, to pretend like nothing was wrong, to say, *I'm fine*, and to kiss her shining mouth again. As if Amber could sense her desire, she leaned forward and reached for Reese's hand, pulling it from where it was clenched into a fist on her thigh. She loosened Reese's fingers, interlacing them with her own. Reese felt betrayed by her own body, because even though she knew that she was just an assignment to Amber, all of her shivered at Amber's touch. But as Amber bowed her head to hers, Reese couldn't bring herself to forget the businesslike tone in Amber's voice as she asked Dr Brand, *What do you want me to do in the meantime?*

Reese jerked her hand out of Amber's and pushed back her chair, the legs screeching against the floor. Standing up and putting space between them was like wrenching herself free from a powerful magnet, and she still felt pulled toward Amber, who seemed stunned by her abrupt leap out of the chair.

'What's wrong?' Amber asked.

Reese went to the sink, putting nearly the entire length of the kitchen between them, and turned on the tap to pour herself a glass of water. She heard Amber push back her own chair and stand as well, but when Reese turned, Amber had stayed on the other side of the kitchen. She looked utterly perplexed.

Reese took a deep breath and asked, 'How do you know Dr Brand?'

Surprise spread over Amber's face. 'Who?'

Anger flared in Reese at Amber's pretense of ignorance. 'Dr Evelyn Brand,' she said slowly, enunciating the name clearly. 'How do you know her?'

Amber shook her head, the confusion on her face deepening. 'I don't know who you're talking about. What do you mean?'

'Don't lie to me,' Reese said harshly. She put down the water glass. 'How do you know Dr Brand?'

Amber raised her hands. 'Reese, I'm not lying to you!'

She sounded so sincere that Reese almost believed her.

'I swear I'm not lying,' Amber insisted. 'Who is this person? Why are you asking me this?'

'I saw you yesterday. Outside your house. I saw you with her.'

Amber's eyebrows rose. 'I don't know what you saw, Reese, but it's not what you think. I'm not dating anyone else—'

'I don't think you're *dating* her!' Amber's effort at turning her question into an accusation of infidelity infuriated her, and for a second she could see through Amber entirely. The person who stood before her, wearing so perfectly the face of a beautiful young woman, was a total stranger to her. Reese had thought it didn't matter that she knew so little about Amber. She had thought their physical connection made up for it. But what did it ultimately mean? Only that

270

Amber knew how she liked to be kissed.

Reese was disgusted with herself for being so blind. 'You know who I'm talking about.' Her voice sounded rough and hard. 'Tell me how you know her. Dr Brand.'

Amber's expression of confusion changed into indignation. 'No, I *don't* know who you're talking about. You're acting crazy. What is going on?'

Amber's flat denials made Reese burn with frustration. 'I came by your house yesterday morning, and I saw Dr Brand leaving. You followed her outside. You talked about what I painted on my wall. She told you to continue with your *assignment*. Does that ring a bell?'

Amber's cheeks flushed. She crossed her arms defensively. 'I don't know what you saw or heard, but the only person I talked to yesterday besides you was my mother. I have no idea who this Dr Evelyn Brand person is, and I don't know why you think it's so important.'

Reese was devastated. Amber was obviously just going to continue to deny it all, and the worst part was, the more she denied it, the more it made Reese wonder if she really was going crazy. Had she imagined it all? Was this another side effect of whatever had happened to her at the hospital?

'Come on, Reese,' Amber said, as if she sensed Reese's self-doubt. 'I swear I don't know this woman. And you're not an assignment. I care about you.' She stepped closer to her, stretching out one hand to touch Reese's arm tentatively. There was a pleading look in her gray eyes. 'Please believe me.'

But Amber's words had stopped Reese cold. 'I never said that I was the assignment.'

Amber's face turned white.

Reese pulled away from her. 'You're a liar. You should leave.'

'Reese, please—'

'Get out.' Reese turned her back on her, going to stand at the kitchen window. She couldn't bear to look at Amber anymore.

After a long moment of uncomfortable silence, she heard Amber pick up her bag and walk out. A minute later, the front door closed with a click.

CHAPTER 29

Reese went back to bed, but she had slept too much already, and all she could do was toss and turn as the conversation with Amber replayed itself over and over in her mind. She was stunned that Amber had flat-out denied knowing Dr Brand. If Amber hadn't slipped up at the end, Reese might have given in to the fear that she had hallucinated the whole thing. But now she knew that Amber was part of whatever had happened to her and David in the Nevada desert. She began to wonder how Amber had managed to arrange their supposedly accidental meeting on the corner of Nineteenth and Dolores. Everything, now, seemed incredibly deliberate.

The doorbell rang, startling her.

She sat up. Was Amber back? Even though Reese was instantly nauseated at the idea of seeing her again so soon, a thread of hope yanked her out of bed to the top of the stairs, where she looked down at the quiet, empty hallway. The doorbell rang again, followed by knocking and someone calling her name.

It wasn't Amber. It was Julian.

Reese ran down the stairs and opened the door. Julian's sunglasses were pushed up into his curly hair, his brows drawn together as he scowled at her. 'Why aren't you answering your phone?'

'What? My phone hasn't been ringing.' She let Julian in and ran back up to her room.

Her phone was still and silent on her desk. When she picked it up, she saw that the ringer had been turned off. She had missed four calls – two from Julian, one from David, one from Amber – as well as several text messages. She clicked on Julian's message from yesterday as she heard his footsteps coming up the stairs.

> I left my jacket in your car. I need to
> come over and get it. Are you
> around?

'My mom must have turned off the ringer,' she said to Julian. 'I've been asleep. And I have your jacket.'

He leaned against the doorframe. 'You've been asleep since yesterday? Are you sick?'

'No, I—' She cut herself off, rubbing a hand over her eyes. She felt groggy. 'Do you want to go get some coffee?'

Julian regarded her thoughtfully for a minute. 'Sure.'

She pulled his jacket from her desk chair and held it out to him, then quickly laced on her sneakers. 'Let's go,' she said, pocketing her phone and grabbing her wallet.

'What's going on?' Julian asked as he followed her out of the house. 'You're acting all weird.'

She locked the front door behind them and headed down the path to the sidewalk. 'I just need some caffeine.' She couldn't bring herself to tell him about Amber yet. 'Sorry I didn't hear your calls. What's up?'

Julian fell into step beside her as they walked east toward Church Street. 'I looked into that company, EC and R. That's why I called you. Apparently they were acquired a couple of years ago by this corporation called Allied Research Associates, which is headquartered in San Francisco.'

'What kind of research do they do?'

'Military, engineering, stuff like that. They're a big government contractor that now owns a bunch of other government contractors, including EC and R. Anyway, I was looking into EC and R because I wanted to find out what projects they handled. I was right; a lot of those projects supposedly took place at Area 51. They started out working for the Atomic Energy Commission way back during the Manhattan Project, when the US was building its first atomic bomb, and they kept on doing stuff for the government.'

Reese glanced at Julian curiously. 'Where did you find all this out? Is it just online?'

'No, but this journalist did an exposé on Area 51 a couple of years ago, and a lot of this info on EC and R is in her book. Most of the book is about the development of spy planes like the U-2, but that's probably because that's all she could get her sources to talk about.'

'Do you think EC and R is also behind that Project Plato thing I told you about?'

'I don't know. I looked that up too, but I couldn't find much beyond what you said. If it's a real government project, it's highly classified. But I did find out that EC and R was involved in a DARPA-funded project to create super soldiers who could heal really fast from combat injuries.'

'You mean regeneration?' she said, giving Julian a startled look.

'Yeah, and also other things, like not needing to sleep or eat for long periods of time.'

They turned onto Church Street and headed for the doughnut shop. 'We need to figure out what Plato is and whether EC and R is involved with it,' she said. 'That hospital bracelet is the one real piece of evidence I have.' She needed more information before she could understand what had happened to her and David, and she was growing impatient. 'You said EC and R is owned by some company headquartered in San Francisco?'

'Yes, Allied Research Associates. They're downtown.'

'We have to go there.' She opened the door to the doughnut shop.

Julian raised his eyebrows, following her inside. 'What, just walk in and demand answers?'

'Can I help you?' said the middle-aged Asian woman behind the cash register.

Reese ordered a glazed old-fashioned and a coffee with cream, and Julian ordered a chocolate frosted and a black coffee. They took their sugar and caffeine outside and found an empty bench in the square where the farmers' market set up on weekends. She peeled off the lid of her coffee and blew on it before taking a sip.

'Obviously we aren't going to walk into their headquarters and demand answers,' Reese said, picking up their conversation. A sense of urgency gripped her. 'We'll have to figure out some way to sneak in or hack their system.' She took a bite of her doughnut, the sugar glaze crumbling onto her tongue.

Julian pulled his cigarettes out of his pocket. 'You smoked like half the pack,' he chided her.

'No, I didn't. You shouldn't be smoking anyway. I'm saving your life.' She watched him strike a match and light up. 'Do you know anyone who can, you know, help us break in?'

He gave her a wary look. 'You're starting to freak me out, Reese. I don't know if we should be breaking in anywhere now that we know you're being tailed by men in black.'

'You mean the guys in suits? I thought *Men in Black* was just a movie.'

'It is a movie, but I'm not talking about Will Smith. The men in black are real. They're special agents who work for a branch of AFOSI.'

'The what?'

'Air Force Office of Special Investigations.'

'What is it with the government and stupid acronyms?' Frustration gnawed at her. 'Whatever, I don't care who's following me. I have to find out what really happened to me and David, and that means I have to figure out what Plato is. Besides, somebody clearly broke into my house to put those recording devices in the walls. Why should I obey the law if they won't? We need to find a way to get into that office; there's got to be some information there on who's doing this.' Her voice rose, and several passersby turned to glance at her. Julian was watching her as if she were a firecracker about to explode.

'Reese, what is going on? You're not acting like yourself.'

She glared down at her coffee, her fingers squeezing the paper cup. 'Amber knows Dr Brand,' she said in a low voice.

'What are you talking about?'

She explained what had happened the day before, and how Amber had come over this morning, only to deny it all. She made her voice hard, dismissive. 'She's totally lying, and she expects me to believe her.'

'That's crazy! You mean she – she—' Julian sounded stunned.

Reese couldn't look at him. Her throat closed up. A rush of something desperate and achy swept through her, and she swallowed, trying to force it down. 'Can I have a cigarette?' she asked, putting the coffee down onto the bench beside her. Silently, Julian handed her the pack, then struck a match for her. She cupped her hand around the flame and inhaled, the taste of the cigarette bitter against the back of her throat. 'Thanks.'

They sat together quietly while she smoked, the nicotine

buzzing through her body and making her head woozy. Someone had dropped a muffin on the sidewalk a few feet away, the crumbs trailing toward the gutter. She realized, with a start, that she hadn't seen a pigeon since before the car accident. 'Are they killing the pigeons?' she asked.

'They've been killing them since June.' Julian ground out his cigarette beneath his shoe and got up to toss it in the trash can nearby.

When he returned, Reese said, 'I don't know who Amber is.' She took all the hurt that was gnawing at her and fisted it into a hard, angry shield. 'Who *is* she? Why would she lie about – about everything?'

'I don't know,' Julian said, shaking his head. 'Fuck. I'm so sorry.' He put an arm around her shoulders and tugged her closer. But she didn't want to lean against him. If she gave in, she would turn into a wreck. She couldn't give in. She had to wall everything up and shut herself off. Otherwise she'd never have the nerve to keep searching for the answers to all these questions.

She bent over to put out the cigarette on the sidewalk, leaving a smudge of black ash behind. 'I have to find out,' she said, taking a shaking breath. 'I have to.'

Reese and Julian parted on the corner of Church and Twenty-Fourth. 'Leave your phone on,' he called to her as he started across Church Street. 'I'll call you later.'

She headed south on Twenty-Fourth, pulling out her cell to call David. But he didn't answer, and his phone kept ringing until she realized the voice mail wasn't going to pick up either. She ended the call, wondering if she had the wrong number.

She was preoccupied with thinking about how they could get inside Allied Research Associates when she arrived at home and unlocked the door. Inside, the house was dim and quiet. She hung her keys on the hall tree and walked past the archway to the living room on her way to the kitchen.

She halted.

There were three men in the living room, all in black suits. Agent Forrestal stood and gave her a tight smile. 'Hello, Miss Holloway.'

Her mouth fell open.

Agent Forrestal took a step forward, his polished shoes clicking smartly across the wooden floorboards. 'I see that we've startled you.'

'What are you doing here?' Reese glanced at her keys, still swinging on their hook. The front door had been locked, hadn't it? 'How did you get in?'

He folded his hands behind his back. 'Your lock wasn't secure.'

'But you can't just come in. It's against the law.' Forrestal gave her a slightly dismissive smile, and her face burned. Obviously that made no difference to them. 'What are you doing here?' she demanded again.

'We're here to take you into protective custody,' Agent Forrestal answered. 'We have to leave immediately.'

'Leave? For where? I'm not going anywhere with you.'
She backed away until her foot struck the wall behind her.

'It would be easier for you – for everyone, really – if you don't resist.'

She glanced behind Forrestal at the other two men in black. One had sandy hair and freckles; the other had skin the color of mahogany. Neither looked like they'd have any problem subduing her if she resisted.

'Agent Kowalski, take Miss Holloway upstairs to pack,' Forrestal said. The sandy-haired man stepped forward.

'I'm not going anywhere,' Reese said again, her muscles tensing.

Kowalski hesitated, looking at Forrestal. 'Would you rather we pack for you?' Forrestal asked.

'Pack to go *where*?' Reese asked angrily.

'That's classified,' Forrestal answered. 'Kowalski—'

'My mom will call the police,' Reese interrupted. 'You can't kidnap me.'

Forrestal's jaw tightened. 'Do you really think the police will be able to do anything?'

Reese felt the lump of her phone in her back pocket as it pressed against the wall. Before she could second-guess herself she lunged for the front door.

It happened so fast that she could barely register what was going on. Someone grabbed her arm, twisting it back painfully. She yelped, turning her head to see Kowalski holding her still with one big hand. His hair was buzzed so short that she could see his white scalp through it. He had

281

something that looked like a pen in his other hand, but then Reese saw the slender tip of it and realized it was a hypodermic needle.

'I'm sorry,' Kowalski said, and his sharp blue eyes held a trace of sympathy as he plunged the needle into her arm.

She felt the sharp stab, and then a thick coldness rushed through her body. Kowalski's face spun in her vision; the smooth lines of his clean-shaven cheeks blurred. Behind him Agent Forrestal loomed like a phantom, and then she saw nothing.

CHAPTER 30

Reese woke to the sensation of the world falling away beneath her. She blinked her eyes open and saw a blackened window. Her stomach heaved and she tried to bend over but discovered she was strapped to a seat. Two seat belts ran diagonally across her body and over her shoulders, pinning her in place. Her ears popped, and she realized that she must be on an airplane.

She turned her head to the other side and saw David sitting across the aisle, hands gripping his armrests. 'David,' she said, her voice sounding muffled.

Behind her a man said, 'She's awake.'

She heard someone getting up, and a moment later Special Agent Forrestal was leaning over her. 'You – you drugged me,' she said. A fog was blanketing her mind; everything she saw seemed slightly out of focus.

He was studying her face. 'The sedative affected you more strongly than we expected.' He reached overhead and took down a waxed paper sack, handing it to her. 'We'll be landing soon, so take this in case you need it.'

It was an airsickness bag. 'Where are we landing?'

'I think you'll find it familiar,' he said, and then returned to his seat.

'Reese?' David said. His face was pale, and he looked like he might need an airsickness bag too.

'Are you okay?' she asked. His face swam in her vision, and she blinked, trying unsuccessfully to clear her head.

'I'm feeling . . . a little weird.'

'Yeah, me too.' She leaned back, trying to breathe steadily as the plane descended. Why did her body feel so disconnected? It was as if her nerves were all gummed up, making everything she did unbearably slow.

'I think it's the drugs,' David said.

Through the haze of the sedative she stared at the blackened window. There were a couple of scratches in the paint, and through them bright light glowed. It was still daytime. She wondered if her mom had figured out that she was gone yet. The plane's descent seemed to accelerate, and she heard machines grinding as the wheels dropped. She gripped the edge of her seat and closed her eyes, sweat breaking out on her forehead. She had never been airsick before, but this landing might precipitate her first time. When the wheels finally touched down, she heaved a sigh of relief and immediately began to fumble with the buckles to release herself from the seat. But her fingers were clumsy, and she couldn't do it.

'Hold on, Miss Holloway,' Agent Forrestal said as the plane taxied down the runway. 'We're almost there.'

284

But it seemed like forever before the plane came to a stop and Agent Forrestal pressed a button overhead that released her seat belts. They retracted automatically as another agent opened the door. Bright daylight flooded into the small cabin of the plane, making Reese squint. She got up, clinging to the top of her seat for balance. Her head spun. Beside her David stood as well, and she heard him say "Whoa" as he banged into the wall.

Agent Forrestal came back. He put a hand on her arm, and at first she tried to pull away, but his fingers only clamped down more firmly. 'Let me help you out,' he said, and she winced at the grip on her elbow.

'Fine, jeez,' she mumbled. He prodded her down the steps of the plane and into a brilliant, hot afternoon.

It looked exactly like the airstrip in Nevada. It *smelled* exactly like the airstrip in Nevada: gasoline on concrete; and dry, dusty air. She jerked away from Agent Forrestal and turned around in a daze, staring at the purplish mountains in the distance, the wide expanse of brown desert, the beige and tan buildings that nearly blended into the ground. She thought she should be terrified – she recognized this dimly in her brain – but instead she felt as if someone had pressed a mute button on her emotions. She saw David climbing down from the plane, eyes narrowed against the glare, and she asked, 'Are we here? Is this the same place?'

'Reese,' David said. She could barely hear him, but she recognized the shape of her name on his lips. His body seemed to waver in the sunlight as if he were a mirage. She blinked again, but it only made her dizzy. She bent over, hands on her knees, as she sucked in a breath of hot air and tried to will herself out of the sedative haze. From the corner of her eye she saw Agent Forrestal talking to Agent Kowalski. Another man in black was carrying duffel bags out of the plane. She heard a car engine approaching and straightened to see a Humvee pulling up to the edge of the airstrip.

Agent Forrestal was beside her. 'You'll need to get into the vehicle,' he said.

She flinched away from him, bumping into David. He put his arm around her waist, and that seemed to help a little. Agent Forrestal's face came into focus. His forehead wrinkled, forming a straight line over his nose.

'. . . into the vehicle,' Forrestal was saying.

'I'm going,' she heard David say. His voice was so close to her that she could feel the vibration through the side of her body.

They walked together, legs scrambling at first so that she nearly tripped over his feet. His arm tightened around her. A charge ran from where his fingers pressed into her hip and all the way through her body. She slipped her arm around him to balance herself, her hand sliding across the muscles of his back. He was warm, and she could smell the slight tang of metal from the sweat on his skin. Beyond her physical sense of him, there was something deeper – something that she remembered to be afraid of. But fear too was muffled by the sedative, and it didn't seem nearly as important as the fact that when she leaned on David, she felt more like herself.

When they reached the Humvee, Agent Forrestal opened the back door and she had to separate herself from David to climb in. She was startled by how wrong that seemed. The haze returned, making her clumsy again, and she slid awkwardly across the giant seat. David followed her in, and then Agent Forrestal closed the door and climbed into the front passenger seat. The Humvee began to move.

They were driven past a row of low buildings that Reese thought might be the Plato facilities, but they never drove close enough for her to make out the signs. They headed down a pale, dusty road that led in a ruler-straight line toward what looked like an airplane hangar. As they approached Reese saw a cluster of shorter buildings in front of the hangar, and this was where the Humvee stopped.

A black man in a white button-down shirt emerged from the nearest building, and Agent Forrestal went to meet him while Reese and David got out of the vehicle. 'Miss Holloway, Mr Li, this is Special Agent Malcolm Todd,' Forrestal said. 'He'll be taking over from here.'

'Good afternoon,' Agent Todd said. There was something familiar about his face, but she couldn't put her finger on what it was. 'Please follow me.' He opened the door to the building, gesturing for Reese and David to enter.

She glanced at David, who shrugged slightly. She knew what he meant. Behind them Agent Forrestal and the driver of the Humvee – another man in black – were watching them. All around, the desert rippled with heat. There was nowhere else for them to go.

CHAPTER 31

The interior was as nondescript as any ordinary office building, but there appeared to be only one thing in it: an elevator that had no call buttons. A camera was mounted above the sliding doors, and Reese gazed up at its blinking red light, the hairs on her neck rising.

The elevator arrived with a soft, nonthreatening *ding*. Agent Todd gestured for them to enter. As she stepped into the elevator, the fear she thought she should be feeling began to pulse inside her, and she knew the sedative was wearing off.

'Where are we going?' she asked.

'Medical evaluations are first,' Agent Todd said. His dark eyes regarded her straightforwardly, as if he had nothing to hide. But she was certain – absolutely certain at that moment – that he did. He broke their gaze before she did, and she stepped back as if she had been pushed, banging into the wall of the elevator.

David touched her elbow. 'Careful,' he said.

Her senses zoomed in on the pressure of his fingertips. 'I'm fine.' She stepped away, and she didn't look at Agent Todd so closely again.

When the elevator doors slid open they were in a hallway identical to the one above, but this time the air was noticeably cooler. Agent Todd took them down the long, white corridor, and they passed a number of locked doors, each one fitted with a lock like the ones Reese remembered from the Plato facility. Finally Agent Todd led them through a set of double doors into a larger space that looked like a hospital ward. There was a central area with a large, U-shaped counter, and around the perimeter were glass walls. On the right side were offices; on the left were exam rooms. At the far end the glass walls were frosted, and Reese saw a sign for a restroom. Several men in lab coats were working in the area, and as Agent Todd led Reese and David through the space, most looked up to watch them pass.

Todd stopped in front of one exam room, and a panel in the glass wall slid open. 'Go inside, Miss Holloway. You'll wait here.'

'What about David?'

'Mr Li will be examined next door. Go on in.'

David gave her a slight nod, and reluctantly she stepped into the room. The glass panel whooshed shut immediately. 'Hey!' she cried, but she couldn't figure out how to get the door to slide open. There were no handles. Agent Todd led David away, and Reese saw all the lab coats in the central area staring at her. Their scrutiny was like dozens of fingers touching her at once. She shuddered and turned her back on them.

The room was a perfect white cube, with the polished glass wall behind her. There was a hospital bed; a counter with a sink; and a bank of computers, monitors, and other machines along the back wall. One chair, molded out of hard, clear plastic, was pulled up beside the counter. She sat in the chair, looking resolutely at her hands. Out of the corner of her eye she could see the men moving behind the glass wall. She felt utterly exposed, like a lab rat in a cage.

She didn't have long to wait. It was barely a few minutes later when the glass wall slid open again and two lab coats came in. One was a woman – the first Reese had seen here – who carried a tablet computer; the other was a thin white man who held a fancy-looking camera. The woman said, 'Clarice Holloway? I'm Dr Singh, and I'll be examining you today. This is Dr Anderson, who will be assisting me. The first thing we need you to do is take off your clothes.'

Reese had stood when they entered, and now she crossed her arms. 'What?' The last traces of the sedative must have left her system, because she felt as if all her senses were on high alert. She could practically smell the scent of curiosity radiating off these people.

'Take off your clothes,' Dr Singh said again.

'No. I don't know you.'

Dr Singh pursed her lips. Her dark brown hair was pulled back in a severe knot. 'We can't do the exam with you fully clothed.'

'Too bad,' Reese snapped. 'I'm not taking my clothes off.'

'It would be a lot easier if you cooperate,' Dr Singh said.

'The last time someone said that to me they drugged and kidnapped me.'

Dr Singh frowned. 'That's regrettable. I'm afraid they had no other option. I'll ask you one more time: Can you please remove your clothes for the exam?'

'No.'

Dr Singh's light brown cheeks darkened. She said over her shoulder, 'Sergeant Harris.'

A tall, burly man in fatigues came into the room and approached Reese. She backed away until she was in the corner, trapped between the bed and the bank of machines. 'Don't touch me,' she warned, but it didn't stop him. He put his hands on her and forced her toward the hospital bed. 'Let go of me!' she screamed, trying to struggle. But he was so strong, she was like a minnow wriggling on a giant hook, and he pulled her easily across the floor. There was something unusually alarming about his touch too. His hands were unnaturally still as she twisted in his grip, and she had the impression of a dense blankness inside him that chilled her to the bone. It was that blankness even more than the threat of being forcibly stripped that made her cry out, 'Stop it, I'll do it! I'll get undressed, just let me go.'

Sergeant Harris abruptly released her, and her legs nearly buckled in relief.

'Thank you,' Dr Singh said. 'You're dismissed, Sergeant.' As he left, Dr Singh removed a remote control from her jacket pocket and pressed a button that caused the glass wall to become an opaque, frosted white. Then she went to the counter and pulled a hospital gown out of the top drawer. She laid it on the bed. 'Put that on.'

Reese crossed her arms over her chest, glancing at Dr Anderson. 'Does he have to be in here?'

'I'm sorry, but we have no other technicians available right now. Your arrival was a bit unexpected.' Dr Singh looked at the male doctor. 'Why don't you turn around while she gets undressed?'

Dr Anderson nodded. He looked a bit apologetic, but Reese didn't know why it made a difference if he turned around. Wasn't he going to photograph her after she took off her clothes? Her face burned as she peeled off her jeans and T-shirt. She left on her underwear, and Dr Singh didn't seem to object. The hospital gown had the same pattern as the one she had worn at the Plato facility.

'Climb onto the bed,' Dr Singh said.

Reese lay down, her heart still racing from the encounter with Sergeant Harris. 'Why are you examining me?'

'You received medical treatment recently at a classified military facility. This is a follow-up exam.' Dr Singh removed a headset from the counter and placed it over her hair, angling the microphone so that it was in front of her mouth. The headset was plugged into a digital recorder that she slid into her pocket.

'If you wanted me to come in for a checkup, you could've called me instead of kidnapping me.'

Dr Singh didn't answer, but her lips drew into a thin line. She pulled on a pair of plastic gloves and plugged her stethoscope into her ears. 'Let's begin,' she said, turning on the digital recorder. Dr Anderson came over with his camera.

As Dr Singh slid the cold stethoscope under the hospital gown against her skin, Reese felt cool, processed air blowing on her bare arms and legs from a vent in the ceiling. In one corner of the room she saw a blinking red light. It was attached to a video camera. Dr Singh began to speak into her microphone, reporting her observations about Reese's body. After she had recorded Reese's pulse, she moved to Reese's head, where she pulled back her hair.

'There are no visible scars on her scalp line,' Dr Singh said. Dr Anderson leaned over and photographed her, the camera clicking several times in quick succession. Reese closed her eyes so that she wouldn't have to see either of them.

Dr Singh's hands moved over her body, feeling along her ribs and pressing against her abdomen. 'The chart says that she had surgery to repair a ruptured spleen, but there is no residual scarring.' The camera clicked and clicked, and Reese flinched as Dr Singh prodded at her belly. She was just a lump of flesh to these people: a scientific specimen splayed out on the hospital bed like an insect with its wings pinned to a piece of paper. Tears pricked at the edges of her eyes, and she fiercely willed them to dry up.

'Her right leg was broken, but again, there is no scarring,' Dr Singh said. Her hands touched her legs, examining her knees. *Click, click, click.* 'This chart has to be omitting something,' Dr Singh muttered.

Reese was startled when fingers pried her eyelids open, forcing her to look into a bright light. When the light was removed, she saw Dr Singh putting it back into the pocket of her lab coat.

'Halfway done,' Dr Singh said.

Reese glared at her and turned her head away, only to find herself facing Dr Anderson's stomach. She looked up at the ceiling instead and began to count the ceiling panels in the room. Dr Singh was debating with Dr Anderson whether Reese's chart was incorrect, and part of Reese thought she should pay attention – it was her medical history, after all – but she couldn't focus on their voices. It was all she could do to prevent herself from dissolving into a frightened, exhausted mess. She went back to counting the ceiling tiles. She ignored the blinking light of the video camera. At some point Dr Singh inserted a needle into her arm and extracted several vials of blood. Reese didn't watch, but she could feel the liquid seeping out of her, leaving her chilled and weak.

At last Dr Singh said, 'Miss Holloway, we have to bring you to the lab to run an MRI. Will you come voluntarily?'

Reese allowed herself to look at Dr Singh. She knew it would be useless to fight back right now. They could easily overpower her; they already had. She would let them run the MRI, and then she would figure out a way to get out of here. 'I'll come voluntarily,' she said.

Dr Singh didn't smile, but her face softened the tiniest bit. 'Thank you.'

CHAPTER 32

Agent Todd was sitting in the clear plastic chair when Reese returned from the MRI, clutching the open-backed hospital gown shut behind her. 'Where's David?' she asked.

Agent Todd stood. 'He's not finished with his evaluation yet.' He glanced behind Reese at Dr Singh. 'Everything all set?'

'For Miss Holloway, yes,' Dr Singh said. She pointed to the duffel bag on the floor at Todd's feet. 'What's that?'

'Miss Holloway's clothing.' Todd looked at Reese and explained, 'Agent Forrestal had some things packed for you.'

Dr Singh asked, 'Why is that here?'

'She's going to have to stay here for now,' Todd said.

Dr Singh shook her head. 'We can't have her in the medical bay overnight. We're not equipped for that. The exam rooms have no attached bathrooms and she can't be wandering around the offices.'

'There's no other option,' Todd said. 'One of the staff can

keep an eye on her and Mr Li, and they can use the main restroom.'

'What about the barracks?' Dr Singh pushed.

'Neither of them is cleared to stay in the barracks. I'm sure you understand.'

Dr Singh seemed irritated. 'I'll have to lock everything down.'

'I'm sorry about that,' Todd said.

'I would have liked a bit of notice, you know.' She sighed. 'I'd better go see to that.'

After she left, Reese asked, 'What do you mean I have to stay here?'

'Just what it sounds like. I brought you some food from the mess hall. I know you haven't eaten all day.' He gestured to a tray of covered dishes on the counter. 'Tomorrow we'll run some other tests, but we're done for today. You can change into your clothes in the bathroom if you want some privacy.' He nodded to the glass wall, which was crystal clear again.

'I need to call my mom,' she said.

'That's not possible right now.'

'Right now?' She gritted her teeth. 'When will it be possible?'

His face was as unreadable to her as his body language. 'I'll let you know. Would you like to follow me to the restroom?' He picked up the duffel bag and offered it to her.

There was nothing threatening in his tone, but Reese understood that his question was merely a courtesy; he expected her to do what he wanted. She was too tired to chance fighting him, and besides, she did want to get dressed. She took the duffel bag and slung it over her shoulder. 'Fine.'

He led her out of the exam room to the frosted walls opposite the main entrance to the medical bay. The glass panel that was marked with a RESTROOM sign slid open automatically when they approached.

'You heard Dr Singh,' Todd said. 'Please don't wander around the offices here. When you're finished, go back to your room. One of the staff will let you in.' He gestured to the U-shaped counter, where two lab coats were sitting in front of computer monitors. 'I suggest you eat and get some sleep. I'll be back in the morning for you and David.' He left her standing in front of the open door. She watched him walk around the perimeter of the medical bay toward the exit until one of the lab coats caught her eye. Something about the way he was looking at her – as if she were a particularly puzzling science experiment – set her on edge. She spun on her heel and stalked into the bathroom. The frosted glass door slid shut behind her.

Inside was a stainless steel counter holding two sinks, and a long mirror on the wall above reflected her image, the shapeless hospital gown hanging loosely over her frame. To the right were two shower stalls hung with white plastic curtains, and to the left were two toilet stalls. She looked up at the ceiling; wide fluorescent panels lit the room, but she did not see any video cameras. Maybe it was against military protocol to record people in the bathroom. She carried the duffel bag into one of the toilet stalls and dropped it on the floor. She unzipped it and found jeans and T-shirts and even a pair of pajamas. It creeped her out to think about the agents pawing through her underwear, but at the same time, she was glad to have some familiar clothing to put on. As she riffled through the bag in search of socks, her hand struck something hard and plastic. She pulled it out.

It was her phone.

She stared at it, not quite believing it was real. The last time she remembered having it in her possession had been at home. They must have taken it off her at some point when she was unconscious. But why would they give it back to her? She peered under the wall of the toilet stall, making sure she was still alone, and then she turned the phone on.

There was no signal – not even one measly little bar. Of course, they were who knows how many stories underground; why would there be any reception? As she looked down at the screen, she noticed that the icons were in different places than they had been before. She paged through the screens, mentally cataloging the various applications. Mail, phone, calculator, calendar, a few games, e-reader, photo album . . . where was the camera? She clicked through the applications several times, but as far as she could tell, the camera function had been removed. She opened the photo album, wondering if somehow that would get her a working camera. She froze at the first photo that appeared.

There was Amber on Ocean Beach, smiling that teasing,

movie-star smile. The sunlight made her short blond hair glow white-hot.

Reese knew that she should close the album. She shouldn't look at the photos. She could already feel the ache beginning to spread from her gut like a seeping stain on a white cloth. But she couldn't help it. She swept her finger across the screen.

The next photo showed Amber standing in front of the ocean, hand raised to her mouth as she blew her a kiss. Reese's stomach knotted up as she flipped through the dozen or so photos. The girl in the pictures seemed like a figment of Reese's imagination. No wonder the whole thing felt so much like a dream. Amber had been putting on an act. None of it had been real.

She paused on a photo of a wall. She didn't recognize it at first, but as she zoomed in she realized it was the bathroom stall in that club Amber had taken her to. The memory of it flooded back into her, and she could practically smell the place again: the sharp tang of disinfectant not quite masking the lingering odor of spilled alcohol. She centered the picture on the haiku graffiti inked onto the stretch of blue wall beside the toilet.

You broke my heart and
Changed my life. Now I'm a dyke
Lovesick on the floor.

Abruptly, she powered off the phone and buried it deep in

the duffel bag. She knelt on the floor, the cold tile biting into her knees as she wrapped her arms around herself. It felt as though someone had punched her, their fists landing deep and hard in her abdomen, and she was having trouble breathing.

You're not an assignment.

Reese choked on a sob. The whole day seemed to rush through her in instant replay, all of its humiliations piling up one after another in a quivering mess. Had it only been that morning that Amber had been standing in her kitchen? It felt like a lifetime ago. Tears streaked down her cheeks and into the corners of her mouth, hot and salty. She remembered the shock of seeing Agent Forrestal in her home; the hard jab of fear in her belly as Agent Kowalski grabbed her. In a way, the sedative had been welcome, because it had staved off her terror – at least until Dr Singh had examined her like a guinea pig in a mad science experiment. Now the terror was running free in her system, mixing with the shame of being taken in so completely by Amber. She almost wished she hadn't cooperated with Dr Singh for the MRI; maybe then they would have sedated her again. She just wanted to curl up in a ball in the corner and cry herself to sleep.

'Reese?'

Her head snapped up at the sound of David's voice. She saw bare feet beneath the door of the stall.

'Are you all right?' he asked.

'I'm fine,' she said quickly, dragging toilet paper from the dispenser to wipe her wet eyes. 'I'm – I was getting dressed.'

She scrambled to her feet and pulled clothes from the bag, paying little attention to what they were.

'You sure?'

'Yeah.' Her breath hitched into a sob, and she covered her mouth with her hand.

'I'm getting dressed too. Wait for me?' David went into the next stall, and a duffel bag that matched hers dropped onto the floor.

'Okay.' She put her clothes on as quickly as possible, conscious that David was doing the same thing two feet away from her. There must be only one restroom; she hadn't seen signs for men or women. She tossed the hospital gown into the duffel bag and then remembered the phone. She picked it up again and hesitated for a second before sliding it into her pocket. Just in case. She grabbed another wad of toilet paper and blew her nose before zipping up the duffel bag and leaving the stall.

Her reflection was not a welcome sight. Puffy eyes gazed back at her from a blotchy face. She turned on the sink and splashed cold water on her cheeks, gasping at the temperature. She heard David come out of the stall while she was reaching blindly for the paper-towel dispenser.

'Here,' he said, and pressed several paper towels into her hands.

'Thanks,' she mumbled as she dried herself off. When she finished, her face was still blotchy, and David was leaning against the side of the counter and watching her with concern.

'Rough day, huh?' he said gently.

She started to laugh, but it came out in a sob, and her eyes grew hot again. 'Understatement of the year,' she muttered, sniffling.

'Reese,' he began, then stopped as indecision crossed his face.

'What?'

'Did they do something to you?'

The question was weighted with a disturbing tone, and she flushed with self-consciousness. 'No,' she said. David's face was hard-edged with worry, and she had the feeling that if she had said yes, he would have gone out into the medical bay and done something about it. 'No,' she said again, flustered. 'I mean, it sucked, but it wasn't – what did they do to you?'

'Nothing,' he said quickly. 'Don't worry. They just made me put on a hospital gown and then examined me and said a bunch of things about my chart that I didn't understand.'

She took a deep breath. 'Yeah. That's what they did to me.'

The glass wall behind them slid open, and one of the lab coats came inside. 'You can't be loitering in the restroom,' he said. 'If you're finished with your business, you need to go back to your exam rooms.'

Reese scowled at him. 'You can't keep us locked up like prisoners.'

The lab coat looked at her as if she were being an idiot. 'Believe me, you're not prisoners. If you were, you'd know it. Come on, get your bags and go back to your rooms.'

Reese lifted the covers on the dishes and saw a mound of mashed potatoes and what looked like cold meat loaf. She wrinkled her nose. It didn't smell that great, but her stomach growled at the sight of the food. She sat down on the plastic chair and balanced the tray on her knees, picking up the fork to take a bite. It didn't taste as bad as she expected, but she suspected her hunger helped.

Afterward she climbed onto the bed, still dressed in her jeans and T-shirt, and turned her back to the glass wall. She hadn't seen a single light switch in the room. The overheads were probably controlled by a remote like the one Dr Singh had used to frost the glass, and Reese supposed she could ask the lab coat in the medical bay to turn them off, but she didn't want to talk to anybody. She pulled the thin beige blanket over her head and hunkered down in the dimly lit tent that it created. Her phone dug into her hip as she tried to make herself comfortable on the creaking gurney. That sharp ache she felt every time she thought about Amber twisted in her gut again.

She should delete those photos. Maybe that would make her feel better. She could erase all evidence of Amber from her life.

She wriggled the phone out of her pocket, making sure to keep it under the cover of the blanket. But just as her finger was about to press the photo album icon, she hesitated. It didn't make any sense for them – whoever *they* were – to return her phone to her. Did it?

She studied the phone's home screen. The icons were in

303

different places from where she had left them. For one thing, the e-reader was on the first screen instead of the second. She clicked on it and saw that the library, which should have been empty since she hadn't downloaded any books yet, contained one item: *PBB Status Report 23*. She touched its icon, and a document opened in the e-reader.

Project Blue Base
Status Report 23
Submitted to the Members of the Board of
the Corporation for [Name Redacted]
Eberhard, Carlyle & Reed
June 2014

Her heart began to race. This definitely had not been on her phone before. She swiped to the next page to skim the text.

Executive Summary

As established in the Blue Base Protocol of 1991, the primary objective of Project Blue Base continues to be the development of genetically enhanced operatives, incorporating the Combat Endurance Initiative (CEI) and the Regenerative Process Initiative (RPI). Over the past year, progress on the CEI component of PBB has accelerated beyond expectations, and test subjects have responded favorably to multiple test conditions. CEI test subjects will be ready to be seeded throughout combat operations within twelve months. Unfortunately progress in RPI continues to be stalled this year. Test subjects have not reacted favorably to new test protocols, and mortality rates have increased. Further research should be placed on hold pending Corporation recommendations.

Reese did not understand much of the report – most of it consisted of spreadsheets full of data and medical jargon – but several things became clear as she read. First, Dr Singh worked for Project Blue Base; her name was all over the report. Second, the attempt to develop some way for humans to regenerate tissue, like salamanders are able to do, had been a massive failure. She shuddered at the descriptions of some of the side effects the scientists had encountered in their research. She thought about her own disappearing scars and the rapid healing of the abrasions on her palms and realized that whatever had been done to her and David, it wasn't this regeneration procedure. She and David had received some other kind of medical treatment: one that worked.

She suddenly understood what Dr Singh had meant during the exam when she questioned whether Reese's chart was accurate. Dr Singh couldn't see how Reese could have recovered from surgery so quickly, without leaving scars on her body. Dr Singh didn't know what had happened to Reese at Plato. That meant that Plato was separate from Blue Base. There were two regenerative projects going on – the

305

one that had failed, at Blue Base, and the one that had succeeded, at Plato.

And that brought Reese back to the questions she still could not answer. What was Plato, exactly, and what had they done to her and David?

The lights in the exam room unexpectedly went off, and the cell phone screen glowed up at her beneath the blanket. She quickly turned the phone over; if the room was dark, the cell phone light would be clearly visible now. She poked her head out from beneath the blanket and glanced over her shoulder. The medical bay lights were still on. Maybe the lab coat working out there thought she had gone to sleep and turned off the overheads in her room. Under the blanket she felt for the power switch and turned off the phone. She couldn't look at it now; it would be too obvious in the dim room, and she was particularly conscious of the video camera mounted in the corner.

She found it difficult to fall asleep. She kept worrying over the questions the report had raised. It wasn't until she began to doze off that something else occurred to her. Someone had put that document on her phone, and they had made sure she got it back after it had been taken from her on the journey here from San Francisco. Whoever it was wanted her to know about Blue Base. The question was: Who?

306

CHAPTER 33

Reese woke up when the overhead lights came on. She groaned and dragged the thin blanket over her head as she remembered where she was. She heard the glass wall slide open and footsteps click across the floor.

'Time to get up, Miss Holloway.' It was Agent Todd. 'I brought you some breakfast and some things to wear.'

She opened her eyes warily, rolling over as something heavy landed on the bed beside her. She saw a pair of dark green shorts, a gray T-shirt, and a pair of the ugliest green-and-brown running shoes she had ever seen. 'Why do you want me to wear that?' She squinted across the room at Agent Todd, who was depositing another tray on the counter.

'We're putting you and Mr Li through a few tests this morning. Eat your breakfast. You'll need it.'

After she ate the food – bland oatmeal and overly sweet orange juice, accompanied by a cup of disgusting coffee – she grabbed the new clothes and the duffel to go to the bathroom. One of the lab coats was keeping an eye out for her, and when she approached the glass wall it whooshed open.

The exam room next to hers was empty, but when she entered the bathroom she found David brushing his teeth at the sink. He was dressed in the same outfit she was about to put on. 'Hey,' she said. 'Where did you get that toothbrush?' He gestured to a folded towel at the far end of the stainless steel counter. A toothbrush and mini tube of toothpaste lay on top. 'Thanks.' She desperately needed to pee, but she didn't want to do it while David could hear. She decided to brush her teeth first.

To her relief, when he finished he said, 'I'll see you in a few,' and left the bathroom. As soon as the glass doors slid shut, she hightailed it into the stall, dragging her duffel bag with her.

After using the toilet, she took off her clothes, taking care to conceal her cell phone in the pocket of her jeans and folding them so that the phone wouldn't fall out. The new clothes did fit, sort of, but she was sure the getup made her look like a complete frump. Whoever had packed her duffel bag must have had a twisted sense of humor, because even though they had seen fit to throw in a sports bra, they had only included black socks. She clomped out of the stall in the heavy new shoes and caught a glimpse of herself in the mirror. She did look frumpy, not to mention possibly crazy, what with her long, tangled hair and eyes bruised from a fitful night's sleep. *Great*, she thought sourly, and resigned herself to looking like a dork.

Out in the medical bay, Agent Todd was standing by the U-shaped counter with David. The clothes that made her look awful made David look good – in an I'm-training-with-the-military kind of way, at least. On her, the T-shirt was too big in the wrong places and made her look pudgy in others; on him, it emphasized the breadth of his shoulders. Plus he had white socks. David noticed her staring at him and said, 'Hey. You ready?'

She colored. 'I have to put this bag back in my room.'

'Go ahead,' Agent Todd said.

When she returned a moment later, Dr Singh was coming out of her office pushing a cart with a computer on it. 'I'm going to attach these to your chest and temples,' she said to David, holding out what looked like shiny metallic stickers.

'What are those?' David asked.

'Sensors to measure your heart rate and other physical reactions.' She pushed up David's shirt and stuck one over his heart and two on his temples. Then Dr Singh came toward Reese and said, 'Now you.' Once Reese was similarly outfitted, Dr Singh went back to the cart and typed something into the computer. 'I'm ready. Let's go.'

Agent Todd led the way out of the medical bay, and Dr Singh trundled the cart after Reese and David. As they walked down the pristine white corridor, Reese noticed video cameras attached to the ceiling, red lights glowing. They passed two of the cameras before Todd stopped outside a set of double doors marked BBTC1. He stepped up to the scanner and keypad, and after he entered the code, the doors clicked open. Reese gaped at what lay beyond them.

It was a huge, multistory gymnasium lit by gleaming overhead lights as bright as midday. An oval track was laid around the perimeter, and in the center was a series of obstacles: climbing walls and sand pits; unidentifiable structures that resembled medieval torture devices; and even a couple of pools, one of which looked muddy. Windows lined the upper walls near the black ceiling. Through the glass, Reese saw white hallways, offices, and in one wide expanse, what appeared to be a cafeteria. There were people too, some gazing down into the gym but most going about their business. Many were dressed in uniforms or fatigues.

'What is this place?' she asked.

'Training Center One,' Agent Todd said. 'We're going to put you through some basic training and see how you do today.' Reese pictured young men in buzz cuts doing several hundred push-ups in a field. Her stomach sank. She hoped he didn't mean that kind of basic training.

While Agent Todd conferred with Dr Singh in a low voice, David edged closer to Reese and whispered, 'Do you think we're going to have to do those obstacles?'

She gave him a dubious look. 'You realize you actually sound kind of excited by that possibility?'

He grinned. 'I like a good obstacle course. Don't you?'

'Are you kidding? I hate gym class.'

'Beats getting another physical exam.'

'Good point,' she said, but she felt a little queasy. She wasn't the worst kid in gym class, but sports were definitely not her thing, and she suspected there was going to be more to this basic-training test than a game of kickball.

Agent Todd returned from his consultation with Dr Singh. 'We've set up a level one obstacle course for you to complete.'

'I knew it,' Reese said.

Dr Singh came over, holding something out in her hand. 'Here. You might need this.'

It was a dusty-looking black scrunchie. 'Thanks,' Reese said. She tried to avoid thinking about where it had come from as she used it to pull back her hair into a ponytail. There probably weren't too many long-haired super soldiers in training down here. She bet they all had buzz cuts, even the women – if there were any.

'The obstacle course begins over there,' Agent Todd said, gesturing to a marker on the ground to the left of the track. 'We'll tell you when we're ready for you to begin.'

Reese walked over to the marker and stood next to David, who was crouching down in a runner's stretch. As he shifted from his right leg to his left, she crossed her arms over her chest, thinking about the cigarettes she had smoked in the last couple of days. David would sail through this. She hoped that she didn't collapse into a hacking mess.

'Ready?' Agent Todd called. 'Go!'

It began innocently enough, with a series of rings embedded on the floor like Reese had seen football players run through. She felt ridiculous as she jumped through the rings – which were spaced out for men with longer legs than

311

she had, she was sure – but she made it through without mishap. David had let her go first, but by the time she was finished, he had already caught up with her.

'Come on, you're not gonna let me win so easy, are you?' he teased her. He slipped around her, tugging on her ponytail as he ran ahead to the next obstacle. She felt the tug all the way through to her toes.

It spurred her on to the set of hurdles he was already sailing over. She took a flying leap at the first one and made it over without falling, surprising herself. Track and field had definitely been her least favorite part of gym class, and she had plenty of memories of face-planting on the ground after tripping over a hurdle. She jumped over the next few cleanly, but before she could get too cocky, her foot caught on the last hurdle and brought it crashing down. She sprawled onto the ground and her cheek skidded over the dirt. David turned back, calling, 'Reese?' The wind had been knocked out of her, but she didn't want to look like a wimp. She waved him off and pushed herself to her feet, brushing the dirt from her face. She winced slightly when she felt a stinging sensation on her cheek. She wondered if the scratch would be gone by the time she finished the obstacle course.

Ahead of her, David was vaulting over what looked like a chest-high wall covered in tan vinyl. She had seen him take a running jump at it, hands hooking over the top to haul himself over, but when she tried, she had a more difficult time. It took a few attempts before she managed to jump high enough to reach the top and slide over. She landed in a pool of muddy water, and she cursed in surprise as it splashed all over her. At the end of the rectangular pool was a fifteen-foot climbing wall outfitted with two ropes and a number of hand- and toeholds. David was already halfway up the wall.

She waded over to the free rope, tugging on it experimentally. It seemed securely attached. She watched David using the rope to help himself move from one toehold to the next as he made his way toward the top. He made it look easy, but when she fitted her foot into the first toehold, she realized this wasn't going to be any fun. She didn't have the upper-body strength he did, so she had to figure out how to get herself up the wall without relying so much on the rope to pull herself. By the time David made it to the top, she had climbed only a couple of feet, and her arms felt like they were about to fall out of their sockets.

He swung his legs over the top of the wall, straddling it, and looked down. 'Do you need some help?'

'I can do it,' she said through gritted teeth, reaching for another handhold while simultaneously clinging to the rope to prevent herself from falling into the muddy water. Bit by bit she inched up the wall, her muscles burning so fiercely that she felt tears spring to her eyes.

A few feet from the top of the wall she miscalculated – her arms were clumsy with fatigue – and she slipped. She shrieked, grabbing at the rope, and it scorched against her sweaty palms until something suddenly halted her descent. David's hand was wrapped around her left wrist, all five fingers digging painfully into her forearm. His grip opened a conduit between them, and suddenly she could sense his entire body: the muscles of his right arm and shoulder burning as he struggled to hold her, the edge of the wall cutting into his left wrist as he hung on. The connection was so open and so clear that it stunned her, and for a moment she just dangled there, feet hanging several feet above the water.

'I'm slipping,' David said, his voice rough. 'You have to give me your other hand. I'll pull you up.'

She twisted her head to look up at him. He was lying flat on his stomach on the top of the wall. A droplet of sweat that was clinging to his nose plummeted onto her face, striking her cheek in a tiny spark. If she didn't grab on to him, she would fall right back to the bottom of the wall. With a groan of effort, she launched her other hand up and grasped his arm. The sensation of connection between them magnified, as if he came fully into focus. The strain of hauling her up tore into the muscles of his upper back, and his abdomen contracted to steady himself. She gasped as she too felt the pain that arced through him. Even if he was in way better shape than she was, he still wasn't accustomed to pulling girls over fifteen-foot walls.

She kicked at the wall with her dripping shoes, trying to push herself so that he wasn't bearing all of her weight. His body pulled back, counterbalancing her as gravity tried to drag her down. It was an awkward, precarious scramble, and she was sure that she was going to slip out of his grasp at any second and plunge down into the shallow pool. But by some miracle – or maybe just stubborn persistence – she managed to throw herself over the top of the wall.

The instant he let go of her she felt ripped away against her will. Her upper body was hanging over the far side and her butt was in the air somewhere in the vicinity of David's face. 'That was shitty,' she said, her voice sounding hoarse.

David wheezed. 'Don't make me laugh.'

She carefully eased herself around so that her stomach was on the top of the wall and she was facing David. He was sitting up, straddling the wall and rubbing the arm she had been holding. 'Thanks,' she said, dazed. She gingerly pushed herself up. 'Now how the hell do we get off this thing?'

He tugged the rope toward him and tossed it over the far side of the wall. 'That should be the easy part.' He swung his legs over the side and began to rappel down, hopping from one toehold to another with ease.

She groaned. 'This is going to kill me.'

When David splashed down – there was a pool on this side too – she grabbed the rope and began the process of easing herself over the top of the wall. Her hands were sore from the rope burn she had gotten when she nearly pitched into the water on the other side, and it was hard to hold on. Halfway down the wall, she skidded. The skin on her palms parted, smearing blood on the rope. She winced. The blood – combined with the sweat on her hands – made the rope slippery. She knew she was going to lose her grip, but she hoped to make it down another few feet before it happened.

She didn't get her wish. All of a sudden she fell, an involuntary scream tearing out of her throat.

David tried to catch her, but he wasn't prepared, and the two of them went down in the water. It was freezing cold on this side of the wall, and when it sluiced over her she gasped in shock. She landed on top of David, tangled in his arms and legs, and the connection was there again – *snap!* like a light switch – and she couldn't breathe for a minute. This time she knew he felt it, because she sensed the surprise inside him. All the aches in his body from the climbing wall were thrust aside as astonishment rippled through him.

His hands tightened over her as he tried to make sense of what was going on. One hand was on her back and the other, embarrassingly, was on her butt. Water streamed over her face as she raised herself up on her hands and knees, trying to extricate herself from him. She was leaning over him now, her hair dripping onto his chest while he was still half-submerged in the water. She could see the outline of the sensor over his heart through the soaked material of his T-shirt. Seeing him from the outside as well as the inside was surreal. When she saw his chest rise, she also felt his lungs expand. The pressure of his thigh against hers sent a startling surge of heat through her. She wanted to stay right there, in this freezing cold water, and – and—

The same surge of heat went through David. Feeling it in someone else was the most dizzying, delirious, frightening thing she had ever experienced. She dragged herself away, breaking their connection.

'I'm sorry,' she said, her voice shaking.

He pushed himself up from the pool, shoving back his wet hair. Water streamed from his clothes, plastered over his body. The gray T-shirt material was pretty revealing when it was wet. 'Are you hurt?' he asked, breathless.

She didn't let herself think about whether her own clothes were as see-through as his. And she definitely wasn't letting herself think about what had just happened. 'Not really,' she said, and averted her eyes from him. Agent Todd was watching from the edge of the obstacle course. 'We should keep going,' she said.

A beat. Two beats. And then David got up and waded away, the water sending ripples against her legs. She let out her breath in relief.

'Looks like there's one more,' David called back.

At the end of the pool was a concrete cylinder submerged lengthwise. Agent Todd was waiting on the other side, watching them. 'What are we supposed to do with that?' she asked.

David examined the cylinder. 'I think we're supposed to go through it.'

'Underwater?'

They glanced at Agent Todd, who nodded. 'All right,' David said. 'Hold your breath.'

'Ugh.' She had never been claustrophobic before, but the cylinder didn't look very roomy, and the thought of submerging herself beneath the chilly water to get through it made her gut clench.

'You want me to go first?' he offered.

'If you want to.' She pushed a few strands of wet hair away from her face. 'But it doesn't mean that you automatically win.' He smiled, and something in her belly fluttered as she saw his eyes move over her. She crossed her arms over her chest and gave him a challenging look.

He laughed. 'All right. I'll see you on the other side.' He placed his hands on the lip of the cylinder, which rose a couple of inches above the surface of the water, then threaded his legs inside and lowered himself underwater. She watched him propel himself through by pushing hard against the edge of the cylinder. The water on the other end churned as his feet kicked out, followed by the rest of his body. Finally his head popped free and he surfaced, gasping for breath.

Reese didn't let herself wait after she saw him emerge; she had to do this before she lost her nerve. She held on to the concrete rim of the cylinder as David had done and climbed in feetfirst. Her fingers slid on the wet concrete. She took a deep breath and ducked her head underwater.

It was like sliding into a coffin, and she flailed in sudden panic, her knee striking the inside top of the pipe so hard that her leg went numb. She shrieked, sending a stream of bubbles toward the surface. The water stung her eyes, and she couldn't see much beyond the dark gray underside of the concrete. No light, no air. Her heart was an echoing drumbeat in her ears.

She remembered being trapped beneath the car. The ton

of warped metal pinning her down, the shattered safety glass of the windshield littered over her, glittering like diamonds in the light of the weirdly angled high beams. Beside her David was silent – so silent. She tasted blood in her mouth. She was screaming.

She blinked furiously to shake herself out of the memory. Water streamed past her ears, magnifying every sound. Her hands found the inside walls of the cylinder and pushed. The goal was simple: Get out and breathe again. There was no room for anything else. Her knees banged against the opposite end of the pipe. Her feet found the bottom of the pool. David's hand wrapped around hers – *snap!* – and she burst out of the water, sputtering and gasping and clutching at him as if he were a life preserver. His shirt was wet and cold, and her teeth were chattering against his shoulder, her fingers digging into his upper back. David.

She was clinging to him like some half-drowned helpless maiden. She pulled away, shamefaced and self-conscious. He reached for her but stopped, his hand halting in midair. On the side of the pool Agent Todd was observing them. Reese scowled, hoping that the water was so cold, she couldn't possibly be blushing, and said, 'Are we done yet?'

Agent Todd took her snappish tone in stride. 'We're done.'

'Thank God.' She climbed out of the pool and didn't let David or Agent Todd give her a helping hand.

CHAPTER 34

Reese was still dripping when she walked into the bathroom, her duffel bag slung over her shoulder. David was right on her heels. She took the shower stall farthest from the door and pulled the plastic curtain closed behind her, the rings rattling, then turned on the water. She heard David drag the other shower curtain shut. Hastily she unzipped her duffel bag and rooted around with her wet hand until she found her jeans. She pulled out the cell phone and stepped out of her shower stall and into David's.

'Shh!' she warned him. She tried to ignore the fact that he had been in the process of unbuttoning his shorts.

'What are you doing in here?' he whispered, his face flushed.

'I had to give you this, and I didn't know when else I would be able to.' She showed him the cell phone, and his eyes widened.

'Does that work?'

'No. There's no reception. But it's my phone, and

somebody here made sure that I got it back.'

'Why?'

'There's a new document on the e-reader. You need to read it. I think it's about this place.'

He took the phone from her, and she moved to leave, but he said, 'Wait.' He grabbed her shoulder, and she jerked as the connection between them surged. 'What is going on?'

She didn't have to ask him what he meant; she could feel it, the charged link that made her aware of the way he was breathing from the inside out. 'I don't know what's going on,' she said. David's wet hair sent droplets down his neck, and his Adam's apple bobbed in his throat. Her mouth went dry. Her pulse seemed to accelerate to match his, each throb doubled. It was too much; she couldn't handle this. A piercing pain shot through her skull.

He dropped his hand from her as if he had been burned.

The water was steaming up the shower stall, clouding the air in hot, white mist. She backed away, her hand fumbling at the edge of the shower curtain. 'Read it,' she said. 'It's important.'

She backed out and stumbled into her own shower stall. The water was too hot now, but she didn't care. She was deeply chilled and quaking. She climbed fully dressed under the water and closed her eyes, letting the spray pelt her until she finally stopped shivering. Only then did she peel off her waterlogged clothes and drop them on the floor, shuddering as the hot water sluiced over her skin.

We're different, David had said to her that night after the trip to the warehouse.

No shit, she thought.

She wondered if the tests that Dr Singh was running would pick up on this difference, whatever it was. Somehow, she doubted it. She was increasingly convinced that Dr Singh and the other scientists here at Blue Base were at least three steps behind Dr Brand and Plato. They were running all these tests because they didn't know what Dr Brand had done. But as far as Reese could tell, none of these tests could detect how she and David had changed. When they touched, it was as if she could cross the gulf between their two bodies and know how he was feeling. But how was that even possible? Was it some weird kind of telepathy? Reese had no idea how that could be tested. Would they bring in paranormal investigators? She had a brief vision of jumpsuited ghost hunters descending on the medical bay, carrying equipment that looked like some sort of paranormal ability-detecting seismograph.

She heard David's shower go off, but she continued to stand under the hot water until he left the bathroom. Her mind went back to that moment on the obstacle course after she fell into the pool with him. Her belly quivered in memory. As if that memory triggered another, just like that she was back in the Holiday Inn in Phoenix, hiding in her hotel room after that boy had egged David on. *Kiss her already*.

She was so afraid of what she felt. The fear rose up in her

like a clammy-fingered ghost, and she put her hands flat against the tiled wall of the shower and gasped as the water beat down on her back. She could barely even admit to herself, alone, how she felt about David. The wall she had built around those feelings, locking them inside, was so high and so strong that merely thinking about opening the door paralyzed her. And everything had a consequence. Look at what had happened with Amber – and she had barely known her. Amber had been so unexpected and so direct, like an injection of a drug straight into her veins. There had been no time for her to put up her defenses, and Amber had walked right in and turned everything upside down.

How much worse would it be with someone like David, whom she had known for years? He could hurt her that much more. The mere thought of it – of everything going wrong, the way she knew these things inevitably did – made her want to throw up.

But you trust him, said a voice inside her. *He's not like her.*

She slammed off the water, grabbing the towel from the hook outside the shower curtain and rubbing it roughly over her head. It had been barely thirty-six hours since she had last talked to Amber. No wonder she was freaking the hell out. It was too damn soon. Maybe, once she and David got out of this place, she would let herself face her feelings. But for now, she had bigger problems.

She got dressed in jeans and a T-shirt, and wrung out the wet clothes she had worn on the obstacle course. When she opened the shower stall door, the bathroom was full of steam. She went to the sink and wiped away the condensation on the mirror with one hand. Her face emerged from the fog, drawn and tired, and she suddenly remembered the painful descent from the climbing wall, her palms scraping open on the rope. But when she looked down at her hands, the cuts were gone already. All that remained were a few pale white lines on her skin.

Out in the medical bay, Agent Todd was waiting outside Reese's room.

'What are you doing here still?' she asked. She thought he had left after bringing the two of them back.

'I have to take you for your debriefing.'

'Where's David?' she couldn't help asking.

'I already took him. You were in the shower a long time.' He nodded to her room. 'Leave your things in there. We're late.'

'Nobody told me I had anything to be on time for,' she snapped. His face was expressionless. She sighed and stalked into her room to drop off the duffel. When she returned, finger-combing her wet hair away from her face, she said, 'I'm ready. Take me to your leader.'

He smirked, and for the first time, she kind of liked him.

He led her out of the medical bay and down the long corridor, heading away from the training center. After they passed the elevator, he went through a door into another hallway, this one much shorter and lined with more doors. He opened one, revealing a square room outfitted with a small table, two chairs, and a one-way mirror. At least, it looked just like the one-way mirrors she had seen on TV.

Todd gestured for her to take a seat at the table facing the mirror. 'I'll be right back.'

She sat down and looked at her reflection. Her wet hair was dripping onto the shoulders of her black SFPD T-shirt. Her mom had given her that shirt – Reese suspected it had been a freebie she got at work – but she never wore it. The sole reason she was wearing it now was because there had only been three T-shirts in her duffel. The one she had worn yesterday, this one, and a Disneyland T-shirt with a picture of Minnie Mouse on it that her grandparents had bought for her last year. Silently she cursed whoever had packed that duffel bag.

Todd returned a few minutes later with a white man wearing black-rimmed glasses. He was wheeling a cart that had various devices on it, including a computer. 'This is John Brennan,' Todd said. 'He'll be asking you some questions this afternoon.'

Todd began to leave the room, and Reese asked, 'Where are you going?'

'I'll be back to get you when Mr Brennan is finished,' Todd said, and shut the door.

Brennan uncoiled a number of wires from the computer, and as he approached her with them, she scooted away. 'What are those for?' she asked.

'Routine. We're recording your answers but also your physical reactions. It's not painful.'

'I didn't ask if it was painful,' she said, but she let him stick the sensors to her temples and wrists.

He sat down across from her and entered something into the computer. A moment later he asked, 'How was your day?'

'Are you serious?'

He blinked. 'Of course.'

'It would've been better if I wasn't trapped here against my will and being forced to do weird obstacle courses.'

He had no reaction. 'What did you eat for breakfast?'

The change of subject startled her. 'What?'

'Breakfast,' he said again. 'What did you eat for breakfast?'

She sat up, giving him a sharp look. 'Is that a lie detector test?'

His expression didn't change. 'What did you eat for breakfast?' he asked again.

She looked behind him at the one-way mirror. 'This isn't going to work out too well if you won't even answer a simple question,' she said in a loud voice. She shifted her gaze back to Brennan. 'Are you giving me a lie detector test?'

He hesitated.

She raised her eyebrows pointedly.

'Lie detector tests can be very inaccurate. This is a more sophisticated sensor. As I said, we're recording your physical reactions as well as your vocal responses.'

'So it's a lie detector test.'

'You could call it that,' he finally admitted.

Getting the answer out of him was satisfying, but it didn't

do anything to change the situation. She clenched her fingers over the edges of her seat, shoulders tight. She said: 'For breakfast today, I had a bowl of seriously bland oatmeal and a cup of disgusting coffee. But it was nice to get it delivered to my room. My mom never lets me order room service when we're on vacation.'

Brennan almost smiled, but he seemed to catch himself just in time to cover it with a frown.

He asked her about where she lived in San Francisco, what grade she was in, the names of her parents – a long, boring list of facts that she knew he could look up online. She was wondering when it was going to get interesting when he finally asked her about the car accident in Nevada and what she remembered from her time at the hospital afterward.

'Not much,' she said. Brennan asked her the same question several different ways, and then moved on to how she had felt after leaving the hospital. This made her nervous, because she wasn't sure how much she wanted to tell these people. She didn't trust that they would help her if she told them the truth, so she told him about having headaches but avoided describing the other experiences she'd had. She half-expected him to accuse her of lying, but he didn't. Instead, he turned the computer around so that she could see the monitor. There was a collection of photos on the screen – a dozen in all – that looked like mug shots. They had been taken with each individual standing in front of a flat white wall, the bright light making their faces wan and grayish. Reese immediately recognized Dr Brand, but there was another person she recognized too. In the lower right corner of the screen was a photo of Amber.

Reese's stomach dropped, all the color draining from her face.

'Do you recognize anyone in these photos?' Brennan asked.

She made a show of scanning all the images as her heart raced. There were six women and six men in total; Dr Brand was the third photo from the left. Reese swallowed. 'I recognize that woman,' she said at last.

'Which woman?'

Reese pointed. 'Dr Evelyn Brand. She was at the hospital after the accident.'

'Is there anyone else you recognize?'

'No.'

She remembered Amber standing in her kitchen in Noe Valley, a defensive look on her face, denying that she knew who Dr Brand was. But here she was, in a lineup of mug shots that included Dr Brand. Amber had definitely lied to her, and Reese felt the betrayal anew like a sharp stab in her belly. So why did she want to protect Amber? Why was she lying for someone who had lied to her?

The people in the photos were all wearing orange jumpsuits, as if they were prisoners. Some of their faces were blank, their eyes glassy as if they had been shot full of a sedative. Others, including Dr Brand, looked directly at the camera with unmistakable anger. Reese didn't know when they had been taken, but Amber's hair was blond, which suggested her photo had been snapped recently, maybe even since yesterday morning. And Amber didn't look happy. She had an expression on her face that Reese recognized instantly as fear. Her gray eyes were wide, her mouth partly open, as if someone had just said something that terrified her.

However much the sight of her pained Reese, she didn't like what the look on Amber's face suggested. What if Amber was imprisoned somewhere along with Dr Brand and these other people? What would happen to Amber if Reese admitted that she knew her?

'Are you sure there's no one else you recognize?' Brennan pushed.

Reese's mouth was dry, her tongue like sandpaper. 'I'm sure,' she whispered. 'There's no one.'

CHAPTER 35

Reese headed straight for the restroom when she returned to the medical bay. 'I have to go,' she called over her shoulder to Agent Todd, but once she was in the stall with the door locked, she simply sat down and put her head in her hands. She couldn't bear to be in that exam room right now, where she was completely exposed behind the glass walls. She needed to be alone.

Seeing the photo of Amber was more than unsettling. It scared her.

There were clearly two sides to whatever she and David had stumbled into because of their car accident. On one side was Dr Brand and all those people in the mug shots, including Amber. On the other was Dr Singh and Project Blue Base. There were some irregularities that she still hadn't figured out – the men in black, in particular, seemed to move between sides – but it was obvious that she and David were caught in the middle. Each side had an interest in them, but neither was telling them the whole truth.

Everybody was lying, and now that she had denied knowing anyone in the photos besides Dr Brand, she was lying too.

The even scarier part was that she wanted to do it to protect Amber. Her brain thought that was about the stupidest move she had ever made – probably unduly influenced by memories of making out on the beach – but her brain was powerless against the stubborn, feet-planted-wide instinct inside her that said: *Amber is entirely freaked out in that photo. You do not want to support anyone who did that to her.*

A Klaxon blared, the noise shattering the quiet of the bathroom. Reese jumped up, opening the stall door. People were running past the frosted glass wall, and she heard shouting. The door slid open as she walked toward it. She saw several doctors sprinting through the medical bay, grabbing supplies as they headed for the exit. Two of them pushed a stretcher between themselves as Dr Singh came barreling out of her office and followed. One of the last remaining attendants in the room typed something rapidly into a computer until the sirens abruptly ceased, and then he hurried after Dr Singh, the door slamming shut behind him.

He had left the remote control that operated the exam-room doors on the U-shaped counter.

Reese hurried out of the restroom and grabbed the device, spinning around to scan the rest of the medical bay. The only other person she saw was David, who was standing in his room with his hands pressed against the glass. It looked like he was shouting something, but she couldn't hear him through the wall. She looked at the remote and then back at his room. There was a small plaque affixed to the glass that read exam room b, and the remote had buttons from A to H, as well as Open. She pointed the remote at David and pressed Open B. The wall slid back, and David ran out into the medical bay.

'What happened?' she asked. 'When did you get back?'

'A minute ago. I was just wondering where you were when the sirens went off and everyone started running for the exit. I think they forgot about us.'

'They're all gone—' she started, and as if the same idea occurred to the two of them at the same moment, they both headed for Dr Singh's office. Reese opened the glass door with the remote and they went inside.

The desk, adorned by a plaque that read DR AMELIA SINGH, was quite neat. There were two low stacks of file folders, a jar of pens, Post-it notes, a computer monitor, and a keyboard. Several tall filing cabinets lined the wall beside the desk, and behind that was a table outfitted with a printer. David went directly to the closest file cabinet and yanked open the top drawer. Reese began to sift through the files on the desk. They were labeled with patient names, but she didn't recognize any of them. She opened one of the folders to see what it was about and found a chart listing a bunch of medical issues she did not understand.

'Crap, why didn't I like bio more?' she muttered. She moved on to the next stack and noticed that on the corner of each chart were the words BLUE BASE, followed by a number like a serial code. 'I think these must be soldiers in that project I read about on my phone. Did you read that document yet?'

'I only had a chance to look at it really briefly in the bathroom, but yeah, I think these files are about that too,' he said, still riffling through the cabinets. 'There's a ton of them. Like, literally, hundreds of patient files.'

She shuffled the mouse attached to the computer, but it only turned up a login screen. Dr Singh must have locked it before she left. Reese turned to the printer station and saw a stack of papers sitting in the output tray. When she touched them, they were still warm. She lifted them out. On the first page was her name.

'I found something,' she said, her heartbeat quickening. It was a report – written in normal English, thankfully – containing results from the various tests she had undergone since arriving yesterday. She began to skim the executive summary.

Report on Status of Clarice Irene Holloway
Dr Amelia Singh
Blue Base Medical Lab
July 31, 2014

Examination of subject Clarice Irene Holloway, identified as patient 83 (PA83) from her Project Plato chart, reveals that injuries sustained during the car accident on June 20 were treated with experimental medical procedures not authorized for use on civilians.

David banged the filing cabinet shut and joined her, leaning over her shoulder.

'This says – oh my God, this is crazy,' Reese said.

Subject's sample contains clear evidence of nonhuman DNA, potentially extraterrestrial (Imria). Further analysis is needed, but preliminary results suggest a successful hybrid procedure has been performed. It is recommended that subject be retained for additional testing that may provide information beneficial to Project Blue Base and future genetic enhancement initiatives.

As Reese flipped through the report, stunned, David shuffled through the rest of the printouts until he found a report on himself. 'It's the same,' he said, scanning the document. 'It says the same thing as yours.'

The doors to the medical bay suddenly banged open, followed by the sound of frantic voices.

'Shit, give me your papers,' Reese said. She tried to stuff the documents back into the printer output tray, but she was too late. Footsteps pounded into the medical bay and through the open door into Dr Singh's office. Someone grabbed Reese's arm, twisting it behind her and dragging her away from the printer. The papers fell on the floor in a cascade of sheets.

'This is why they should not have been kept here!' Dr Singh shouted. 'The medical bay is not equipped to contain prisoners.'

Reese saw David struggling nearby in the grip of a man in black – it was Agent Kowalski – and across the medical bay two doctors rushed inside with a man on a stretcher. There was an oxygen mask on his face and blood all over his abdomen.

'We'll take them into custody,' said the man holding Reese, and she realized it was Agent Forrestal. 'But you should have locked your door—'

'It was an emergency!' Dr Singh exploded.

Agent Todd came through the medical bay doors. 'What is going on?' he demanded.

Dr Singh turned on him. 'Your charges broke into my office and accessed classified information—'

'Those reports were about *us*,' David cut in.

'And you won't tell us anything,' Reese said. 'What do you expect us to do, wait around until you decide what to do with us?'

Nobody answered her. In the background she heard doctors reeling off the bleeding patient's stats as they called for various drugs and equipment. In the distance someone was screaming. The doors burst open, and the screaming came into the medical bay, emanating from a person strapped down to a second stretcher, his legs thrashing wildly.

Agent Todd said, 'Let's take them over to internal for now.'

'They need to be in containment,' Dr Singh said. 'You don't know what they're capable of.'

Agent Todd gave her a dark look. 'That's not possible right now.' He looked at Kowalski and Forrestal. 'Follow me.'

Reese stumbled as Agent Forrestal pushed her along. 'Where are you taking us?' she asked.

'Just move along,' he said, his hand squeezing her arm so tightly that it made her wince.

Powerless to resist, she followed Agent Todd out into the corridor. As she passed the screaming patient, she saw an ugly gash in his side so deep, she glimpsed internal organs. She shuddered. He looked like he had been clawed open.

Once the medical bay doors closed behind them, the sound of the screams was muffled. She glanced over her shoulder; David was being shoved along by Agent Kowalski. Agent Todd led them down the corridor and back to the interrogation rooms they had used earlier. Agent Forrestal directed her into the same room where she had been questioned by John Brennan, and the door was pulled shut. She heard a lock click, and when she rattled the handle, it wouldn't turn.

She backed away from the door and sat down in the chair. In the one-way mirror she saw her reflection: the color on her cheeks heightened, her hair a mess.

Nonhuman DNA, potentially extraterrestrial. A successful hybrid procedure.

Intellectually, she understood what the words meant, but

336

they seemed to echo in her mind like meaningless syllables shouted in a vast cavern. *Extraterrestrial. Nonhuman. Hybrid.* They circled around and around like buzzards over a kill. Like UFOs dancing in the night sky. Julian would have a field day with this.

She groaned, running her hands through her hair and tugging it away from her face. She couldn't seem to get a firm grasp on what she had read in that report. Maybe she was just too freaked out to allow herself to comprehend the words. It was easier to sit here, staring at her reflection in the one-way mirror, and make jokes to herself about aliens.

Because if that report was true, it meant she was no longer human.

CHAPTER 36

The door opened, and Reese lifted her head from her arms. She had fallen into a doze, but it was hard to sleep deeply with the overhead lights on. She was groggy and hungry and confused, and when she saw Agent Todd come into the interrogation room, she asked, 'What's going on? How long are you going to keep me in here?' She had been alone for hours, except for the five minutes they had let her out – accompanied, embarrassingly – to use the bathroom.

'I've brought someone here to talk to you,' Agent Todd said. 'But this is entirely unauthorized, so you'll need to keep this to yourself.'

His words swept away the grogginess. 'What do you mean unauthorized?' she asked sharply.

'You'll know soon enough.'

'Who is it?'

'Amber Gray,' he said.

Her heart seemed to stop entirely. 'What?'

He held open the door, and Amber walked into the room.

The moment Reese saw her, it was as though every nerve in her body switched on, and she couldn't tell if she was angry or frightened or hurt or all of the above. She stood up, her chair crashing onto the floor.

A hint of a smile floated across Amber's face. 'Hi,' she said. The fluorescent overhead lights made her skin look washed out and emphasized the dark shadows beneath her eyes. But on her, it somehow just looked like her eye makeup had smudged, more morning-after than imprisoned-against-my-will. She was wearing an ill-fitting orange jumpsuit with a serial number printed on the right breast.

'You have fifteen minutes,' Todd said. 'I'll be outside.' He pulled the door shut.

Amber took a step toward Reese, but when Reese backed up, Amber stopped. The half smile on her face disappeared, and she looked away from Reese as if the sight of her were painful. 'I'm sorry that I had to lie to you,' she said in a low voice.

The apology was so unexpected that Reese was speechless.

Amber turned her face back to Reese after a moment. Her eyes were sad and shimmering. 'I really am sorry.'

Reese couldn't look at Amber. She picked up the chair and set it upright. 'Why did you lie to me?'

'I had to,' Amber whispered.

'Because I was an assignment,' Reese said in a flat tone of voice.

Amber shook her head. 'No.'

'I heard you on the street with Dr Brand. She told you to

continue with your assignment. Wasn't that me?' She braced herself for Amber's response.

'No. It's not what you think.'

'Then what was your assignment?' Reese snapped, raising her gaze to Amber's face.

'I was supposed to – to keep an eye on you. Because—'

'You went above and beyond the call of duty.'

Amber flinched. She backed up until she banged into the door, and she slid down to the floor, knees bent. 'You're asking the wrong questions.'

'Oh, really,' Reese said, sarcasm twisting her words. 'What am I supposed to be asking, then?'

'This isn't about you and me,' Amber said gently. 'This whole thing – it's way bigger than just the two of us.'

Reese was stung. 'I'm not saying—'

'Listen to me,' Amber interrupted. 'I know you're angry about what happened. I'm sorry. I really am. I would apologize a million times if I could. But you and me – we're just at the end of a really long string of events that had nothing to do with us to begin with.'

Reese sat down. 'What events?'

'I can't tell you everything right now. But you should know that we're here to help you.' The expression on Amber's face pleaded with Reese to believe her.

'Who's "we"?'

'Everybody who was in Nevada at the Plato facility. And me. We're here to help you, but your government is going to kill us.'

Reese's eyes narrowed. 'What? That doesn't make any sense. My government is your government too.'

'No, it's not. Your government did not approve what we did to you at Plato. They weren't supposed to find out – at least, not yet. But things got messed up. I messed up.' Amber sounded extremely disappointed with herself, and Reese inexplicably wanted to reassure her.

Irritated with herself, Reese said, 'So the Plato people – they're not with Project Blue Base, right?'

'I didn't know you knew about that. But no, it's not the same thing. The biotechnology being developed at Plato is not the same, but Blue Base wants it. And they think that you – and your friend David – carry that information in your DNA now.'

'How do you know all this? How do you know Dr Brand?'

'It doesn't matter. The point is: Your government wants to use you and David as guinea pigs. That's why you're here.'

Reese gave Amber a frustrated look. 'But why are you here?'

Amber's chest rose and fell as she took a deep breath, wrapping her hands around her knees. 'Because you were being monitored by your government in San Francisco, and I wasn't careful enough. They found out about me. The morning I came to your house – the morning you asked me about Dr Brand – I was followed by some men in black. On my way back to where I was staying, I called in to report that you had connected me with Dr Brand' – Amber flushed a little – 'and the agents must have intercepted the call. They

341

were waiting for me back at the flat. They kidnapped me and brought me here along with everyone else from Project Plato. They think we're expendable now because they have you and David. They think they don't need us anymore. So they're going to execute us all. It's scheduled for the day after tomorrow.' Amber seemed strangely calm for someone who had just said that she was about to be killed.

'I don't understand,' Reese finally managed to say. 'I can't believe the US government would execute you. What have you done? What is Plato? And why are you involved with it?'

Reese saw Amber hesitate. Her face had gone so pale. When she spoke, her voice was barely above a whisper. 'Plato is a US government project that was supposed to establish diplomatic relations with my people, the Imria. We're...not from Earth.'

Reese couldn't absorb Amber's words. 'You've got to be joking.'

Amber's face darkened. 'I've been imprisoned in a military bunker for twenty-four hours, and I'm scheduled to be executed in two days. Why would I joke about this?'

'But – but you speak English,' Reese said, and immediately flushed.

Amber raised an eyebrow. 'You don't think we can learn foreign languages?'

'And you look exactly like us!' Reese said defensively. 'How can you be a – how can you be *not from Earth*? I'm having a hard time believing you.'

Amber pushed herself to her feet. 'Believe me or not, but

342

listen to what I'm telling you. My people are coming for us. They won't allow us to be executed. It will happen tomorrow, so you should be prepared.'

'Prepared for what?'

'We're leaving, and we want you to come with us. For your own safety.' A drop of perspiration slid down Amber's temple. 'The only way to get out of here is to trip the bunker's emergency override to the security system. That means that every door will be unlocked to allow everyone out, but you'll only have an hour to evacuate before everything here is permanently shut down. The whole place will be sealed off and destroyed automatically. So when the emergency override begins, you'll need to get to the surface as quickly as you can. Bring David.'

Reese crossed her arms. 'You sound crazy. Why would you expect me to believe you? Why should I do anything you ask me to do? You still haven't even told me how you know Dr Brand. You lied to me before. You could still be lying.'

Amber closed her eyes briefly, drawing in a shallow breath. When she opened her eyes again there was a hard glint in them. 'The woman you know as Dr Brand is my mother. That's how I know her.'

Reese was stunned. 'Your mother?'

'We are watching out for you – I swear. I know this is totally confusing and weird, but I asked Todd to allow me to talk to you for a reason. Because tomorrow everything in this world is going to change. You will understand it all soon

343

enough. But right now, I can't tell you more than this. The only thing you need to know is that if you believe what your government tells you, you will spend the rest of your life as a guinea pig. We want to help you. I swear you can believe me. I'll never lie to you again.'

Before Reese could respond, the door opened. Amber moved out of the way. 'Time to go,' Agent Todd said.

'Tomorrow,' Amber said. 'Reese, tomorrow. When the chance comes you have to get up to the surface.'

Reese stood. 'What chance? How will I even know?'

'You'll know.'

Amber's mouth was set in a hard line, her gray eyes trained insistently on Reese. The Amber she had known in San Francisco – the girl with the smile that made Reese's knees weak – had disappeared. All the flirtation was gone, replaced by a fierce demand that Reese believe her.

Agent Todd touched Amber's elbow. 'Come on.' He began to leave the room.

'Agent Todd,' Reese said quickly, 'I have to talk to David. If she's telling me the truth, he needs to know it too.'

He considered her request. 'All right. I have to return Miss Gray to her cell, but I'll come back when I'm finished.' He opened the door and stepped into the hall.

Amber turned to go, but at the last moment she looked back. 'Reese. I never lied to you about the way I feel about you. I swear.'

Heat shot through Reese. She remembered the first time she had seen Amber, with her pink hair and her skateboard.

From the very beginning, there had been something unusually precise about her. Not a hair out of place. She knew what she was doing.

She still did.

Even beneath the unforgiving fluorescents; even dressed in that ridiculous jumpsuit; even with her face bare of makeup – or maybe because of it – she was magnetic. Reese remembered thinking that pretty was too bland of a word to describe Amber. And it was true; Amber wasn't pretty. She could be cute, if she wanted. She could be beautiful too. But in her heart, she was a chameleon. And now she presented the face that she wanted Reese to see: naked, artless.

Reese wanted to believe her. But she didn't trust her.

Looking away was one of the hardest things she had ever done.

CHAPTER 37

When Agent Todd returned twenty minutes later, Reese was pacing in front of the one-way mirror. 'I can give you fifteen minutes with David, but that's all,' Agent Todd said. 'There's a limit to how long I can fool the security system.'

Fifteen minutes wasn't a lot, but she would take it. 'Fine.'

'Follow me.'

She stepped out of the room into the hallway. 'Who are you?' she asked.

He looked at her. 'Malcolm Todd.'

Reese shook her head. 'You know what I mean. You're not one of them – like Agent Forrestal – are you? A man in black.'

'I work for the Air Force Office of Special Investigations,' Todd said. He led her down the hall to another interrogation room.

'Why did you want me to talk to Amber? Whose side are you on?'

He didn't hesitate. 'I'm on your side.'

Frustration burned through her. 'If you're on my side, you'll tell me the truth. Who—'

He cut her off. 'Amber Gray has already told you the truth. All I'm here to do is make sure you're in the right place at the right time.' He entered the code to unlock the door. 'Any other questions?'

She shook her head. He opened the door.

David's interrogation room was identical to hers. He had managed to fall asleep under the bright lights, head nodding against his chest. His feet were propped up on the second chair, which he had dragged around the table.

'David,' she said.

At the sound of her voice, he awoke with a jerk, feet falling off the chair. He squinted at Reese, and then glanced around the room. It was empty but for them. 'What are you doing in here?'

'We have fifteen minutes,' she said, sitting on the edge of the table.

He rubbed a hand over his face. 'What do you mean?'

'Agent Todd is giving us fifteen minutes together. I have to tell you something.'

He rubbed his eyes and sat up. 'What is it?'

Reese hadn't had much time to plan what she would tell David about Amber, but she knew there were some things she wanted to keep private. 'Did they show you a bunch of mug shots today during your debriefing?'

'Yeah.'

'They showed them to me too. Agent Todd just had me

talk to one of the people in the photos.' Quickly, she told him what Amber had said about Project Plato versus Blue Base. When she reached the part about the Imria, David raised his eyebrows but didn't question her. It wasn't until she explained the instructions to evacuate the next day that he spoke.

'You trust this person?' he asked.

She squeezed the back of her neck with her fingers, trying to loosen some of the tension. 'Not entirely,' she admitted. 'But if there's a chance to get out of here, don't you think we should take it?'

'And run straight into the arms of the – what did you call them? Imria? That was in those reports on us, wasn't it?'

'Yeah. What else are we going to do? I don't want to wait here for who knows what. You read the reports too. They want to retain us for more tests. How long does "retain" mean? And it's not like they've been treating us that well.' She glanced around the locked interrogation room. 'I don't trust *them*, that's for sure.'

'You'd rather trust Dr Brand and these Imria from Project Plato, even though they apparently did some crazy medical procedure on us that they still haven't fully explained?'

She sighed. 'Well, when you put it that way...' Was she just being played by Amber again? Now that she wasn't locked in the same room with her, Amber's explanations did seem a little bizarre. More than a little.

David shifted in his seat, the chair squeaking. 'Who's Amber?'

She froze. She hadn't mentioned Amber's name. She had made sure to not mention it. David was watching her calmly, though she saw the dark vein in his temple that meant he wasn't exactly having a Zen moment. 'How do you – I didn't say that name. Did I?'

His face went pale. 'You didn't say that name out loud?'

'No.' She got up. She had to move around. She couldn't look at David. Thoughts rushed through her mind like a flock of birds beating their wings. And then she realized what had happened. 'Could you hear me thinking about her? Can you hear my thoughts?'

'No, it's not like that,' David said, excitement rising in his voice. 'Do you think that's what's happening when I hear those voices? Remember when I told you about that?'

'You said it was random – that it was like changing channels on the TV or something.' She ran a hand through her hair nervously. 'Is that what it's like still?'

'Yeah, it's random. I don't know when it's going to happen. But that name – I heard it so clearly, and I swear I thought you said it out loud. It's the first time that's happened.'

Reese paced back and forth. If he was developing the ability to hear thoughts, she wouldn't be able to hide anything from him. Panic spread through her in cold waves.

'Reese,' David said.

She didn't know what to tell him. She didn't know how much she wanted to tell him.

'All I heard was the name. Amber. And…you seemed

kind of confused. I swear I can't read your thoughts, if that's what you're worried about.'

Out of the corner of her eye she saw him turning to follow her progress across the room, but she couldn't bring herself to meet his gaze. He wasn't Julian; she couldn't just come out to him. What if he judged her? Straight guys could be weird about bisexual girls. He might think that she'd be up for threesomes or that she'd dump him for a girl. Not that they were together, but hypothetically... How much did he really need to know? Maybe she could tell him that Amber was some random girl, so he wouldn't think she was—

And then she realized she was contemplating lying to him, and she was horrified at herself.

'Reese?' he said. When she didn't answer, he got up and came to her, reaching for her arm. She pulled away, bumping into the table. His hand caught hers, holding her fast, and she had to look at him. *Snap*. She felt his heartbeat, his breath.

'What are you doing?' Her voice trembled.

'It might help if... we're touching,' he said, and a flush crept over his face.

'It might help?' she said, and it came out with a half-choked laugh.

'So you know that you can trust me.'

The edge of the table pressed against the back of her thighs. Through the touch of his hand, with his skin against hers, she was inside him. This intimacy still frightened her, but David wouldn't let go. And this time, his interior landscape was less foreign. She recognized the shape of him, and she realized that he was trying to show her something. It unrolled slowly at first and then more quickly as she instinctually grasped what was happening. She was seeing something inside his mind: a series of images, like an old-fashioned home movie but blurrier – more like the images she saw when she dreamed. David, looking down at her from the top of a wall. It was the memory of the obstacle course from his perspective. His arm extended to her. There was no doubt in his mind. He would catch her.

And she knew that he was right. She could trust him. She had known him since freshman year. He had never given her any reason to think he would laugh at her or make offensive assumptions. He was fine with Julian. He would be fine with this. She had to stop being afraid of it. She would tell him the truth.

She took a deep breath. 'Amber is the person that Agent Todd took me to see just now. Amber Gray. I met her in San Francisco after we got back from the accident, and we … we had a thing.' She couldn't bring herself to say that they had a relationship. Did one week count as a relationship? But she knew that David understood what she meant, because she was holding his hand and she could sense his comprehension as clearly as she could sense her own anxiety about it. 'I didn't know she was a – an Imria,' Reese continued. 'I thought she was just a girl. And now it's over.' She felt as if she were bracing herself for a car crash.

David's fingers squeezed hers. 'I'm sorry.'

'Do you think I'm a freak?' she whispered. 'I mean, she's—' The truth of it struck her in the gut. 'Oh my God, she's an alien.' She had been making out with an alien. All the blood in her body seemed to rush to her head. A hysterical giggle rose to her mouth, and she pressed her free hand over her lips to stifle it.

David smiled slightly. 'I don't think you're a freak.'

'I *am* a freak,' she insisted, feeling dizzy. An *alien*.

'If you are, then so am I, because I'm kind of jealous.'

She gaped at him. 'You're what?'

'Jealous. Of Amber.' He still had that half smile on his face, and it made her insides quiver. 'You must have pretty strong feelings about her for her name to come through so clearly.'

'You're jealous?' A tingle ran down her spine.

He reached for her other hand, lacing his fingers through hers. 'Can't you feel it?'

She *could* feel it. It was like a hot, hungry little tug, as if he had crooked his finger around a cord attached to her belly and pulled at her. She was grateful that the edge of the table was pressed against the back of her legs, because it gave her something to lean on. Her heart was beating way too fast. So was his.

'Reese,' he said, his voice low.

'What?' she whispered.

He didn't answer, but he ran his hands up her arms, making her shiver. He cupped her head, his fingers buried in her hair as his thumbs stroked her temples. *He's going to kiss me.* The knowledge came to her with such certainty that it was almost as if it had already happened, and heat flared through her whole body. Her breath hitched into her lungs as his mouth skimmed over hers.

The door opened. 'Your time's up,' Agent Todd said.

They sprang apart guiltily, and Reese was sure that she was beet red as she spun around to see the amused expression on Agent Todd's normally blank face.

'Did you come to any conclusions?' Todd asked. He was clearly enjoying their embarrassment.

All Reese could hear was the pounding of her heart. She pressed her fingers against the bridge of her nose, trying to breathe. They hadn't decided what to do. They had gotten distracted.

'We did,' David said, sounding remarkably calm.

She shot him a puzzled look.

'There's no good reason for us to stay down here if the whole place is going to self-destruct,' David said. 'We're getting out of here. But whether or not we go with the Imria...' He trailed off and glanced at Reese as if he were tossing her a ball he expected her to catch.

Just like debate, she thought, and all at once she knew exactly what to say. 'We'll make that decision tomorrow.' She looked at Agent Todd. 'You've given us no proof that what Amber said is the truth. She hasn't exactly been honest with me in the past. So tomorrow we'll see what happens, and we'll decide then. If it turns out she's telling the truth,

353

then we'll consider her offer. Otherwise, no deal.'

Agent Todd regarded the two of them for a long moment, his eyes traveling from David to Reese and back again. Finally he said, 'All right. That seems fair. Tomorrow when the evacuation begins, I'll come and get you. For now, Miss Holloway, you'll need to return to the other interrogation room.'

CHAPTER 38

Reese's least favorite activity in the world was waiting. It was even worse, she discovered, when locked in an empty interrogation room with nothing to do except think.

She hadn't slept much after she and David finished talking. She couldn't get comfortable on the hard chairs, and every time her head nodded off, she jerked awake, certain she was about to fall onto the floor. Eventually she lay down directly on the cold tiles, pillowing her head on her arms, and attempted to sleep that way. But her thoughts kept spiraling back to David in the room next door, and the look on Amber's face when she left, and...

When the door opened, she bounded up expectantly, only to see Agent Todd carrying in a breakfast tray. 'I know you didn't eat last night,' he said, sounding apologetic.

Her stomach growled, but she had other needs too. 'I have to use the bathroom.'

He put the tray on the table and then held open the door. 'After you.'

Afterward she ate the rapidly cooling oatmeal, shoveling it down even though it was as flavorless as it was yesterday. As soon as she got out of here, she was eating a burger, medium-rare with tons of onions and mushrooms and melted sharp cheddar. And fries. Lots of fries, from that diner on Twenty-Fourth, salty and crispy and dipped in their special extra-vinegary ketchup. The overhead lights buzzed, flickering as her spoon scraped against the bottom of the bowl. The oatmeal wasn't nearly as good as that burger would be, but at least it was filling. She pushed it away and began to think through what she knew of the layout of the bunker, mentally sketching it out in case she and David had to find their way to the surface without Agent Todd. She wished she had a pen and a piece of paper. The lights buzzed again, as if an insect had burrowed its way through the wiring and was trapped against its will.

She closed her eyes and tried to visualize the floor plan of the area near the interrogation rooms. The elevator was to the left. There must be stairs somewhere nearby. The buzzing sound overhead sharpened, and something snapped. Startled, Reese sat up.

The lights went out.

For several breathless seconds, the room was pitch-dark.

A blue light hummed on over the door. Sirens began to wail, softly at first, but then increasing in volume. Reese ran to the door and twisted the handle. It was still locked. She put all her weight behind it, trying to yank the door open, but it didn't budge.

Glancing around the room, she looked for something she could use to hammer the door open, but there was nothing. She heard footsteps running past the door and voices shouting, but nobody came to let her out. She grabbed one of the chairs and slammed it against the handle. It bounced off, leaving only a scuff mark on the metal surface. She slammed the chair against the door again and again until sweat stuck to her T-shirt, but the door remained locked.

She heard a deep, loud *boom*. It was just like an earthquake she had experienced a couple of years ago, when nothing shook at all, but she had looked up in class and wondered whether something had exploded. For a few seconds she stood frozen, wondering if the bunker was about to go up in flames with her trapped in this room. Impulsively she tried the door again. This time, the handle turned.

All the lights in the short corridor were blue, and there was no one there. Had they forgotten about David and her? She ran to the other interrogation room and turned the handle. David had a chair raised over his head, ready to strike. He lowered it when he recognized her and asked, 'Where's Agent Todd?'

'I don't know. There's nobody out there.'

He brushed past her into the empty hall. 'Should we wait for him?'

Over the blaring sirens, a computerized voice announced through the intercom system: 'Emergency shutdown procedures initiated. All personnel must proceed to exit stations.'

'I don't want to wait,' Reese said.

'I agree.'

Together they sprinted toward the door that opened into the main corridor, also bathed in blue light. 'Let's head for the elevator,' Reese said, turning left.

But they had gone only a few feet before soldiers burst into the hall through a side door. They were dressed in fatigues and wore helmets outfitted with what looked like night-vision goggles. They also carried weapons that were aimed directly at Reese and David.

She froze in her tracks. David grabbed her arm and tugged her in the opposite direction before she had time to think. 'Where are you going?' she shouted.

'Away from them,' he called over his shoulder.

She glanced back; the soldiers were about fifty feet behind but were rapidly closing the distance. David ducked down a hallway on their left, sprinting past unmarked doors. 'We have to find a way up!' she cried.

'I know!' He was throwing open doors left and right but only discovering empty offices with no way out.

'This one!' Reese had started opening doors too, and through one of them was a long room that looked like a science lab. Black-topped counters ran down the center and were covered with collections of test tubes, as if they had been abandoned mid-experiment. She ran inside the lab and ducked beneath one of the counters. David squeezed in next to her, reaching out to pull a wheeled stool in front of their hiding space. There wasn't much room under the lab bench.

The entire right side of Reese's body was pressed up against David, and after a moment of uncomfortable maneuvering, he freed his left arm from where it was trapped between them and wrapped it around her shoulders. It was both more comfortable and more unnerving, because now she felt surrounded by him, and she could feel his panic – an acidic rush in his gut – as much as her own.

Footsteps pounded into the lab. A light swept across the floor. Reese saw it bobbing over the stool in front of them, and she knew it was only a matter of seconds before the soldiers found them. What had made her think this would be a good hiding place? David's hand tightened on her shoulder, and she tried to calm down.

'There's motion all over this room,' said one of the soldiers over the sirens.

'Is that machine working properly?' said another.

'Yeah, look – the motion detector is picking up tons of activity.'

The lights swept over the room again, and suddenly there was a burst of noise, like a flock of birds screeching in unison.

'Shit! What the fuck is that?'

A new voice came into the room. 'It's the avian lab. That's why there's so much motion. They're not in here – let's go.' Reese could swear it was Agent Todd.

She held her breath as the soldiers left. They waited until the birds stopped calling, and finally she whispered, 'I think they're gone.'

David pushed the stool away, and they crawled out, peering carefully around the bench to the door. It was wide open, but no one was there. Reese scrambled to her feet, glancing around the room. Along the walls, glass-fronted shelves reflected the blue overhead lights.

'We should go,' David said.

Something moved behind the glass.

'Wait a minute,' Reese said. She approached the shelves slowly. In the dim light she saw that the glass was punctured with air holes, and that what she had thought were shelves were actually rows of cages made of Plexiglas.

'What are you doing?'

'Just a second.' The soldiers' words had sparked her interest, and she couldn't help but think of the birds she had seen plummeting to the tarmac at Phoenix Airport. Another memory flashed in her mind: eyes glowing in the high beams before the car accident on the empty desert road. Was this where that bird had come from? It was hard to see inside the cages; the blue light made everything murky. She paused less than a foot from one of them, peering into the dark space. She stepped a few inches closer.

A bird rammed itself against the Plexiglas, its beak pecking at one of the air holes as if it were a bird feeder.

Reese jumped back as the bird began to beat its wings. 'Oh my God.'

It was as if one bird set off a chain reaction all down the wall of cages, and other birds began to throw themselves at the Plexiglas as well, their beaks banging out a frantic, staccato drumbeat.

'What are they doing with all these birds?' she asked.

David began to pull out drawers from the lab benches, riffling through papers and lab equipment. 'Look,' he said.

She ran to his side as he flipped through a stack of reports. She grabbed one of them and squinted in the dim light at the first page. Again she cursed herself for not paying more attention in bio class, but judging from what she was reading, even bio wouldn't have prepared her to fully understand these reports. 'It's like Project Blue Base, but with birds,' she said.

David was skimming through another one. 'They're altering the birds genetically.'

'With Imria DNA,' Reese said, reading through the summary of the report she had picked up. 'Why would they do that?' The overhead lights turned red, and she glanced up in alarm. 'I don't think that's a good sign.'

David ripped several pages out of the report he was reading and stuffed them into his back pocket, and she copied him. 'Come on,' he said, 'we have to get out of here.'

They went to the door and peeked out into the hallway. There was no one in sight, but the red light made everything look the same. Reese couldn't remember which direction they had come from.

'It's this way,' David said, going to the right.

'Are you sure?'

'Yes!'

'How do you know—' She cut herself off when she saw

361

someone she recognized turn into the hallway up ahead. 'It's Agent Todd. I think he led those other soldiers away from us earlier.'

Reese headed toward him, but when two tall shapes came into the corridor behind him, she halted, and David bumped right into her.

'What the hell are those?' he said.

The two figures walked like humans, and their bodies had the same general shape, but their skin was metallic, and to Reese's horror their heads appeared to have no eyes.

'You need to come with me,' Agent Todd said as he approached. 'We only have fifteen minutes left to get out of here.'

Reese pointed at the creatures. 'What are those things?'

'They're erim – Imria soldiers,' Todd said. 'They're robots; you don't need to be afraid of them.'

'They're creepy,' she said, but she followed Todd down the empty corridor at a jog. The robots turned and fell in behind them, running so smoothly, it was almost as if they were gliding on wheels.

When they rounded the corner, Reese recognized the main hallway onto which the medical bay and the interrogation offices opened. The elevator that had brought them underground was waiting, the interior bathed in the same hellish red glow that lit the corridor. Reese and David entered the elevator, and the erim followed, standing at attention on either side of the door while Todd flipped open the cover to a keypad embedded in the wall. As he entered a

362

code, Reese studied the closest robot. Her fear turned into curiosity as she realized it wasn't eyeless, exactly. There was a band of some sort of darker metal circling the center of its head.

The doors slid shut, and the elevator began to move. 'How do they see?' she asked Agent Todd.

'They don't need eyes like you and me,' he explained. 'They use a combination of infrared-heat sensing and radar.'

'They have eyes in the back of their heads,' David said.

'And in the front and the sides,' Todd said, smiling slightly.

Reese studied Agent Todd. There was something about him that reminded her of Dr Brand. 'You're one of them, aren't you?' she said.

He turned his gaze to her. 'What do you mean?'

'You're one of the Imria.'

'Yes,' he said.

'Where are the rest of you?' She thought of Amber. 'Did everyone get out?'

'Yes. That's why I was late coming for you two – there was a glitch in the security system, and I had to modify it somewhat. But everyone is out. When we get to the surface, a ship will come for us, but there may be some resistance from the Blue Base soldiers. You'll need to stay with me. Do not veer off in any direction on your own.'

As the elevator slowed to a stop, the erim raised their arms. They held snub-nosed devices in their jointed metal fingers that looked like oddly cutoff handguns. David

363

stepped closer to Reese, and she didn't need to touch him to feel the tension radiating from his body.

The doors slid open.

They were in the same nondescript corridor they had walked through when they first entered the underground bunker three days earlier. Then Reese's senses had been blunted by the sedative Agent Kowalski had injected into her. Now she felt as if every nerve in her body was vigilant. The sirens from below couldn't be heard up here, and the relative silence rang in her ears. Daylight pooled along the floor from the window in the door at the end of the hall. She could smell the outdoors immediately, and after several days of breathing recycled, refrigerated air, she inhaled greedily as she stepped out of the elevator into the warm hallway.

The erim loped ahead of them to the exit. Agent Todd said something that Reese didn't understand, and as the robots crouched down, she realized it was because he had spoken in a different language. One of the erim pushed the door open while the other swung outside, weapon raised. The sun glinted off their metal skin, and hot air rushed in along with the sound of shouting.

'Stay with me,' Agent Todd said, giving Reese and David a sharp look.

Heart racing, she followed Agent Todd out of the building.

The blast of heat on her face was a shock. She reeled back involuntarily, holding her arm up to block the midday sun. As her pupils contracted against the brightness, she saw dozens of people take shape like mirages solidifying out of the shimmering desert. There were soldiers – human ones in fatigues, carrying weapons – and civilians in lab coats and suits, and in the distance, a clump of people in orange jumpsuits. They were all running away from the building that still shadowed Reese. Straight ahead was a wide, paved area that abutted a hard-packed dirt road. She remembered climbing out of the Humvee onto that road, leaning against David while fighting off the last dregs of the sedative. Beyond the road was the brown, rocky desert. Heat rolled in waves over the dry ground. In the sky, at about two hand spans up from the horizon, a black object was approaching. It was too far away to see clearly, but the orange jumpsuits were striking out across the desert toward whatever it was.

A brown-and-tan military transport truck roared down the road, screeching to a stop in front of Reese and David. Soldiers poured out of the back and formed a line that blocked them from crossing the road to follow the orange jumpsuits. The soldiers all raised their weapons and began to advance on them. David reached out and grabbed Reese's hand, dragging her back against him. Agent Todd had a gun too, and he was shouting something in that foreign language again.

It all happened so quickly that Reese barely had time to make sense of it. The erim lifted their snub-nosed guns and fired a series of short, sharp bursts. The human soldiers fell like a row of dominos, none having a chance to discharge his weapon. At the same time, the ground rumbled. Reese swayed on her feet, her fingers slipping out of David's grasp.

There was a giant shudder as if something deep underground had convulsed, and the desert floor itself tilted. A gust of wind blasted out from the building behind her, knocking her off her feet as if she were a paper doll.

She sprawled on the ground, hands and knees scraping against the asphalt as the force of the explosion shoved her forward. She hissed in pain and covered her head with her arms, stunned and breathless. The pavement was burning hot against her cheek. When the ground seemed still again, she raised her head carefully. She had been thrown almost to the edge of the pavement; the rocky brown dirt was only a few feet away. Her hands were bloody, the knees of her jeans torn, and she winced as she gingerly pushed herself up with her elbows.

David rolled onto his back a few feet away, blood trickling from his temple. She couldn't see Agent Todd anywhere, but the erim were already standing. Behind her the building had not entirely collapsed, though the roof was severely buckled and the door hung on one hinge. She got to her feet, knees shaking. Someone was calling her name, and her ears seemed stuffed with cotton. She turned. A person in an orange jumpsuit was running toward her. Reese recognized the blond hair. Amber.

Beyond Amber, the black object in the sky had grown closer. It was triangular in shape, and it moved with an unearthly silence and precision. It did not appear to have wings or engines like a normal plane. Instead it traveled in an unnaturally straight line over the desert, rotating into position near the largest group of orange jumpsuits, and then began to descend. Clawlike landing gear emerged from the bottom as the craft floated to the ground. A ramp lowered from the shortest end of the triangular ship, and a squadron of erim began to march out.

As Reese stared openmouthed at the spacecraft, time seemed to slow down. It was as if the air had suddenly thickened, making every movement take twice as long as it should.

Amber was only a few feet away, sunlight crowning her head. Her hand was outstretched, and a plea was on her lips. She wanted Reese to come with her.

David was on Reese's other side, and she heard him say something about soldiers and weapons. The urgency in his voice made her turn away from Amber. Another truckload of soldiers had arrived – where had they come from? – and their weapons were raised, fingers on the triggers.

Amber screamed at her. *Get down*.

Reese couldn't move fast enough – her body seemed stuck in quicksand – and Amber leaped at her, shoving her down to the hard ground. She heard gunfire. Amber's body fell, warm and heavy, against her own.

Pain exploded in her body. Her muscles spasmed in shock. She screamed, her voice hoarse and guttural as it tore out of her throat.

But she wasn't the one who was shot.

CHAPTER 39

Amber's body was weighting her down, muscles slack, limbs inert. Reese was dimly aware that the pain she was feeling wasn't hers. It was Amber's.

A voice was screaming at her, but she couldn't understand it. All of her senses were overwhelmed by Amber's pain. Reese felt as if she were battling through some kind of thick, fuzzy haze.

All of a sudden the weight on her lightened as Amber's body was pulled away. Reese drew in a ragged breath and pushed herself up onto her elbows. She felt David's hand on her shoulder – she knew it was him – and the gunfire stopped as abruptly as it had started.

Amber lost consciousness. Reese felt it as a sudden cessation of pain, and she looked up in confusion. David was leaning over her, his face smeared with dirt, and he asked, 'Are you shot?'

'I'm—' She saw Amber barely a foot away from her, lying on her back with her arms flung over her head as if they had been used to drag her there. A dark red spot was spreading from her abdomen, and Reese sucked in her breath and crawled to her, pressing her hands down on the wound. 'Oh my God, she's shot!' Amber's blood pulsed beneath her hands. Reese looked around wildly. The soldiers who had shot her had collapsed near their truck, their weapons on the ground. The erim that had emerged from the spacecraft stood in a line between Reese and the fallen soldiers, snub-nosed guns pointed down. Several of the orange jumpsuits had turned away from the ship and were running toward Reese and Amber.

'She's shot!' Reese screamed. 'Somebody help her!'

David knelt down across from Reese on the other side of Amber, and he pressed his hands over the wound as well. Amber's blood leaked out over their entwined fingers, warm and slippery.

And then Dr Brand was there, saying, 'You need to move out of the way. You need to move!'

Reese looked up at her, dazed from the residual effects of Amber's pain. Dr Brand was wearing an orange jumpsuit, and a purplish bruise ran up her left cheek and into the shadows beneath her eye, as if she had been punched in the face. Blood trickled from a cut in her lip.

'Reese,' Dr Brand said, 'please – please move. She's my daughter.' Two of the erim approached.

David scrambled to his feet first and reached for Reese's arm, tugging on it gently. 'Come on,' he said.

Reese pulled her hands from Amber's wound and let

369

David help her up. She watched numbly as the robots carefully lifted Amber into their gleaming metal arms and carried her across the desert toward the spacecraft.

'Come with us,' Dr Brand urged as she headed back to the ship. 'You can't stay here.' But Reese couldn't seem to move; she felt as if all her energy had drained out of her when Amber was taken away. Her feet weighed a million tons. She looked down at her bloody hands. David put his arm around her. He was whispering in her ear, but she couldn't hear him. *Is Amber going to die?*

Dr Brand turned back when she reached the ramp. 'Reese! David!' she shouted. The command in her voice made Reese take a step away from David, but then Dr Brand's expression changed to one of shock.

Someone grabbed Reese's arms, twisting them behind her. Something hard was pressed against her temple. 'Don't move,' said a curt voice.

There was a gun to her head. Terror roared inside her like an ice-cold waterfall.

'Let them go!' Dr Brand cried, but the man holding Reese captive did not loosen his grip.

Reese felt her captor's voice rumbling through his body and into hers as he said, 'You can take your people and leave, but these kids are ours.'

Dr Brand took a step away from the craft, and the gun at Reese's temple clicked. She could feel every millimeter of the weapon's nose as it slid against her sweat-dampened skin.

370

'They're ours!' the man said again. 'If you come one step closer, they'll be dead.'

Dr Brand stopped. Her face closed into a cold, angry mask. 'You don't know what you're getting yourself into. When you want answers, you'll come back to us.'

She marched up the ramp into the spacecraft, followed by the remaining erim. They moved swiftly and silently, backward, pointing their weapons in Reese's direction the entire time. The ramp lifted into the belly of the triangular craft, and a moment later the ship floated up from the ground, the landing gear retracting.

Reese watched the ship spin soundlessly, and then it sped away, accelerating until it disappeared into the bright, blue-white sky.

The man who put the gun to Reese's head was a stranger to her. He had gray hair worn in a buzz cut, and he was wearing a camouflage uniform like the other soldiers from Project Blue Base. He tied her wrists together with a plastic strap and shoved her into the back of a Jeep. David, who was similarly cuffed, was dragged away to another vehicle.

The desert seemed to bounce outside the window as the Jeep rattled down the dirt road away from the bunker that had exploded. All she could feel was a distant, frozen terror. She knew if she let herself go, she would break down, so she concentrated on the iciness that had descended on her as she was being led away. She could still feel the aftereffects of

Amber's gunshot wound: a phantom ache in her abdomen. It was the only thing that felt alive in her.

The Jeep pulled to a halt in front of a low, beige-colored building that she recognized. The plaque on the door read BUILDING 5 – PLATO. She saw David climb out of a nearby Humvee. The wound on his head had bled spectacularly, leaving a delta of blood on the side of his face. The soldier in charge of Reese pushed her, and she stepped back into the hospital facility she had thought she would never see again.

She didn't know if they put her in the same room she had been in after the car accident, but it was definitely the same layout. Bed, medical equipment, one window, one bathroom. They cut off her wrist restraint and locked her inside.

Knees wobbling, she slid down onto the floor, her back against the door. She bent forward to put her head in her hands but stopped at the sight of dark red smeared over her palms.

Her stomach heaved, and she lurched across the linoleum to the bathroom, barely making it to the toilet in time. She threw up until her throat was burning and raw.

Afterward, she went to the sink and scrubbed the blood off her hands, wincing as her fingers rubbed against the shallow scrapes on her palms from sliding across the desert ground. She was struck by déjà vu. How many times had she cut her hands since she had last been in this place? The thought made her dizzy, and she retreated to the bed, curling

372

up on top of the blanket with her knees drawn to her chest.

In her mind's eye, she saw Amber running across the desert toward her, the triangular spacecraft hovering in the distance. She saw Amber's mouth moving, and she heard David shouting, and then Amber knocked her down, the thud of impact swallowed by the eruption of pain tearing through her body – no, it was Amber's body. She had felt the bullet strike Amber just as surely as if it had struck herself. She had never been able to sense Amber's feelings – not the way she could sense David's. Had she?

She remembered the night in Dolores Park on the swing set, the way it felt as if she could breathe through Amber's lungs when they kissed. The memory of it shot through her in a gut-wrenching pang. Everything with Amber had been so magnified. Was it because of this ability she had acquired? Maybe some of those emotions hadn't been her own. That would mean that Amber truly hadn't lied about the way she felt.

But as seductive as that thought was, something didn't add up. The bullet tearing into Amber's body – that had the same all-encompassing, wholly immersive feeling that she had with David, as well as that time with her mom. But the rest of her experiences with Amber weren't like that.

No. All those feelings had been hers. Amber was still a liar. It still hurt.

Reese woke up with a start. The room was dark except for the marginally lighter square of the window. An unfamiliar sensation crept through her, like someone whispering inside her brain. She shivered.

She rolled onto her side, gazing toward the window. She wondered what time it was and how long she and David would be locked in these rooms.

David. She wished she could talk to him.

Last December, after they had won their first tournament as debate partners, they had hugged each other ecstatically on the stage during the award ceremony. Someone had snapped the photo of them that she had pinned to her bulletin board at home. She still remembered his arm around her, squeezing her close. She had felt his touch burning all the way through to her toes. That day she had dismissed her feelings as a fluke. But maybe the only person she had fooled was herself.

David. I hope you're okay.

She heard it again: the whispering in her brain. Her spine went rigid.

Reese.

'Oh my God,' she whispered. The hairs on her arms stood straight up. *David?* She closed her eyes and tried to picture him in her mind: the shape of his eyes and mouth, the way his hair fell across his forehead when he turned his head. The rhythm of his heartbeat, matching hers.

She felt like she was being dragged down into quicksand. She let herself sink.

David?

She could sense his physical presence forming at the edge

of her perception. Pulse. Breath. Flesh and bone. A dull pain in his head where he had been injured. His hands, clenched against the thin blanket just like hers. He was in the next room.

I can hear you.

Five days later

CHAPTER 40

Reese stepped out of the airplane onto the top step of the rolling staircase. Down below on the tarmac of Travis Air Force Base, a cluster of people waited behind a rope, their faces turned toward her. She saw at least two television cameras, several photographers pointing their glinting lenses in her direction, and dozens of uniformed military personnel lined up to create a path across the runway.

She had been awakened that morning by Agent Forrestal. He walked with a slight limp, and she wondered if that was the only injury he had sustained when the bunker exploded. He informed her that due to unforeseen circumstances, she and David were to be released to their parents later that day. But first he gave her a towel, a stack of clean clothes, and a small toiletry kit, and told her to make herself presentable. There had even been a mirror, and as she combed out her wet hair in the bathroom, she wondered what all this to-do was for.

Now she knew. The press was here.

Their curiosity pricked at her like birds pecking at worms in the ground, and as she descended the staircase, it only got worse. She clutched the railing, keeping her gaze down so that she wasn't blinded by the strobe effect of dozens of cameras flashing in her direction.

'Reese!' a woman cried. It was her mom, and Reese looked up to see her break through the cordoned-off area and run across the tarmac. The crowd behind the rope burst into excited chatter, their attention temporarily diverted. But when her mom reached the bottom of the stairs, they all turned back to Reese. Her breath was knocked out of her by the strength of their interest. She forced herself to focus on her mom, shutting out the cacophony on the tarmac. Her mom's face was pale, with rough red spots on her cheeks and dark shadows beneath her eyes. She looked as if she wasn't entirely convinced it was her daughter emerging from that plane.

Reese took the last few steps quickly and pulled her mom into a tight embrace. 'I'm all right, Mom,' she said, pressing her face into her mother's wavy brown hair. Something inside herself that had been knocked off center by five days in that hospital room finally shifted back into place. For the first time in days, it felt safe to let herself relax. But when she did, she wasn't prepared for the result.

Her mother's emotions were a riot of anxiety and exhaustion and relief. It was almost suffocating to experience. Beyond that, the shouted questions of the reporters were like stones striking her.

'How does it feel to be back?'

'What were the last few days like for you?'

'Will you be pressing charges?'

She stiffened and pulled away.

'Reese?' Her mom looked alarmed.

'I'm sorry,' she said, gasping. Her shoulders hunched defensively as she tried to block out all the mental noise.

Out of the corner of her eye, she saw David coming down the stairs, heading for his parents. During the time they had spent locked in those rooms at Project Plato, their only contact with other people had been when meals were delivered by an armed guard. That had left the two of them plenty of time to practice their newfound ability. At times it had felt as if she only existed on a level of disembodied consciousness, connected to David by an invisible cord. But now, with all her defenses up and pushing against the crowd, she couldn't sense him at all. She was herself alone again. It was strange: as if she were separated from the world by a glass wall.

Before her accident, this was how she had always lived. She had never been aware of that glass wall until today.

Her mom reached out and smoothed Reese's hair away from her face. This time, she felt only the simple, physical touch of her mom's hand. 'Welcome home, honey,' her mom said.

Reese smiled faintly. 'Thanks.' She was startled to recognize the man hovering behind her mom's shoulder. 'Dad?'

381

'Hi, sweetie.' Rick Holloway had the kind of square-jawed, craggy face that aged well on men, but Reese had never realized his dark hair was turning gray. She let him hug her. He smelled faintly like the tea-tree soap in her mom's bathroom, and to her shock it made her want to cry.

'What are you doing here?' she mumbled into his shoulder. 'I mean—'

'I think your mom should tell you that,' he said as she pulled away.

She was about to ask him why when she saw another familiar face waiting behind her father. 'Julian?'

Julian squeezed her into a hug and said, 'Welcome back.'

'What is going on?' she asked as he released her. 'Why are all of you here?' She looked around at the gathered group. David and his parents, Winston and Grace Li, were nearby, along with his twelve-year-old sister, Chloe, who was watching everything with barely contained excitement.

A vaguely familiar-looking woman in a navy-blue suit stepped forward, escorted by Reese's mother. 'Reese, David, let me introduce you to Senator Joyce Michaelson,' her mom said.

'Hello, Reese,' the woman in the suit said, extending her hand. Her dark blond hair was styled in a short, wavy cut, and she wore a triple strand of pearls around her neck.

'Hi.' Reese shook the woman's hand as the cameras flashed.

'Hello, David,' the senator said.

David looked wary but polite as he also shook her hand.

382

He was wearing the same outfit that Reese was: khaki pants and a long-sleeved blue T-shirt. She wondered who had picked out their clothes, even managing to get their sizes about right. It would have looked pretty bad for them to be on camera in the stinking, bloody clothes they had been wearing for the last five days. Now they looked like they had come straight from a Gap store.

'Senator Michaelson helped us get you home,' Reese's mom explained. 'We're very grateful to her.'

'I'm so happy I could be of assistance,' Senator Michaelson said, a concerned look on her face. 'I was so worried when Cat contacted me with your story. Let me be the first to extend apologies to the both of you on behalf of the United States government for any distress you may have been caused in the last few days.'

Distress? Reese had no idea how to respond to that. The reporters, the cameras, her family – it was all overwhelming.

Her mom put an arm around Reese's shoulders, steering her away from the reporters. 'You ready to go home?'

'Please,' Reese said. 'But what about David?'

'He's coming too. I've already arranged it with his parents.'

The reporters followed them to the edge of the tarmac, where several cars were parked. Reese heard her father saying, 'We're not taking any questions now. We'll issue a statement later.' Then he and Julian closed ranks around her, and she couldn't see the reporters anymore as they herded her toward her mom's car.

* * *

383

They left Travis Air Force Base with a police escort, blue lights whirling with the occasional blip of the siren to cut through traffic. David's car was directly behind theirs.

'How are you feeling, honey?' her mom asked as she drove. 'How did they treat you? Senator Michaelson wasn't clear on where you were being held.'

'I'm just . . . tired,' Reese said. She didn't want to discuss it yet. 'Can we talk about it later? What's been going on? Why were you all here to meet us?'

Her mom glanced at her in the rearview mirror. 'The day you were taken, I came home to find a letter from the Air Force Office of Special Investigations stating that you were being removed for additional testing – a follow-up to your accident. I called the number on the letterhead, but nobody would tell me anything. That's why I contacted Senator Michaelson. I knew her from when I worked for her fresh out of law school at the DA's office. She agreed to look into it. I was still waiting for an answer when Julian called me on Saturday morning.'

Julian was sitting next to Reese in the backseat. 'That's when a video was posted on the Hub,' he said. 'Things went crazy when it hit, and Bin 42 got a billion links to it, so Keith asked me to reformat it for the site in case it was taken down.'

'Why would it be taken down?'

'Because it was surveillance-camera footage from a classified military base. It had location data embedded in it that corresponds exactly to the coordinates for Area 51. And

384

it had you and David on it.' He looked at Reese and hesitated.

'What?' she prompted him.

'It also had Amber on it.'

She braced herself and asked, 'What does the video show?'

'It shows the desert, and in the background this spaceship is landing. And then you see you and David running toward it, and suddenly Amber knocks you over, and – are you okay?'

Reese rubbed her clammy hands over her new khaki pants. 'I'm fine. What else is on the video?'

'It shows these silver things coming out of it – they look like robots – and they come and take Amber into the ship and then it lifts off.' Julian couldn't hide his excitement. 'It's amazing, Reese. It's freaking amazing. It's evidence of extraterrestrials.'

'Let's not jump to conclusions,' her mom said.

'What else could it be?' Julian asked. 'We don't have the technology for a ship like that. The way it moved was insane.'

'The technology is pretty advanced,' her dad said from the front passenger seat. 'But that's still being analyzed by aviation experts.'

'Anyway,' her mom said, 'after Julian called me to say he saw you on this video, I asked your father if he could help find out if the video was genuine.'

'I contacted an expert I've worked with in the past, and they determined that it wasn't a hoax,' her dad said.

'Then I contacted Senator Michaelson again and told her about the video,' her mom said. 'I also sent it to CNN.'

Reese's eyes widened. 'You sent it to CNN?'

'It never would have made as much of an impact on Julian's website—'

'It's not really *my* website—'

'—as it did on CNN. Your father's expert went on the air to explain how he had determined its authenticity, and then I went on the air along with your father and David's parents to identify the two of you and Amber, and to demand that the government explain what was happening in the video.'

'When did you do this?' Reese asked.

'It aired on CNN four days ago, on Monday,' her mom said. 'Right afterward, Senator Michaelson tried a different angle in getting information on your whereabouts. She's on the Senate Armed Services Committee, and she eventually took this to the Secretary of Defense and had a meeting with him yesterday. This morning she called me and said that you and David were coming back today.'

The police lights ahead flickered, as blue as the emergency lights in the bunker. Something was still unexplained, though. 'Who uploaded the video?' Reese asked.

'Nobody knows,' Julian said. 'That's the big mystery. I think somebody was working on the inside like a double agent.'

'That's just speculation,' her mom said.

'There's been a *lot* of speculation,' her dad said.

'The media went crazy over the video,' Julian said. 'Not

only do you have a genuine image of a spaceship landing, you have the revelation that Area 51 actually exists—'

'The government is still denying that's where the video was shot,' her dad said.

'It was totally Area 51,' Julian insisted. 'And then you've got you and David, two ordinary high school students, running out of Area 51 toward a spaceship, and then this mysterious chick Amber basically throws herself in the line of fire to prevent you from getting shot, and—'

'Wait,' Reese interrupted, staring at him. 'She did what?'

'It's the big story,' Julian said, as if he were pitching a feature to their journalism teacher. 'The cable channels, the news sites, they all think Amber is the hero, blocking the bullet from hitting you.' Julian paused, giving her a sympathetic look. 'They all want to know who she is and why she saved you.'

Reese's stomach fell. 'Did you tell them anything?' She had never expected she might be outed in the national media.

But Julian shook his head. 'Only her name.'

'It's up to you if you want to say anything more, honey,' her mom said. 'The press hasn't been able to find out much about her. She was enrolled as a student at Winthrop Academy in Massachusetts and at the Hunter Glen School in Arizona, but her parents haven't come forward.'

Reese turned her head to look out the window. She tried to remember what exactly had happened that day, but all she could recall was the impact of Amber's body on hers, pushing her onto the ground. Then the pain that tore through her abdomen as if someone had reached inside and ripped out her guts. She hadn't known where the gunshot came from. She hadn't known Amber had taken the bullet for her. But now all she could think of were Julian's words: *They all think Amber is the hero*.

CHAPTER 41

There was a mob of reporters outside the house in Noe Valley. Two television-station vans were parked on the street, and cameras flashed as Julian, Reese, and her parents climbed out of their car. David and his family were right behind them, and Reese tried to shield herself from the flurry of questions tossed at them as she hurried up the steps to the house. Her mom unlocked the door, and then they all crowded inside, shutting out the press.

'They're quite aggressive, aren't they?' David's mom, Grace, observed.

'We'll give them a statement later tonight, once we've talked things over,' Reese's dad said.

Reese slipped into the living room while her mom asked David's parents if they wanted anything to drink. The coffee table and couch were strewn with empty takeout containers and newspapers, as if her mom had been besieged here for weeks. Reese picked up one of the papers as she heard her mom and the others head down the hall to the kitchen. It

389

was Tuesday's front page, and a giant black-and-white photograph – slightly grainy as if it had come from a security camera – took up the entire top half. It showed a spacecraft lifting off from the rocky desert, its landing gear still not fully retracted. A smaller inset photo focused on three people: one lying on her back on the ground, and two others crouched over her. With a shock, Reese recognized David, Amber, and herself.

David had followed her into the living room, and he leaned over her shoulder to look at the newspaper. His closeness made her unexpectedly uncomfortable. She handed him the paper and moved away to sit on the edge of the couch. He gave her a short, questioning look, but she busied herself by collecting the empty takeout containers. Why did she suddenly feel shy around him?

'My parents told me about what happened,' he said. 'Did yours?'

'Yeah,' she said. She stacked the containers on the end table and started to gather together the newspapers.

David sat down beside her and dropped a hand on her knee. His touch made her stiffen, and he pulled away. She flushed. What was wrong with her? After all they had gone through, she was still acting like a jerk. She was relieved when Julian came into the living room and sat down in the armchair. 'Is that the picture?' he asked.

'Yeah,' David said, passing it to Julian. 'My parents said you played a big role in getting us out of there.'

Julian shrugged, but he was obviously pleased. 'Nah. I

just saw the video and called Reese's mom.'

'Did you ever get anything from the video we shot at the warehouse?' David asked.

Julian shook his head. 'It was too dark. I tried to lighten it up, but I couldn't see much. The only thing I got was the license plate of that car, and I haven't been able to look it up.'

'Oh my God, I almost forgot,' Reese exclaimed, dropping a pile of newspapers on the floor. She reached into her bra and pulled out a folded piece of paper. 'I didn't want them to take it off me if we were searched today,' she said self-consciously. She spread out the paper on her knee; it was the first page from the report she had read in the avian lab.

'I totally forgot about that,' David said. 'The pages I took must still be in my pants back at the hospital.'

'What is it?' Julian asked.

Reese passed the paper to him. 'I think it's connected to the June crashes.'

Julian's eyes widened as he read. 'No, I think this is the June crash.'

'We found a lab full of birds at – at Area 51,' Reese said. 'That's where that report came from.'

Her mom came into the living room with a tray full of teacups. She set it on the coffee table and asked, 'What report?' David's parents and sister came into the living room as well, and Reese's father followed, carrying folding chairs.

'Reese lifted a top-secret document from Area 51,' Julian said.

Her mom frowned. 'Let me see that.' She took the wrinkled paper from Julian and scanned it. 'I don't understand. This is about birds.'

'They're genetically altering birds with alien DNA,' Reese said. David's sister, Chloe, sat down on the couch beside David, who scooted over to make room for her. His leg brushed against Reese's. She forced herself to hold still.

'Alien DNA?' her mom said skeptically. 'And who's 'they'?'

'Project Blue Base,' Reese answered.

'Shit, are you serious?' Julian cried. 'Sorry,' he said to the assembled parents.

'What's Project Blue Base?' her mom asked.

'It's a classified defense project to create genetically enhanced soldiers. Super soldiers,' David explained. 'That's where they were holding us.'

'I thought you were being held at Area 51?' Grace said.

'Wait, start at the beginning,' Reese's mom said, sitting in one of the folding chairs next to her ex-husband. 'What does this paper mean?'

David's father, Winston, held out his hand. 'Let me take a look,' he said. 'I'm not a geneticist, but I might be able to figure it out.'

'He's a biochemist,' Grace said. 'So modest.'

Winston read through the short document. 'This is very odd,' he concluded. 'It says that these birds are being genetically modified to make them more intelligent. But why? Do they need to train them for some reason? And what is this word, Imria?'

Reese felt David's leg tighten, and his tension radiated throughout her whole body. She had known she would have to explain what had really been done to her at Project Plato, but now that the moment had come, she wasn't sure if she was ready. Would her parents even believe her?

Julian's phone buzzed, and he pulled it from his pocket. 'We have to turn on the TV,' he said. He lunged for the remote that was half-hidden behind the stack of takeout containers and switched on the television. It was already on CNN, and a silver-haired announcer was saying: '– going to a live feed from the White House in a couple of minutes. We're told that President Randall will address the nation regarding the video footage containing the unidentified flying object.'

President Elizabeth Randall appeared unusually nervous as the camera opened onto a marble hall in the White House. Reese had never liked President Randall – she thought the woman was too much of a slick politician – but today she showed some rougher edges. Standing behind a podium decorated with the presidential seal and flanked by the Joint Chiefs of Staff, the president's hand shook slightly as she adjusted her glasses.

'My fellow Americans,' President Randall began, 'I know that the events of the past couple of days have shaken many of you and caused some of you to question whether your own government has been keeping secrets. Well, this is an unprecedented situation, folks, and I'm going to cut through all the PR speak and tell it to you like it is – which is just what I promised you I would do when you elected me two years ago.'

'Bullshit,' Reese's mom snapped.

The president looked gravely at the camera. 'The truth is: Yes, your government has lied to you. It has been lying to you for decades, because it believed that you were better off not knowing the truth. But as soon as I stepped into office, I began working to stop the lies. And today I'm going to tell you the truth.' She took a deep breath. 'Yes, it's true: We have been visited by extraterrestrials.'

'I can't believe she said that,' Julian said, leaning forward.

'They first visited us in 1947, and some of that visit was leaked by mistake to the public and became popularly known as the Roswell Incident.' The president smiled self-deprecatingly. 'But they're not little green men, or gray aliens, as many conspiracy buffs believe. The people who visited us—' She paused dramatically. 'There's no other way to say it. They look like us. The people you saw in the video who were running into the spacecraft – those people were our extraterrestrial visitors.'

Reese already knew this, but hearing the president say the words out loud still made a chill run down her spine. She glanced at Julian to see how he took it; he was gaping at the television.

The president adjusted her glasses again, then tucked a strand of hair behind an ear. 'Since 1947 the United States has been cooperating with these extraterrestrial visitors, who identify themselves as the Imria. We have set up a research agreement with them, exchanging scientific knowledge and developing a relationship. The United States government decided to keep this relationship classified because in 1947, the world was reeling from the aftermath of World War Two, and we were fighting the rise of Communism. If I had been president then, I can promise you I wouldn't have done the same thing.'

'Whatever,' Julian said. 'She wouldn't have made a statement if that video hadn't been leaked. It forced her hand.'

'In recent days, it has become clear to me that the time for secrecy has passed,' the president continued. 'In order to move forward into the future – a future in which interplanetary contact is no longer a thing of science fiction – you deserve to know who these Imria are. The release of the video earlier this week showed me that you are ready for the truth. But my fellow Americans, I am afraid that the truth is not entirely pretty. After the ship that you saw in the video lifted off, we have had no further contact from the Imria. At this point, we are alone, again, on our planet. So, I say this to the Imria: If you are watching, I invite you to make public contact with us. We will meet at a global summit. We will begin our relationship anew.' She paused. 'And to my fellow Americans, I offer my heartfelt apologies. On behalf of all the administrations before mine that kept this secret from you: I am sorry. I hope we can move forward into a more truthful and open future.'

CNN cut back to the newsroom, where the anchor began to summarize the president's words. 'That's it?' Julian said. 'She lays that on us, and that's it? No follow-up?'

'That's quite a lot on its own,' Winston said.

Julian and David's father began to debate the ramifications of the president's announcement, but Reese wasn't listening. Her eyes were fixed on the television, where the anchor was now turning to a panel of experts to discuss what had just occurred. In a smaller picture embedded in the upper left corner of the screen, CNN was playing the video from Area 51.

It was a black-and-white image, and the desert looked like something out of a 1950s B movie, especially with the black triangle hovering in the sky. Reese recognized David and herself and even Agent Todd running toward the spacecraft as it lowered itself effortlessly into a perfect landing. She knew what was coming, and her muscles tensed in anticipation as she watched a girl break away from the group of people closer to the spacecraft. She ran back toward the camera, and though her face was so tiny in the inset video it was unrecognizable, Reese knew it was Amber. Just before Amber reached David and Reese, she stretched out a hand and seemed to throw herself at Reese, knocking her to the ground. As they fell, Reese's body twisted so that her face turned toward the camera, hair flying. The letters on her SFPD T-shirt stood out in stark contrast for a fraction of a second, and then Amber's body jerked, struck by a bullet from offscreen.

Reese flinched as she saw Amber slump over her, head lolling forward. She couldn't stop watching, even though it was making her queasy. She watched David dragging Amber off her. She watched herself crawl over to Amber as the dark stain on her belly spread. She watched herself press her hands over the wound, and then David joined her and did the same. The sight of the three of them on the ground, connected by the seeping blood from Amber's abdomen like some kind of morbid triptych, seemed to burn itself into her mind's eye.

And then Reese had to get up and leave, because she couldn't stand to see it anymore.

CHAPTER 42

Reese ran upstairs to her bedroom, closing the door between herself and everyone else. She leaned against the door for a moment, pressing the heels of her hands over her eyes as if that would rub out the image that hovered there. She became aware of a sound in the distance, like rotors whirring.

Her room was dim; the blinds were drawn shut. But she could make out the gleam of plastic attached to the wall that she had painted to look like her dream. The sound came closer, and she went to the window, separating the blinds to peer out. Down on the sidewalk the crowd of reporters only seemed to have grown, and some of them were looking up at the sky. A helicopter was circling overhead. As it turned, Reese could read what was printed on the side: EYEWITNESS NEWS.

She let the blinds fall shut and backed away, striking the edge of her desk with her hip. She felt trapped, and all of a sudden the accumulated stress of the last few weeks seemed to tower over her in a precarious pile of conflicting emotions and confusing facts. She sank down to the floor, leaning against the side of her desk, and wrapped her elbows around her knees. She couldn't break down. Her parents – her father! – and Julian and David's family and David too were all downstairs, and there was a mob outside the front door, salivating for her to tell them what had happened.

She tried to breathe in to calm herself, but it only seemed to make things worse. Now she wanted to burst into tears. She buried her head in her arms, her body shuddering as she tried to contain the panic roaring in her. Hot tears slid out of her eyes, dampening the dark blue cotton of the shirt Agent Forrestal had given her. She wiped her eyes against the material, hating it for what it represented. They were trying to turn her into their nicely washed puppet, trying to obscure the fact that she and David had been kept in virtual isolation for days. During that time she had clung to her newfound connection with David – it had been the only thing that was good about it – but now that she was out, she didn't understand how she felt about him. It was like she missed him, but simultaneously she was afraid of the fact that she missed him.

There was a knock on her door. *David*. 'Reese? Can I come in?'

No.

He pushed open the door and came inside, switching on her desk lamp. He sat down on the floor in front of her, the toe of his sneaker touching hers. He said softly, 'It was rough to see that video, wasn't it?'

399

'She's the hero,' Reese blurted out, raising her head. 'That's what Julian told me. The media thinks she took a bullet for me.'

'You mean Amber.' His voice was gentle, and she couldn't bear the way he looked at her, as if she were a broken doll.

'Yes, I mean Amber.' She angrily wiped away the tears from her face, then rubbed her damp fingers over her pants.

'What do you think?' David asked. 'Do you think she's the hero?'

'I don't know. I think she's still a liar. Can you be both?'

'I have no idea.' He paused. 'Is that what's bothering you? You still have feelings for her?'

She was startled by the bluntness of his question. His mouth was drawn down at the corners, and a sharp line formed in the middle of his forehead, betraying his tension. She knew he deserved an answer, but more than that, *she* deserved an answer. 'I don't know,' she said, frustrated. 'I don't know how I feel. I wish I did. Everything is so crazy out there. Those reporters – what are we supposed to tell them? And what's going on with the government? You think they're just going to let us out of Area 51 without doing anything else to us? Who are we anyway? Are we even still human?'

David's face relaxed slightly. 'You're just as human as I am. And we're going to figure out all this stuff together. You're not alone in this, you know.'

The shyness that had made her so twitchy downstairs

came back. Everything they had gone through at Area 51 had forced them into such quick intimacy. Not physical intimacy – Reese thought that might have been easier to deal with – but mental and emotional intimacy. He knew how she felt because he could feel it too. But she wasn't used to anyone knowing that stuff about her. She was used to being on her own, being independent, figuring things out by herself.

Abruptly, she said, 'I don't know if I can do this with you.' The words sounded unexpectedly harsh, and Reese tried to backtrack. 'I mean – I'm just not used to – to—'

He put a hand lightly on her foot, the barest contact, and yet even through her shoe she felt the solidity of him. Reassuring. 'Do what?' he asked quietly.

There was nothing aggressive in his question; she knew she could make a joke and brush it off, pretend like she had been talking about something else, and he wouldn't push her. But then she would be a liar, and she didn't want to lie to him. For one thing, he would know, and besides, she would feel like a jerk. She was still afraid to face her feelings for him; she felt them twisting inside her like knotted ropes. She had to find some way to unknot them or else they would hang her. She imagined herself sitting here in the corner of her bedroom forever, strangled by this lump of emotion in her throat.

The only way she could get beyond it was to force herself to move. She scrambled to her feet and went to the windows. She grabbed the cord to pull up the blinds, but then stopped.

She could still hear the helicopter rotors. All those reporters were waiting outside.

'What I mean,' she began, her back turned to David, 'is that I don't know how to date anyone. I never wanted to date anyone until – until recently.' She heard him get up, but she still didn't turn. 'I'm not good at this. I don't know how to act, and I'm pretty sure I'll freak out at some point, and then you'll think I'm crazy. I already freaked out on you in Phoenix, and it messed us up at the finals and it was all my fault.' She dropped the cord and turned to face him. 'So maybe it's not a good idea for us to...get involved.'

He seemed both startled and a little pleased. 'Are you saying that you got so upset in Phoenix because you *liked* me?'

She turned bright red. 'I'm – I—'

'Because I totally did not get that from you. I thought you were freaked out because you realized that *I* liked you.' His cheeks were pink. 'So I backed off.'

'But you almost kissed me in that interrogation room.'

'I thought *you* almost kissed *me*,' he objected.

'What are you saying?' she said, confused. 'That you don't want to kiss me?'

His eyebrows rose. 'No.' He smiled slightly. 'That is not what I'm saying.'

Warmth spread through her, loosening the knotted rope inside. 'Then what are you saying?'

'I'm saying that we can take it really slow.'

'But what if it doesn't work out?' she said in a low voice.

'What if you end up hating me?' To her horror, tears sprang into her eyes. 'I don't want that to happen.'

'Maybe you're getting ahead of yourself,' he said. 'We haven't even started anything yet. Why are you already assuming it's not going to work out? And you could end up hating me, you know. You're not the only person involved.'

'I wouldn't end up hating you.' *You're not like Amber*. But she didn't let herself speak the sentence out loud.

If he heard her thoughts, it didn't show. He simply reached for her hands, which she had clenched into fists at her sides. Their fingers laced together, and she felt her defensive walls melting. 'How slow did you want to go?' she asked, something in her stomach fluttering maddeningly.

'As slow as you want.' He slid his hands behind her back, her fingers still twined in his. As the space between them closed, she pulled her hands free and curled them over the nape of his neck.

He was right there at her fingertips. She could let go. She could let him in. And she wanted to. All of her fears were still there, hovering in the background like swirling fog, but right now – in this moment – they were less significant than the fact that this was David, right here, and she trusted him.

He was worth the possibility of getting hurt.

She let down her guard. In an instant he was so much more than a physical presence next to her; it was like going from two to three dimensions in the blink of an eye. Now he was fully formed. His body was filled with a curling heat that made her knees weak.

He bent his head and kissed her.

His lips were harder than Amber's, but he was gentler. When he pulled her close, it was as if her whole body gave a long, shaking sigh. Dimly she heard some kind of racket outside – people were shouting – but she was too distracted to pay attention. She opened her mouth beneath his. His hands pressed her closer, and there was a single, jarring moment when she realized how different his body was from Amber's. He was all long planes and muscle, and she splayed her hands over his upper back, mapping out the shape of him against her.

'Oh shit, I'm sorry!'

The sound of Julian's voice made her and David spring apart, breathless.

Dazed, Reese looked at the door. Julian was holding it half open, his eyes averted as his face darkened with embarrassment. 'I'm really sorry,' he said again. 'I totally didn't mean to interrupt, um, but there's someone here to see you.'

Reese's skin tingled. She *knew*, with an uncanny certainty, who it was. She crossed the room on wobbly legs and grabbed the door handle. She pulled it all the way open. Julian stepped aside.

Amber was standing in the hall. There was no trace of the bullet wound on her. She looked just like she always had, wearing faded jeans and a white tank top beneath her red hoodie with the racer stripe. Her white-blond hair was perfectly styled, and she had even put on makeup: smudged eyeliner, lip gloss in that candylike shine.

'Hi, Reese,' she said, a ghost of a smile on her face. 'Bad time?'

CHAPTER 43

Reese could tell right away that this conversation wasn't going to go well.

She could feel David's tension rising as he crossed the room to join her just inside the doorway. Julian looked like he was torn between fleeing the scene and holding out to see what was going to happen next.

'What are you doing here?' Reese asked.

'I was hoping you'd be at least a little bit happy that I'm not dead,' Amber said. She was obviously going for sarcasm, but the undertone of hurt was unmistakable.

'That's not fair,' Reese said. 'You know I'm happy that you're alive.'

Amber's cheeks reddened slightly. 'Yeah? Well, now I do.'

The words stung, but David spoke before Reese could formulate a retort. 'Amber, right?' he said. 'I don't think we've ever been properly introduced.' He extended his hand to her.

Amber looked at it, startled, as if no one had ever offered to shake her hand before. 'Hi. You must be David.'

'Yeah.'

Reese didn't want to be aware of the way the two of them felt when they shook hands: surprised, wary. She didn't want to notice the way they looked at each other: like adversaries. She shook her head in annoyance and asked, 'Are you going to tell us why you're here?'

Amber raised one eyebrow. 'Impatient much?'

'Don't fuck with me,' Reese said.

The smile disappeared from Amber's face. She crossed her arms and entered the room, brushing past Reese and David. 'I'm here to tell you the truth.'

'Just like the president?' Reese said.

'She's a liar,' Amber said.

Reese had to bite her tongue to prevent herself from snapping, *And you're not?* It was David who asked, 'What's the truth?'

'Well, first of all, obviously we have not left the planet,' Amber said.

'So, why are you still here?' Reese asked.

'Because of you,' Amber said, then shifted her eyes to David. 'And you.'

'What do you mean?' he asked.

'The thing that happened to you in Nevada after your car accident – you're both different now.'

'Yeah,' Reese said. 'We found our medical records. We have extraterrestrial DNA now.' She heard Julian utter an

407

exclamation behind her.

'Sort of,' Amber said. She pulled out the desk chair and straddled it, elbows resting on the back. 'What the president said about the United States government working with the extraterrestrials on scientific research – that's only half right. My people, the Imria, have been here for decades doing research. That's true. We've agreed to help you with advancements in biotechnology, but your government hasn't been too eager to wait. It's been stealing that biotech for decades. That's what they've been using in Project Blue Base. But that technology is not meant for those purposes.'

'The June nineteenth crashes,' Julian said. 'It's the government's fault, isn't it? Because they were modifying birds in a way that was never supposed to be done. They're like Dr Frankenstein.'

'Except they weren't trying to reanimate dead birds,' Amber pointed out, 'but yeah, basically. You can't just start injecting Imria DNA into ordinary birds and expect the birds not to freak out. It doesn't work that way.'

'Wait a minute,' Reese said. 'This technology that the government is using the wrong way. What exactly is it for?'

Amber took a deep breath. 'My people, under the guise of Project Plato, have been developing an adaptation procedure that would basically upgrade human DNA.'

'Upgrade? How?' David asked.

'We have certain abilities that you don't. We, meaning the Imria. We wanted to find a way to give you guys those same abilities through this adaptation procedure. But it's

408

been really, really tricky to do. We've been working on it basically forever. You and David were actually, um, test subjects.'

Reese stared at her. 'Are you serious? We didn't give our consent.'

Amber looked uncomfortable, but she said, 'You would have died if you weren't given the procedure. Your accident was pretty bad. The procedure saved you.'

'But you had no right to do that to us,' David said. 'You should have at least contacted our families and gotten their permission.'

Amber rolled her eyes. 'There was no time. It wasn't ideal, but sometimes things happen for a reason.'

Reese gave her a puzzled look. 'What's that supposed to mean?'

'I'm just saying that we've been testing this procedure for a long time and—'

'They weren't the first test subjects?' Julian cut in. 'David and Reese. You've been testing this procedure on other humans?'

'Yes.' At the expression on Julian's face, she said, 'Don't freak out on me; they've mostly been consenting subjects. You two were an exception.'

'Mostly?' Julian said.

'Let's not get off track here,' Amber said. 'The point is, you had the accident; the procedure saved you. Both of you took really well to the adaptation chamber.'

'The what?' Reese remembered overhearing Dr Brand say

those words that day in front of Amber's house. 'What is that exactly?'

Amber gestured to the painting on the wall. 'This thing you painted – it's a pretty good depiction of the adaptation chamber.'

Reese gazed at the red and yellow paint, the light gleaming off the plastic in the center. '*This?*'

'Yeah. The adaptation chamber is kind of like an incubator. After you went through the procedure you were pretty beat up, and this chamber enabled you to heal faster. It also prevented your body from rejecting the Imria DNA. It helped you to adapt.'

Reese crossed her arms. 'So David and I had this procedure. What does it do exactly?'

'It introduces Imria DNA into your mitochondrial DNA,' Amber said. 'It enables you to have certain abilities that most humans don't.'

'Like telepathy,' David said.

'Telepathy?' Julian cried. 'You're telepathic now?'

Reese made a face. 'Well, sometimes. It doesn't always work.'

'Your abilities can be enhanced through training,' Amber said. 'I was supposed to keep an eye on you to track how you were developing and to make sure you didn't have any unexpected side effects.' She looked at Reese. '*That* was my assignment. To make sure that you were okay.'

'Why didn't David get assigned someone too?' Reese asked.

'Initially we didn't think the procedure worked with him,' Amber admitted. 'He didn't test positively after the procedure, but you did.'

'Obviously you guys were wrong,' Reese said.

Amber shrugged. 'Yeah, we were wrong. We don't know everything. But now we know that it worked with both of you. And we want to make you an offer. You can stay here and be a government guinea pig if you want, or you can come with us.'

'Why would it be any better to be a guinea pig for the Imria than for the US government?' David asked.

'You wouldn't be our guinea pigs,' Amber insisted. 'Don't you understand? You guys are the first truly successful adapted humans. We don't want to treat you like guinea pigs. We want you as partners.'

Reese gave her a skeptical look. 'For what?'

Amber made a frustrated face. 'To help you. We want to help humanity, not destroy it. But your government has different plans. It's using that biotech to make weapons and soldiers. Those weapons could wipe out all of your civilization. Do you really want to be a part of that?'

'Why should we trust you?' Reese asked. 'You lied to me.' She remembered something that had been puzzling her for some time. 'If I have this crazy telepathy adaptation now, why did it never work with you? The only time I ever felt it with you was when you got shot.'

Amber's eyes flickered from Reese to David and back. 'I guess it's worked with David?'

'Yes.'

Amber looked uncomfortable. 'When I first met you, I didn't want to overwhelm you. For us – for the Imria, and now for you – it only works if both people are open to it. Humans don't have this ability, so they're kind of open to it by default because they don't know any better. Some humans are more open than others. But now that you have this ability, if you decide that you don't want to let someone into your mind, you don't have to.'

'Like shutting them out?' Reese said.

'More like keeping things to yourself. When I first met you, I knew that you didn't have any experience with this ability, so I . . . I kept things to myself. If I'd let you see everything, it probably would have freaked you out. It's not exactly like what you think of as telepathy. It's kind of a deep thing.'

'That's an understatement,' Reese said. 'But it was also convenient, wasn't it? If I couldn't see inside you, I couldn't tell that you were lying to me.'

Amber stood up and crossed the room, reaching for Reese's hand as if they were alone. 'I'm not lying to you now. I'll show you.'

Reese went rigid and jerked her hand away. 'No. You don't get to see inside me.'

Amber's face went white. 'Reese—'

'Look, it doesn't matter if you're lying or not. This isn't about you. If we have this new ability, we need to be in control of it – not the US government, not your people.' She

412

turned to David. The vein in his temple was back. 'Do you agree?' she asked him. *We do this on our own terms.*

'Yes,' he said immediately. 'I absolutely agree.'

'But if you don't accept our help, your government won't allow you to go free,' Amber said, her voice rising. 'You think you're here on your own terms now, but you're not. They're parked right down the street with machine guns. They're not going to let you go.'

Julian cleared his throat. 'Sorry to interrupt, but I think there might be a solution to this.' Reese, David, and Amber all looked at him. He was still standing in the doorway. He squared his shoulders. 'Since there is a whole mob of reporters out in front of your house, you might try talking to them. Power of the media, you know. That's how your mom got you back from Area 51.'

'You mean, we go out there and tell them about everything?' Reese said. 'The birds and the adaptation procedure and how the government and the Imria are fighting over us?'

'We're not fighting—' Amber objected.

'Basically, yes,' Julian interrupted. 'I think your parents were only going to give a brief statement, like 'We're happy to have our children home' sort of thing, but if you tell all, you'll get the press on your side, and you'll also expose the government for being totally crappy to you. They'll probably fall all over themselves to deny it and let you have your freedom.'

David said, 'I think we should do it.'

413

Amber's eyebrows drew together. 'You don't know what you're getting yourself into,' she warned them. 'The media isn't exactly a neutral party.'

'But it's the best option, isn't it?' Reese said. 'If you were me, isn't that what you would do? I can't imagine you just giving in to anyone.'

'It's not giving in. It's in your best interest.'

Reese turned to David. 'We can tell them together.'

'Together,' he agreed.

Reese headed for the doorway, brushing past Amber and Julian with David on her heels. Their parents and Chloe were clustered at the bottom of the stairs, and Reese's mom asked, 'What's going on? Where are you going?'

'We're going to tell the press the whole story,' Reese said.

Her mom grabbed her arm. 'Honey, wait. We should think this through more carefully. There are repercussions to revealing classified information.'

Reese pulled away. 'We have to do it, Mom. How else are we going to make sure the government doesn't take us again?'

'David,' his father said, 'do you think this is a good idea?'

'I don't think there's any other choice,' David answered.

'Come on,' Reese said. Now that they were doing this, she wanted to get it over with.

She opened the front door and stepped outside. The sky was pale blue, with clouds scudding in from the west. Directly overhead a triangular spacecraft hovered motionless.

David joined her on the top step. The murmur of voices

from the mob of reporters on the street below rose as they noticed the two of them.

Amber came outside too. 'Reese, please listen to me.'

Reese started down the steps. The police officers at the bottom turned toward her, followed by the reporters, and she was buffeted by the uncanny but now familiar sensation of dozens of people looking at her. They began to shout questions at her. They wanted to know what had happened to her and David, why the spacecraft was over their house, why the army was waiting at the end of the block, whether that blond girl at the top of the steps was really the girl in the video—

The force of their curiosity was so strong – an avalanche bearing down on her – that Reese almost wanted to run back inside. But David was there beside her. He reached out and took her hand.

Snap.

ACKNOWLEDGEMENTS

Thanks to my agent, Laura Langlie, for supporting this crazy book idea from the beginning. Thanks to my editor, Kate Sullivan, who barely blinked when I told her what was going to happen in the end (shh!). Thanks to my friend Cindy Pon, for her sharp-eyed critiquing and for being the best writing cheerleader ever (fuzzy hugs to you!). Thanks to my brother, John, for talking me through many conspiracy theories and for reading an early draft. Thanks to my friend Dr Vincent Smith, for answering my weird medical questions. Any errors – medical or conspiracy-related – are my own. And as always, thanks to my partner, Amy, for being there in good writing days and bad. I couldn't have done this without you.

Q&A with Malinda Lo

What inspired you to write *Adaptation*?

The idea for *Adaptation* came to me in a dream.

I know, I know. Such a cliché, right? But I swear I'm not lying. Like many writers, I keep a journal, and the morning I woke up from the dream that became *Adaptation*, I ran to my desk and scribbled it down as fast as I could. Here is that journal entry in its entirety:

Saturday, Jan. 11, 2009

I had a dream that would make a great beginning to a postapocalyptic novel. I was on a plane that stopped for a layover in Texas. Outside the windows suddenly these spacecrafts started shooting into the sky – like UFOs, and then hundreds of birds started falling from the sky dead. We were all very scared. Eventually it stopped and the plane took off. On the news we were told it was just an antivirus thing – killing off cancer-causing animals. Even

Bill Clinton was shown standing outside in the falling birds, unharmed. Wouldn't it be great to send a group of high school kids on a school trip where they encounter this? And although the government says it's OK, it's really not.

Two main things survive from that dream in the book: it starts in an airport, and birds are falling dead from the sky. Sadly, I was not able to integrate Bill Clinton in a shower of dead birds into *Adaptation*.

But the last two lines of that journal entry were actually my first attempts at figuring out what a book inspired by this dream could be about. I was a little startled to realize that I haven't strayed from that initial idea. Those last two lines are exactly what *Adaptation* is about.

You did graduate research into *The X-Files*. Have you always wanted to write a sci-fi novel?

I've always wanted to write all kinds of novels: fantasy, science fiction, and mysteries particularly. I was a huge Nancy Drew fan as a kid! I think of *Adaptation* as less a straightforward science fiction novel than a sci-fi-tinged mystery – which is also what *The X-Files* is, in a way.

What songs would be on the *Adaptation* soundtrack?

I listen to music to cue up the mood of what I'm writing, and for *Adaptation* I had a giant playlist filled with tons of electronic music from groups such as The Glitch Mob,

Stateless, and Bassnectar. I also tend to identify each of my books with a particular sound, usually from one band, and for *Adaptation* that band was Metric. I listened to their album *Fantasies* countless times while thinking about and writing *Adaptation*.

Which character in the series do you most relate to?

I relate to all of the characters because they all reflect some part of me. Reese has very strong emotions that she doesn't yet understand how to deal with, which is something I've certainly experienced. David faces some issues specific to his race that I've definitely encountered as an Asian American. And I've had moments in my life where I felt like Amber, although those moments were fleeting!

Which author do you most admire, and why?

I don't have a single favorite, but among the authors I admire are Sarah Waters, because she writes wonderful literary fiction about queer women that is still quite accessible and commercial; Tana French, because the level of detail in her crime novels brings her characters to life so vividly; and Holly Black, because she makes her novels read effortlessly – and I know that takes a ton of effort and skill.

Is there a book you wish you had written?

When I read a book that I really love, I never wish I'd written it; I'm grateful that someone else did so I can simply enjoy it. Recently I felt that way about Curtis Sittenfeld's *American*

Wife. It was completely gripping and amazing, and as a writer I found it so inspiring.

What advice would you give to aspiring young writers?

Read a lot. Read widely, in every genre if you can, and don't be limited by what so-called authorities (like your English teachers or book critics) claim is "good". Discover what's "good" for yourself. Most importantly: Don't give up. Many people will question your desire to be a writer, but if you truly want to write, then write. Don't give up on your dream.

Where do you like to write?

I have a very nice office at home where I spend most of my writing time, but sometimes I also like to sit in one corner of the couch in the living room with my laptop. However, unlike what seems like most authors, I absolutely hate writing in cafés. All I want to do in a café is drink frothy beverages and surreptitiously study the other patrons. I can do no writing there!

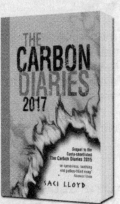

Ash

CINDERELLA AS YOU'VE NEVER KNOWN HER

Alone with the sheer misery of
her stepmother's cruelty, greed
and ambition in preparing her
two charmless daughters for
presentation at court,
orphaned Ash befriends a fairy
– a mysterious, handsome man
who grants her wishes and
restores hope to Ash's life –
even though she knows there
will be a price to pay.

But then Ash meets Kaisa,
a huntress employed by the
king, and it is Kaisa who truly
awakens Ash's desires for both
love and self-respect.

Ash is a fairytale like no other...

978 0 340 98837 4 PBK   978 1 444 90371 3 eBook

**Also available
as an ebook**

WWW.HODDERCHILDRENS.CO.UK